THE FIELD GUIDE TO
NORTH AMERICAN
MONSTERS

THE FIELD GUIDE TO NORTH AMERICAN MONSTERS

Everything You Need to Know
About Encountering Over 100
Terrifying Creatures in the Wild

W. HADEN BLACKMAN

Three Rivers Press
New York

Published by Three Rivers Press, a division of Crown Publishers, Inc., 201 East 50th Street, New York, New York 10022. Member of the Crown Publishing Group.

Random House, Inc. New York, Toronto, London, Sydney, Auckland
www.randomhouse.com

THREE RIVERS PRESS and colophon are trademarks of Crown Publishers, Inc.

Printed in the United States of America

Library of Congress Cataloging-in-Publication Data
Blackman, W. Haden.
    The field guide to North American monsters : everything you need to know about encountering over 100 terrifying creatures in the wild / W. Haden Blackman. — 1st ed.
p.   cm.
Includes bibliographical references (p. 247).
1. Monsters—North America. I. Title.
QL89.B58   1998
001.944'097—dc21   97-43243
                                                                                         CIP

ISBN 0-609-80017-5

10 9 8 7 6 5 4 3 2 1

First Edition

For Mom and Dad,
who never discouraged.

And for all things that dwell in the dark,
may you never be pulled from the shadows.

CONTENTS

ACKNOWLEDGMENTS

Monsterology is a demanding endeavor, and to succeed monsterologists must rely heavily upon family and friends. I am extremely grateful to everyone who has helped me see this project to completion.

I reserve a special thank-you for my supportive family, especially Barbara Blackman, who graciously copied photographs, and Steve Cravens, who instilled within me a profound fear of the Bogeyman. My deep appreciation to Jan and Dave Bonfilio for food and shelter; and to the Karchers for living next door. For friendship and black humor, I thank Matt Ragland, Joe Harrop, James and Rose Ann Lang, Matt Brophy, Kim Carlson, Todd Platt, Lara Thompson, and Larke Brost.

I was fortunate to have three wonderful editors in Candice Fuhrman, Wendy Hubbert, and Jessica Schulte, all of whom I thank for their effort and patience.

I also extend my gratitude to fellow monsterologists Loren Coleman and Janet and Colin Bord for their aid on this project. And I thank all those who helped me conduct research by donating texts, including Sue Driscoll, Michelle Bonfilio, Lauren Christopher, and Adelaide Bonfilio.

Without certain skills, I would not have been able to embark upon my quest to write about monsters: thank you to David Swanger, Kate Toll, Anne Busenkell, and John Barnes for teaching me the basics and beyond.

Both monsterology and writing require constant inspiration, so I thank Tom Petty and the Heartbreakers for shattering the monotony of silence.

Finally, a heartfelt thank-you to Anne-Marie Bonfilio, who listened to a million monster stories well past the witching hour and provided all the intangibles far beyond the point of patience.

INTRODUCTION

MONSTERS ARE EVERYWHERE.

They hide beneath our beds, in our closets, and in attics; they roam mountain peaks and lonely roads; they dwell beneath bridges and skulk in the shadows that creep ever closer. And, most important, they lurk in our imaginations. We peer into the darkness of a cave or into the impenetrable blackness of the ocean and know that something must be there, waiting. Most of the time, we believe that unknown "something" to be horrible and gruesome; on rare occasions, we envision it as truly wondrous, magical, and exquisitely unique.

Because humans have the ability to find monsters virtually everywhere and in every shape, the world is replete with intricate monster stories from all eras. In North America, monsters were first encountered by the Native American and Inuit Indians, who discovered a host of terrifying creatures in lakes, caves, forests, and mountains, and even in the sky above. A quickly moving shadow followed by a clap of thunder became the ominous **Thunderbird,** while the howl of the winter wind became the **Wendigo**'s fearsome cry. Such encounters were integrated into Native American artwork, song, and oral tradition, forming the foundation of North America's modern monster folklore.

As European settlers began to arrive in the New World, they too found monsters in the hills and fields. Diseases, plagues, unsolved homicides, and mysterious disappearances all pointed toward a legion of invisible ghosts, man-eating monstrosities, and enigmatic entities haunting the continent. Settlers migrating into the wild lands in the western part of the continent found monsters behind every bush and tree, and these fearsome beasts also became an integral part of early American folklore.

Lumberjacks and explorers added to this folklore, preserving encounters with a host of horrible monsters through songs and hair-raising campfire stories. African slaves, pirates, cowboys, prospectors, farmers, and immigrants from all parts of the world also spread similar legends throughout the continent.

And, just as our ancestors did, we continue to find monsters everywhere. Some are preserved in modern monster myths, often known as urban legends or campfire tales, which relate the exploits of the **Bogeyman,** the notorious **Hook,** and an assortment of vengeful ghosts. More surprising, in modern times, many people are actually encountering monsters as well. Some witnesses are even filming or photographing horrifying and inexplicable creatures in the woods and lakes of North America.

This book attempts, for the first time, to catalog a wide spectrum of the strange creatures described in Native American legends, American folklore, and modern sightings. From the lake monsters stalking Inuit Indians long ago, to the hairy humanoids spotted just yesterday, *The Field Guide to North American Monsters* reveals the rich diversity of monstrous life living in North America, a continent virtually overrun by every manner of supernatural terror and sublime beast.

Although this book's ultimate goal is to expose the monsters in our midst, it will also allow interested readers to become monster researchers, commonly known as monsterologists. Monsterology, the study of monsters, is a modern science descended from several other related fields, most notably cryptozoology and supernaturalism.

Cryptozoology is the investigation of unknown animals, also known as cryptids or possible animals. Cryptozoologists commonly have solid backgrounds in the natural sciences and tend to gravitate toward investigating creatures that strongly resemble animals already in existence, such as the baffling giant squid or the elusive **Bigfoot.** Cryptozoologists focus a great deal of attention on physical evidence, including footprints and hair samples, but they will also analyze legends and lore for evidence of monsters throughout history.

Supernaturalism, in contrast, focuses on the metaphysical world. Ghosts, ghouls, and the products of witchcraft and magic are typical areas of supernaturalist study. Supernaturalists devote most of their efforts to investigating the psychic state of witnesses; sacred sites and power points located near a monster's habitat; auras; and occult lore.

Somewhere between the world of the cryptozoologist and the supernaturalist resides the monsterologist. Monsterologists combine a command of the natural sciences with an in-depth knowledge of the supernatural world in order to analyze the wealth of information related to monsters. Such researchers study every aspect of a given case, including data gathered from firsthand accounts, folklore, sightings, trace evidence, and any possible supernatural influences.

Monsterology is not, however, synonymous with "monster hunting," a disparaging label that suggests those who seek out monsters want to capture, kill, or exploit the world's mysterious creatures for personal gain. In actuality, most monsterologists wish only to observe, describe, and understand monsters and their habits. It is the dream of every monsterologist to one day run free through the forest in the company of a Bigfoot or swim alongside a sea serpent. This book is intended to aid monsterologists in realizing such dreams.

HOW TO USE THIS BOOK

THE BOOK IS DIVIDED INTO

eight major chapters, each exploring a prominent monster type or species native to the continental United States and Canada. The first chapter describes *hairy humanoids,* such as **Bigfoot;** the second chapter discusses *lake monsters* and *sea serpents;* and the third chapter explores *flying monsters,* including the **Thunderbird.** The fourth chapter features *dwarves* and *giants,* the smallest and tallest known monsters; while the fifth chapter focuses on unidentified or mutant animals, commonly known as *cryptid animals.* The sixth chapter deals with the strange and unruly *beastmen and beastwomen,* human-animal hybrids roaming backwoods and lonely roads; and the seventh chapter is home to the *supernatural monsters,* including a few ghosts. The eighth chapter, which deals with *enigmatic entities,* offers a small collection of monsters that do not fit easily into any other category.

Each chapter begins with a brief overview of the characteristics common to the monster type and then goes on to describe in detail an assortment of monsters representative of the category. (Note that some monsters display characteristics of more than one monster type: **Mothman,** for example, is both a flying monster and a beastman. Such monsters have been categorized based upon their most prominent features.) Finally, each chapter ends with a brief overview of other monsters belonging to the specific monster type.

As encounters with monsters frequently require quick thinking, each monster entry in the eight major sections begins with a Vital Statistics box, which will allow you to instantly recognize a monster and predict its behavior. Each box contains the following information:

DISTINGUISHING FEATURES: Traits that set the creature apart from other monsters.

HEIGHT/LENGTH: An estimate measured in feet.

WEIGHT: An estimate measured in pounds (lbs).

RANGE AND HABITAT: The terrain and geographical areas preferred by the monster.

POPULATION SIZE: An estimate of the number of individuals in existence.

DIET: The monster's feeding habits, listed as either carnivore (eats meat), herbivore (eats plants), omnivore (eats both meat and plants), or anthropophagus (eats people).

BEHAVIOR: A brief description of the monster's common habits.

SOURCE: The major folklore traditions or fields of study that document the monster.

Specific tribes, peoples, or groups involved with the monster's folklore are listed when available.

ENCOUNTERING: The number of appearing immediately after this heading reflects the likelihood of actually spotting the monster in the field, ranging from one (the chance of an encounter is extremely slim) to four (the possibility of an encounter is extremely high).

The Vital Statistics box is followed by a more detailed description of the monster's appearance, special abilities, behavior, and history. Each entry ends with a few paragraphs imparting advice for successfully finding and surviving an encounter with the creature discussed.

After the eight major chapters, the book contains a "bonus" chapter on becoming a monsterologist, which offers general advice for advancing in this exciting and vibrant field.

The supplemental information provided at the back of the book includes two appendices, a glossary, and a selected bibliography. If you come across an unfamiliar term or concept while reading the book, refer to the glossary, which contains many important monsterology terms. Appendix A provides a sample questionnaire for monster witnesses, while appendix B lists the major monsters as they appear by U.S. state or Canadian province. Throughout the text, the names of monsters contained elsewhere in the work are set in **boldface** type, signifying that these creatures have their own individual entries.

THE FIELD GUIDE TO
NORTH AMERICAN
MONSTERS

HAIRY HUMANOIDS

THE HAIRY HUMANOIDS, a group of monsters that includes the famous Bigfoot (or Sasquatch), are a collection of bipedal hirsute creatures found across the continent.

They are the most unified monster type, as all hairy humanoids are almost identical to one another in appearance and behavior.

In many respects, hairy humanoids resemble erect and rather large apes. They are covered head to toe in hair about an inch in length, with minute bare patches around the mouth, nose, and ears. The soles of their feet, which are rough and padded, and the palms of their hands are also hairless. Usually, a hairy humanoid's hair is dark brown or black, but witnesses also describe such monsters with white, russet, red, beige, gray, and even silver-tipped hair.

The average hairy humanoid stands close to seven feet tall, but exceptional members of this monster type can reach heights of twelve feet or more. They have extremely long arms, which are often capable of uprooting trees. Most hairy humanoids weigh between three hundred pounds and a whopping half ton, and they move with an awkward, lumbering gait.

Hairy humanoids frequently emit a rank odor, often compared to the spray of a skunk or the smell of burning tires. In addition, they are noted for a wide variety of eerie vocalizations: mournful wails, disturbing shrieks, and ominous bellows are all common to hairy humanoid encounters. A large number of hairy humanoids are also reported with red or green glowing eyes. They leave little physical evidence of their existence, save large footprints, which can exceed two feet in length. From these recovered prints, researchers know that most hairy humanoids have five toes, but a fair share only have three or four toes, with the "three-toed" variety seemingly most common in the southern portions of the United States.

Despite their hair-covered bodies, many witnesses describe hairy humanoids as more human than beast. In fact, hunters are often unable to shoot these creatures because of their evident human traits. Most often, these observers cite the hairy humanoid's eyes, which reveal an almost human intelligence. The gestures, mouths, and voices of many of these monsters have also been described as "human" or "humanlike."

Hairy humanoids exist in virtually every area of the continent, but they are almost always found in only the most remote wilderness areas. Bigfoot, for example, is rarely sighted outside of isolated regions of the Pacific Northwest, where the creature enjoys roughly 125,000 square miles of uninhabited terrain. The dense forests and rugged mountains are marked by countless tree hollows, canyons, caves, and lava tubes, providing Bigfoot with ample sanctuary. Other hairy humanoids prefer dense swamps or the tangled shores of lonely lakes, where they find similar isolation.

Because of the demands of their chosen terrains, the survival skills of the hairy humanoids far outstrip those of humankind. These creatures have keen night vision, superhuman smell, and an innate sense of direction and location. They are also incredibly strong: witnesses have described these beasts effortlessly hefting oil drums, toppling telephone poles, ripping metal doors from their hinges, and carrying away prize hogs. A hairy humanoid's rippling muscles allow it to climb sheer cliff faces and run through even the most difficult terrain with ease.

In the past one hundred years alone there have been well over a thousand reported sightings of hairy humanoids, the most commonly encountered type of monster, from as many as five hundred locations across the continent. Witnesses come from every walk of life and include single mothers, woodsmen, biologists, loggers, hikers, housewives, police officers, construction workers, motorists, hunters, teachers, writers, and children.

Hairy humanoids are only rarely considered dangerous, and most modern reports indicate that these monsters attempt to flee immediately upon seeing humans. If they do allow themselves to be approached, they are cautious and occasionally curious, but rarely violent. There may be a few rogue hairy humanoids that are much more dangerous, but the vast majority of these creatures pose little threat to humans unless provoked. There are, however, reports of hairy humanoids attacking humans when threatened by gunfire, mobs, or fire.

They may also become vicious if confronted by domestic dogs or in defense of their offspring. And, in recent years, attacks on automobiles have been a commonly reported form of hairy humanoid violence.

BIGFOOT

VITAL STATISTICS

DISTINGUISHING FEATURES: Foul stench and huge feet with five toes

HEIGHT: 6–12′

WEIGHT: 200–2,000 lbs

RANGE AND HABITAT: Forests of Idaho, Washington, northern California, Oregon, and British Columbia, collectively known as the Pacific Northwest

POPULATION SIZE: Unknown, but presumably less than two thousand

DIET: Omnivore

BEHAVIOR: Generally shy and peaceful, Bigfoot usually remains hidden from humans, but can be provoked to violence in extreme circumstances. It spends most of its time foraging for food, but has kidnapped or attacked humans on occasion.

SOURCE: Native American mythology, American folklore, cryptozoology

ENCOUNTERING BIGFOOT:

The most well-known and widely recognized of North America's monsters, Bigfoot is the quintessential hairy humanoid. The creature is often referred to by the Native American term Sasquatch, roughly translated as "hairy giant," which describes the towering monster to perfection. Bigfoot shares all the traits of the typical hairy humanoid, but it is most noted for its large footprints, which prominently display five thick toes.

As "Sasquatch," Bigfoot first appeared in Native American tales long before the arrival of the early settlers. By the late 1700s, explorers, lumberjacks, trappers, and hunters traveling through the forests of the Pacific Northwest also began to report sightings of the hairy, apelike creatures.

The most widely publicized early Bigfoot encounter occurred in 1884, when several men collared a stocky, hairy beast along the Fraser River, just outside Yale, British Columbia. Local papers dubbed the monster Jacko and described him as a brawny humanoid with "apelike" features. No one was able to determine Jacko's true identity or origin, and the creature was eventually entrusted to the care of George Telbury. Telbury alternately vowed to tour England with the beast or sell him to the Barnum and Bailey Circus, but Jacko eventually disappeared, and his ultimate fate remains unknown. It is possible that he was murdered and his body unceremoniously discarded, but perhaps he was set free by Telbury, who, it has been reported, did develop a bond with the monster.

After the disappearance of Jacko, reported sightings of Bigfoot continued sporadically until the 1950s, when a resurgence in Sasquatch-related incidents attracted the attention of numerous cryptozoologists and professional monsterologists. These researchers have since managed to amass a vast trove of data, including hair samples, perfect footprint casts, audio recordings of the creature's unearthly howls and shrieks, hundreds of firsthand reports, and rare photographs.

Possibly the most important (and controversial) piece of Bigfoot evidence is the Patterson-Gimlin film, which allegedly captures a live Bigfoot on the move and in full color. The film was recorded on October 20, 1967, when two trackers named Roger Patterson and Bob Gimlin stumbled across a female Bigfoot near Bluff Creek, California. Patterson leapt from his startled horse and ran after the creature with a rented handheld movie camera. Although brief, Patterson's 16mm film clearly shows a large, hair-covered biped with pendulous breasts, a trademark of a female Bigfoot, and an awkward gait.

The Patterson-Gimlin film has never been convincingly debunked, and the countless biologists and zoologists who have studied it have been uniformly noncommittal about the identity of the creature. Film experts and individuals experienced with hoaxes have been unable to find evidence that the movie is a fabrication. In addition, Bluff Creek was a hot spot of Bigfoot activity before the film and has continued to produce numerous footprints and sightings well into the 1990s.

The film's veracity is further supported by the fact that neither man profited from the footage. Patterson sold stills from the film in an

attempt to raise funds for an expedition to a monastery in Thailand, where he believed a hairy humanoid was being held captive, but he contracted Hodgkin's disease and died just five years after shooting the controversial footage. He held to his story until his death. Gimlin, who is still alive, has never contradicted himself or Patterson.

Still, the film has its detractors. Some skeptics claim that the Bigfoot was merely a man in a suit constructed by special-effects wizards from Hollywood. According to this theory, Patterson and Gimlin (both destitute in 1967) rented the expensive suit from its

Cliff Crook

Rene Dahinden

A still from the Patterson-Gimlin film.

the mainstream media, and the creature's likeness and name have been used to promote everything from pizza to beer.

However, despite the wealth of information gathered from the thousands of sightings, Bigfooters are still uncertain about many of the monster's habits. For example, it is not known whether Bigfeet have any social structure. The majority of encounters involve only one Bigfoot, but in a small percentage of cases, these monsters have been observed in family units consisting of three or four individuals. Because of this contradictory data, some Bigfooters believe the monster to be a solitary wanderer, while others contend that the creatures maintain a small tribal society.

Bigfoot researchers are also divided on the issue of whether or not the monster poses a threat

maker to fabricate the film. In less damning theories, Patterson and Gimlin are viewed as merely the victims of an anonymous third party's cruel hoax.

Regardless of the Patterson-Gimlin film's legitimacy, it has been credited with propelling Bigfoot into the public consciousness. Since the film's release, literally thousands of people have come forward with stories of their own Bigfoot encounters. Today, Bigfoot continues to be observed several times each year, and Bigfoot researchers, who are commonly known as Bigfooters, pursue the monster with a fervent passion. Bigfoot has also invaded

to humans. Some view the creature as a gentle giant, but other researchers believe that Bigfoot, like humans, is prone to emotional outbursts and can be easily motivated toward violence.

Native American stories about Sasquatch suggest that Bigfoot is not entirely peaceful. In the Yakama tradition, for example, Sasquatch was an outcast who became an evil spirit known as Qah-lin-me, the devourer. The monster's hatred of humanity twisted its appearance and made it extremely dangerous. The Hupa Indians also called the beast by a terrifying name: Omah, the demon of the wilderness.

Sasquatch was also greatly feared by Native Americans for its tendency to kidnap humans. In 1871, seventeen-year-old Seraphine Long, while away from her village searching for firewood, was abducted by a male Bigfoot. She was taken to a hidden cave, where the creature lived with his elderly parents, and held captive by the beast for over a year. She eventually took ill, and her captor reluctantly allowed her to return to her family. However, when she reached her village, it was discovered that she was carrying the creature's child. She gave birth to the Bigfoot's baby, but the child only lived a few days.

Although a high percentage of abductees are female, women are not the only victims of the hairy kidnappers. In the summer of 1924, woodsman Albert Ostman was searching for a lost gold mine near the Toba Inlet in British Columbia, when he awoke one night to find himself being carried away from his campsite. Trapped in his sleeping bag, Ostman could

What Does Bigfoot Eat?

No one is quite sure, but the Pacific Northwest is a rich environment that provides an intelligent creature such as Bigfoot with numerous food sources, including:

FISH AND OTHER SEAFOOD: salmon, trout, mussels, minnows, clams, shrimp

INSECTS AND RELATED: crickets, grasshoppers, spiders, potato bugs, leeches, earthworms and other annelids, slugs, snails, moths, butterflies, termites, caterpillars, big mountain angleworms, grubs, maggots, ants, beetles, larvae, bees

RODENTS AND OTHER SMALL MAMMALS: pikas, gophers, mice, rabbits, woodchucks, squirrels, marmots, rats, moles

RED MEAT: deer, goats, sheep, domestic dogs and cats, elk, foxes, moose, bear cubs, mountain lion cubs, wolf pups

BERRIES AND OTHER FRUITS: blueberries, blue and red huckleberries, wild cherries, tomatoes, salal berries, Oregon grapes, manzanita fruit, peaches, apples, boysenberries, blackberries

PLANTS AND OTHER FOLIAGE: spruce and hemlock tips, grasses, ferns, leaves, roots, bark, water plants, shoots, mushrooms, cauliflower fungus, white chanterelles, licorice ferns, saplings, corn, turnips, lima beans, wild onions, sweet grass, tubers, pinecones

FOWL AND OTHER WHITE MEAT: geese, ducks, Canada honkers, jays, woodpeckers, eggs, stolen pigs, boars

OTHER: acorns and other nuts; frogs, tadpoles, toads, and other amphibians; feces, honey, sap, humans (especially children)

only wait throughout the long hours of travel until he was finally dumped at the feet of a large male Bigfoot. Much to his surprise, Ostman discovered that he was the guest of a family of four monsters living within a secluded valley, where he would remain for the next several days.

During his stay, the Bigfeet were extremely curious about Ostman and his belongings, but they never tried to harm him in any way. Due to the family's hospitality, Ostman began to sense that he had been kidnapped to breed with the Bigfoot's young daughter. To escape, Ostman fired his rifle into the air, startling the family, then bolted from the valley.

Bigfeet do not stop at simply kidnapping humans, and the notion that this monster occasionally turns to humans for food is ex-

Loren Coleman

A Native American mask thought to be a likeness of Sasquatch.

tremely common in Native American accounts of the beast. While exploring the British Columbia coast in 1792, the naturalist José Mariano Mozino interviewed locals who were terrified of the "Matlox," a large, hairy humanoid with huge feet, sharp teeth, and hooked claws known to devour any humans it captured. As recently as 1854 the tribes living near Mount St. Helens claimed that their Sasquatch neighbors dined on human flesh, and Californian tribes living near Elk Creek similarly feared a cannibalistic Sasquatch, known locally as the Seatco, who carried a staff made of human shinbones.

One of the first written accounts of a murderous Bigfoot appears in Theodore Roosevelt's 1893 book, *Wilderness Hunter*. In that tome, Roosevelt relates the tragic tale of a hunter who was stolen from his campsite at the head of Idaho's Wisdom River in the early 1800s. The kidnapper was reported to be a hairy monster with a terrible stench. Shortly after the hunter disappeared, his corpse was discovered nearby amid several giant footprints: his neck had been broken and his throat had been savagely torn out.

Although such vicious murders are rare, since the 1800s there have been dozens of reported Bigfoot attacks on humans. The most dramatic assault was the Ape Canyon Affair of 1924. That year, a group of miners working in a valley near Mount St. Helens, Washington, reportedly shot and wounded a Bigfoot. After sunset, several apelike creatures standing over seven feet tall descended into the valley and rained stones and boulders upon the miners' cabin. According to the miners, the monsters' eerie howls and wails echoed throughout the canyon until dawn. As soon as the sun appeared, the terrified miners made their escape, dodging thrown boulders and tree limbs. Today, the area is known as Ape Canyon in recognition of Bigfoot's presence.

Despite the wealth of evidence casting Bigfoot in a negative light, individual Bigfeet have also exhibited a much more benign aspect. They have been known to rescue animals in danger and on rare occasions to aid humans lost or injured in the woods. Fortunate is the man or woman who happens to befriend one of these monsters through some twist of fate, as they are extremely loyal and will take great pains to repay any debt.

Indicative of the creature's fealty is the story of a Native American fisherman who encountered an emaciated Bigfoot near Tulelake, California, in 1897. The man took pity on the monster and gave the beast his recent catch, despite his own suffering appetite. A few weeks after the encounter, the fisherman awoke to find several fresh deerskins neatly arranged outside his cabin. In the months that followed, the nocturnal visitor left prodigious amounts of firewood, pelts, and berries and other fruit. Eventually, the gifts ceased and the fisherman came to believe that his silent, hairy friend had finally left the area. However, years later, the fisherman was bitten by a rattlesnake and fell unconscious in the forest. Miraculously, he awoke a few hours later to find himself being shouldered by three large Bigfeet. He looked to his wound and saw that the snake bite had been neatly wrapped in a moss that neutralized the poison. The mon-

> Everything we know about [Bigfoot] tells us that if it exists, it is infinitely more peaceful and nonviolent than the other great ape occupying the continent.
>
> —Robert Pyle,
> *Where Bigfoot Walks*

sters returned the man to his cabin and, the old debt paid in full, disappeared into the forests forever.

Sadly, Bigfoot may have much more cause to fear humans than we have reasons to fear this hairy giant. As a direct result of man's interference with the environment of the Pacific Northwest, Bigfoot must now contend with numerous threats to its habitat.

The largest danger to Bigfoot's survival is the lumber industry's wanton destruction of the old-growth forests of the Pacific Northwest, which the monster depends upon for food and shelter. This habitat is further plagued by such man-made ills as acid rain, chemical dumping, erosion, and landfills. Finally, the monster must also face armed humans seeking the beast for fame and fortune. Although usually ill-equipped, such monster hunters force local Bigfeet to migrate, and many of these monsters may lose homes and reliable food sources in the process.

A few local governments have taken steps to protect Bigfoot. In 1969, Washington's Skamania County passed an ordinance that prohibits the wanton murder of any bipedal hairy creatures. Whatcom County, Washington, and areas of California, Oregon, and even Pennsylvania and Arkansas also have ordinances protecting Bigfoot and other hairy humanoids;

from 1974 to 1980, but it failed to produce anything more than a bear and a wandering hippie. The baits were eventually removed and the trap was left to rust in the forest, where it remains to this day.

Should We Kill Bigfoot?

Most researchers advocate leaving Bigfoot in peace, but Dr. Grover Krantz, an anthropologist at Washington State University, argues that only a Bigfoot corpse will prove the existence of the creature beyond all doubt. Yet even Krantz admits that Bigfoot's killer would face many problems in the aftermath of the murder: Namely, how would the massive body be transported in secrecy, where could it be studied, and who should be trusted with the find? These difficult questions, as well as the legality of murdering something with possible ties to humanity, face anyone who manages to bag a Bigfoot.

---

and Bigfoot has been declared an endangered species by Siskiyou County, California.

Unfortunately, Bigfoot will only be completely protected once its existence has been proven and accepted by the federal government. While the Army Corps of Engineers once listed "Sasquatch" as part of the natural fauna of Washington, the U.S. Fish and Wildlife Service has refused to officially include the creature on the endangered species list until concrete evidence, in the form of a live or dead Bigfoot, can be obtained.

One of the most widely publicized attempts to meet the federal government's strict requirements occurred in 1969, when North American Wildlife Research of Eugene, Oregon, sought to capture the beast in a ten-foot steel cage. The cage, which was placed near the site of recent Bigfoot activity, was kept baited

Numerous expeditions have also set out in search of Bigfoot, and these too have fared poorly. In 1960, the wealthy oilman Tom Slick organized the Pacific Northwest Bigfoot Expedition, the most formidable group of Sasquatch-seekers ever assembled. Most of the men involved were seasoned trackers, and many had spent time in Tibet searching for the Yeti (or Abominable Snowman), a creature often considered to be one of Bigfoot's far-flung relatives. Nevertheless, the group could not find Bigfoot. Slick, who was the unifying force behind the group, died in a plane crash in 1962, and the Pacific Northwest Bigfoot Expedition disbanded soon after.

In 1970, Robert W. Morgan tried to continue Slick's work when he formed the American Yeti Expedition, which consisted of an archaeologist, a cinematographer, at least one psychic, several biology students, and George Harrison, the editor of *National Wildlife*. Partially funded by the National Wildlife Federation, Morgan and his crew traveled to the Mount St. Helens region, where they employed jeeps, night-vision goggles, and other advanced gadgetry in their quest to find the creature. Morgan found no sign of the creature and, in desperation, resorted to baiting his traps with a nude female volunteer. Eventually, after spending over $50,000 in his failed pursuit of the beast, Morgan was forced to dissolve the expedition.

The most recent "failure" in the quest for Bigfoot involved a research project led by Peter Byrne, who played a significant role in Tom Slick's 1960 expedition and is notorious for being one of the few well-funded Bigfooters. Until recently, Byrne's Oregon-based Bigfoot Research Project was financed by the Academy of Applied Science of Boston and made use of a variety of technology ranging from digital global positioning equipment to motion and heat sensors. The most important device in Byrne's possession, however, was a special biopsy dart, specifically designed to take small blood, hair, and tissue samples without injuring Bigfoot. Byrne reasoned that the data gained from these darts would have provided viable DNA samples, which, when combined with the wealth of sightings and footprints, could conclusively prove the monster's existence. Unfortunately, Byrne and his team never managed to find Bigfoot, much less shoot the creature with a biopsy dart. As of this writing, the Bigfoot Research Project has been dissolved.

Despite the difficulties inherent in the search for Bigfoot, numerous hikers and hunters do encounter this creature each year. Therefore, Bigfoot should be one of the principal subjects for budding monsterologists. If you decide to seek Bigfoot, limit your search to the Pacific Northwest, specifically those areas with prodigious amounts of rain. Plan your expedition for the fall months as the bulk of sightings occur from August to October. In addition, conduct most of your research at dusk, dawn, or in the dead of night, when Bigfoot is most active.

Trekking through the forest is the most successful method for spotting Bigfoot, but be sure to visit caves and lava tubes as well. Be certain to study riverbanks and patches of mud for Bigfoot's footprints, which can be identified by their incredible size, a lack of claw marks, and a distinct big toe; and always carry a small quantity of gypsum cement to make casts of any prints you may find. Also have on hand tweezers, rubber gloves, and plastic containers for collecting hair samples. Novice hikers wary of venturing into the forest should drive along logging roads at night to catch Bigfoot in their headlights.

During a sighting, remain motionless and attempt to observe the creature's appearance, actions, and general demeanor. Always remain entirely passive unless the monster exhibits aggression. Flee from a violent Bigfoot with great haste.

When peaceful Bigfeet are encountered, offer flowers or food to establish a bond, which will allow for closer study. Avoid sudden movements or loud noises, and always speak calmly. Never convey fear, and if you wish to leave the area, do so by backing away slowly. Any attempts to photograph or film Bigfoot should be made from a great distance, as the camera might alarm, frighten, or enrage the monster, especially if equipped with a flash.

It should be noted that some Bigfeet actually approach isolated cabins, trailer parks, and other abodes. If a Bigfoot does come near your home, gently close all doors and windows, and quiet dogs and children. Most important, do not feed the Bigfoot, as it will come to associate human dwellings with food and may return to kidnap loved ones or pets.

THE CHICKEN MAN

VITAL STATISTICS

DISTINGUISHING FEATURES: Deformed hand and love of raw chickens

HEIGHT: 7′

WEIGHT: 600 lbs

RANGE AND HABITAT: Rural areas of Oklahoma

POPULATION SIZE: One

DIET: Omnivore

BEHAVIOR: The Chicken Man routinely raids henhouses at night and steals chickens, but otherwise remains hidden and reclusive.

SOURCE: Cryptozoology

ENCOUNTERING THE CHICKEN MAN: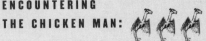

In December of 1970, El Reno, Oklahoma, was rocked by a wave of mysterious raids on chicken coops. The unidentified assailant always attacked late at night and tore through wooden doors and chicken wire to reach its prey. It left the coops littered with feathers and pools of blood, and was known to consume several dozen fowl in a single night. Authorities blamed the raids on small predators such as weasels or foxes, until victimized farmers discovered huge footprints and handprints at several attack sites. Authorities were completely stumped by the chicken coop raids, which continued well into 1971, but locals began referring to the unknown assailant as the Abominable Chicken Man.

Because the footprints found in and around the violated henhouses strongly resembled those created by **Bigfoot** and other hairy humanoids, the nightly attacks eventually attracted the attention of cryptozoologists. These investigators theorized that the assailant was in fact a wayward Bigfoot, perhaps born with physical deformities. To support this assertion, researchers collected numerous handprints, which were found in huge numbers at the sites of the attacks.

When Lawrence Curtis, the director of the Oklahoma City Zoo during the height of the Chicken Man's activities, studied a handprint left on the door of a coop by the monster, he confessed to being completely perplexed. Although he was confident that the print belonged to a large primate, he could not ascertain the exact identity of the animal. Furthermore, the monster's hand, which measured seven by five inches, showed signs of deformity: the thumb appeared unusually crooked and extended from the hand at an odd angle.

Cryptozoologists investigating the case soon uncovered Howard Dreeson, a man who claimed that he had befriended a large, apelike monster in 1967, near Calumet, Oklahoma, only about ten miles from El Reno. For three years, Dreeson fed the monster a steady diet of bananas and oranges, and his descriptions of the creature agree with the descriptions of young Bigfoot.

Eventually, Dreeson attempted to capture the beast, but when his traps failed, he relented and ceased feeding the creature altogether in 1970, shortly before the wave of chicken coop assaults began. Perhaps the Chicken Man became reliant on Dreeson's handouts and, when this food source suddenly disappeared, was forced into stealing chickens.

Patient monsterologists in search of the Chicken Man would do well to stake out chicken coops near El Reno. Conduct field research from late November to early February, as the monster strays closer to humanity during the harsh winter months. When you spy the creature, offerings of apples, oranges, bananas, grapes, corn, and of course chickens will entice it to approach for closer study.

The Chicken Man should not be considered dangerous, but like all hairy humanoids, it may have violent tendencies. Specifically, if driven by hunger, the Chicken Man could murder and consume humans.

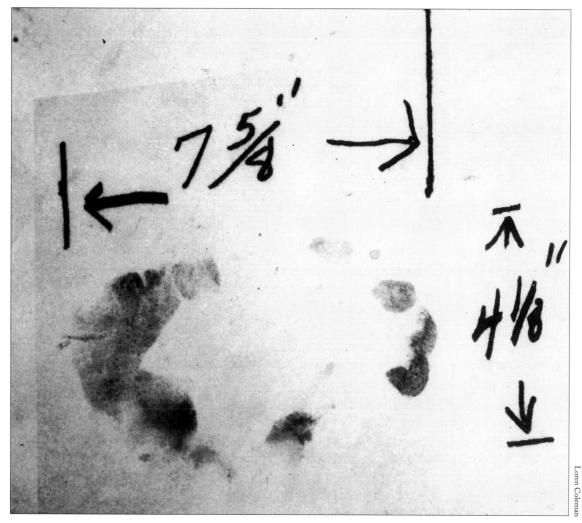

Loren Coleman

The abominable Chicken Man left this strange handprint behind after one of its daring midnight raids.

THE FOUKE MONSTER

VITAL STATISTICS

DISTINGUISHING FEATURES: Red eyes, hooked claws, extremely haunting cry, and large three-toed footprints

HEIGHT: 7'6"

WEIGHT: 600 lbs

RANGE AND HABITAT: Swamps and waterways surrounding Fouke, Arkansas

POPULATION SIZE: One

DIET: Omnivore

BEHAVIOR: The Fouke Monster has been known to steal prize shoats, frighten motorists, assault trailers, and stalk hunters; but it generally remains deep in the heart of the Arkansas swamps.

SOURCE: Cryptozoology, cult film *(The Legend of Boggy Creek)*

**ENCOUNTERING
THE FOUKE MONSTER:**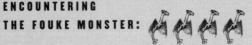

The Fouke Monster is famous among cryptozoologists because, after its well-publicized appearances in Fouke, Arkansas, in the 1970s, the creature attracted the attention of filmmaker Charles Pierce, who featured the beast in his pseudodocumentary *The Legend of Boggy Creek* (1972). Today, the film is a minor cult classic, and the tale of the Fouke Monster is still widely retold in monsterology circles.

The Fouke Monster first gained widespread notice on May 1, 1971, when it reached through the living room window of Bobby and Jean Ford. Bobby grabbed his rifle and chased the creature into the night, but was attacked by the beast. He escaped the encounter with only minor cuts and bruises, but both of the Fords were hospitalized for hysteria, shock, and uncontrollable fear. The couple described the Fouke Monster as a towering ape with shaggy black hair, blazing red eyes, and hooked claws. The Fords' neighbors, who had heard the monster's eerie cries, corroborated the couple's incredible story.

After the Fords' encounter, a major hunt for the Fouke Monster produced a string of hoaxes and several lost monster hunters, but the beast could not be tracked. Cryptozoologists now believe it escaped into the dense swamps where Boggy Creek and the Sulphur River Bottoms meet, where the monster spends the bulk of its time.

However, in mid-May of 1971, a motorist almost collided with the hairy humanoid when it reemerged from the swamps and strode onto Highway 71. All three occupants of the car claimed to have seen the beast before it slipped out of sight. That very same night, at least two other witnesses spotted the Fouke phenomenon, and in the days to come, dozens of locals would encounter the monster or hear its awful cry.

The Fouke Monster's repeated appearances

throughout May and the following months caused panic, mental anguish, and stress among the community. To protect the town, county authorities organized another monster hunt, complete with trained dogs and hordes of armed men. Although the creature again eluded capture, someone did find a huge footprint in the mud at the edge of Boggy Creek. The footprint, which had only three toes, measured fourteen inches long and five inches wide.

By August, over two hundred people had reported sightings of the Fouke Monster. In one incident, the creature was seen lifting prize shoats (hogs) from their pens. The monster also attacked a trailer full of teenage girls, cavorted through large fields, and tore down barbed-wire fences; and its howls continued to drift through Fouke daily, causing uncontrollable and inexplicable fear in all who heard the beast. The monster was shot by hunters several times, but it could not be slain.

Reports of the Fouke Monster and its ominous cries continued unabated until 1972, when Charles Pierce and his crew descended on Fouke to interview the populace and search for the mysterious man-beast. The resulting documentary, *The Legend of Boggy Creek,* was released to mixed reviews, but has since become an important component of the video library of any serious monsterologist. While Pierce's interviews with witnesses are insight-ful, the most vital pieces of evidence provided by the film are the monster's actual cries: while exploring the swamps, Pierce allegedly heard and recorded these sorrowful screams.

Shortly after the release of *The Legend of Boggy Creek* the Fouke Monster simply disappeared. For several years, it remained in the depths of the swamp, refusing to roam close to humanity until June 1978, when it appeared in Crosset, Arkansas, just over one hundred miles from Fouke. Since 1978, the creature has spent long periods in seclusion, but it does continue to emerge from time to time. It is still encountered regularly in and around Fouke, and any sighting of a big, hairy humanoid throughout Arkansas may in fact be a meeting with the Fouke Monster.

To reliably track the Fouke Monster, listen for its eerie call, which some witnesses claim sounds like the cry of a wounded cow. While traveling the Fouke wilderness, remain near the water, for the Fouke Monster always travels the waterways and is never found very far from the edge of a bayou, creek, or river.

Upon encountering the Fouke Monster, remain calm and motionless. Observe the creature's behavior and react accordingly. Never fire on the monster, as this usually prompts it to attack. The Fouke Monster is incredibly strong and has proven extremely vicious when angered. Fools who do incite the creature are likely to be dismembered.

THE HONEY ISLAND SWAMP MONSTER

VITAL STATISTICS

DISTINGUISHING FEATURES: Incredibly foul stench, hideous scream, three toes, and "evil aura"

HEIGHT: 7–10′

WEIGHT: 600–800 lbs

RANGE AND HABITAT: Honey Island Swamp, Louisiana/Mississippi

POPULATION SIZE: Unknown

DIET: Omnivore

BEHAVIOR: A sinister and imposing monster, the Honey Island Swamp creature hides deep in the swamps, only appearing to humans for brief moments before slipping away into the wilderness again.

SOURCE: Cryptozoology

ENCOUNTERING THE HONEY ISLAND SWAMP MONSTER:

As its name implies, the Honey Island Swamp Monster inhabits the Honey Island Swamp, only two hours outside New Orleans, where the Pearl River flows away from the Mississippi and enters the Gulf of Mexico. It is one of the most demanding swamplands in North America, and even experienced trackers have difficulty navigating this wilderness. The swamp is inhabited by alligators, bears, boar, and several species of poisonous snakes. There are few natural trails and even fewer man-made paths. Tourists frequently become hopelessly lost, but many hunters, explorers, hikers, and fishermen have also gone missing in the dense swamp. Some of those lost have never been seen again.

The Honey Island Swamp Monster limits its diet to raw flesh. It enjoys fish, deer, rodents, wild boar, snakes, and even alligators and bears. It's possible that the creature may dine on humans, given the number of people who have never returned from a trip into the swamp.

By all accounts, the Honey Island Swamp Monster is a hulking figure, even more striking than most hairy humanoids. In fact, many witnesses describe being overcome by its sinister presence. Its dingy gray hair is exceedingly long, especially on the head, sometimes reaching two feet in length. The monster's body bulges with muscles, and its chest and shoulders are positively massive. Its face is cruel and square, two rows of sharp teeth jut from its thick jaw, and it exudes a nauseating stench. The monster can also be identified by its horrifying shriek.

Like other hairy humanoids, the Honey Island Swamp Monster has been encountered on several occasions throughout the past century. The most reliably documented sighting occurred as recently as the early 1970s, when a hunter named Harlan Ford ran across the beast. Ford, who had spent most of his life in the wilderness, frequented areas of the Honey Island Swamp rarely entered by humans.

Honey Island Swamp.

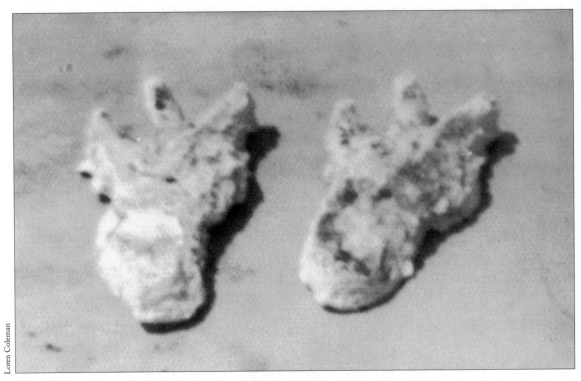

Casts of the three-toed Honey Island Swamp Monster's footprints.

In fact, on the day of the encounter, Ford and a friend were hunting in a region where fewer than a dozen men had ever set foot. When the monster suddenly appeared, the men were startled by its staggering proportions, and its evil aura filled them with dread. Frozen with shock, they stared at the creature for a full two minutes, until it ran into the woods and disappeared. When Ford related his tale, he was met with skepticism, but in the following weeks, he repeatedly returned to the site and collected several giant footprints to support his claims.

Since Ford's encounter with the monster, there have been numerous reported sightings. While witnesses note the monster's foreboding presence, the creature has yet to attack. Instead, it allows witnesses a brief glimpse, then darts into the forest, where it disappears for several years.

Though the Honey Island Swamp Monster occasionally appears near shores of the Pearl River and Lake Borgne, anyone seeking the creature should be prepared to travel into the most inaccessible and dangerous areas of the swamp. Do not travel through this area without an experienced guide and always carry extra supplies, including antivenin formulas and a compass. Also, bring along a camera or video recorder and be ready to photograph the monster at a moment's notice, as it usually disappears quickly. Fortunately, the Honey Island Swamp Monster has thus far failed to live up to its fearsome reputation and is not likely to injure witnesses. But if it does appear aggressive, flee immediately.

THE MINNESOTA ICEMAN

VITAL STATISTICS

DISTINGUISHING FEATURES: Frozen in block of ice, missing right eye, and shattered skull

HEIGHT: 6'

WEIGHT: Approximately 175 lbs (6,000 with ice)

RANGE AND HABITAT: Block of ice quartered near Winona, Minnesota

POPULATION SIZE: One

DIET: Unknown

BEHAVIOR: Clinically dead and encased in ice, the Iceman doesn't do much of anything, but his keeper occasionally travels the country with the corpse. However, before his death, the Iceman may have assaulted and even raped humans.

SOURCE: Cryptozoology, creative taxidermy, urban legend

ENCOUNTERING THE MINNESOTA ICEMAN:

hairy humanoid encased in ice, the Iceman has been on display at carnivals, shopping malls, and fairs since the late 1960s. Its grotesque appearance has attracted hordes of curious onlookers, who pay to glimpse the beast, and its possible authenticity has intrigued numerous well-known cryptozoologists.

The Minnesota Iceman is disturbing to behold. The creature has fairly normal human proportions, but his body is covered with three-inch-long dark brown hair. The monster's flesh, where visible, is a pale white, and the flat pug nose sits above a wide mouth. A single yellowed tooth is evident within the creature's maw, and its apelike head is set atop an exceedingly short neck. The Iceman also has human hands with long thumbs. Most surprising are the gunshot wounds that gape from the Iceman's chest, skull, and right arm. The bullets responsible for these wounds also destroyed the monster's right eye, dislodged its left eye, and fractured its right arm.

Since long before P. T. Barnum created an art form out of the carnival sideshow, cagey showmen have been playing on humanity's fascination with monsters. Through "creative taxidermy," these entrepreneurs have fashioned the corpses of alleged mermaids, unicorns, and two-headed snakes. However, while most monster hoaxes are easily debunked, the corpse of the Minnesota Iceman defies skeptics, even today. Reputed to be the body of a

The history of the Minnesota Iceman is possibly one of the most convoluted yet intriguing tales from the annals of monsterology. The beast first came to the public's attention in May 1967, when Frank Hansen began presenting the Iceman to crowds at carnivals and fairgrounds throughout the United States.

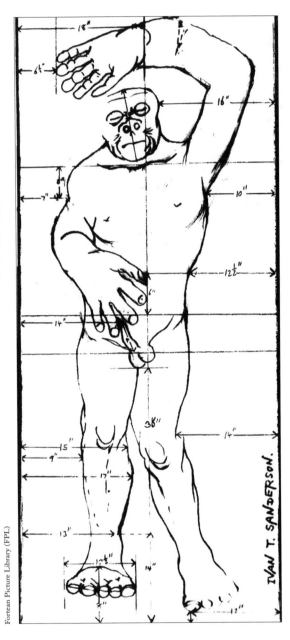

Ivan Sanderson's sketches of ...

He charged patrons thirty-five cents for a chance to glimpse the corpse. At the time, Hansen claimed that the Iceman was a relic of the last Ice Age and had been discovered perfectly preserved in a block of ice somewhere in the Bering Strait.

Eventually, the famous cryptozoologists Dr. Bernard Heuvelmans and Dr. Ivan Sanderson heard of the Minnesota Iceman and decided to investigate. In December 1968, the two stalwart monsterologists visited Hansen's farm near Winona, Minnesota. For several days, they studied the Iceman, which they nicknamed Bozo.

The conditions for the survey of the Iceman were horrendous. The monster's refrigerated coffin was kept inside a small, dimly lit trailer. The confines of the room forced Sanderson to lie on top of the coffin's plate-glass lid to study and sketch the monster. Nevertheless, Heuvelmans and Sanderson were able to compile a general description of the Iceman and became convinced that the creature was a genuine specimen of some unknown hominid.

During their study, Heuvelmans and Sanderson deduced that the monster had been shot twice by large-caliber bullets. The first bullet entered the Iceman's chest, prompting the frightened creature to raise his right arm just as the second shot was fired. The second bullet passed through the Iceman's right arm, fracturing the forearm, and then entered the monster's right eye socket. The impact of this second bullet shattered the back of the creature's skull, killing him.

When the researchers questioned Hansen about the gunshot wounds, which could not have been suffered during the Ice Age, Hansen confessed that the monster had not been rescued from the Bering Strait but had, in fact, been murdered. Unfortunately, he refused to elaborate.

Concerned over the murder of an unidentified humanoid, Heuvelmans and Sanderson urged the FBI to investigate Hansen and his frozen find. Although the Bureau never actually approached Hansen, he immediately changed his story yet again and alleged that the Iceman actually belonged to an enigmatic "Mr. X," an anonymous Hollywood filmmaker and millionaire. According to this version of the tale, the frozen Iceman was recovered from the Sea of Okhotsk by Russian sealers and was transported to Hong Kong. There, one of Mr. X's agents purchased the corpse. The creature was then transported to the United States by Japanese whalers and Chinese merchants. Hansen acquired the Iceman in 1967 when Mr. X decided that the entire country should be allowed to view the frozen find.

In 1969, at the height of the furor caused by the Sanderson and Heuvelmans investigation, Mr. X allegedly ordered Hansen to take the Iceman on tour again. However, skepticism soon began to coalesce around the Iceman Affair. First, the Smithsonian Institution was denied a request to subject the Iceman to extensive X rays. Next, Hansen admitted to researchers that Mr. X had funded the construction of at least two latex models resembling the Iceman. According to Hansen, these reproductions were to be kept in reserve in the event the real Iceman was stolen, lost, or subjected to undue scrutiny. But many researchers began to believe that a "real" Iceman had never even existed.

Undaunted by the negative publicity, Hansen did indeed tour in 1969, advertising the Iceman as the "Siberskoya Creature—a Manmade Allusion [sic] . . . As Investigated by the FBI . . . Creature frozen and preserved

Fortean Picture Library (FPL)

. . . the Minnesota Iceman.

forever in a coffin of ice." Those involved in the 1968 investigation of Bozo, the original Iceman, also studied the monster that toured during 1969 and agreed that it was indeed a latex model. Bozo, however, could not be located.

The next major development in the Iceman Affair occurred in 1970, when a woman named Helen Westring told the *National Bulletin* of her harrowing encounter with a hairy humanoid similar to the Iceman. In an article titled "I Was Raped by the Abominable Snowman," Westring claimed that, in 1967, she was confronted by the creature while hunting alone in the forests near Bemidji, Minnesota. The monster burst from the foliage and knocked her to the ground. It used its immense strength and long arms to tear the clothes from her body and, after staring lewdly for a long moment, sexually assaulted her. During the attack, Westring managed to recover her rifle and shot the beast through the eye. The bullet penetrated the back of the monster's skull and killed it. Helen fled the scene, leaving the body behind.

In July 1970, perhaps after reading Westring's account, Hansen approached *Saga* magazine and confessed that *he* had actually murdered the Iceman in the woods in the early 1960s while on a hunting trip in northern Minnesota with fellow Air Force officers. He then secretly transported the body to his Air Force base and stored it in a freezer unit. Seven years later, Hansen shipped it home to his farmhouse and then began his publicized tours in 1967.

In the past twenty years, Hansen has not changed his story significantly and has sporadically toured with the Iceman. He reportedly alternates between displaying the various models and the original creature in attempts to confuse, frustrate, and trick the press, the public, scientists, and monsterologists. As recently as 1982, Bozo and the replicas were on display at shopping malls across the United States.

Today, discovering the original Iceman's whereabouts is the most difficult task facing monsterologists interested in this hairy humanoid. The threat of FBI involvement, the sudden increase in attention from the public and the scientific community, and the difficulties inherent in transporting and protecting this amazing find may have forced Hansen to retire the original Iceman forever. The creature could be anywhere: it could easily be on display within the home of some wealthy Hollywood producer or hidden in a storm cellar somewhere in Minnesota.

Nonetheless, those wishing to see the original Iceman or its replicas are advised to frequent carnivals, sideshows, circuses, and shopping malls in the hope of stumbling across the bizarre beast. The authentic Iceman can be identified by its single yellowed tooth, while all the models possess four teeth.

Monsterologists should also consider the possibility that the Iceman is not a unique individual or a freak mutation, but rather an errant member of a larger group of monsters. Living Icemen may be encountered in densely forested areas of the Great Lakes region, especially northern Minnesota. Their range could include much of central and northern Canada, or any other cold and desolate wilderness across the continent. However, as Helen Westring's distressing account illuminates, any bipedal hairy humanoid matching the Iceman's general description should be approached with extreme caution.

MOMO, THE MISSOURI MONSTER

VITAL STATISTICS

DISTINGUISHING FEATURES: Slender fingers, exceedingly long hair, an unholy stench, and three toes

HEIGHT: 7–10'

WEIGHT: 500–1,000 lbs

RANGE AND HABITAT: Area surrounding the town of Louisiana, Missouri, specifically the Marzolf Hills

POPULATION SIZE: One to five

DIET: Omnivore

BEHAVIOR: One of the most frightening hairy humanoids, Momo only emerges from hiding to mutilate animals, steal dogs, and approach young adults and children in suspected kidnap attempts.

SOURCE: Cryptozoology, Native American mythology

ENCOUNTERING MOMO:

Since at least the 1940s, people living in Missouri have reported glimpses of a towering hairy humanoid lurking in the swamps. Today, this creature is known as the Missouri Monster, or Momo. It has been observed by hundreds of people in the past fifty years, and its existence is further supported by a wealth of physical evidence, including footprints.

Momo is even more hirsute than most hairy humanoids: black hair covers its entire body, except for its palms and forearms, and its face is usually concealed by long locks. Its other discernible traits include three-toed footprints and unusually long fingers.

Momo first appeared in the early 1940s in southeastern Missouri, where it haunted the swamps for several years. During that time, it was blamed for dismembering numerous cows and horses. Finally, a hunter spotted the giant, shambling mound of hair and fired at it, but Momo escaped into the swamps and went into hiding for almost three decades.

In July 1968, Momo appeared again, in the St. Louis suburb of Kinloch. The massive creature stepped from the woods and into the backyard of a home, where it grabbed a four-year-old child. Fortunately, the child's aunt spied the monster and ran shrieking into the backyard. Momo dropped its captive and sprinted away, the family dog nipping at its calves. Police were unable to track or find the beast, and it escaped into the wilderness again.

Momo made another kidnap attempt in the summer of 1971, when it cornered two teenage girls, Joan Mills and Mary Ryan, just north of Louisiana, Missouri. The pair had been driving along Route 70 when they decided to stop along the road for a quick lunch. They smelled a terrible stench, then the

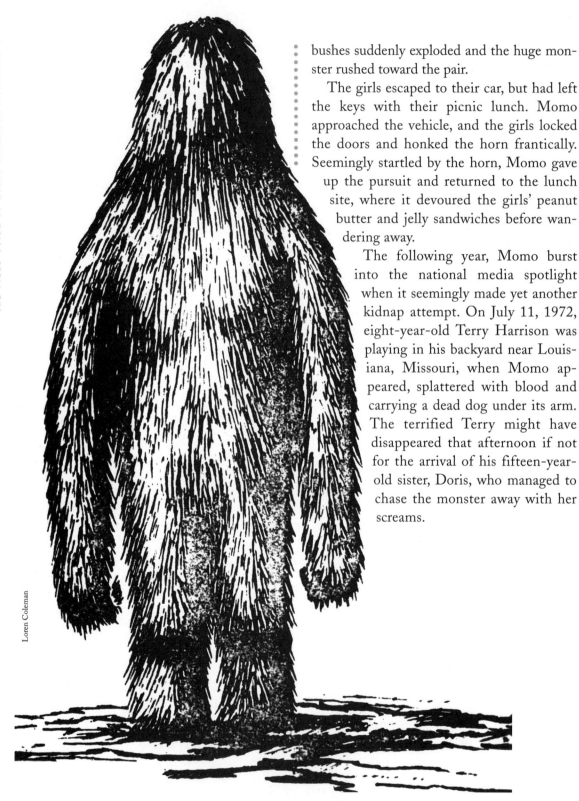

Loren Coleman

bushes suddenly exploded and the huge monster rushed toward the pair.

The girls escaped to their car, but had left the keys with their picnic lunch. Momo approached the vehicle, and the girls locked the doors and honked the horn frantically. Seemingly startled by the horn, Momo gave up the pursuit and returned to the lunch site, where it devoured the girls' peanut butter and jelly sandwiches before wandering away.

The following year, Momo burst into the national media spotlight when it seemingly made yet another kidnap attempt. On July 11, 1972, eight-year-old Terry Harrison was playing in his backyard near Louisiana, Missouri, when Momo appeared, splattered with blood and carrying a dead dog under its arm. The terrified Terry might have disappeared that afternoon if not for the arrival of his fifteen-year-old sister, Doris, who managed to chase the monster away with her screams.

Terry's father, Edgar, scoured the backyard and found several footprints and large clumps of black hair. Horrified that a monster had come so close to his children, Edgar vowed to find the creature before it returned. Theorizing that Momo lived in the Marzolf Hills, prime wildland directly behind the family's home, he combed the region for twenty-one consecutive nights, searching every gully and limestone cave he could find. During the hunt, he discovered a shack filled with a terrible odor and detected the monster's scent on the wind several times. On one occasion, after being exposed to Momo's severe smell, Edgar's trained dog began vomiting and its eyes became bloodshot and raw. The canine retched for four hours, until Edgar calmed the animal's stomach with milk and bread.

While Edgar Harrison struggled in vain with the mysteries of the Marzolf Hills, Momo continued to terrorize the small community of Louisiana, Missouri. One day, it confronted a group of boys and roared ferociously at them, then later tried to overturn a motorist's vehicle with the driver trapped inside. There were also more sightings of Momo carrying dead animals, including sheep.

Encounters with Momo continued until the late fall of 1972, when the monster completely vanished for a while. It probably went into seclusion in one of the many caves in the Marzolf Hills in an attempt to escape humanity. Or, it may have migrated away from Louisiana, Missouri, to protect its young. This theory is supported by the testimony of hunters who have stumbled across a pair of Momo tracks next to each other, one set considerably larger than the other.

Whatever the case, Momo has appeared and sightings in recent years have confirmed that Momo has returned to its favorite stomping grounds. The creature is most active during the summer months and can best be observed during the early evening. In proximity to human settlements, Momo might be lured into the open by a child or basket of food left seemingly untended near the edge of the monster's vast habitat. It can be observed in garbage dumps digging through trash in search of food and at pet cemeteries, where it exhumes and eats animal corpses.

Because Momo has been easily startled in the past by screams, car horns, and other noises, carry a loud whistle with you whenever you search for the beast. If Momo displays aggression or tries to grab you during an encounter, blowing the whistle may frighten the monster away. If it attempts to flee, allow it to do so unhindered.

There is a strong possibility that prolonged exposure to Momo's odor can cause nausea and violent illness. If affected by the creature's stench, consume large quantities of milk and bread until the sickness subsides.

Most important, remember that in many encounters Momo's actions have implied a disturbing hidden agenda. It may try to kidnap you and pull you into the swamps for its own dark purposes.

> We'd have difficulty proving that the experience occurred, but all you have to do is go into those hills to realize that an army of those things could live there undetected.
>
> —Witness Joan Mills

ORANGE EYES

VITAL STATISTICS

DISTINGUISHING FEATURES: Orange hair and luminous orange eyes

HEIGHT: 11′

WEIGHT: 1,000 lbs

RANGE AND HABITAT: Lovers' lanes in central Ohio

POPULATION SIZE: One

DIET: Carnivore

BEHAVIOR: For its own perverse amusement, Orange Eyes spends most of its time spying on couples necking in cars parked along secluded roads.

SOURCE: Urban legend

ENCOUNTERING ORANGE EYES:

Almost every community in North America has a secluded road or far-removed path known to the local populace as a lovers' lane. Teenagers frequent lovers' lanes to socialize, engage in courting rituals, or watch the skies. Unfortunately, such secluded roads also attract a wide variety of malevolent creatures, known collectively as the Monsters of Lovers' Lane, which enjoy stalking and slaughtering teenagers. In central Ohio, the resident Monster of Lovers' Lane is the infamous Orange Eyes, a towering and perverted hairy humanoid.

Orange Eyes is an eleven-foot bipedal monster covered in a coat of long orange fur. Its most salient feature is its brightly glowing orange eyes, which light up the darkness and can be spotted from several miles away. Al-

though not as bloodthirsty as some other voyeuristic monsters, Orange Eyes does peer into cars to watch as impassioned teenagers kiss. The monster has been known to drool on windows and howl with delight at the sight of naked flesh. Frightened lovers have stabbed, shot, and driven over the creature, but none of these attacks seem to have injured the beast, and it has always reappeared, much to the discomfort of Ohio's teens.

One of Orange Eyes' first appearances may have occurred on March 28, 1959, when three teenagers observed a huge hairy monster rise from the ground fog at the Charles Mill Reservoir, near Mansfield. In 1963, the creature reappeared in Mansfield, where it was witnessed by several people. An organized search party could find no sign of the beast, which was described as a massive, hairy monster with ominously glowing eyes.

Although researchers are unsure where Orange Eyes lives, a tunnel in Cleveland's Riverside cemetery may have been the abode of this monstrous hairy humanoid for over twenty-five years, according to a host of sightings that placed the beast in the cemetery's vicinity between the 1940s and the 1960s. When highway construction destroyed the tunnel in the late 1960s, Orange Eyes reportedly relocated to a stretch of forest directly behind the Cleveland Zoo. There, Orange Eyes might have lived in peace, if not for a group of children who invaded the creature's habitat on the

Lonely roads like this one are the favorite haunts of Orange Eyes and other Lovers' Lane monsters.

W. H. Blackman

night of April 22, 1968. The children spotted the monster and began to chase it, at which point the creature knocked one of its pursuers to the ground and viciously scratched another.

In response to this attack, a horde of teenagers armed with flashlights, baseball bats, and ropes poured into the forest to capture or kill the monster. They found no sign of the hairy humanoid, but did discover a scorched white sheet and a pile of chicken feathers. The hairy giant never reappeared in that area again. However, Orange Eyes may have manifested itself as recently as June 1991, when a hairy humanoid charged past two people fishing near Willis Creek, terrifying the pair before it vanished.

As with any monster that haunts a lovers' lane, the best way to spy Orange Eyes is to park alongside a remote and rarely trafficked road, preferably in an area with dense concealing foliage. Ruggles Road, near Blue Bridge, is a likely site. If Orange Eyes' curiosity is piqued, the monster will approach.

Be aware that, while a real Orange Eyes does exist, several pranksters and mentally disturbed individuals have capitalized on the Orange Eyes legend. The most notable copycat is a clinically insane hermit who is said to manufacture Orange Eyes' trademark feature by nailing two round, orange bike reflectors to a stick. Teenagers have likewise used Christmas tree lights, flashlights, and torches to frighten one another. Upon sighting a pair of "orange eyes," immediately verify that the glowing orbs belong to an eleven-foot hairy monster, rather than a creepy recluse or a group of rowdy teens.

Orange Eyes has yet to prove a direct threat to humans, but the creature's sudden appearance and tendency to peer into steamed windows can cause intense fear, lasting nightmares, and possibly heart attacks or other physical maladies. If molested, the giant could easily kill even the largest and most robust monsterologists. Researchers are advised to proceed with caution until Orange Eyes' motives and general demeanor can be ascertained.

PENELOPE

VITAL STATISTICS

DISTINGUISHING FEATURES: Fangs, claws, and terrifying appearance

HEIGHT: 7'

WEIGHT: 600 lbs

RANGE AND HABITAT: Sierra Nevada

POPULATION SIZE: One

DIET: Omnivore

BEHAVIOR: Penelope wanders through the wilderness aimlessly, savagely killing anything she encounters, including humans.

SOURCE: Urban legend, campfire tales

ENCOUNTERING PENELOPE:

Penelope is by far the most vicious and terrifying of all the hairy humanoids roaming North America. This may be because, unlike the other monsters in this group, Penelope was once a normal human, who was horrifically mutated into her current terrible form.

Penelope's tragic tale begins late one winter eve, when she and her husband ventured into the Sierras by car, only to be caught in a sudden snowstorm that swept them from the road and into a deep gulch. When Penelope regained consciousness, she realized her husband had been decapitated in the collision and his head had landed in her lap. In shock, Penelope fled from the vehicle, ran deep into the forest, and became hopelessly lost. Throughout the following days, she wandered farther

astray and only survived by eating berries and insects. As time passed, she grew more desperate and took to hunting birds and rodents, quarry she was forced to eat raw.

By the week's end, the snowstorm had returned and Penelope found herself searching for shelter. She stumbled upon several large metal drums halfburied in the snow and was able to squeeze into one to escape the elements. Exhausted, Penelope fell into a deep slumber. As she slept, however, the remnants of a toxic substance once stored in the drum seeped into her open wounds. This radioactive material combined with her recent diet of raw meat to begin a horrible transformation.

When Penelope woke, her body ached and her mind was clouded. No longer concerned about finding help or being rescued, she simply wanted to eat. The Penelope that struggled from the metal drum in search of food was no longer wholly human. She had become a giant savage, with feral eyes, jagged fangs, and hooked claws. Much of her body was covered in a coat of shaggy, tangled hair, and her mouth watered for the taste of raw flesh.

Without thinking, Penelope successfully stalked and killed a deer with her bare hands. After consuming the animal, she began to realize that she had changed somehow. Penelope gathered her courage and peered at her reflection in a puddle of melting snow, but when she saw what she had become, the last vestiges of sanity fled from her already fractured mind.

Over the next several months, Penelope embarked on a spree of sadistic violence that carried her throughout the Sierra Nevada. She is credited with derailing a logging train and killing its passengers, dismembering campers and hikers, and slaughtering forest rangers. On the anniversary of her transformation, she rampaged through a trailer park, overturning mobile homes and stealing their occupants into the night. Witnesses to Penelope's savagery could barely describe the beast, her appearance too gruesome for words.

Horrified by the violent monster roaming the mountains, authorities from several states and counties launched massive but futile efforts to find Penelope. Finally, an exasperated FBI hired a group of several dozen seasoned bounty hunters to kill the wild beast. The hunters soon cornered Penelope in a box canyon, but she decapitated or disemboweled the bulk of her pursuers.

The remaining hunters eventually surrounded Penelope and forced her farther into the canyon until her back was quite literally against the wall. Frantically, Penelope turned to the cliff face and began climbing. She endured numerous gunshot wounds, but miraculously managed to disappear over the canyon's rim, presumably forever; her body was never recovered.

Although many researchers would like to know Penelope's fate, monsterologists are strongly urged to avoid searching for this savage monster. As has been clearly shown by her previous encounters with humans, Penelope is a lethal and proficient killer. Guns are useless against her, and the monster's brutality is truly legendary. Her initial blow, which moves with such speed as to be almost invisible, will knock you to the ground and divest you of your senses. The attacks that follow will spill your intestines onto the ground and deliver your heart into her hands.

However, if you are foolish enough to seek Penelope, the monster might still survive deep in the Sierra Nevada, where she could be lured into the open with offerings of raw deer meat. But her history proves that she would rather consume human flesh and is therefore likely to turn on you instead.

THE SKUNK APE

VITAL STATISTICS

DISTINGUISHING FEATURES: Terrible stench, green aura, green eyes, and three toes

HEIGHT: 7–9′

WEIGHT: 700–1,000 lbs

RANGE AND HABITAT: Florida swamps and wilderness

POPULATION SIZE: Three

DIET: Omnivore

BEHAVIOR: Although known to attack humans and animals on rare occasion, the Skunk Ape is most frequently observed simply standing around and emitting an overwhelmingly rank odor.

SOURCE: Cryptozoology

ENCOUNTERING THE SKUNK APE:

The most odorous of all the hairy humanoids studied by cryptozoologists is Florida's Skunk Ape, also known as the Abominable Swamp Slob, the Green Chimp, the Everglades Ape, and the Holopaw Gorilla. A bipedal creature standing well over seven feet tall, the robust monster trails a strong scent that dogs will not follow and humans find nauseating. Skunk Apes are frequently surrounded by a greenish hue, which may be a result of their natural body odor.

Skunk Apes also have bright green eyes and reddish brown hair. They leave three-toed footprints seventeen inches long and eleven inches wide, and can weigh close to a thousand pounds. Skunk Apes are extremely sturdy and can easily survive gunshot wounds, collisions with automobiles, and attacks by natural predators.

Humans first encountered the Skunk Apes in the 1920s, when trappers, fishermen, explorers, and tourists began reporting confrontations with this rank monster. For the next forty years, the Skunk Ape continued to appear regularly. However, it was not until the heyday of monster identification, the 1960s, that cryptozoologists officially recognized the possible existence of this creature.

In 1963, the Skunk Ape made a dramatic appearance near Holopaw, Florida, when it attacked hunters at the Desert Ranch. The men shot the beast, but it escaped and later ransacked a house on the ranch, breaking furniture and leaving bloodstains on the walls and floors. The Skunk Ape returned to Holopaw in 1966 and 1967, when it again eluded capture.

The Skunk Ape's greenish hue was first noticed on November 30, 1966, by a woman who found herself face-

> The thing had a rancid, putrid odor like stale urine.
>
> —Witness
> Bud Chambers

to-face with the monster while changing a tire near Brooksville, Florida. On this occasion, the Skunk Ape was more curious than aggressive, and it wandered back into the woods when another motorist appeared on the road.

The year 1966 was important for Skunk Ape sightings along Florida's western coast. In April, Brooksville townsfolk began hearing the monster's cries on the outskirts of town. The howls continued until late 1967, even though the monster had been shot at and attacked by hunting dogs several times. Meanwhile, in Elfers, Florida, Ralph "Bud" Chambers claimed to have encountered a Skunk Ape on his front lawn on two separate occasions: once in the summer of 1966 and again the following year.

Skunk Ape sightings in 1967 took on an even more ominous tone. In January, four teenagers parked on a lovers' lane near Elfers were horrified when a Skunk Ape leapt onto the hood of their car and stared into the windshield with its glowing eyes. Throughout May of the same year, the monster raided ranches near New Port Richey, where it spirited cattle away into the night. In addition, decapitated chickens, raccoons, rabbits, and other smaller animals were frequently found in the Skunk Ape's range, surrounded by the monster's huge footprints.

By 1970, the Skunk Ape had become something of a celebrity. It began attracting scientifically minded investigators, such as H. C. Osborn, an engineer and archae-

ologist, who became a prominent figure in the Skunk Ape search after he bumped into the creature during the spring of 1970 while excavating a Native American mound in Florida's Big Cypress Swamp. Osborn's account of the event was substantiated by the discovery of gigantic footprints in the area of the sighting. Frank Hudson, who observed the Skunk Ape with Osborn, uncovered further proof of the monster when he interviewed locals who had seen the Skunk Ape in their youth.

Loren Coleman

Map of Skunk Ape sightings.

Trailer Park Monsters

Trailer parks attract a host of monsters, including virtually every known hairy humanoid, from **Bigfoot** to the **Fouke Monster**. Other monstrous visitors to trailer parks include **Mothman**, the **Jersey Devil**, **Phantom Felines**, **Phantom Kangaroos**, various **Bogeymen**, a host of ghosts and specters, UFOs and their alien occupants, **Gremlins**, and even the Devil. As trailer parks are generally located in rural or wild areas, many monsters simply share their habitats with these human settlements and occasionally venture within their boundaries to satisfy curiosity about humans. Hungry monsters are attracted to a trailer park's untended garbage and children, while flying monsters and UFOs may be lured to the parks by the proliferation of radio and television antennas.

In August 1971, Skunk Apes, like so many monsters, turned to invading trailer parks. At least two of the creatures descended upon the King's Manor Estates Trailer Court in Broward County. A rabies-control officer, Henry Ring, was the first authority to respond to the panicked calls of the trailer park's residents. Upon arriving at the site, he found numerous footprints and a few knuckle prints, but the monsters had evidently disappeared.

From 1973 to 1977, Skunk Ape encounters reached an all-time high after a motorist collided full-on with a pungent monster and watched in shock as the humanoid form limped away from the road. Investigators recovered blood and hair samples from the dent in the motorist's car. Though this vital evidence has since disappeared, the report was credible and received national attention from such media giants as Walter Cronkite.

Finally, in 1978, Florida (like many other parts of the country) was gripped by a hairy-humanoid frenzy after the release of the movie *Sasquatch*. Skunk Apes were reportedly spotted hundreds of times, especially in Charlotte County, where the towering terror was briefly cornered by a member of the Charlotte County Sheriff's Department.

Between 1977 and 1997, the Skunk Apes spent most of their time hidden well within the Big Cypress Swamp or the Everglades. They continued to lurk on the outskirts of small towns, at the edges of trailer parks, and near the shores of lonely rivers, but encounters with the creature were infrequent. However, in 1997, the Skunk Ape returned in dramatic fashion. Throughout the summer, the monster appeared to dozens of tourists and tour guides throughout the Big Cypress Swamp, and as of this writing it has shown no signs of retreating into the wilderness again.

Because of the rash of recent sightings, the Skunk Apes have become one of the most frequently sought monsters on the continent. However, monsterologists should remember that Skunk Apes are seasonal creatures that come out of hiding most often during July and August, when they migrate along Florida's west coast, traveling from the southern tip of the state and continuing as far north as Brooksville. Any area along this path is a prime site for Skunk Ape research throughout the summer. In August, you may also want to focus your efforts on the shores of the Anclote River, near Elfers, where the Skunk Apes have been encountered quite often.

When searching for Skunk Apes, be alert for their signature stench and footprints. The latter can be found in wet mud, tall grass, or sand and can be identified by their size and three prominent toes.

To date, no one has successfully enticed a Skunk Ape with food or other gifts, nor has a Skunk Ape displayed any desire to communicate with humanity. For the most part, Skunk Apes wish to remain hidden and unmolested; any attempt by monsterologists to make contact with these monsters may be seen as an invasion and could produce a lethally violent response.

THE WINSTED WILDMAN

VITAL STATISTICS

DISTINGUISHING FEATURES: Thin hair and no discernible odor

HEIGHT: 6–8'

WEIGHT: 200 lbs

RANGE AND HABITAT: Connecticut wilderness, especially near Winsted

POPULATION SIZE: Unknown

DIET: Omnivore

BEHAVIOR: The Winsted Wildman lives on the outskirts of humanity, where he roams quarries, lakes, and lonely roads at night, but he rarely, if ever, interacts with humans in any meaningful way.

SOURCE: American folklore, urban legend, cryptozoology

ENCOUNTERING THE WINSTED WILDMAN:

The Winsted Wildman is a curious discovery, even by standards of modern monsterology. At first glimpse, he appears to be yet another hairy humanoid, similar to **Bigfoot**. He has a large and powerful body covered in thick hair alternately described as yellow, blond, brown, and black. He also has a chilling cry, which has been known to cause severe apprehension in all who hear it; and, as with **Momo** and others, the creature is greatly feared by animals, especially dogs, although its diet does not seem to include domestic pets.

However, although grouped with other hairy humanoids here, the Winsted Wildman is slightly shorter and much thinner than the average hairy monster. And unlike the vast majority of hair-covered bipeds, he does not exude a heavy, pungent scent; nor has he been known to attack automobiles, animals, or humans. In addition, the Wildman roams urban areas of Connecticut, while Bigfoot and others prefer to remain in inaccessible forests or swamps. The Wildman's territory is much smaller than that of most hairy humanoids, being limited to Litchfield County, specifically the town of Winsted in northern Connecticut.

The first encounter with a Winsted Wildman took place in August 1895, as reported by the *Winsted Herald*. According to the paper, Riley Smith was picking blueberries near Colebrook when his normally fearless bulldog suddenly bolted from the bushes and cowered between Riley's legs. In a few seconds, a huge naked man covered head to toe in blond hair burst from the foliage and sprinted past Riley. The Wildman hooted and shrieked as he ran, then disappeared into the forest.

Similar encounters continued with a fair amount of frequency for the next century. Then, in 1972, there was an incredible surge in sightings as the Wildman began boldly approaching human settlements. The most memorable of these encounters occurred in the early-morning hours of July 25, when the creature was sighted by Wayne Hall and David Chapman as he emerged from the forest surrounding the Crystal Lake Reservoir. The two young men watched the creature from the safety of Chapman's home for over forty-five minutes. During this time, the Wildman repeatedly entered and exited a barn, scratched his head several times, and finally wandered back into the woods on the edge of Crystal Lake. Both men were most impressed by the monster's weird, haunting cry.

In 1974, the monster began roaming lovers' lanes in the Winsted area, a habit typical of many hairy humanoids. On September 27, two couples parked on a secluded road near the Rugg Brook Reservoir observed a large, hairy man lurking nearby. They drove away and immediately fetched the police. While authorities found no trace of the monster, they did report that the couples were genuinely distraught and shaken by the encounter.

The most recent reliable sighting occurred on October 29, 1989, when the Winsted Wildman approached a target range in Bristol, Connecticut, only twenty miles from Winsted. The creature roamed about for several minutes in full view of witnesses, then silently wandered away. Although everyone at the range was armed, no one shot at the Wildman because he seemed far too human. Throughout the encounter, those unaware of the monster's presence continued to fire at their targets, but the sound of gunfire did not seem to disturb the Wildman, a trait totally inconsistent with almost all other hairy-humanoid reports.

Fairly easy quarry for all monsterologists, the Winsted Wildman can be sought in the northwestern areas of Connecticut year-round. While Winsted is the best place to begin any quest for this hairy creature, Bristol, the Crystal Lake Reservoir, and the Rugg Brook Reservoir might also yield sightings. In addition, it would be wise to explore the shores of the Connecticut River and the lower reaches of the Green Mountains.

As it is likely that the Wildman is far more closely related to humanity than most monsters, monsterologists should attempt to communicate with him in whatever manner possible if an encounter occurs. Keep your distance, however. Although he has yet to exhibit any hostility or aggression, we do not know what might enrage such a creature.

As in many encounters involving hairy humanoids, you might offer the Winsted Wildman food to establish a bond. Keep pets at bay, avoid any show of aggression, and do not pursue the creature while armed. Above all, watch the Wildman carefully for the sudden mood swings common to hairy humanoids. It is likely the monster is a peaceful and retiring feral human, but there is no guarantee that he will not suddenly turn on a monsterologist.

> It sounded like a frog and a cat mixed together . . . a real weird sound like when a frog blows up and makes a lot of noise.
>
> —Witness
> Wayne Hall

THE LAKE WORTH MONSTER

VITAL STATISTICS

DISTINGUISHING FEATURES: White hair, long beard, scaly skin, and goatlike legs

HEIGHT: 7′

WEIGHT: 500 lbs

RANGE AND HABITAT: Shores of Lake Worth, Texas

POPULATION SIZE: One

DIET: Omnivore

BEHAVIOR: An easily incited beast, the Lake Worth Monster is prone to extremely violent outbursts and has been known to attack humans, cars, and animals.

SOURCE: Cryptozoology, Native American mythology, urban legend

ENCOUNTERING THE LAKE WORTH MONSTER:

The case of the Lake Worth Monster is one of the most interesting and exciting in the annals of cryptozoology. Described as a hairy "goat-man," the creature made a dramatic appearance in the summer of 1969, resulting in a monster craze that swept the Lake Worth, Texas, area. The numerous sightings that followed confirmed that the Lake Worth Monster is a bizarre creature with the upper torso of a fearsome hairy humanoid and the lower body of a large and virile goat. It has yellow eyes and a long, white beard. The beast lurks on the shores of Lake Worth, Texas, but it is not truly an aquatic monster: its only aquatic adaptation appears to be a layer of scales visible on its hands and face.

Like many hairy humanoids, the Lake Worth Monster possesses long arms, frequently makes low, guttural noises, and emits an unpleasant odor. Because of its unique physiology, the Lake Worth Monster moves with a loping gait and is capable of leaping massive distances or running at amazing speeds. Its bestial lower extremities do not hinder its ability to swim, as the Lake Worth Monster moves almost as rapidly in water as it does on land.

The vast majority of Lake Worth Monster encounters are incredibly dramatic. The creature first appeared in modern times on July 9, 1969, near Fort Worth, Texas, when the shaggy humanoid jumped onto the hood of a car occupied by three terrified couples. The beast angrily raked the vehicle with its claws, leaving long scratch marks on the car, then vanished into the foliage. Just a few hours after this initial attack, a motorist traveling the same stretch of road heard a monstrous roar, then rounded a bend and saw a huge hairy form throw a tire at least five hundred feet before it leapt into the bushes and disappeared.

Sightings continued the following day, when at least six people near Greer Island in Lake Worth observed the hairy creature roaming the reservoir's shores. On July 11, over thirty people observed the monster on a bluff near the lake's Nature Center. Soon after, the community found itself gripped by a monster frenzy that lasted for three months. Hundreds of people caught fleeting glimpses of the bearded beast, and their reports attracted hordes of monster hunters, cryptozoologists, journalists, and curiosity-seekers. The monster was also mentioned on the national news and in newspapers across the country.

During the height of the craze, monster hunters spent days beating bushes, frightening local wildlife, and accidentally discharging their weapons. At least thirty people sighted the monster, but no one managed to shoot it. A tall teenager wearing white overalls was mistaken for the creature, however, and shot in the shoulder. After this incident, guns were banned at the lake, but the monster hunters merely took up clubs, knifes, baseball bats, and other weapons.

By the end of summer, the Lake Worth Monster began to live up to its monstrous appearance. Rumors claimed that the creature had savaged and mutilated several dogs and livestock, and it frequently screamed vehemently at witnesses. After each such report surfaced, the monster hunters set out after the creature with renewed vigor, but they continually met with failure.

Only one dedicated researcher, Sallie Ann Clark, actually succeeded in the quest for the Lake Worth Monster. Clark managed to spot the monster on at least four different occasions, a success rate far higher than that of many seasoned monsterologists. Her first sighting occurred in July 1969, when the monster sprinted in front of her car as she was driving toward her home. Inspired by this sighting, she doggedly searched the lake armed with only a camera, notepad, and tape recorder. When away from the field, she interviewed hunters, locals, and other

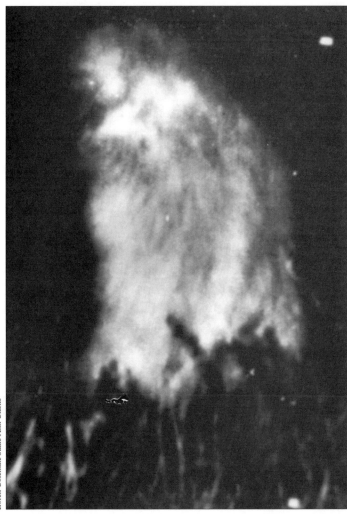

Loren Coleman/Sallie Ann Clarke

witnesses. Finally, during her last encounter, Clark snapped a photograph of the large, white humanoid as it raced past her.

Since Clark's success, the Lake Worth Monster has remained largely invisible. It faded from sight in late 1969, after it attacked Charles Buchanan on November 7. Buchanan was camped on the shores of Lake Worth when the beast yanked him from the back of his truck, where he had been sleeping, and threw him to the ground. Although overwhelmed by the monster's terrible stench, Buchanan managed to reach into his pack and grab a bag of chicken, which he handed to the beast. Seemingly placated, the monster put the bag into its mouth, leapt into the lake, and swam toward its home on Greer Island, where it has remained hidden to this day.

Although rarely seen in modern times, the Lake Worth Monster remains an alluring subject for monsterologists because sightings provide such intense thrills. The search for the monster should begin in the vicinity of Greer Island and expand to include the rest of Lake Worth. Upon failing in this limited exploration, consider the possibility that the Lake Worth beast has migrated to a new habitat. Lakes and rivers within three hundred miles, including the Brazos River (which is also home to a serpentine monster) and Lake Texoma, could provide a suitable home for the Lake Worth Monster.

If the Lake Worth Monster is discovered, approach with caution. It is unpredictable and prone to sudden and terrible acts of violence. Offerings of food might mollify the monster, but if driven into a frenzy, it could easily dismember a human with its bare hands.

Other Hairy Humanoids

Virtually every state in the United States and every province of Canada has recorded some sort of hairy-humanoid activity. Most notable is southeastern Ohio, known to many as Sasquatch Valley due to the high number of monster sightings in the area. Pennsylvania also reports a high density of hairy-humanoid encounters; unlike hairy monsters from other areas of the continent, these creatures leave behind three- and five-toed prints and have been seen exiting UFOs!

Other hairy humanoids include:

- **Big Muddy Monster:** The resident hairy humanoid along the banks of the Big Muddy River in Illinois.

- **The Booger:** A tall, hairy monster sighted repeatedly in and around Clanton, Alabama.

- **Brush Creek Bigfeet:** A collection of hairy humanoids found roaming Brush Creek, near Pacific, Missouri.

- **Hawley Him:** A hairy humanoid native to Peerless, Texas, and the Sulphur River Bottoms, extending from Arkansas to eastern Texas.

- **Old Yellow Top:** A shaggy hairy humanoid with a yellow mane and pronounced limp found wandering mines near Cobalt, Ontario.

- **Peg-Leg:** A hairy humanoid with a wooden leg spotted along highways in Georgia in the 1970s.

LAKE MONSTERS AND SEA SERPENTS

AQUATIC MONSTERS HAVE been spotted by humans throughout time and in virtually every part of the world.

Internationally, the group includes such recognizable creatures as mermaids, giant squid, and multihumped sea serpents. In North America, encounters with aquatic monsters are just as frequent, especially in the hundreds of lakes spread out across the continent, where strange creatures have been observed since long before white settlers arrived on North American soil.

Aquatic monsters come in two general varieties. The first is the giant serpent. Usually over twenty-five feet in length with an oblong head and dark hide, these monsters are typically marine animals. They move with an undulating motion, and portions of their bodies often break the water, creating the illusion of "humps." Some sea serpents have flippers, fins, scales, horns, tusks or fangs, and other adornments.

The second type of aquatic monster is the saurian, which is most commonly found in lakes. The most famous saurian is the Loch Ness Monster; like all saurians, the Loch Ness Monster resembles an extinct reptile known as

the plesiosaur, which vanished from the earth over 60 million years ago. Saurians typically have long, thin necks topped by tiny bulbous heads that are often described as "horselike." Their bodies are round and they usually have long tails, small eyes, and either flippers or stubby legs. Many saurians have fleshy protrusions jutting from their foreheads, which are often called horns but more closely resemble the antennae of snails. Like sea serpents, saurians may also have further adaptations, including tusks or scaly hides.

Lake monsters typically live in large, deep, cold lakes. Most of these are murky and difficult to navigate, and many were, at one point, far removed from humanity. Sea serpents have access to whole oceans, although they frequently make a specific bay, cove, or stretch of beach their home. Many aquatic monsters, both marine and freshwater, are also capable of short forays onto land.

All aquatic monsters can breathe underwater or hold their breath for extended periods of time. They can also survive in cold environments and withstand the effects of pressure while in the depths of their chosen lake or ocean. Aquatic monsters are fairly reclusive and skittish, rarely surfacing when humans are present. During many sightings, these creatures are seen cavorting wildly until they realize they are being watched, at which point they quickly sink beneath the surface.

Sightings of aquatic monsters typically occur in short yet dramatic spurts. Most of these creatures only surface once every few years, at which point they are observed dozens of times within a short period before disappearing again. Each monster's cycle of surfacing seems to vary, but few remain in the public

eye for more than a month, and most reappear at least once every decade. Because of their long absences, it is likely that many aquatic monsters can hibernate for years at a time.

Almost all aquatic monsters are extremely long-lived, sometimes surviving for centuries. They are also notoriously hard to capture or kill: many of these beasts continually reappear even after being shot, harpooned, hooked, or rammed with boats. Because of this seeming immortality, many aquatic monsters have been rumored to possess supernatural powers, but this claim has never been verified.

There is still some debate over whether or not water monsters are actually dangerous. About half of these creatures have been known to attack and kill humans, while the other half have proven completely benign. Unfortunately, size or appearance is not an indicator of aggression: some exceedingly large and grotesque monsters have failed to act belligerently, while small and seemingly innocuous aquatic monsters can prove quite lethal.

In centuries past, lake monsters and sea serpents were generally feared by humanity, regardless of their behavior. However, in recent decades many of these creatures have been adopted by their human neighbors as beloved local mascots. In fact, many lakeside communities boasting aquatic monsters build models of their resident cryptid creatures, include the beasts in their annual parades, or hold festivals to honor the animals.

THE ALKALI LAKE MONSTER

VITAL STATISTICS

DISTINGUISHING FEATURES: Incredibly ghastly fetor, hideous appearance, and a huge mouth

LENGTH: 300′

WEIGHT: 120 tons

RANGE AND HABITAT: Alkali (Walgren) Lake, Nebraska

POPULATION SIZE: Unknown

DIET: Carnivore

BEHAVIOR: Although a rather introverted creature, when the Alkali Lake Monster does surface, its stench slays all who near it, and the beast's hideous appearance drives the few survivors mad. It also tends to swallow anything in its path.

SOURCE: Native American mythology, cryptozoology

ENCOUNTERING THE ALKALI LAKE MONSTER:

Many monsters have unpleasant odors, but only Nebraska's Alkali Lake Monster has a stench that is fatal. The creature was first reported by Native Americans living near the lake, who claimed that anyone attempting to capture or kill the monster would be overpowered by its noxious fumes. The beast was also feared for its huge mouth and rapacious appetite. In one report, a group of Native Americans fleeing the beast sought sanctuary on a small island in the center of the lake, but the monster merely opened its mouth and swallowed both the island and the terrified humans.

The monster's visage is almost as terrible as its stench, and a glimpse of the creature can crack the mind and bleach the hair. The beast is reptilian and similar to an alligator in overall appearance, but measures a whopping three hundred feet from head to tail. Its snout is blunt, and a long horn projects from the space between its flaring nostrils and its beady eyes. The behemoth's stocky body is dull brown in color, and it moves with a quickness that belies its massive size.

The monster spends the bulk of its time in Alkali Lake (also known as Walgren Lake), which is a few miles south of Hay Springs, but is not strictly aquatic. It can come ashore whenever it pleases, most often to feed on livestock.

Foul-Smelling Monsters

Like the Alkali Lake Monster, many monsters emit terribly noxious odors, which can be the result of a monster's origins, habitat, or hygiene. In the case of many lake monsters, a horrible stench is often the result of rotting plant or animal matter, which attaches to the hides of these creatures. Hair-covered monsters, such as the aptly named **Skunk Ape** or **Werewolves,** develop gaseous auras as a result of dried sweat, natural body odor, wet hair, and a high-fiber diet. Some incredibly vile monsters, including the **Jersey Devil,** exude evil in the form of toxic fumes, which are described as smelling like brimstone or sulfur. **Zombies, Vampires,** and other monsters that are actually dead have the smell of death hanging over them, while the bad breath reported in a wide range of monsters may be the result of a diet consisting of raw flesh.

The Alkali Lake Monster is well documented in Native American accounts, but it has also been observed in recent times. The earliest modern sighting occurred in the fall of 1922, when J. A. Johnson and two companions spied the creature rising from the lake. Johnson, and every other witness since, noted the strong and unpleasant odor that lingered for minutes after the monster disappeared beneath the water. Following Johnson's sighting, at least thirty others came forward with similar encounters.

In 1939, the Federal Writers Project compiled a history of the monster sightings in and around the lake and named the beast *Giganticus brutervious*. After the Project released its report, the lake was abuzz with eager monster hunters, and the number of annual sightings of the monster diminished rapidly as the monster went into hiding. Some contend that the creature actually died or moved away during the early 1940s, but given the smattering of sightings since 1940, it is more probable that the Lake Alkali Monster periodically hibernates. Perhaps it is waiting for humans to forget that it ever existed, at which point it will emerge from the lake and devour whole towns, its stench spreading a swath of death wherever the monster roams.

Regardless of the monster's current whereabouts, the beast's colorful history is much appreciated by locals, who have erected a statue of the monster in the center of the lake.

Since the Alkali Lake Monster's stench is believed to be deadly, it should not be used as a means to track the creature. Always wear a protective mask or some sort of self-contained breathing apparatus whenever approaching the lake in search of the beast. Due to these protective measures, you will be stripped of your sense of smell and must rely heavily on other senses, notably sight and hearing. Watch and listen for the telltale commotion caused by the surfacing of a large aquatic monster.

Once encountered, beware the Alkali Lake Monster's fearsome mouth, which can swallow large objects, including most boats. After documenting your observation of the behemoth, quickly flee the scene before you find yourself awash in the monster's stomach.

> When the monster appears, the earth trembles and the skies cloud over. . . .
> When he comes ashore, to devour calves it is said, a thick mist covers the shore around him.
>
> —Peter Costello,
> *In Search of Lake Monsters*

THE BEAR LAKE SERPENT

VITAL STATISTICS

DISTINGUISHING FEATURES: Four legs, enormous mouth, dark brown scales, and beige fur

LENGTH: 90'

WEIGHT: Over 75 tons

RANGE AND HABITAT: Bear Lake, Utah/Idaho

POPULATION SIZE: One to twelve

DIET: Carnivore

BEHAVIOR: Known for startling Mormons, the Bear Lake Serpent is especially fond of coming onto land and swallowing horses and groups of humans whole.

SOURCE: Native American (Shoshone) mythology, Mormon folklore

ENCOUNTERING THE BEAR LAKE SERPENT:

The Bear Lake Serpent is one of the few monsters recognized and studied by Mormons. The creature was first encountered by Joseph Rich, the son of Bear Lake's founder, apostle Charles Colson Rich. According to Rich's account, he was attacked by the beast in the late 1860s as he was riding along the shore of the lake on his father's favorite horse. The horse was consumed, but Rich managed to escape and returned to town to tell of his harrowing ordeal. Many incredulous researchers have claimed that Rich invented the story about the monster and its attack to conceal that he had actually lost his father's horse while gambling, but as pious Mormons do not gamble or lie, this theory is unlikely. Furthermore, Native American legends and numerous sightings of the Serpent seem to confirm Rich's assertion that something monstrous does indeed dwell in Bear Lake.

Rich's description, which has been thoroughly supported by other witnesses, portrays the Bear Lake beast as a serpent at least ninety feet in length. Its most impressive trait is its huge mouth, which enables it to swallow humans and large animals whole. While its head and face are vaguely lupine and covered in a short coat of beige fur, the rest of its burly body is covered in dark brown scales. Its forked tongue flickers constantly, and on cold days it emits clouds of steam from its distended nostrils. Two muscular growths, likely ears, protrude from the sides of its head. When enraged or hungry, the beast bellows like a bull.

The Bear Lake Serpent has four thick legs, each eighteen inches long, allowing it to move on land. It also has two small flippers a few feet behind its head, and an incredibly strong tail with which it moors itself to the bottom of the lake when it wishes to remain stationary. When mobile, the monster can outrace horses and locomotives, moving at speeds of approximately a mile a minute.

After Joseph Rich's initial encounter with the terrifying creature, he spent much of his life collecting and chronicling sightings of the beast. According to Joseph's reports, confrontations with the monster became legion. From 1868 to 1875, the Bear Lake Serpent was spied by hundreds of people, including a host of Mormon church presidents. Due to these sightings, the monster quickly became one of North America's foremost curiosities during the late 1800s.

Aside from firsthand reports, Rich also gathered numerous Native American legends about the creature from the Shoshone Indians living near the lake. The Shoshone called the monster the "beast of the storm spirits," and they claimed that it had plagued them long before the white settlers had arrived. Their tales asserted that the monster rose from the lake during the months of the harvest moon and attacked nearby villages. With a single bite, it could engulf a dozen men within its mouth, and countless maidens and braves were thus consumed by this monster.

The Shoshone also told Rich that, aside from humans, buffalo formed the staple of the monster's diet. However, after the local buffalo herds were destroyed in a snowstorm in 1830, the creature vanished. Many of the Shoshone hoped that it had actually starved to death, but the Mormons arrived at the lake with herds of livestock, which evidently prompted the Serpent's return (and subsequent attack on Rich) in the 1860s.

Despite Rich's extensive research and numerous modern sightings, the Bear Lake Serpent has never been captured, although many have tried. One hunter, Phineas Cook, formulated a plan to catch the Serpent by baiting a monstrous hook with a live sheep or a Native American. The Shoshone did not take kindly to this concept, and Cook was forced to abandon the chase.

The creature's famed elusiveness may be due, at least in part, to its habitat. Bear Lake, which straddles the border between Utah and Idaho, is roughly 100 square miles in size. Most researchers claim that the lake only reaches about two hundred feet at its deepest point, but legends contend that portions of the lake are actually bottomless and may even provide portals to other realms.

Although a live specimen has not been hooked and the depths of the lake remain difficult to plumb, physical evidence has been recovered to support the existence of an entire species of Bear Lake Serpents. On September 10, 1925, the Utah Power and Light Company drained portions of the lake, revealing large stretches of previously covered shoreline. Utah's secretary of state was on the shore during this project and stumbled upon a three-inch-long tooth buried in the muck. Zoologists verified that the tooth belonged to a huge aquatic carnivore, but could not conclusively identify the animal.

Several years after the tooth surfaced, a nearly complete skeleton was uncovered about a mile west of Ideal Beach. Because it was much larger than any other animal living in the vicinity of the beach, researchers could only assume that the skeleton belonged to one of the Bear Lake creatures. The skeleton had stubby legs about ten inches long, a unique backbone, and a thick skull, all traits consistent with sightings of the Bear Lake Serpent.

Given the reported deaths and the discovery of skeletons and other remains, it is unknown how many monsters still exist in Bear Lake. Because of recent sightings, including a well-publicized encounter in 1981, it is safe to assume that at least a few of the monsters survive.

Study of the monster may be dangerous, but it offers an acceptable success ratio. A wide variety of people have witnessed the Bear Lake Serpent, especially in recent years, but historically Mormons have been the most successful researchers. Therefore, atheists, Satanists, and others with widely divergent belief systems may not be able to compel the monster to surface. In addition, while drunks and alcoholics constitute a major faction among monster witnesses in general, the Bear Lake Serpent *never* appears before anyone who has imbibed . . . unless the Mormon witnesses are lying about their sobriety.

Although a relatively minor monster, the Beast of 'Busco is a favorite subject among cryptozoologists because of the long string of colorful sightings that surround the creature. The monster first came to light in the late 1940s, when people living near a large pond outside Churubusco, Indiana, began coming forward with incredible stories of encounters with an enormous turtle. These tales attracted the attention of researchers, who have since collected numerous eyewitness accounts.

According to most sources, the Beast of 'Busco's presence was first detected in 1948, when the pond's fish population declined drastically. The pond's owner searched the pond for any signs of a large predator and was astonished to see ducks disappearing from the water's surface, as if pulled under by a beast swiftly striking from below. His reports attracted others to the pond, and the first official sighting of the monster occurred soon afterward.

THE BEAST OF 'BUSCO

VITAL STATISTICS

DISTINGUISHING FEATURES: Giant turtle with huge beak and thick shell

SIZE: 12–50' in diameter

WEIGHT: 3 tons or more

RANGE AND HABITAT: Large pond near Churubusco, Indiana

POPULATION SIZE: Unknown

DIET: Omnivore

BEHAVIOR: The Beast of 'Busco spends its solitary life at the bottom of its pond, only surfacing at night to feed, but will attack when threatened.

SOURCE: Cryptozoology

ENCOUNTERING THE BEAST OF 'BUSCO:

The Beast, who is commonly known as Oscar, is said to be a giant turtle measuring anywhere between twelve and fifty feet in diameter. One witness likened Oscar's size to that of a pickup truck. In all other respects, Oscar is identical to other large turtles and possesses a thick, durable shell that deflects bullets and protects him from all predators. Turtles are notoriously patient, and Oscar is no exception: he only emerges at night to feed on ducks or plants near the water's surface.

After the initial sightings, which described Oscar in detail, several attempts were made to capture the Beast. Turtle hunters gathered with baited hooks, rifles, and nets made of thick rope and chains. Oscar easily avoided entanglements, warily stole baits, and never appeared to an armed individual. However, in 1949 a few men managed to loop a chain around Oscar's midsection. The chain was attached to a team of four strong, healthy horses and a tug-of-war ensued. Oscar would not budge, and eventually the chain broke. The Beast disappeared shortly thereafter, and despite the fact that a giant turtle corpse was never recovered, the hunters involved claimed that he must surely have died from exertion.

Oscar remained in seclusion for several decades, refusing to surface again until recent years. Since the 1960s, the creature has been spotted on a few occasions. Many modern witnesses only glimpse Oscar's snout as he rises for air. A small faction claim that the creature enjoys eating children, but this report has not been confirmed. Fortunately, most locals feel that Oscar is harmless, and an annual Turtle Days Festival is held in Churubusco in honor of the Beast.

Today, Oscar remains difficult to study or spot, despite the relatively small size of its habitat. The lake was even drained sometime during the last century, but Oscar was not found. In recent years, he may have migrated into the nearby Eel River. Still, begin any search at the pond near Churubusco, as Oscar may still lurk at the bottom of this pool. Any ripple in the water should be studied with great interest, but never approach Oscar directly. When agitated, he could conceivably become incredibly dangerous, and Oscar would probably have little difficulty engulfing a human head within its sharp beak.

THE BLACK RIVER MONSTER

VITAL STATISTICS

DISTINGUISHING FEATURES: Dark brown body, protruding eyeballs, and fingers on flippers

LENGTH: 15'

WEIGHT: 500 lbs

RANGE AND HABITAT: Black River, New York

POPULATION SIZE: One

DIET: Unknown

BEHAVIOR: The Black River Monster, which only appears during electrical storms, occasionally startles onlookers but largely remains indifferent toward humans.

SOURCE: Cryptozoology, supernaturalism, Fortean studies

ENCOUNTERING THE BLACK RIVER MONSTER:

The Black River Monster is a large, enigmatic serpent living in New York State's Black River, about two hundred miles north of New York City. Although many cryptozoologists have studied the beast since it was first spotted in 1951, little is known about the creature. It has surfaced only a handful of times, averaging about three appearances every ten years. From these encounters, however, cryptozoologists have gleaned the most important piece of information known about the Black River Monster: it only manifests during electrical storms.

When it does appear, the Black River Monster is described as a serpentine behemoth with a thick, tapered body, dark brown skin, and large eyes that protrude grotesquely from its skull. Unique among river monsters, the flippers of the Black River Monster actually possess fingers and an opposable thumb.

Several theories explain the Black River Monster's connection to electrical storms. Cryptozoologists have speculated that the beast is actually a supernatural entity from another dimension. It travels to Earth by opening a dimensional gateway, and the energy released by this rift in the fabric of the universe disrupts weather patterns and causes electrical storms. Alternately, the Black River Monster may inhabit our dimension, but possess vast powers allowing it to control the weather and summon storms, perhaps in an attempt to conceal its passing.

When searching for the Black River Monster, listen to local weather forecasts for predictions of severe atmospheric turbulence. When such warnings are broadcast, rush to the banks of the Black River and establish an observation post. While tromping about in the electrical storm, however, be cautious of sudden and potentially fatal lightning strikes. Wear several layers of insulation and rubber boots. Avoid carrying cameras, video recorders, or rifles, which can act as conduits for lightning.

Little evidence has been gained from inter-

NYS Department of Economic Development

Rafting on the Black River in New York during electrical storms may provide a glimpse of the Black River Monster.

actions with the beast, and it is therefore difficult to predict how the monster will respond toward humans. During a 1951 encounter, Wash Mellick threw rocks at the Black River Monster, which only stared at him with indifference. For the most part, the aloof monster seems to care little for humanity. When sighted during a storm, it will go about its business and eventually disappear beneath the waters as the thunder and lightning fade away.

CADDY, THE CADBORO BAY SEA SERPENT

VITAL STATISTICS

DISTINGUISHING FEATURES: Black body, bulbous eyes, and mottled hide

LENGTH: 80–100′

WEIGHT: 90–120 tons

RANGE AND HABITAT: British Columbia coastal waters

POPULATION SIZE: Unknown

DIET: Omnivore

BEHAVIOR: Caddy is an extremely active and benign sea serpent that makes frequent appearances off the shores of Vancouver Island.

SOURCE: Cryptozoology, Native American mythology

ENCOUNTERING CADDY:

Caddy, more properly known as cadborosaurus, is a sea serpent living in Cadboro Bay, between Vancouver Island and the British Columbian mainland. Like all sea serpents, he is slender and long, but Caddy also has two large flippers. A jagged dorsal crest, frequently mistaken for a mane, provides Caddy with ballast. His large head, usually described as "horselike," rests atop a slender neck about two and a half feet thick. Caddy's flesh has been variously described as black, dark brown, bluish green, mottled gray, and creamy yellow. The monster also has small, insulating patches of short, soft hair.

The physiology of the cadborosaurus is extremely well suited to high-speed travel, and witnesses uniformly describe the monster's movement as being rapid and streamlined. When Caddy swims at maximum speed, his dorsal fin often breaks the water's surface. During more leisurely trips, large portions of the monster's body rise above the water at irregular intervals, creating the false impression that he has several humps or coils. Whenever molested, Caddy immediately dives.

Caddy's most unusual physical trait is his face, which is alternately described as horrific or lovable. Caddy has no visible ears or nostrils, but long whiskers hang from his jaw and cheeks. The monster's eyes are black and bulbous and cast a reddish green "eye-shine" when viewed under certain conditions; they have been variously characterized as sinister or endearing. Caddy's mouth harbors eight-inch fangs, rows of sharp, fishlike teeth, and a serpentine tongue.

Despite appearances, Caddy has yet to pose a danger to humans or other animals. In 1934, one witness observed Caddy swallow a wounded duck, but such hunting is rare. Caddy's diet consists largely of kelp and other sea plants, only occasionally supplemented by such fare as fish and waterfowl.

Caddy was originally encountered centuries ago by the Chinook Indians. His first documented appearance before white settlers occurred in the mid-1920s, when he was called the Sea Hag because of the fear he inspired. However, in 1933, Archie Wills, the editor of the *Victoria Times,* began promoting the beast as a local mascot. He sponsored a "name the monster" contest and selected "cadborosaurus" from the entries. Caddy, as the sea serpent quickly became known, was promptly adopted by the residents of Cadboro Bay and the surrounding areas. The monster has since been observed hundreds of times, with appearances as recent as 1992, and has become a much beloved neighbor.

Ernest Lee, who hunted Caddy throughout the 1940s, can attest to the locals' undying affection for their creature. In the spring of 1943, Lee rammed the hapless serpent twice with his motorboat. After the second blow, Caddy stopped moving and sank below the water, presumably dead. If Caddy had not emerged just two weeks later, the public outrage over the monster's death could have cost Lee his freedom or even his life.

Despite the fact that Caddy has resisted capture, more than enough evidence suggests that the creature does exist. The sheer wealth of sightings lends the most credence to claims of the monster's reality, and the list of people who have spotted Caddy is rife with dignitaries and respected citizens. In August

1932, F. W. Kemp, an official at the Provincial Library at Victoria, was one of the first non-natives to spy the beast. In October of the following year, Maj. W. H. Langley, a clerk of the British Columbia Legislative Assembly, and a well-known barrister and amateur marine biologist, also glimpsed the creature. Judge James Thomas Brown, who had spent over thirty years as the highly respected chief justice of the King's Bench in Saskatchewan, observed Caddy from a distance of less than 150 yards.

Caddy sightings are still more impressive because, on many occasions, the monster is observed by a group of witnesses. In February 1953, for example, at least ten people watched for over an hour as the cadborosaurus cavorted throughout Qualicum Bay. The following February, near Nanaimo, Caddy repeated this performance for a group of no less than thirty people.

Such amazing sightings, which are difficult to dismiss as hoaxes or mass hallucinations, have inspired a handful of scientists to investigate cadborosaurus. Most notable are the marine scientists Paul LeBlond, from the University of British Columbia, and E. L. Bousfield, from the Royal British Columbia Museum. They have determined that Caddy is an enormous reptile with mammalian traits. They have also been credited with baptizing cadborosaurus with his scientific name, *Cadborosaurus willsi,* and in

> The Thing's presence seemed to change the whole landscape, which makes it difficult to describe my experiences. It did not seem to belong to the present scheme of things, but rather to the Long Ago when the world was young.
>
> —Caddy witness
> F. W. Kemp

December 1992 Bousfield brought Caddy's existence to the attention of the American Society of Zoologists.

The efforts of researchers such as Bousfield and LeBlond have also unearthed sightings of a cadborosaurus lacking whiskers and a visible dorsal fin. This creature, dubbed Amy, is believed to be Caddy's mate. The female serpent is smaller than Caddy, reaching only sixty feet in length, has darker skin, and remains much more reclusive than her paramour.

Caddy and Amy have evidently produced offspring, as Capt. Bill Hagelund testified to capturing an infant cadborosaurus while fishing in Pirate's Cove in 1968. The small, eellike creature was sixteen inches long and roughly one inch in diameter. Its lower jaw contained a full complement of sharp, tiny teeth. The young cadborosaurus also had underdeveloped flippers, a spade-shaped tail, and a layer of yellow fuzz on its underbelly.

Hagelund had initially thought to take the baby monster to scientists at Departure Bay, but he became fearful that the serpent's frantic efforts to escape would result in its death, and thus he released it back into the wild. Unfortunately, not all of Caddy and Amy's progeny have been so fortunate: several cadborosauri have been fired upon by frightened witnesses. In all such cases, the assaulted serpent's body was never recovered.

Caddy's kin have also fallen prey to natural

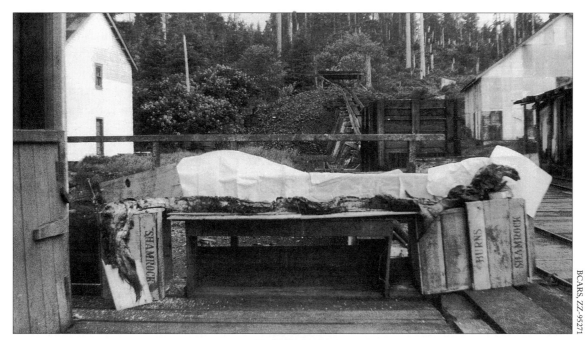

BCARS, ZZ-95271

The Caddy corpse.

predators, as graphically revealed in October 1937 when the corpse of a young cadborosaurus was extracted from a sperm whale's stomach. The cadaver was taken to a Naden Harbour whaling station in the Queen Charlotte Islands, British Columbia, where it was extensively studied. Although decay prevented more thorough descriptions of the creature's exterior, the rotting mass was roughly ten feet long, possessed a horselike head, and had a serpentine body. Sadly, as is the case with so many finds integral to monsterology, this corpse has disappeared.

While the famed "Caddy corpse" has vanished, the living creature has not. In 1996, there were over a dozen sightings of Caddy, and in June 1997 Caddy was spotted in a much publicized encounter as he surfaced near Desolation Sound.

Novice monsterologists are urged to pursue Caddy because he appears frequently. The creature has been known to roam the entire northern-Pacific coastline, but prefers the haven of Cadboro Bay, and monsterologists are advised to study Caddy from this locale. The monster is most often spotted from boats on the bay, but can also be observed from the shores of Victoria on Vancouver Island and nearby Chatham Island.

Caddy is neither murderous nor aggressive, but always approach the monster slowly, using every effort to avoid startling or confusing the creature. Do not make sudden movements and do not attempt to touch the monster. Provide the creature with a comfortable distance and always leave him with an escape route. Never approach within one hundred feet of a small cadborosaurus, as Caddy may construe this as an attack on his offspring and will surely use every means to defend his child.

CHAMP, THE LAKE CHAMPLAIN MONSTER

VITAL STATISTICS

DISTINGUISHING FEATURES: Horselike head, slick flesh, long neck, humped back, and green eyes

HEIGHT: 40′

WEIGHT: 2,000 lbs or more

RANGE AND HABITAT: Lake Champlain, New York/Vermont/Quebec

POPULATION SIZE: Unknown

DIET: Omnivore

BEHAVIOR: Although once mischievous and prone to clashes with humanity, Champ is currently one of the most tranquil of all lake monsters and is usually encountered as it gracefully glides across the surface of Lake Champlain.

SOURCE: Cryptozoology, Native American mythology

ENCOUNTERING CHAMP:

Next to **Ogopogo,** Champ may be the most widely known and recognized lake monster in North America. It is also one of the most substantiated monsters, boasting literally hundreds of sightings, at least one photograph, and supporters within the scientific community. Few cryptozoologists deny the possibility of Champ's existence, and many openly accept the creature.

Champ's natural habitat is Lake Champlain, a body of water straddling the New York/Vermont border and extending into Quebec. Roughly 125 miles long and 13 miles wide, the lake reaches depths of over four hundred feet. At 436 square miles in size, it is the largest body of fresh water in the United States aside from the Great Lakes. It is also home to over eighty species of fish, including huge sturgeon, and offers more than adequate space and food for a large, unidentified beast.

Champ is the archetypal saurian: it has a long neck, small head, and large body often described as "thick as a barrel." It also possesses the horselike head typical of so many other lake monsters, including Ogopogo. Champ's gray skin is slick and coated by a thin layer of algae, and the monster looks out on the world through a pair of brilliant green eyes.

Champ was originally reported by Native Americans living on the shores of Lake Champlain, who called the creature Chaousarou. Europeans observed it in July 1609, when the famed explorer Samuel de Champlain encountered and described the monster. Since settlers arrived on the shores of Lake Champlain in the early 1800s, there have been nearly four hundred recorded sightings of the beast. Between 1870 and 1900 in particular, there were over twenty separate encounters, most involving witnesses of impeccable character. Nineteenth-century accounts of the monster were so vivid that P. T. Barnum was compelled to post a

$50,000 reward for the monster's carcass.

In 1873, Champ clashed with settlers when it began stealing livestock from the shores of Lake Champlain near Dresden, New York. Enraged farmers searching for the monster allegedly discovered the creature lurking in a cave on the edge of the lake, but its glowing green eyes and guttural growls frightened the hunters away. Champ was later fired upon by the crew of a steamship, and the beast, bleeding from superficial wounds, sank beneath the water. The brush with humanity evidently concerned Champ so greatly that the creature retired to the depths of the lake for several years.

Champ resurfaced on July 9, 1887, and charged a beach near East Charlotte, Ver-

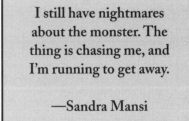

> I still have nightmares about the monster. The thing is chasing me, and I'm running to get away.
>
> —Sandra Mansi

mont, forcing terrorized picnickers to flee. The creature swerved shortly before running aground, a wickedly sly "flyby" maneuver that left witnesses trembling in its wake. The monster was finally observed in its full glory when, in 1915, the beast found itself stranded in the shallows near the entrance of Bulwagga Bay. Champ eventually freed itself and fled immediately to the bowels of the lake.

Champ materialized many times in the early to mid-1900s. Two tourists, Mr. and Mrs. Charles Langlois, struck the monster with an oar when it neared their small rowboat in August 1939. In 1945, Champ stunned the passengers and crew of the SS *Ticonderoga* when it appeared during a bridge-opening ceremony.

Loren Coleman

Artist's rendering of Champ.

By the 1970s, Champ had become an established resident of Lake Champlain, and its notoriety would only continue to increase. The creature was finally caught on film on July 5, 1977, when a vacationing Sandra Mansi spotted the huge creature rising from the lake. She snapped a photograph of the behemoth, but hid the image for fear of ridicule. By the time Mansi came forward in 1980, the negative had been lost (or stolen). However, extensive tests on the image revealed that the photograph had not been tampered with in any way.

Encouraged by Mansi's photograph, researchers took to the lake in search of Champ. A wealth of new sightings poured forth, and the creature continues to appear before dozens of witnesses each year. In 1981 alone, over twenty-one witnesses came forward with tales involving Champ.

Champ has also attracted much interest from the scientific community. In 1981, a conference focusing on the existence of the aquatic reptile was held in Port Henry, New York, where Champ has long been protected by law. In August of that same year, a similar meeting convened in Shelburne, Vermont. Titled "Does Champ Exist?" the conference was led by noted cryptozoologist Joseph Zarzynski, the founder of the Lake Champlain Phenomena Investigation.

In 1982, Zarzynski introduced a resolution in the Vermont House of Representatives and the New York State Senate designed to grant Champ greater legal protection. The resolution passed in both states, ensuring that anyone who willfully kills, injures, or molests Champ will be fully prosecuted.

Today, the monster is revered by locals along the shores of Lake Champlain. In Port Henry, the creature's image is printed on everything from T-shirts to coffee mugs. Similar ventures, including special Champ sight-seeing cruises, can be found throughout the Lake Champlain area.

Those who have successfully spied Champ claim that observing the beast can be akin to looking back into time, as the monster is clearly prehistoric. With its impossible size, glowing green eyes, and regal bearing, Champ is a mercurial monster of epic proportions. Some witnesses suffer psychological aftershocks following their encounter, while others feel a deep affinity and connection to the creature and spend the rest of their lives yearning for another glimpse.

For all the above reasons, Champ is much sought after by intrepid researchers. Fortunately, the lake's resident leviathan is far less difficult to study than other North American monsters. Although the lake is large, cities and towns on its shores offer gracious amenities, and searching for Champ may become a series of afternoon pleasure cruises through sparkling bays. Plan your travel to Lake Champlain during the summer, specifically late July and early August, when Champ most often rears its saurian head.

Champ is rarely dangerous, but monsterologists should still avoid cornering or pestering the beast. Aside from the threat of legal action, anyone who does harm Champ could face the monster's full wrath and strength. After surviving gunshots, collisions with large craft, freezing temperatures, and centuries of human contact, Champ has evolved into a hardy and robust monster. It could easily smash through a bothersome researcher's boat and drag the pest into the lake's icy depths.

THE FLATHEAD LAKE MONSTER

VITAL STATISTICS

DISTINGUISHING FEATURES: Black hide and no fins

LENGTH: 30′

WEIGHT: 2 tons

RANGE AND HABITAT: Flathead Lake, Montana

POPULATION SIZE: One

DIET: Unknown

BEHAVIOR: A fairly congenial creature, the Flathead Lake Monster has been known to approach people in boats and on shore, but it has never displayed any aggressive tendencies.

SOURCE: Native American mythology, American (seaman) folklore, cryptozoology

ENCOUNTERING THE FLATHEAD LAKE MONSTER:

Montana's Flathead Lake Monster is a fairly typical aquatic serpent in all respects. It measures about thirty feet in length and possesses a vaguely serpentine shape. Most descriptions depict the monster as large, black, and ominous. Like many sea serpents and lake monsters, it moves through the water with an undulating motion, leaving a large wake behind it. The monster is also known for throwing its head about and spouting jets of water into the air.

Unlike many of its contemporaries, the Flathead Lake Monster lacks fins of any type, an omission that leaves researchers wondering just how the animal reaches its top speed of forty miles per hour while maintaining its equilibrium. Observers also note that the creature is extremely graceful, and it appears that the beast is completely mute.

The Flathead Lake Monster's home is one of the largest bodies of water in the northwest United States, about 188 square miles in size. It stretches for twenty-seven miles and reaches widths of fifteen miles. However, because it is fed by so-called glacial rivers, the water in the lake is extremely cold, stunting the development of microorganisms, which in turn prevents the growth of any large fish populations. Fish such as salmon are common, but seldom reach any notable size. Thus, the exact nature of the Flathead Lake Monster's diet remains unknown. In recent years, there have been rumors that the lake has been injected with sturgeon from other lakes in an attempt to boost the tourist industry, and these fish could form the bulk of the monster's diet. Yet only one sturgeon of any noteworthy size (7.5 feet) has been caught.

The Flathead Lake Monster was first spotted several centuries ago by Native Americans, who mentioned the monster in a small number of legends about the lake, but its existence was not seriously considered until sightings began anew in the late 1800s. The first officially reported sighting occurred in 1885, when James Kern, the skipper of the *U.S.*

Travel Montana/Donnie Sexton

Flathead Lake, Montana.

Grant, spotted what he believed to be another boat coming toward him. As the two vessels converged, Kern realized that the approaching object was organic, and given its size, he assumed it was some sort of whale. Kern continued on his path, closing the gap between the *Grant* and the beast. In the ensuing panic, at least one passenger fired on the creature, which escaped beneath the water.

The *U.S. Grant*'s encounter was followed in 1919 by a phenomenal sighting almost unmatched in the history of monsterology. While aboard the *City of Polson,* at least fifty individuals saw the behemoth swim directly in front of the boat. In the eighty years since the *Polson* sighting, the monster has also been spotted by dozens of fishermen, tourists, bathers, and ship passengers and personnel. Around 1920, fishermen began coming forward with complaints about "something" tearing through their nets, a problem that still

occurs today. Even those nets used to catch enormous bull trout are shredded, convincing many locals of the presence of a "monster fish" in the lake.

By 1959, annual sightings of the Flathead Lake Monster had dramatically increased, but the 1960s would be the creature's most active period to date. The most notable of the decade's sightings occurred in September 1960, when Mr. and Mrs. Gilbert Zigler encountered the monster on the shore near the Polson country club. The creature was reclining beneath a pier, rubbing its massive body against a piling. Mrs. Zigler was overcome with horror upon observing the monster, which she described as inordinately ugly. Gilbert sprinted to the country club to fetch his rifle, but by the time he had returned, the monster had moved into the center of the lake and was well out of range. Before the week came to a close, the Ziglers would sight the monster once again, as would numerous other witnesses, many of whom refused to come forward for fear of ridicule.

The year 1963 was almost as eventful. On the clear afternoon of July 15, twelve people watched the Flathead Lake Monster cavort in the lake; and on September 8, two upstanding high school teachers also became primary witnesses.

As a result of the sightings of the 1960s, numerous attempts were made to photograph, capture, or kill the monster. Several dive teams entered the lake, and at least one diver spent four full days scouring the waters for the monster. The syndicate Big Fish Unlimited, which was formed to hook the Flathead Lake Monster, offered a reward of $1,400 to anyone who managed to catch any fish over fourteen feet in length. The *Flathead Courier* promised $25 for the first photograph of the creature, and a local Realtor extended a reward of $100 per foot to anyone who caught the Flathead Lake Monster, a prize that could total $6,000 or more if the beast is as large as many believe. None of these rewards have been claimed.

Since the end of the 1960s, the Flathead Lake Monster has become more reclusive, but sightings do occur every few years. It is likely that the beast has haunts at the bottom of the lake where it whiles away months at a time.

Because it surfaces so rarely, study of the Flathead Lake Monster is difficult. However, researching the lake proves far more worthwhile. Flathead Lake is located near Polson and is bordered by several pleasant towns and small cities, including Elmo, Big Arm, and Rollins. The area is scenic and relaxing. Flathead Lake is also an enjoyable research location because of the Flathead Lake Rock Art, a large geometrical drawing that survives as western Montana's only petroglyph.

The design seems to have been intended to cover a series of red pictographs, and the overall message of the rock art is totally unclear. It has been postulated that some element of the petroglyph or the underlying paintings may be an obscure warning to others that the lake is inhabited by a monster. But if the rock art was intended to be a warning, the Flathead Lake Monster has yet to live up to any fearsome reputation. It is safe to assume the beast does not pose a significant threat, and monsterologists are encouraged to study the monster and lake extensively.

Sturgeon: The Lake Monster Through the Eyes of Science

Sturgeon are capable of reaching such massive proportions that they have often been misidentified as monsters by the untrained observer. Throughout Russia, many lakes support sturgeon that range from twenty to twenty-six feet in length and can weigh over two tons. Across the United States and Canada, sturgeon have been known to reach lengths of twenty-five feet or more. Possibly the largest sturgeon are found in Seton Lake, British Columbia, where there are tales of fish that surpass thirty-five feet in length.

THE GLOUCESTER SEA SERPENT

VITAL STATISTICS

DISTINGUISHING FEATURES: Thick, black scales and prominent humps

LENGTH: 100'

WEIGHT: Unknown

RANGE AND HABITAT: Atlantic Ocean

POPULATION SIZE: Unknown

DIET: Omnivore

BEHAVIOR: The Gloucester Sea Serpent only appears in the summer months, when it presumably nears the shores of New England to lay eggs.

SOURCE: Cryptozoology

ENCOUNTERING THE GLOUCESTER SEA SERPENT:

Possibly the most famous marine monster of all time, and certainly one of the most well-documented by sightings and witness testimony, the Gloucester Sea Serpent is a serpentine animal of enormous proportions. Estimated at between 80 and 140 feet long, the monster has dark, leathery skin marked by small white streaks. Its head, which is about six feet in length, is flat and snakelike. The creature has a large dorsal fin, often described as a mane or a row of spines racing down the length of its back. Its mouth is lined with rows of tiny, hooked teeth about three inches long, which are more akin to the teeth of a pike than the fangs of any serpent. It swims with an un-dulating motion and can outpace most boats.

The Gloucester Sea Serpent was originally sighted in Broad Bay, Maine, in 1751 and Penobscot Bay, Maine, in 1779, but moved to Gloucester, Massachusetts, in 1815. After brief forays into the waters off the coast of Gloucester in the summers of 1815 and 1816, the monster finally became well-known in August 1817, when fully one hundred people observed the serpent in just weeks.

Witnesses like Amos Story, who watched the serpent for over an hour on August 10, 1817, spawned initial interest in Gloucester's aquatic inhabitant. The creature was formally recognized by the press on August 22, when a pamphlet titled "A Monstrous Sea Serpent: The largest ever seen in America" was published. Between these two events, the monster was spotted dozens of times by a wide range of witnesses. It was seen near a lighthouse and near a windmill and Fort Point. The Gloucester Sea Serpent was also seen frequently from the shore; one Col. S. G. Perkins reportedly observed the beast reclining in the shallow waters off a public beach.

In mid-August 1817, during the height of the sightings, a group of amateur investigators formed the Linnaean Society of New England with the intention of researching and validating the sightings of the Gloucester Sea Serpent. Membership included a judge, a physician, and a naturalist. Using an extensive questionnaire, the group interviewed firsthand witnesses immediately after sightings occurred and later attempted to organize this information to create an accurate image of the monster.

Unfortunately, the Linnaean Society eventually suffered several blows to their credibility. First, the group constructed nets and traps in the hopes of catching a live specimen. These attempts failed. Next, the Linnaeans theorized that the monster must come close to the shore during summer to deposit its eggs in the warm sand. With the intention of finding a nest or a clutch of eggs, the Society made a publicized search of the shores, which also produced nothing.

In September 1817, just as the sightings of the Gloucester Sea Serpent were beginning their annual decline, a group of boys discovered a three-foot black snake with prominent humps on a beach about fifty feet from the shore. The creature, which had thirty-two distinct humps, fit the Linnaeans' projections of the Gloucester Sea Serpent's offspring. After extensive study and a thorough dissection, the investigators declared that they had discovered a new species and renamed the Gloucester Sea Serpent *Scoliophis atlanticus,* or the Atlantic humped snake. To prove the veracity of their find, the Society prepared a detailed report, complete with illustrations of the snake's major organs and skeletal structure.

According to the Linnaeans, the so-called Atlantic humped snake is a close relative of the common blacksnake, *Coluber constrictor.* Unfortunately, when the French naturalist Alexandre Lesueur heard of the find, he instantly refuted the Linnaean Society's evidence and asserted boldly that the infant snake was, in fact, a common blacksnake. The humps, the naturalist

Giant Squid

Many researchers have suggested that witnesses who claim to have seen sea serpents have actually observed a giant squid. Sometimes referred to as the Kraken, the giant squid was long relegated to the realm of fable and fantasy. In modern times, however, even zoologists recognize the existence of these behemoths, which can reach documented lengths of sixty-five feet (some researchers place the largest squid at ninety feet). The giant squid spend much of their time on the ocean floor, where they often fall prey to voracious sperm whales. Giant squid have been known to attack humans, and they are capable of using their powerful suckers and long tentacles to inflict huge wounds. However, sightings are rare, and monsterologists and other scientists most often encounter giant squid when the animals are beached upon death.

A giant squid found beached at Plum Island, Massachusetts, in 1980.

Loren Coleman

argued, were a result of deformity or disease and were probably tumors of some sort. After Lesueur's rebuttal, the Linnaean Society became the target of intense ridicule. Humiliated, they discontinued their admirable research into the Gloucester Sea Serpent.

Although the Linnaean Society disbanded late in 1817, the Gloucester Sea Serpent and the controversy it engendered continued. The following summer, the monster arrived again on the shores of New England, presumably to deposit eggs. One Samuel Cabot watched the creature from Nahant, Massachusetts, about twenty miles from Gloucester, and skippers sailing Massachusetts Bay claimed that they had been forced to flee from the onrushing giant.

By 1819, the people of Gloucester as well as

many tourists knew to expect the sea serpent's arrival each summer. Early in the summer of 1819, several dozen beachgoers in Nahant watched as the monster approached to within a few yards of the shore. A vacationing marine biologist who spied the monster maintained that it was not any known aquatic animal. Later in the summer of 1819, the captain and first mate of a schooner called the *Concord* gave formal statements before a justice of the peace, testifying that they too had seen the Gloucester monster. A Rev. Cheever Finch gave a description that perfectly matched those of other witnesses and claimed to have observed the creature for over thirty minutes.

Similar sightings of the Gloucester Sea Serpent continued every summer from 1817 to 1847, constituting at least thirty years of consistent and reliable appearances by the immense sea snake. Unfortunately, on May 15, 1833, Capt. W. Sullivan and several other military men were traveling between Halifax and Mahone Bay, Nova Scotia, in a small yacht when they spotted the Gloucester Sea Serpent and fired upon it. Following this encounter, the sea serpent exhibited much greater caution in its dealings with humans.

After 1847, reported sightings began to taper off dramatically, and by the late 1880s, many feared that the monster had died. Fortunately, the Gloucester Sea Serpent suddenly returned during the summers of 1886 and 1887, when it was seen at Rockport, Cape Cod, and Gloucester, Massachusetts, as well as various other locations along the East Coast. On August 13, 1886, one G. B. Putnam used his marine glass to watch the monster rise out of the water multiple times. News of this sighting prompted P. T. Barnum to offer a $20,000 reward for any sea serpent,

alive or dead. To this day, the purse has gone uncollected.

Gloucester Sea Serpent sightings continued with regularity into the twentieth century as well. In August 1905, for example, the monster was encountered off Wood Island, Maine, where Maj. Gen. H. C. Merriam of the U.S. Army watched it undulate through the water. And, although much less active in modern times, the Gloucester Sea Serpent did appear in Cape Elizabeth, Maine, on June 5, 1958.

In July 1963, a group of scientists aboard a research ship were in the water near New York City, where they watched a huge serpent pass beneath the boat. A monstrous, slime-covered black serpent also surprised fishermen in Bronx, New York, in March 1969 and reappeared days later in Little Neck Bay, Queens. Although neither of these sightings has been directly linked to the Gloucester beast, the possibility should not be ruled out.

In recent years, reports of the giant Gloucester Sea Serpent are rare. There are, however, infrequent sightings of smaller black serpents on New England beaches and in the water.

Summer is still the best time to visit Gloucester in pursuit of the fabled sea serpent, and the entire month of August should be devoted to watching the Atlantic ocean for the emergence of the snake as it comes ashore to lay its eggs. Do not molest the sea serpent during this process, as it could become extremely aggressive in defense of its young.

The Gloucester Sea Serpent may present other dangers not commonly considered by many monsterologists. Though not particularly hostile, like numerous aquatic reptiles it may be venomous. It has also been known to charge small craft. If cornered or injured, it could lash out with terrifying consequences.

THE ILIAMNA LAKE MONSTERS

VITAL STATISTICS

DISTINGUISHING FEATURES: Blunt heads and vertical tails

LENGTH: 1–30′

WEIGHT: Varies

RANGE AND HABITAT: Lake Iliamna, Alaska

POPULATION SIZE: Unknown

DIET: Carnivore

BEHAVIOR: The Iliamna monsters use their thick heads to capsize passing boats, so that they might consume the passengers as the crafts sink.

SOURCE: Aleut Indian mythology, cryptozoology

ENCOUNTERING THE ILIAMNA LAKE MONSTER:

Unlike many of North America's monster lakes, which only play host to a single entity, Iliamna Lake in Alaska boasts an entire population of strange aquatic creatures. The Aleut Indians, who had been living on the shores of the lake before white settlers arrived, first encountered the deadly species, much to the tribe's dismay. Beginning early in the nineteenth century, the lake's monstrous inhabitants terrorized the human populace by overturning canoes and devouring braves. After futile attempts to defeat the monsters, the Aleut Indians abandoned the area.

Only a few decades later, white settlers began exploring the region and eventually ran afoul of the Iliamna creatures as well. In more recent times, numerous sightings by bush pilots and the efforts of investigators such as Tom Slick, who led an expedition to the lake in the middle of this century, have propelled the Iliamna Lake Monsters from the realm of Native American mythology and into the world of cryptozoology.

Evidence gleaned from Aleut accounts and modern sightings has allowed monsterologists to construct a physical description of the Iliamna Lake Monsters, which generally resemble the common barracuda. The beasts vary radically in size, with the smallest representatives only measuring a scant foot in length and the largest reaching lengths of thirty feet or more. Regardless of size, all of these monsters possess blunt heads, vertical tails, slender bodies, and dull, metallic skin.

The Iliamna Lake Monsters hunt a wide variety of prey, including birds, fish, and small mammals, but they are patently dangerous because they prefer human meat above all other fare. They stalk humans by floating just a few feet beneath the water's surface, patiently waiting for boats to enter the lake. Using their blunt heads, the monsters easily capsize canoes, sailboats, and even small motorboats. Anyone who is thrown into the water in this manner is quickly torn apart by a pack of these bloodthirsty fish.

Unless hunting, the Iliamna Lake Monsters avoid humans whenever possible, refusing to surface or allow themselves to be caught. Tom Slick's expedition, which had the aid of U.S. naval officers, ultimately failed to produce concrete evidence; and in 1966, an intrepid photographer from New York ventured out onto the lake to capture the monsters on film but found the creatures far too elusive. On occasion, trustworthy fishermen profess to hooking one of the Iliamna brutes by using heavy tackle and raw meat as bait, but even under these circumstances the tenacious monsters cannot be pulled from the lake and soon escape their predicament.

The Iliamna Lake Monsters may remain so elusive because the lake, which is about eighty miles long, is connected to the ocean via the surprisingly deep Kvichak River. With this outlet readily available, it is likely that the monsters travel freely between the lake and the sea. In fact, the monsters may only enter the lake to spawn.

The Iliamna Lake Monsters are a difficult challenge for researchers because of Alaska's unforgiving elements and harsh terrain. Inexperienced or poorly equipped monsterologists will surely be defeated by a vicious windchill, sudden snowfall, or roaming predators before reaching the lake's shores.

Although surrounded by dangerous terrain, the lake is a monsterologist's dream because it has amazingly clear waters. Therefore, the creatures are best observed by plane on clear, calm days. However, never strike out across the lake's surface. Once the monsters detect your presence, they will surely attack en masse, overturning your vessel and sending you into the cold waters. After you have been unseated in this manner, hypothermia and shock will render you helpless. But before the lake can claim you, the monsters will flock to your sinking body and tear it into a thousand bloody pieces.

MANIPOGO, THE LAKE MANITOBA MONSTER

VITAL STATISTICS

DISTINGUISHING FEATURES: Extremely noisy

LENGTH: 35–60′

WEIGHT: Over 10 tons

RANGE AND HABITAT: Lake Manitoba, Lake Winnipeg, Lake Winnipegosis

POPULATION SIZE: Fewer than six

DIET: Unknown

BEHAVIOR: An extremely boisterous monster, Manipogo spends most of its time making strange noises, which echo across Lake Manitoba. When it is actually spotted, Manipogo usually flees immediately.

SOURCE: Cryptozoology, Native American mythology, immigrant (Icelandic) folklore

ENCOUNTERING MANIPOGO:

Manipogo is often overlooked in discussions on lake monsters, usually obscured by better known lake monsters such as **Ogopogo** or **Champ.** Yet the creature, which has been encountered for at least the past three centuries in Lake Manitoba, Lake Winnipeg, and Lake Winnipegosis, is extremely well-documented by Native American folklore, immigrant legends, the tales of fur trappers and traders, and a host of modern sightings.

These myriad sources all agree that Manipogo (or Winnipogo, as the creature is known on the shores of Lake Winnipeg) is an im-

mense, serpentine creature similar in shape to a giant eel. It can reach speeds of fifteen miles per hour as it swims. Like the **Alkali Lake Monster** and others, Manipogo's flat head is adorned with a long, slender horn.

The coloration of the monster's hide has alternatively been described as slimy, yellow-brown; brownish black; gray; dark green; and purple. These varied descriptions suggest that Manipogo has the chameleon-like ability to subtly shift shades, perhaps altering its coloration according to season or time of day.

Witnesses also report that the monster has a wide range of vocalizations, which inspire awe and fear. It alternately hollers, weeps, whistles, hoots, screams, laughs, and whispers. The Assiniboin Indians living on the shores of Lake Manitoba were the first to hear the monster's eerie cries, which they believed to be the shrieks of a powerful spirit known as a manitou. They named the lake in honor of the supernatural entity, whose voice they heard almost nightly. During the 1800s, Icelanders settling near Gimli on the shores of Lake Winnipeg claimed that the area was home to a whole race of large serpents known as the *skrimski.* They often reported hearing the call of the *skrimski,* which they described as a rumbling and thunderous bellow. The Cree Indians who lived on the lake before the Icelanders told similar stories.

Evidence gathered from numerous sightings suggests that, unlike **Ogopogo** (a single monster), Manipogo is a representative of an entire species. On August 12, 1960, at least seventeen people saw three different monsters traveling together. By their respective sizes, witnesses identified the group as a family unit consisting of a father, mother, and child.

Manipogo is unusual among lake monsters because of its vast habitat, which includes at least three lakes with a combined surface area in excess of 13,000 square miles. Although most often associated with Lake Manitoba, the creature has also been observed frequently in Lake Winnipeg, the sixth-largest lake in Canada. In addition, Manipogo (or a nearly identical creature) is said to roam Lake Winnipegosis, which is connected to Lake Manitoba by the Dauphin River.

Due to the size of its habitat, a fair share of physical evidence, and a massive number of sightings, Manipogo's existence is strongly supported by many cryptozoologists. Recorded sightings began in 1909, when a member of the Hudson Bay Company witnessed a thirty-five-foot mass progress across Lake Manitoba. In 1935, timber inspectors Charlie Ross and Tom Spence revealed to the *Winnipeg Free Press* that they had also spied a behemoth of epic proportions on the lake.

The first physical evidence to support Manipogo's existence surfaced in the 1930s, when Oscar Frederickson discovered a huge vertebra on the shore of Lake Winnipegosis. The bone, which measured six inches by three inches, was destroyed in a mysterious fire sometime before 1970, but a wooden replica has convinced many cryptozoologists that the vertebra belonged to a Manipogo.

In August 1955, a widely discussed Manipogo sighting by four men prompted a thorough investigation by the Department of Game and Fisheries. The department explored the area for a few months, crossing the lake thousands of times in their noisy boats as they scanned the horizon for any sign of the gray mass. These efforts proved futile, but while the department's investigation was busy wasting time and energy, at least six other witnesses observed Manipogo.

In 1960, Lake Manitoba garnered a record number of sightings. The most phenomenal encounter took place on July 22, when at least twenty people, including a well-respected Canadian official, watched the monster from a beach. Just a

Mike Grandmaison

The shores of Lake Manitoba.

few weeks later, on August 12, a group of seventeen people at the same beach also became Manipogo believers. Tom Locke, a witness to the August 12 Manipogo appearance, attempted to photograph the monster with a handheld movie camera, but discovered he was out of film. Although he did not obtain evidence of the creature, Locke is credited with coining the name Manipogo, no doubt in deference to the world-famous **Ogopogo.** Soon after, the beach where so many sightings took place (and continue to occur) was renamed Manipogo Beach.

The summer of 1960 also marked a significant event in the monsterology of Manipogo when Prof. James McLeod, the head of the Department of Zoology at the University of Manitoba, organized an expedition to find the elusive creature. Unfortunately, the expedition was plagued by malfunctions, poor timing, and the complete absence of concrete sightings. McLeod continued his quest the following summer, but met with similar results. However, his dedication has inspired other monsterologists and validated the search for Manipogo.

While McLeod and other experienced researchers have failed to find Manipogo, seemingly incontrovertible evidence supporting the existence of a large, reptilian creature residing within Lake Manitoba finally emerged in 1962. On August 13, at about four in the afternoon, a tourist named Dick Vincent took several photographs of something strange surfacing on the lake. One of these priceless shots was published in the *Winnipeg Free Press* on August 15. Although fuzzy, the photograph seemingly depicts a large reptilian creature with a dark green hide.

Vincent's photo, initially viewed as a hoax, was validated by the fact that a large number of witnesses also observed Manipogo at approximately the same time and from a variety of vantage points. More than half of these individuals had the creature in view for over fifteen minutes.

Since Vincent's success, the hype and hysteria surrounding the monster has diminished somewhat, but Manipogo sightings still occur regularly. Today, cryptozoologists continue to support the beast's existence, and it remains one of the most widely accepted of all lake monsters.

However, before overeager monsterologists strike out for Lake Manitoba hastily, it must be noted that the sheer size of Manipogo's habitat makes the creature difficult to study. It would be impossible to continually monitor or fully explore the area with even the largest of expeditions. Therefore, monsterologists should content themselves with a few primary locations. Most notable are Graves Point, Overflowing River, and especially Manipogo Beach, where countless Manipogo sightings have occurred since the 1960s. If you can bear the weather, visit these sites during winter. Although the creature is least active during this time of year, its presence is far more easily noted because its huge body tends to crack and heave surface ice as the monster passes below. Also pay close attention to the shores of Manipogo's three lakes. It is quite possible that the monster visits the land at night, leaving behind footprints or other signs of its passing.

Manipogo has yet to prove dangerous, but like all monsters, it should be approached with caution. In most instances, the beast will probably descend to the bottom of the lake at the first signs of human approach. Pay close attention to its cries: if it roars in anger, flee the lake immediately.

OGOPOGO, THE MONSTER OF LAKE OKANAGAN

VITAL STATISTICS

DISTINGUISHING FEATURES: Horns, whiskered chin, and four flippers

LENGTH: 70′

WEIGHT: 100 tons

RANGE AND HABITAT: Lake Okanagan, British Columbia

POPULATION SIZE: Unknown

DIET: Omnivore

BEHAVIOR: In the past, Ogopogo murdered and devoured people with impunity, but in recent years the monster has become mild-mannered and even friendly.

SOURCE: Native American (Okanakane, Shushwap) mythology, cryptozoology

ENCOUNTERING OGOPOGO:

Ogopogo is one of many North American monsters whose history begins with Native American lore and continues well into the twentieth century with modern sightings and induction into the halls of cryptozoology. The belief in Ogopogo originated with the Shushwap and Okanakane Indians living on the shores of Lake Okanagan hundreds of years ago. But by the mid-1800s, the Okanagan Valley had attracted a handful of courageous pioneers, who also began telling tales of en-

counters with a fearsome animal lurking in the lake. Since 1850, well over one thousand people have testified to spying the creature, leading modern cryptozoologists to devote a great deal of time and energy to studying the monster. Today, Ogopogo is one of the most thoroughly documented unidentified lake creatures, second only to Scotland's Loch Ness Monster, and possibly the most famous North American monster aside from **Bigfoot**.

In virtually every account, Ogopogo is described as a long, sinuous creature almost seventy feet long. Its head is usually described as being "sheeplike" or "horselike," due to the general shape of its skull, its large eyes, and its blunt nose. Two large horns erupt from this odd head, and a jagged fin begins at the creature's skull and continues down the length of its body.

Adorning the monster's chin are thick whiskers resembling a beard. The rest of Ogopogo's skin is composed of sizable scales, ranging from dark green to pitch-black in color. Four flippers sprout from the monster's slender body, which is roughly two feet thick. The serpent ends in a long, forked tail capable of propelling the beast at speeds surpassing forty miles per hour. While Ogopogo is largely aquatic, it can also venture onto land. Six-inch "flipper-prints" have been discovered near the lake, and at least one witness spotted the monster lying on a beach.

Loren Coleman

A likeness of Ogopogo in Kelowna, British Columbia.

Lake Okanagan is one of the world's premier monster habitats because it is cold, deep, and large. The lake is seventy-nine miles long with a width that ranges from roughly one mile to two and a half miles. It reaches eight hundred feet at its deepest point, and the total surface area is about 127 square miles. The lake never freezes, but remains a chilly thirty-four degrees Fahrenheit year-round. In comparison, the renowned Loch Ness is only twenty-four miles long, one and a half miles wide, and a constant forty-two degrees Fahrenheit. Although at its greatest depth the Loch is one hundred feet deeper than Lake Okanagan, Ogopogo's home is colder, longer, wider, and much larger overall than the Loch Ness Monster's habitat.

According to both the Shushwap and Okanakane Indians, Ogopogo was originally a violent and unpredictable creature. The monster was known to these peoples as N'ha-a-itk, or "the lake demon,"

> A mighty serpent with the face of a sheep and the head of a bulldog. He struck me dumb with horror.
>
> —American tourist and Ogopogo witness

because they believed that it was an evil supernatural entity with great power and ill intent. To appease this horrible monster, they would carry sacrifices with them whenever they crossed the lake. Such gifts to N'ha-a-itk included lumps of deer meat or live puppies, chickens, and ducks. The sacrifices could be thrown to the monster when it neared or placed in a separate canoe to be floated several feet ahead of the humans.

Native American lore also reveals that Ogopogo allegedly made its home in a cave hidden between what is now known as Squally Point

and a barren island some distance from the shore. The island was dubbed Monster Island, and the waters surrounding it were considered the most dangerous stretch of the lake. Braves foolish enough to land on Monster Island often found it littered with bones, skins, bloodstains, and other signs of the monster's gruesome dining habits.

Ogopogo's attacks on humans continued sporadically throughout the 1800s, but the monster also began a subtle shift in behavior and temperament at about this time. In 1852, Mrs. John Allison became one of the first white Ogopogo witnesses when she glimpsed the creature peacefully basking on the surface of the lake, a sighting that prompted her to diligently collect all accounts of the monster from witnesses and Native Americans. She continued this task until her death in 1928, and much of what she discovered reveals that Ogopogo's tendency to dine on humans waned significantly over time.

By 1924, reported Ogopogo attacks had ceased completely, and the peoples living on the lake were beginning to view the monster in a much kinder light. As fear gave way to curiosity and excitement, accounts of encounters with "the lake demon" became much more lighthearted. While visiting Vernon, British entertainer W. H. Brimblecombe heard many of these colorful stories and was inspired to write a silly song about a creature known as the Ogopogo, a monster spawned from the union of an earwig and a whale. Brimblecombe performed the song at a service-club luncheon in

Kelowna, and Lake Okanagan's resident monster has been known as Ogopogo, or "Ogie," ever since.

As if in recognition of its new name and redeemed reputation, Ogopogo began appearing with much greater frequency after 1924. Sightings have continued unabated throughout this century, and many people still spy the serpent every year. With rare exception, Ogopogo has yet to exhibit the violent demeanor that once terrified the lake's residents. Ogopogo is now much beloved, especially in Kelowna, where a statue of the monster has been erected. The creature has also been made an honorary citizen of Kelowna, afforded all the rights and benefits that all other citizens enjoy, and in 1970 the city formed the Ogopogo Serendipity Society.

Today, Lake Okanagan remains an especially effective training ground for novice monsterologists because the environment presents few hardships. The lake is easy to find and does not present the dangers common to remote or isolated locations. Monsterologists can make use of numerous hotels and other accommodations, boats and docks, and a plethora of supportive locals. Food, like shelter, is easily accessible, and navigating the shores of the lake requires no special skills or physical prowess.

A trip in search of Ogopogo can easily become a vacation, as the lake is a financially feasible destination and the monster is most often seen on sunny days. The lake is also relatively narrow, allowing hydrophobic monsterologists to search for Ogopogo from land-based beach chairs. While a sonar device and a fast boat might be useful, many monsterologists can still meet with success armed with little more than a pair of high-powered binoculars.

However, students of Ogopogo should be warned that the quest also has its difficulties. The few well-manned expeditions that have set out in search of Ogopogo have failed to produce any concrete evidence of the creature's existence. Monsterologists are most often hindered by the noisy boats and hordes of tourists that swarm across the lake and frighten Ogopogo into hiding.

THE LAKE UTOPIA MONSTER

VITAL STATISTICS

DISTINGUISHING FEATURES: Extremely large head and bloody jaws

LENGTH: 100′

WEIGHT: 80 tons

RANGE AND HABITAT: Lake Utopia, New Brunswick

POPULATION SIZE: Unknown

DIET: Carnivore

BEHAVIOR: Despite its namesake, the Lake Utopia Monster is an abhorrent beast that viciously attacks anything that enters its waters.

SOURCE: Native American (Micmac) mythology, Canadian lore, cryptozoology

ENCOUNTERING THE LAKE UTOPIA MONSTER:

The Lake Utopia Monster is yet another reclusive creature that generates great terror with each rare manifestation. Native Americans described it as a terrible, voracious serpent with huge jaws and jagged teeth. According to such accounts, blood drips constantly from the monster's mouth, and particles of tattered flesh dangle from its vicious teeth. This gruesome maw is lodged within a head the size of a large barrel. Modern sightings only seem to confirm this horrible image of the Lake Utopia Monster.

Lake Utopia in New Brunswick, Canada, is a haunting site, the lake monster's presence aside. It is a picturesque and majestic body of water, prone to moments of inexplicable and eerie silence. Nine miles long and three miles wide, it offers moderate space for a lake monster, and it is likely that the beast spends the greater portion of its life at the very bottom of the lake. In fact, the monster often dredges the lake's bed, dislodging old logs, sunken canoes, and large branches. When these objects rush to the surface, they can seriously injure bathers, overturn boats, and create a roiling foam that conceals the monster's presence.

Lake Utopia freezes in the winter, and the monster has been known to push its head through the ice when enraged. Its passing causes huge fissures capable of swallowing anyone treading the ice. In addition, fishermen have long been wary of cutting holes in the ice, for the monster snaps at humans through these openings.

The Lake Utopia Monster has been observed since humans first settled on the lake. The Micmac Indians, in particular, were profoundly affected by the beast's presence, for it often surfaced and consumed braves sailing across the lake. During such attacks, the monster swallowed the unfortunate victim's canoe as well.

The first European settlers also frequently encountered the beast; most residents claimed to have run afoul of the monster at least once, and some spotted the creature on several

occasions. During the late 1800s, sightings became so frequent that several locals in nearby St. George formed a joint stock company with the intention of capturing the monster. In 1870, this organization raised over $200, funds used to buy several large nets. Their efforts proved fruitless, but the excitement generated by the quest ensured that the Lake Utopia Monster would become a popular attraction at the lake for years to come.

Although numerous sightings occurred between 1870 and 1980, none were more memorable than Sherman Hatt's encounter with the creature in July 1982. The monster surfaced near Hatt, who likened the beast to a giant submarine. Hatt was extremely fortunate, as the Lake Utopia Monster showed no signs of aggression before disappearing beneath the waters.

The Lake Utopia Monster, although relatively dangerous, can be safely spotted by ex-perienced monsterologists. Begin your search at night, for the beast appears to be largely nocturnal. To limit the range of your quest, arrive in New Brunswick at the height of winter, after ice has formed on Lake Utopia's surface. Cut a large hole in the ice, position a camera ten feet from this opening, then wait for the monster to surface. Lures, such as large fish or shanks of raw meat, may be dangled over the hole to entice the beast.

If the former tactic does not work, await the first sign of warm weather. After spending an entire winter beneath the ice, the Lake Utopia Monster is half-starved when the ice finally begins to melt and will surface at the first opportunity. However, at this time of year be sure to observe the monster from a distance. Its hunger is so great that it will attempt to consume anything within reach, and the careless monsterologist is easy prey.

WHITEY, THE WHITE RIVER MONSTER

VITAL STATISTICS

DISTINGUISHING FEATURES: Mottled skin and large horn on forehead

LENGTH: 12–65′

WEIGHT: 2–4 tons

RANGE AND HABITAT: White River, Arkansas

POPULATION SIZE: Unknown

DIET: Omnivore

BEHAVIOR: Generally lethargic, Whitey does little aside from drift along Arkansas's White River. However, when approached by humans, the beast can move quickly to escape.

SOURCE: Native American (Quapaw) mythology, cryptozoology

ENCOUNTERING WHITEY: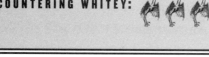

The creature today known as Whitey first appeared in the legends of the Quapaw Indians living on the shores of Arkansas's White River. Most notable are their stories about a large, barren island that would sporadically appear within the river. When one intrepid brave dared to explore the island, he stepped atop the fleshy mound and suddenly spotted a large, ponderous head rising up from the land mass. Frightened, the brave leapt into his canoe and paddled toward shore, but the thrashing monster overturned his little boat. The brave barely survived, and the "island" sank into the depths.

Whitey resurfaced during the Civil War, when it allegedly rammed into the hull of a Confederate riverboat near Newport, Arkansas. The boat, which was carrying several million dollars in gold, promptly sank, severely wounding the Confederacy's war effort. Whitey also emerged briefly in 1850, 1890, and 1917. But the monster did not become a legitimate component of Arkansas's fauna until July 1937, when several reputable businessmen watched Whitey float on the river's surface for several minutes. The most compelling witness was plantation owner Bramblett Bateman, who could describe Whitey in full detail.

According to Bateman and later witnesses, Whitey is a huge river serpent with dull white, blotchy skin. His spine is graced by a large, ridged fin that extends down the creature's back and tail. The beast also has four stubby legs and wide, padded feet. The heel of each foot is armed with a large, sharp protrusion, and a huge horn juts from its forehead. Whitey's size is poorly confirmed. Witnesses have variously described the monster as twelve to sixty-five feet long, and upward of two to four tons. Whitey may be even larger still, as few observers admit to having seen the creature in its entirety.

After his initial sighting in 1937, Bramblett Bateman, who owned riverside land, observed Whitey on over one hundred separate occasions. Eventually Batemen even constructed a viewing pen on the banks of the White River, where he charged visitors admission for a chance to see the infamous creature. Although local officials vouched for Bateman's credibility, no one who paid the quarter admission actually saw the monster. By late 1938, it was clear that Whitey had completely disappeared.

In 1971, Whitey rose from the river again, and several witnesses reported encounters with the monster. One man, Cloyce Warren, was fishing with two companions near the White River Bridge on June 28, 1971, when the water began to boil and bubble around them. In moments, the creature, which the men described as "prehistoric," surfaced nearby. In late June 1971, Towhead Island became the center of the search for Whitey after tracks fourteen inches long and eight inches across were discovered there.

Inspired by these 1971 sightings, the Newport Chamber of Commerce hired a skilled diver from Memphis to search for Whitey and deliver proof of the monster's existence. The diver, armed with an eight-foot harpoon, roamed the bottom of the White River for over seventy-five minutes, but he found nothing.

Whitey seemingly vanished again as 1971 came to a close. However, monsterologists may very well prepare themselves for a new rash of sightings, as Whitey has historically vanished for thirty years or more at a time. If this cycle holds true, the beast will reappear soon after the year 2000.

When Whitey appears, it is excellent quarry for young monsterologists as it is lethargic and totally passive unless pressed into fleeing by attackers or overly inquisitive humans.

Whitey prefers to inhabit the deepest portions of the White River, which reaches depths of sixty feet near Newport, a frequent haunt for the creature. Several even deeper pools are in this area, a few of which are rumored to be bottomless. Whitey prefers to remain curled up within these depths, until it feels the urge to surface again.

To find Whitey, slowly troll the White River, beginning near Roe and continuing north until you reach Newport. This search is best conducted during June and July, as Whitey most often appears during the summer. Be aware, however, that should an encounter occur, Newport and other towns along the White River have deemed it unlawful to kill, injure, or otherwise molest Whitey. Although any monsterologist worth his salt would never harm a monster, always verify the exact nature of such laws with local authorities and be sure that your actions cannot be misconstrued as an attempt to harass the creature.

Other Lake Monsters and Sea Serpents

Almost every lake in North America has produced a few monster sightings, and a great majority of coastal towns have played host to sea serpents. Below is an abbreviated list of notable reoccurring aquatic monsters.

- **Chessie:** A giant wormlike monstrosity seen frequently in Chesapeake Bay in Maryland and Virginia.

- **Colossal Claude:** Oregon's resident aquatic monster, inhabiting the Columbia River.

- **Lake Elizabeth Monster:** A flying frog-faced monster living in Lake Elizabeth, California, whom Mexican ranchers and early American settlers blamed for causing earthquakes.

- **Elsie:** The monster of southern California's Lake Elsinore. The town has honored Elsie

"Elsie by Starlight."

by constructing a huge model in her image, which is floated on the lake during holidays.

- **Hapyxelor (or Mussy):** The monster of Muskrat Lake, one of Ontario's most famous monster habitats.

- **Igopogo:** A dog-faced serpentine monster inhabiting Lake Simcoe, Ontario.

- **Maggot:** A serpent roaming Newfoundland's Swangler's Cove.

- **Memphre:** A giant saurian living in Vermont's Lake Memphremagog and the subject of much scientific investigation.

- **Metro Maggie:** The Lake Ontario water snake, whose stench was once believed to cause illness and death.

- **Old Man of Monterey:** A sea serpent sighted hundreds of times from the beaches of Monterey, California.

- **Oogle-Boogles:** Forty-foot horned serpents living in Lake Watherton, Montana.

- **St. John's River Monster:** A serpent, whose skin appears to have been turned inside out, found roaming Florida's St. John's River.

- **Slimy Slim:** A giant walrus-faced leviathan lurking in Lake Payette, Idaho.

- **Tahoe Tessie:** A lovable green dragon living in the depths of Lake Tahoe, California, and featured in a children's book.

- **Lake Walker Monster:** A creature that once agreed to eat only white settlers who roamed too close to Lake Walker, Nevada, provided the local Native Americans would leave the monster in peace.

FLYING MONSTERS

FLYING MONSTERS ARE a diverse collection of creatures unified by their ability to soar the skies above North America.

An incredibly varied group, flying monsters include humanoids with wings sprouting from their shoulders or arms, while others are simply giant birds. Still others are amorphous orbs of bright light that bob and weave through the heavens; and a small segment are vicious, winged horrors, resembling nothing known to humankind.

Despite their many differences in appearance, flying monsters share a surprising number of traits. The great majority achieve flight through the power of large wings, and almost every flying monster can fly in complete silence, enabling them to better surprise their prey. Most flying monsters have hypnotic eyes or luminous auras, which can mesmerize and stupefy humans who stare at the creatures for too long. Many also possess other supernatural powers as well, such as the ability to become invisible or cause crippling fear in onlookers. Flying monsters usually live in remote, inaccessible places, such as caves hidden high atop treacherous peaks.

Like almost all other monsters, flying monsters are resilient and nearly impossible to kill. In fact, of all the flying monsters discussed in this section, only the **Killer Bees** seem to be vulnerable to human attacks.

Finally, flying monsters are generally malignant and enjoy eating humans. They prefer to hunt at night, and they attack swiftly and without warning. Victims of flying monsters are usually carried into the sky and disappear forever, presumably finding their final rest in the belly of their winged captors.

BIG OWL

VITAL STATISTICS

DISTINGUISHING FEATURES: Giant white wings and huge, glowing eyes

HEIGHT: Varies

WEIGHT: Varies

RANGE AND HABITAT: The Southwest

POPULATION SIZE: One

DIET: Anthropophagus

BEHAVIOR: A shape-shifter, Big Owl is frequently found in the guise of a monstrous owl who swoops onto wanderers and devours them.

SOURCE: Native American (White Mountain Apache) mythology

ENCOUNTERING BIG OWL:

Big Owl is a sentient monster who plagued the White Mountain Apache before the first white settlers arrived. Generally regarded as completely destructive and insatiably cannibalistic, Big Owl is an evil spirit who usually takes the form of a gigantic white owl. Its snowy shape soaring against the blackness of night, Big Owl descends upon men, women, children, and animals, gripping its victims in talons that snap bones and tear away limbs.

Big Owl can also appear in a variety of other forms, including that of a sallow giant with greasy hair and round, yellow eyes. In this form, Big Owl carries a large blood-smattered basket to hold his victims.

In any disguise, Big Owl possesses the ability to mesmerize and paralyze humans with his dreadful glowing eyes.

Big Owl, like a great many monsters, is virtually impossible to permanently destroy. Apache legends hold that Big Owl was in fact wounded several times by his half brother, a demigod hero experienced in vanquishing monsters. Unfortunately, Big Owl eventually managed to recover from these attacks and always returned to torment humans. In many instances, Big Owl went on to decimate whole tribes as an affront to his brave and half-human brother.

Today Big Owl is relatively inactive, but when the creature does roam abroad, he always assaults solitary wanderers. Most victims of the beast never return, and those rare few who manage to escape are left with an incurable sense of dread

Owls and the Supernatural

In many cultures, including the vast majority of Native American tribes, the owl is regarded as a supernatural creature and often an ill omen. The call of the owl foretells death, sickness, and a host of other personal afflictions; and owl behavior and hoots are used to predict bad weather, coming plagues, the death of crops, and natural disasters. Owls are also sometimes regarded as the minions of witches or the Devil.

and nightmares that cripple the mind and strip away sanity. For all these reasons, Big Owl is a monster best left alone, even by the most experienced supernaturalists. However, for those intrepid few, Big Owl can be sought in the skies above the Southwest. He only appears at night, and often beneath the light of the full moon.

If you encounter Big Owl, in any of his forms, you will likely be destined for the monster's maw after considerable suffering. Expect a painful journey to Big Owl's lair, either gripped in his piercing talons or trapped in his stained basket. Big Owl enjoys torturing his captives, sometimes slowly tearing away one limb at a time and devouring this morsel leisurely while the victim painfully bleeds to death.

EL CHUPACABRA (THE GOATSUCKER)

VITAL STATISTICS

DISTINGUISHING FEATURES: Batlike wings, glowing red eyes, fangs, terrible stench, and generally horrible appearance

HEIGHT: 3–4′

WEIGHT: 70–120 lbs

RANGE AND HABITAT: Northern Mexico, Texas, and much of the Southwest, California, South America, Puerto Rico

POPULATION SIZE: Unknown

DIET: Carnivore

BEHAVIOR: The flying vampire beast known as El Chupacabra silently patrols the skies, only descending from the darkness to attack livestock and people.

SOURCE: Mexican-American folklore, urban legend, cryptozoology

ENCOUNTERING THE CHUPACABRA:

One of the most recently discovered monsters, El Chupacabra, or the Goatsucker, is a savage beast known to hunt the skies from South America to Canada. Today, it is most often sighted in the southwestern United States, Puerto Rico, and Florida, although it has also appeared in eastern Texas and northern California as well.

A typical Chupacabra is covered in glossy matted hair and has a feral face. Its long limbs, which end in massive claws, can propel the monster across any terrain at amazing speeds, but it is the creature's powerful batlike wings that allow it to migrate huge distances and carry victims off into the night.

Goatsuckers are deceptively small, standing just three or four feet high. But within this diminutive body lurks a strength that only a monster's hunger could produce. Capable of wrestling full-grown bulls to the ground, the Chupacabra proves far stronger than mere mortals. Once pinned, a victim's neck is neatly pierced by the Goatsucker's huge fangs and the veins sucked dry in minutes. Prey can also be hypnotized by its luminescent red eyes, paralyzed by the creature's horrifying appearance, or overcome by the Chupacabra's terrible stale-urine stench.

The beast has a seemingly unquenchable appetite. In Puerto Rico, where the monster first appeared in late 1995, at least two thousand animals were killed by Goatsuckers in less than eight months. The creature feeds on a wide variety of prey, including lambs, rabbits, sheep, turkeys, dogs, and, of course, goats. In southern Florida, the Goatsuckers are fond of chickens and ducks; in Fresno, California, they prefer puppies, pet cats, and pet roosters. Chupacabras also attack larger animals, including horses, cattle, and bulls.

Chupacabras have no qualms about attacking humans. In São Paulo and Rio, it is believed that the Chupacabras steal children from the slums, drain their victims of blood, and leave the lifeless bodies in dirty alleys. Goatsuckers have hunted children in the schoolyards of Mexico City as well. Terrifying and savage attacks on adults have taken place in as many as five different Mexican states; and in late May 1996, a young nurse near Mexico City reportedly had her arm severed by a Goatsucker. That same year, in the western state of Jalisco, a farmworker displayed prominent fang marks on his body after claiming that he was ambushed by a Chupacabra. Dade County, Florida, suffered a rash of assaults during the summer and early fall of 1996, and Goatsucker attacks continue to be reported throughout Texas and the Southwest.

To stop these creatures before more attacks occur, at least a few people within the Chupacabra's known hunting grounds have at-

tempted to capture or kill the beast. All such endeavors have failed, largely because the creature seems impervious to injury. In late 1996, policemen in northern Mexico cornered a Goatsucker after it had assaulted locals. After firing a hail of rounds at the monster, they were amazed to watch it leap over a fence and disappear, seemingly uninjured.

In other areas of the Chupacabra's range, especially in North America, the Goatsucker is not hunted, but is actually often co-opted and celebrated. The beast's reputation has been thoroughly exploited by advertisers and businesses, who have attached the creature's name to hamburgers, a dance, a professional wrestler, and a Texas blood drive. Varied (and often inaccurate) images of the monster appear on bumper stickers, mugs, T-shirts, posters, Internet sites, and magazines. Several songs have also been devoted to the creature. Clearly, even if the Chupacabra eventually descends into extinction, it will live on in the garish products it has spawned.

Monsterologists interested in glimpsing the Chupacabra should hide near a farm at night, in an area where Chupacabra attacks have recently been reported. As the winged monstrosity drops from the sky, monsterologists equipped with night-vision goggles will be presented with a unique view of these creatures.

However, the Goatsucker's sense of smell is keen, and there is always the danger that it will detect human presence. If the Chupacabra attacks, flee at once, for the monster cannot be reliably countered by any conventional means.

If you are bitten by the Chupacabra but manage to survive the encounter, visit a hospital immediately. There is the strong possibility that the Chupacabra carries various diseases and viruses, including rabies.

THE JERSEY DEVIL

VITAL STATISTICS

DISTINGUISHING FEATURES: Leathery wings, cloven hooves, horns, and an eerie aura

HEIGHT: 3'6"

WEIGHT: 70 lbs

RANGE AND HABITAT: New Jersey Pine Barrens

POPULATION SIZE: One

DIET: Carnivore

BEHAVIOR: The Jersey Devil is fond of kidnapping children and travelers who stray too close to its home in the New Jersey Pine Barrens. It also mutilates livestock and invades homes in search of human prey.

SOURCE: American folklore, cryptozoology

ENCOUNTERING THE JERSEY DEVIL:

The Jersey Devil is a hideous monster with a lithe body, cloven hooves, and a thin neck. Atop this slender neck sways a horrible head that combines the ugliest attributes of three domestic animals. Like a horse, the monster flares large, round nostrils and has broad, yellow teeth; two goatlike horns shoot from the creature's forehead, just above its twitching ears; from its black gums and curled lips, the monster drools like a mangy dog. To take flight, the Jersey Devil unfurls a pair of leathery wings, which cover a span of two feet. As it travels through the night, its body is sheathed in a yellow glow. The monster is also known for its mournful cry.

The Jersey Devil inhabits the Pine Barrens of New Jersey, a thinly populated area largely subject to isolation and poverty. Throughout the Pine Barrens, or Pineys, the Jersey Devil hunts possums, rabbits, and fish. Occasionally, the monster wanders into the surrounding countryside, where it mutilates sheep and cattle.

The Jersey Devil is also known for its daring chimney raids, which were first reported in the 1780s. During such assaults, the monster slips down a chimney and creates havoc within a home by destroying furniture, emptying the pantry, chasing pets, and terrorizing the inhabitants to near insanity. In the most memorable of these raids, the Jersey Devil pulls children from their beds, drags the screaming victims up the chimney, and spirits them away, presumably to devour at its leisure. A guaranteed defense against chimney raids has yet to be discovered, as closed flues, wire barriers, and even flames in the fireplace have failed to stop the monster's descent.

In addition to aggressively attacking people living near the Pine Barrens, the Jersey Devil assaults anyone who enters its habitat. There are numerous reports of teenagers, hunters, and explorers venturing into New Jersey's forests only to be threatened by the monster. Some disappear altogether. The creature frequently manifests near roads leading into the secluded terrain in order to frighten away

THE NEW JERSEY "WHAT-IS-IT," AS NELSON EVANS SAYS HE SAW IT ON HIS SHED ROOF AT 2 A. M.

potential invaders. Cars parked in the Pine Barrens have had their roofs ripped away and their passengers stolen into the night. Locals living on the fringes of the Pine Barrens have long reported eerie shrieks and ominous screams coming from the backwoods, sounds that are the harbingers of doom.

Aside from its ability to fly and its great strength, the Jersey Devil possesses many other powers. It can become invisible at will, giving itself access to even the most heavily guarded livestock or homes. Its fetid breath can curdle milk and kill off all the fish in a lake. The creature is surrounded by an evil aura that causes bad fortune to befall witnesses, and it is also capable of spitting fire from its black mouth.

The history of New Jersey's most gruesome resident begins on the outskirts of the Pine Barrens on a winter night in 1735, when the mistress of a British soldier, a woman known as Mother Leeds, went into labor with her thirteenth child. Mother Leeds had delivered her twelve previous children without a single complication, but from the onset of this unlucky labor, she suffered agonizing pain. In a moment of anguish she cursed her thirteenth child and wished it out of her body. As the hateful words faded from her lips, the infant slithered from her womb. Thus, the Jersey Devil was born.

Upon seeing the baby, the midwife in attendance screamed and died of shock. The Devil's father rushed into the room with his musket raised, but when he looked upon the creature, he fled the house and was never seen again. Through her haze of pain, Mother Leeds sat up to behold her child, and her mind completely snapped at the sight of her horrific offspring.

For a moment the creature stood motion-less, but when it heard one of its siblings wailing in the next room, it bolted toward the sound. With each step, the Jersey Devil's black cloven hooves burned bizarre footprints into the wooden floorboards. Mother Leeds followed the beast into the next room and watched it pluck its tearful brother from a cradle, open its jaws wide, and swallow the child whole. The newborn monster then killed and consumed the remaining eleven children. With its ghastly red eyes, it looked upon Mother Leeds one last time and disappeared up the chimney.

The fate of Mother Leeds has been lost, though it is likely she either died shortly after the incident or spent the rest of her days in an asylum. The tale of her demonic child, however, continues well into the present. The monster that sprang from Mother Leeds was originally known as the Leeds Devil, but it soon became more generally known as the Jersey Devil due to its preference for the swamps and woods of southern New Jersey. In the decades following its birth, the monster spent much of its time rustling bushes, casting strange shadows through windows, tangling clotheslines, and hovering over solitary travelers. While its cloven footprints, often mistaken for those of Satan, were discovered in snowdrifts, fields, and forest paths, the creature itself was rarely encountered.

Still, enough witnesses had come forward by 1740 that a priest decided to bless the Pine Barrens to prevent the monster from continuing to haunt the area. He placed a powerful spell over the habitat meant to keep the Jersey Devil from returning to the Pine Barrens for at least one hundred years. The spell largely failed, as the creature reappeared later that same year.

In 1800, Commodore Stephen Decatur was testing cannons at the Hanover Iron Work when the Jersey Devil made a dramatic appearance. Decatur fired a cannonball toward the flying monstrosity, but watched in horror as the metal ball merely passed through the Jersey Devil's body. From 1816 to 1839, the Jersey Devil was also reported by Joseph Bonaparte, Napoleon's brother and the former king of Spain, who spent many years in and around the Pine Barrens.

In the 1830s and 1840s, the Jersey Devil left the Pine Barrens for brief forays into Virginia, where it began hunting livestock, mutilating and gorging on as many as a dozen cattle in one night. On one outing, it killed two dogs, three geese, four cats, and thirty-one ducks, then tried to snatch several curious children as well.

From the mid-1800s to the early twentieth century, the beast was content to remain deep in the Pine Barrens. In 1909, however, it became tired of hiding and launched a much publicized rampage. Between January 16 and January 23, the monster openly canvassed New Jersey and neighboring states, generating over *one thousand* confirmed sightings. Hordes of people also discovered the Devil's unique footprints on rooftops, along roads, and even inside their homes. Further evidence of the monster's presence included destroyed chicken coops and the mutilated remains of dogs, cats, and livestock. The Jersey Devil's actions were so terrifying that schools in the area closed and children were kept behind locked doors. But after a seven-day spree, the Devil's rampage inexplicably ended, and it disappeared once again into the Pineys.

Throughout the next fifty years, more chilling encounters kept the Jersey Devil's reputation alive. In 1927, the beast boldly leapt onto the hood of a taxicab, squawked furiously, and lifted up into the night sky again. Near Erial, New Jersey, in the early 1930s, a pair of men watched as the Jersey Devil used its powerful wings to lop off the tops of several trees. Soon after, two young girls claimed that they had barely escaped the growling creature.

On November 22, 1951, the Jersey Devil cornered several children at the Duport Clubhouse in Gibbstown, but inexplicably left without claiming a victim. However, according to one witness, the brute's face was covered in fresh blood, indicating that others had met their doom earlier that day within the monster's maw. After fleeing the clubhouse, the monster besieged other areas of Gibbstown. It was ultimately spotted by several hundred people, most between the ages of thirteen and twenty-two.

The Jersey Devil faded from sight in the 1960s, but throughout the 1970s it became the bane of campers visiting the Pine Barrens. At night, they were uniformly tormented by terrible screams and endless shrieks. The monster also rustled bushes, stole tents, and doused campfires until its victims fled in terror. Such activity has continued unabated into the present.

The most recent recorded sighting of the monster occurred in December 1993. Forest ranger John Irwin was driving alongside the Mullica River in southern New Jersey when he found the road blocked by the creature. Irwin described the monster as a six-foot-tall bipedal animal with horns and matted black fur. The ranger and the Jersey Devil stared at each other for several minutes, but the monster opted to disappear into the forest rather than attack.

Concerned authorities attempt to calm a panic caused by Jersey Devil sightings.

be garish fakes and offer little information about the real monster. Until someone dares seek out the beast and observe it more closely, we will never learn how to coexist peacefully with this bizarre predator.

Unfortunately, encountering the Jersey Devil is a frightening prospect. If you do search for it, do so in the Pine Barrens. Always travel with a bright lantern, which a handful of researchers insist can dissuade the monster from attacking. Others claim that holy items, such as the Bible and a crucifix, might also ward off the creature.

Most important, never forget that the Jersey Devil has a wide array of incredible powers and abilities. It can lift you into the sky and rip out your throat with its teeth. Or, it could stalk you and spit fire into your face. If threatened by your presence, it will momentarily become invisible, only to reappear as its claws pierce your belly.

Unlike other North American monsters, the Jersey Devil has not been the subject of massive expeditions, nor have local residents instigated organized searches for their fearsome neighbor. P. T. Barnum and others have exhibited "Jersey Devils," but these proved to

KILLER BEES

VITAL STATISTICS

DISTINGUISHING FEATURE: Huge stingers

LENGTH: 1″

WEIGHT: Almost weightless

RANGE AND HABITAT: Skies of the Southwest and South America

POPULATION SIZE: 900,000 plus

DIET: Herbivore

BEHAVIOR: Killer Bees are large, aggressive insects that have migrated to North America from South America and are capable of delivering painful and often fatal stings.

SOURCE: Urban legend, cryptozoology

ENCOUNTERING KILLER BEES:

Killer Bees received their ominous name from their tendency to aggressively attack people when disturbed or molested, usually descending on hapless victims in frenzied swarms. They sting their victims literally hundreds of times with an enlarged stinger; and their venom acts as a powerful toxin that causes massive swelling, paralysis, respiratory failure, and eventually death.

As they are incredibly agile in flight and can attack from a variety of directions simultaneously, Killer Bees are difficult to elude or destroy. Swarms, which are composed of hundreds of thousands of individuals and can reach over a mile in width, engulf anything in their path. A swarm resembles a churning black cloud on the horizon, but its approach is swift. As the swarm nears, the collective buzz of the bees becomes deafening. When they attack, the members of the swarm become frenzied and fearless; there are even stories about swarms bringing down airplanes and helicopters.

It is largely believed that the Killer Bee is a mutant, the result of radiation or pollution. The insects originated in South America, but since the 1970s, swarms have periodically migrated into Texas, New Mexico, southern California, and Arizona. Killer Bee swarms have also been reported to head directly toward heavily populated areas, as if consciously and purposefully attacking humans.

Although they are often encountered in swarms, Killer Bees must maintain a hive to reproduce and feed. These hives are massive complexes that usually take up several hundred square feet and may be built in such locales as attics, basements, abandoned mines, or caves. A hive should only have one entrance and will always be fairly dark inside.

Killer Bee society is a matriarchy ruled by a queen bee who spends most of her time in a birthing chamber deep within the hive. Because she is responsible for maintaining the size of the swarm, the queen is protected by hundreds of tenacious drone bees.

Direct contact with Killer Bees, either individually or in swarms, should be avoided at all costs. A single sting can result in painful death within hours, and the wrath of the swarm is virtually inescapable. Even when completely protected by an airtight suit, only attempt to view these bees from a safe distance.

If faced with an onrushing swarm, attempt to dissuade the insects with fire, insecticides, toxic fumes, or gasoline. Killer Bees drown easily in any viscous substance, and immersion in water should also provide you with ample protection from even the most determined swarm.

Occasionally, monsterologists are called upon to combat Killer Bees to preserve human lives. If you undertake such an endeavor, you must find the local hive and destroy the queen bee. Enter the hive armed with a flamethrower or insecticide sprayer and thoroughly douse the queen's birthing chamber with fire or poison.

Bees and the Supernatural

Throughout the world, bees have long been regarded as extremely supernatural creatures. In Europe, bees are responsible for notifying the gods whenever a human dies. In the Ozarks, bees are the actual souls of the departed, and they should never be harmed, lest the souls be prevented from reaching the afterlife. Bees, especially in swarms, are powerful omens as well. The sudden appearance of a swarm is extremely bad luck and usually results in bodily injury or death. Bees alighting on a dead tree or appearing in dreams also prophesy imminent demise. However, the venom of bees has been used as a cure for a wide variety of ailments, including rheumatism, arthritis, and neuritis. Bee venom, stingers, wings, legs, and other body parts are also used in potions and spells.

THE MARFA LIGHTS

VITAL STATISTICS

DISTINGUISHING FEATURES: Intense glow and spherical shape

SIZE: 1–10′ in diameter

WEIGHT: Unknown

RANGE AND HABITAT: Area outside Marfa, Texas

POPULATION SIZE: Unknown

DIET: Unknown

BEHAVIOR: The Marfa Lights, one of the most benign of all monsters, simply float about the night sky. They never attack humans but have been known to aid people on rare occasion.

SOURCE: Fortean studies, cryptozoology, ufology

ENCOUNTERING THE MARFA LIGHTS:

The Marfa Lights are a collection of reddish orange spectral lights that mysteriously appear in the skies above Marfa, Texas. Usually described as glowing globes approximately the size and shape of a basketball, they fly at amazing speeds and exhibit an incredible mobility. They can also vary their size, intensity, coloration, and speed at will. Their range extends across the Mitchell Flats area, between Alpine and Marfa, Texas, and they are encountered frequently over the Chinati Mountains and along U.S. Highway 90.

The Marfa Lights have been observed since the first settlers arrived in the Southwest and continue to be spotted in modern times by a wide variety of people, including geologists, film crews, cryptozoologists, ufologists, and hundreds of motorists. They have even been photographed and captured on video.

Despite the wealth of sightings, there are no concrete explanations for the Marfa Lights phenomenon, although theories abound. Mexican and early American settlers claimed that the Marfa Lights are the spirits of Chisos Apache warriors who were sealed in a cave long ago to guard an ill-gotten treasure. Other stories identify them as the ghosts of Pancho Villa and his crew, who are cursed to wander the desert forever. During World War I, locals believed that the government had invented the Marfa Lights as a means to warn of an enemy invasion. Some ufologists argue vehemently that the Marfa Lights are actually the beams, or "flashlights," of flying saucers.

While the Marfa Lights have yet to be conclusively identified, investigators have been overwhelmingly successful in their quest to observe them. One of the earliest Marfa Lights researchers was a cowboy named Robert Ellison, who in 1883 encountered the lights while on several cattle drives in western Texas. Ellison's son-in-law, Lee Plumbley, set out to find the Marfa Lights as well and was rewarded with an encounter in 1921.

During World War II, sightings increased dramatically. In response to such reports, military pilots were ordered into the air to investigate the strange occurrences. The Marfa Lights compliantly appeared and playfully buzzed the planes. (The encounter became rather comical when the pilots attempted to drop "flour bombs" on the Marfa Lights to mark them for future reference. The bombs simply passed through the lights, and the morning after the drop, the populace of the area awoke to find flour dusting the ground like snow.)

After interacting with the planes for a few minutes, the Marfa Lights tired of the game and floated toward Mexico, vanishing altogether a few miles outside Marfa. The encounter was reported to the Pentagon, but because the Marfa Lights did not seem to pose a threat, the Pentagon officially advised all military personnel and government agencies to leave the lights well enough alone. This policy is still in effect today.

The most exciting modern sighting occurred in July 1989 when NBC's *Unsolved Mysteries* targeted the Marfa Lights for investigation. After organizing a research group that included an astronomer, geologist, chemist, and several others, the investigators arranged a series of infrared video cameras to capture the lights on film. At 11:59 P.M., the Marfa Lights appeared to the investigative unit, who filmed the glowing orbs as they changed size and pulsated.

The shocking *Unsolved Mysteries* film is almost impossible to refute, as the investigators

James Crocker/FPL

The Marfa Lights, captured on film by James Crocker in 1986.

took careful precautions to avoid being tricked or misled; for example, fearing that the Marfa Lights were simply the reflected headlights of passing cars, the crew positioned several devices along the nearby road to alert them when vehicles approached. At the time of the filming, the group was stationed far from civilization, no cars were detected on the road, and the area had been scoured for pranksters.

Although usually completely enigmatic, the Marfa Lights have been known to come to the rescue of humans. Early in this century, for example, a rancher attempting to reach stranded cattle in the Chinati Mountains was suddenly caught in a terrible blizzard. When night fell, he became hopelessly lost and was on the verge of death when a group of lights miraculously appeared before him. They led him to a small cave, where one of the larger lights actually provided him with warmth. The rancher fell asleep, awoke healthy and warm, and was able to find his way home easily. After this encounter, the Marfa Lights visited the rancher's land on several occasions and were observed many times by his daughter and other relatives.

Because of their frequent appearances and benign nature, the Marfa Lights are the perfect induction into the field of monsterology, providing eager young monsterologists with a safe and reliable means to view a monster for the first time. Their range is well-defined, they appear regularly, and they can be photographed with conventional cameras and visual recording devices. Aside from being easy to locate and sight, they are completely innocuous. Occasionally, they follow cars and fly close to planes, but they never attack vehicles or people.

To sight the Marfa Lights, visit the area just outside Marfa, Texas, on a particularly dark night when the moon is barely visible. Locals will probably be able to direct you to the most accessible and rewarding locations, which will likely rest somewhere along U.S. Highway 90. While waiting for the lights, do not build a fire, listen to the radio, turn on flashlights, or operate any noisy machinery. Cameras and video recorders should be readied, but use a high-speed film and appropriate filters to avoid employing a flash, which can obscure and frighten the Marfa Lights.

MOTHMAN

VITAL STATISTICS

DISTINGUISHING FEATURES: Massive wings, red eyes, and a high-pitched cry

HEIGHT: 5–7'

WEIGHT: Unknown

RANGE AND HABITAT: TNT Area, Point Pleasant, West Virginia

POPULATION SIZE: One

DIET: Unknown

BEHAVIOR: The cryptic creature Mothman spends most of its time lurking on the outskirts of humanity, seemingly waiting for opportune moments to scare motorists and other travelers. In almost every encounter, he has caused inexplicable fear in all witnesses.

SOURCE: Ufology, cryptozoology, urban legend

ENCOUNTERING MOTHMAN:

Mothman is a complex and much studied entity who has provoked the interest of monsterologists and ufologists alike since his initial appearances in West Virginia in the 1960s. Generally described as a humanoid with huge wings, Mothman's body is dark gray and somewhat wrinkled. His eyes are luminous red orbs that can be seen bobbing through the darkness. Because his eyes burn so brightly, his featureless face is often caught in shadow and has rarely been described.

Unlike large birds and most flying monsters, which require a running start before lifting from the ground, Mothman is able to take directly to flight by leaping vertically into the air. His top flight speed is unknown but exceeds one hundred miles per hour.

Aside from his proficient method of flight, Mothman possesses numerous bizarre powers, including the ability to extend an aura of pervasive fear. Although he has never actually attacked anyone, Mothman witnesses are frenzied and panicked after encountering the creature. Even noted researchers who have faced other monsters feel this dread when wandering Mothman's territory.

Although his origins are unclear, Mothman first appeared in the Ohio River Valley in 1961, where he was initially observed on the edge of the Chief Cornstalk Hunting Grounds by a woman and her father, who watched in amazement as Mothman spread his staggering wings and took to the sky. Mothman disappeared quickly, but both witnesses were struck by the monster's signature aura of dread and quickly sped from the area.

Mothman next emerged in Point Pleasant, West Virginia, on November 15, 1966. Driving through an abandoned munitions dump known as the TNT Area at about 11:30 P.M., Roger and Linda Scarberry and their friends Steve and Mary Mallette suddenly noticed Mothman's glowing eyes. In moments, they had a full view of the winged monstrosity. Roger wisely accelerated the vehicle and tried to escape the creature. Much to the couples' horror, Mothman gave chase, squeaking audibly as he raced

FPL

World War II, when Point Pleasant manufactured high explosives in large quantities. To support the industry, the 2,500-acre McClintic Wildlife Sanctuary, located seven miles from Point Pleasant, was torn up so that munitions manufacturers could build several miles of subterranean tunnels, numerous camouflaged buildings and factories, and at least one hundred concrete domes for storing explosives.

At the war's end, the TNT Area, as the sanctuary had become known, was completely abandoned. By the time Mothman arrived in the mid-1960s, it had become a perfect monster habitat: the concrete domes had been stripped of their green paint, the buildings were dilapidated, and the whole area was charged with the possibility of a haunting. It became a favorite location for cavorting teens, many of whom used Route 62, the single road running through the TNT Area, as the local lovers' lane. Mothman was frequently observed lurking in the concrete domes, and it appeared before many motorists as they traveled Route 62.

The most dramatic of the TNT Area sightings occurred on November 16, 1966, the night after Mothman's first appearance. Marcella Bennet and two adult friends were leaving the home of a friend who lived on the outskirts of the TNT Area when they saw Mothman's dark shape rise from the bushes. The terrified trio were so shaken that Bennet actually dropped her infant daughter. Three children also witnessed the encounter, but by the time police arrived, Mothman had fled. Ironically, over one hundred armed adults had been scouring the

after the car. The flying monster quit the pursuit only after the vehicle neared town. Immediately, the couple sought out authorities and recounted their harrowing ordeal.

After the Scarberry-Mallette sighting, Mothman became a phenomenon, sighted by more than one hundred people over the following months. The monster was seen perched on fences of the National Guard armory at the edge of Point Pleasant and was accused of kidnapping dogs and cats from backyards. Most often, however, it was encountered in the TNT Area.

The TNT Area was first constructed during

TNT Area in search of Mothman only a few miles away.

Mothman sightings continued to be reported throughout Point Pleasant during the next several months, attracting dozens of reporters and researchers to the area. An increasing number of people also spied UFOs directly before or after Mothman encounters, leading many monsterologists to believe that the creature is actually an alien visitor.

The West Virginia Mothman reports climaxed with the collapse of the Silver Bridge on December 15, 1967. During the height of rush hour, the suspension bridge convulsed and snapped, spilling forty-six cars and several dozen shrieking motorists into the Ohio River. In an eerie twist of fate, many of the thirty-eight people who died in the disaster had been primary Mothman witnesses.

Survivors of the Silver Bridge collapse claimed that they observed a flash of light seconds before the bridge fell apart, and rumors implicating both Mothman and UFOs surrounded the catastrophe for years. Engineers eventually determined that the bridge had collapsed because of "metal fatigue and structural failure," which was a logical conclusion as the bridge had been opened in 1928 and was poorly equipped to handle a high density of traffic. Still, many affected by the Mothman affair still believe that the creature was in some way connected to the tragedy.

Mothman fled Point Pleasant after the Silver Bridge collapse, but reappeared in Texas throughout 1976, when it was reported numerous times in and around Harlingen. Unfortunately, Mothman's current whereabouts are unknown. He may be capable of migrating great distances, since similar entities have been seen relatively recently in China and England.

If this is the case, he could be virtually anywhere. However, the legend of Mothman still survives in West Virginia, and perhaps he will one day return to his haunts in the TNT Area.

Although no one knows where Mothman is today, it is likely that he inhabits some remote and seldom visited area on the outskirts of humanity. Visit the TNT Area in Point Pleasant to get a feel for the type of terrain Mothman likes best, then frequent other areas around the country that have similar auras. A junkyard, abandoned mine, creepy forest, run-down factory, or neglected warehouse might provide Mothman with a home. Search such areas at night, watching closely for the monster's glowing eyes.

Upon spying Mothman, even the most courageous monsterologists will be overwhelmed by inexplicable fear and horror. In this situation, first remind yourself that this is a product of the creature's strange aura. Then attempt to show you are unafraid by smiling or waving. Because no one has attempted to communicate with this monster, it is unknown whether Mothman understands English or any other language. Anyone who encounters the creature is urged to ask Mothman simple questions, such as:

1. Who are you?
2. What do you want?
3. Where do you come from?

If Mothman attacks or you are overcome with fear and forced to flee, head toward the nearest populated area. Mothman seems reluctant to pursue people into inhabited regions, but if he does follow you into a city or town, stop running from the monster in a crowded area. Direct bystanders toward the strange being in the sky to ensure a wealth of witnesses to your incredible story.

THE PIASA BIRDS

VITAL STATISTICS

DISTINGUISHING FEATURES: Human face, huge antlers, shaggy beard, extremely long tail, red eyes, and scaled body

WINGSPAN: 10–20′

WEIGHT: 200 lbs

RANGE AND HABITAT: Caves along the Mississippi River

POPULATION SIZE: Two

DIET: Carnivore

BEHAVIOR: Cruel killers, the Piasa Birds do little besides hunt for humans, whom they greedily consume.

SOURCE: Native American (Illini) mythology, Fortean studies, cryptozoology

ENCOUNTERING THE PIASA BIRDS:

The Piasa Birds are terrible monsters first encountered by the Illini Indians, who preserved images of the fearsome creatures in their artwork. The famed French explorer Father Marquette was the first non-Native to spy the Piasa Birds over three hundred years ago when, while sailing the Mississippi between Alton, Illinois, and St. Louis, Missouri, he noticed a painting of two malignant monster birds staring at him from a cliff near the river.

According to the Illini's artwork and Marquette's descriptions, the Piasa Birds are two enormous, brutal avian entities. In the tongue of the Illini, *piasa* can be translated as "the bird that devours men," and the monsters are so named because of their anthropophagous tendencies.

Both Piasa Birds stand over four feet high and wear thorny antlers atop their horrible heads. Their eyes blaze red from their vaguely human faces, and leonine beards dangle from their chins. Sturdy scales cover much of their bodies, and they have extremely long tails capable of winding several times around their bodies. This unearthly appendage ends in two large sharp fins.

Marquette discovered that the Illini had rendered the ominous painting as a warning that the monster birds lived nearby. At the time, the Piasa Birds were said to inhabit a cave near Alton and would dive at anyone sailing down the Mississippi. Victims were captured in the birds' claws, carried back to the cave, and eaten alive. To stave off these attacks, the Illini would leave an offering of tobacco near the picture. Some braves also fired arrows or rifles at the painting as they passed, hoping that such shows of defiance toward the image would deter the birds themselves.

Despite their horrific appearance, the Piasa Birds were not always evil murderers. In fact, according to the Illini, both Piasa Birds were once incredibly fond of humans and protected them from other monsters. However, during a war between two Illini tribes, one of the Piasa Birds tried to rescue in its beak two wounded warriors from the battlefield. When the blood from these dying men touched the bird's tongue, it was overcome with hunger. The

Piasa was compelled to eat the men and found that it greatly enjoyed the taste of human flesh. It convinced its mate to dine on a warrior as well, and thus both birds became devoted man-eaters.

Over the next several decades, the Piasa Birds raided Illini settlements, snatching away men, women, and children to feed their dark appetites. Eventually a courageous brave named Massatoga organized a group of twenty warriors to combat the birds. Acting as human bait, Massatoga lured one of the Piasa Birds from its cave. Massatoga's warriors then ambushed the creature, wounding it with spears and arrows.

Miraculously, the Piasa Bird survived that

> On the flat face of a high rock were painted, in red, black, and green, a pair of monsters, each as large as a calf, with horns like a deer, red eyes, a beard like a tiger, and frightful expression of countenance.
>
> —Father Marquette

attack, and both creatures continued to torment the peoples living along the Mississippi. Many tribes, including the Illini, told stories of the monster birds carrying young boys over high cliffs and dropping the children to their deaths. By the time Marquette visited the Mississippi, the monsters had claimed an untold number of lives.

Fortunately, the Piasa Birds are relatively inactive in modern times. They remain in caves along the Mississippi, only venturing out infrequently in search of prey.

Monsterologists seeking the Piasa Birds should begin by studying the Piasa Rock, near Alton, Illinois. Although the original petroglyph observed by Marquette no longer exists, a replica has graced a bluff in Norma Park since the 1970s. This painting will give researchers an appreciation for the terrifying features and size of these birds.

The flesh-and-blood Piasas are best sought along the shores of the Mississippi, particularly where it runs through Illinois and Missouri. Unlike other monsters, the Piasa Birds cannot be enticed into the open with gifts of food, and therefore monsterologists must boldly enter each cave in search of the creatures.

Once encountered, the Piasa Birds will probably attempt to flee, but these are unpredictable beasts. If they attack, attempt an immediate escape. Slow monsterologists will find themselves torn between the savage beaks of these birds.

FPL

THE THUNDERBIRD

VITAL STATISTICS

DISTINGUISHING FEATURES: Flashing eyes and immense wings that beat the sky like thunder

WINGSPAN: 15–185′

WEIGHT: Varies drastically

RANGE AND HABITAT: Skies over North America, especially the Southwest

POPULATION SIZE: Unknown

DIET: Carnivore

BEHAVIOR: Thunderbirds are confusing entities, alternately malicious and cannibalistic or kindly and peaceful. They generally avoid people, except when compelled to feed on human flesh.

SOURCE: Native American mythology, cryptozoology

ENCOUNTERING THE THUNDERBIRD:

Almost every Native American tribe in North America has claimed encounters with giant birds, many of which were brutal beasts who slaughtered humans for food and twisted pleasure. For other tribes, interactions with these monstrous avians were more beneficial, and the birds were even known to slay local monsters or to aid lost hunters. Today, all of these huge creatures are collectively known as Thunderbirds because the sound of their beating wings often emulates rolling thunder and their eyes flash like lightning.

The average Thunderbird has a wingspan of over thirty feet, and some of these creatures are so huge that entire lakes form on their backs. Others block out the sun when they take flight and are large enough to pluck whales from the ocean.

At their most malign, Thunderbirds enjoy descending upon unsuspecting travelers and sweeping them into the sky. They also eat a variety of other animals, including caribou, moose, horses, and cattle.

The Thunderbird may have been regarded as nothing more than a long-lived and widespread Native American myth if not for reported sightings and attacks throughout the past two centuries. In 1886, a group of ranchers in Tombstone, Arizona, claimed that they had actually shot and killed a Thunderbird. After pinning the dead creature to the side of a barn, they measured its wingspan at about thirty-five feet. Photographs were taken and allegedly published in the *Tombstone Epitaph,* although all records of such evidence have mysteriously disappeared, and the photograph has not been located by even the most thorough researchers.

Just four years later, Arizona was again visited by a Thunderbird, which two cowhands discovered wounded and struggling in the desert outside Tombstone. This bird's wingspan exceeded 185 feet, and its mouth was filled with enormous and deadly teeth. After shooting the bird numerous times, the pair followed the floundering creature until it expired. They wisely measured and examined the monster, then severed a portion of its wing and took it with them. The *Tombstone Epitaph* reported that the men planned to return for the rest of the carcass, but again the story inexplicably ends with the paper's brief article about the amazing find. The wing tip has been lost for decades.

Attacks on humans by giant birds have been recorded since at least 1868, when eight-year-old Jemmie Kenney, a boy in Tippa County, Missouri, was snatched by one of the creatures. As the bird's claws burrowed into Jemmie's shoulder, the screaming boy thrashed violently against his captor. Eventually, the Thunderbird faltered and lost its hold on its prey. Jemmie was killed by the fall, but even if he had survived collision with the ground, his horrified teacher reported that the boy would have died from blood loss. The monster's talons had buried themselves into the boy's shoulder so deeply as to almost sever his arm.

More recently, giant birds appeared over Alton, Caledonia, Richmond Heights, Overland, and Freeport, Illinois, throughout April 1948. They were spotted by an army colonel, farmers, truck drivers, police officers, a chiropractor, and instructors from an aeronautics school. On several occasions, these monsters attempted to snatch livestock and pets.

One of the most well-documented attacks took place on July 25, 1977, when a pair of large birds with ten-foot wingspans suddenly appeared over ten-year-old Marlon Lowe, in Lawndale, Illinois. Marlon was gripped by one of the bird's sharp talons and carried thirty feet before his mother's screams caused the avian to release the boy. Marlon thankfully escaped unharmed.

Many pilots have also told of harrowing encounters with birds as large as airplanes. In May 1961, a pilot cruising above the Hudson Valley spotted what may have been a Thunderbird and was so frightened that he almost lost control of the plane. Such an encounter could have been responsible for the crash of a United Airlines plane in November 1962. When the wreckage was discovered in a wooded area of Maryland, rescuers found no survivors but did stumble upon a mass of bloody feathers. Investigators also noted huge gouges and slash marks on the plane, especially near the tail assembly.

If such attacks on airplanes do occur, the Thunderbird could be the most terrifying monster on the continent. Imagine a bird with talons the size of a human arm suddenly ripping into the cabin of an aircraft, its beating wings drowning out screams and its feathers choking the air. Imagine that monster bird tearing people from their seats to sate its hunger, biting humans in half with its sharp golden beak, then throwing the plane to the earth after consuming most of its passengers. The bird would then disappear into the sky, while the wreckage from the plane would either land in the ocean or explode upon impact with the ground, preventing investigators from determining the exact cause of the crash.

Thunderbirds are best studied from the ground, as air-to-air confrontations provide the monsters with a distinct advantage. In recent years, the Southwest has provided the highest number of reliable sightings, especially in Texas, where the famed "Big Bird of Texas" makes several appearances annually. Thunderbirds might also appear above sacred sites containing petroglyphs honoring the

Loren Coleman

The Lowes show the distance that Marlon was carried before the giant bird released him.

monsters, such as the Writing Rock State Historic Site in North Dakota and Gullikson's Glen Petroglyph Site in Wisconsin.

To spot the monster, set up a comfortable observation station on the desert or open plain, then merely sit back and study the sky. The wait can take months, but it will be impossible to miss a Thunderbird's passing from this vantage point.

Other Flying Monsters

The skies of North America are heavily populated by a host of flying monsters. Flying humanoids have been observed in numerous U.S. states, including New York, Washington, Texas, Mississippi, and Ohio, while giant birds and other flying creatures have been sighted in

virtually every region of North America. Below is a sampling of such creatures:

- **Achiyalabopa:** An avian monstrosity with feathers as sharp as knives who is known for hunting the Pueblo Indians.

- **Bird Women:** A race of beautiful female entities with huge wings sprouting from their backs, allowing them to fly through the peaks of the Rocky Mountains with ease.

- **Coney Island Creature:** Between 1877 and 1880, a tall man with wings and a hideous face performed aerial stunts over Brooklyn and Coney Island, New York. He never harmed anyone and has since disappeared into the vales of mystery.

- **Flying Felines:** Large cats that possess wings and are capable of rudimentary flight. Usually black and menacing, they have been known to attack and mutilate livestock, especially in Ontario, Canada.

- **Marionettes:** Flying orbs of ghostly light, not unlike the **Marfa Lights,** found on the shores of Quebec and generally believed to be the souls of the drowned.

- **Milamo:** A "supercrane" from Texas described as the size of a small ostrich. It only feeds on enormous earthworms the size of inner tubes.

- **Nunyenunc:** A giant avian found only on the highest mountain peaks. Like the **Piasa Birds,** it loves to eat humans.

- **Upland Trout:** Winged fish, encountered by numerous lumberjacks and revered for their ability to breathe outside of water and build nests in trees. Unfortunately, they began to fear water and would not return to streams to spawn, thereby ensuring the extinction of the species.

DWARVES AND GIANTS

THOSE MONSTERS THAT most resemble ourselves often cause the greatest concern.

Such is the case with dwarves and giants, two distinct groups of monsters that are generally human in appearance, but reveal their unusual natures through their size.

Dwarves are usually perfectly formed, but extremely tiny, humans. They typically live in remote wilderness, where they remain hidden from people. In many cases, they wield vast supernatural powers poorly understood by mortals. For example, dwarves are usually impossible to capture, kill, or injure because they possess mystical resilience or can become in-tangible at will. A small number are hairless and have oversize heads (often said to resemble watermelons), and many possess large or glowing eyes. Although easily angered, most dwarves are generally peaceful and choose to live hidden from humanity.

In contrast, giants are almost always excessively brutal entities of great size and strength. Although they too live in remote places, most emerge from their lairs to wantonly hunt humans. The large majority of giants are extremely ugly and display such distasteful traits as bad breath or pus-colored skin. Like dwarves, they often have glowing eyes, are woefully difficult to harm, and possess numerous supernatural powers. Giants are generally considered stupid and dim-witted, but they typically have highly advanced senses and incredible instincts, which make them extremely formidable.

Although their origins vary, a great many dwarves and giants were first encountered by Native Americans centuries ago and are considered part of the natural world. However, the giants and dwarves spotted in more recent times are often believed to be extraterrestrials or visitors from other dimensions.

THE ARMOUCHIQUOIS

VITAL STATISTICS

DISTINGUISHING FEATURES: Exceedingly long arms and legs

HEIGHT: 3′

WEIGHT: 60 lbs

RANGE AND HABITAT: Fertile farmlands around the Great Lakes

POPULATION SIZE: Several hundred

DIET: Omnivore

BEHAVIOR: The Armouchiquois are ancient diminutive entities who have become embittered by the loss of their lands to human settlers and will now attack people with little provocation.

SOURCE: Native American mythology, American (settler) folklore

ENCOUNTERING THE ARMOUCHIQUOIS:

As early American settlers began to expand westward into the Great Lakes region, they were met by Native Americans who warned them against angering the spirits of the land. In particular, the Native Americans referred to the Armouchiquois, a race of stubby humanoids with shrunken heads and skeletal limbs who became enraged whenever disturbed by humans. Evidently, the early settlers did not respect the Armouchiquois, and Native American reports from the Great Lakes region are replete with accounts about these monsters' attempts to exact revenge against the American pioneers. Eventually, the creatures were reported by settlers as well, who blamed almost every misfortune on the stealthy and angry entities. By the late 1700s, it was widely believed that the Armouchiquois were covertly battling humanity in pursuit of the richest lands.

By all accounts, the Armouchiquois are diminutive and thin. Each member of the race stands about three feet high, but most of this height comes from the creature's disproportionately long legs. When an Armouchiquois is sitting, its knees actually extend at least six inches above the top of its head. In many ways, these entities resemble frogs, with their spindly appendages and squat bodies. And like frogs, the Armouchiquois can use their powerful legs to leap great distances. They can also run at mind-boggling speeds and perform amazing acrobatic feats.

The Armouchiquois population is relatively small and only known to occupy the lands around the Great Lakes, where they compete with humans for suitable living space. They will rarely be found in cities, preferring to live on the outskirts of farming communities or completely in the wild. They adapt well to a wide variety of terrains, from swamps to cropland, but they will always be found near a healthy body of water and patches of rich soil.

The Armouchiquois are renowned for their quick and volatile tempers. They are easily angered and their rage knows few bounds. Armouchiquois are enraged when their lands are defiled, and they are driven positively berserk by pollution, landfills, chemical spills, and the like. When such crimes occur near their homes, they band together to pester and harass the offending party through a series of magical spells and enchantments. A victim of the Armouchiquois' wrath might suddenly develop a lingering cough, painful rash, constant muscle spasms, or similar physical ailment that cannot be cured by modern medicine.

When humans attempt to build near the Armouchiquois land, the settlement will be plagued by such nuisances as mysterious fires, faulty equipment, diseased crops and livestock, broken windows, and a host of mechanical failures. In the most extreme cases, the Armouchiquois might steal children or pets.

When encountered by researchers, Armouchiquois should be treated with utmost respect. Although unpredictable, these monsters are not inherently evil and only resort to dangerous tricks to ensure the survival of their species. Like most humans, the Armouchiquois desire the freedom to live unmolested in a land they can call home. If a monsterologist can prove he means no harm, the Armouchiquois may not act with hostility. In addition, offerings of seeds or tools might ease the tensions of an encounter.

If you become convinced that the Armouchiquois are plaguing a farm or house, you should study the afflicted humans' treatment of the land for signs of transgressions against these entities. The human residents should be instructed on methods for living peacefully with the monsters. Portions of the shared habitat should be graciously presented to the Armouchiquois and reserved for their use alone. Again, offerings and gifts can placate the Armouchiquois, as will an increased respect for the land and its inhabitants. If the Armouchiquois do not seem appeased by any of these efforts, however, it is best for humans to move away rather that face the full wrath of this supernatural tribe.

THE CANNIBAL BABE

VITAL STATISTICS

DISTINGUISHING FEATURES: Angelic eyes, cherubic face, and bloody lips

HEIGHT: 1'

WEIGHT: 10 lbs

RANGE AND HABITAT: Forest and brushlands of central North America

POPULATION SIZE: One

DIET: Anthropophagus

BEHAVIOR: The Cannibal Babe hunts by pretending to be a helpless infant abandoned in the woods and then consuming anyone who approaches to offer aid.

SOURCE: Native American mythology, American folklore

ENCOUNTERING THE CANNIBAL BABE:

The Cannibal Babe is a supernatural entity that takes the form of an infant in order to attract victims. Most often encountered in Montana, the Dakotas, and Nebraska, it lurks in the brush, wailing until an unsuspecting traveler hears the din. Anyone who investigates discovers a naked infant, scratched and dirty, sobbing uncontrollably. Only the most coldhearted individuals can resist plucking the baby from the bushes.

After the Cannibal Babe finds its way into a human's arms, it opens its mouth and pleads for a finger to suckle. Often deafened by the child's screams, most adults are happy to appease the baby. Unfortunately, once the monster's lips wrap around the victim's finger, the Cannibal Babe's mouth begins to literally suck flesh and muscle from bone. The horrified victim immediately loses whichever finger has been placed into the baby's maw. Despite the victim's attempts to toss the baby to the ground, the beast's sucking continues to pull skin, muscle, and fat from the naive Samaritan's arm. If the demonic infant is actually dropped, it crawls to the staggering victim and begins sucking a toe or an ankle. Once its prey has been devoured, the infant falls asleep cradled in the victim's empty rib cage, bloody drool oozing from its stained lips.

The Cannibal Babe will sometimes drag portions of the skeleton back to the small cave in which it makes its home, where it can crack the bones and extract the marrow at its leisure. Because of this habit, a Cannibal Babe's den can be recognized by a small pile of shattered and discarded bones near the entrance.

While largely untested, there may be methods for safely studying the Cannibal Babe in the field. If discovered, the Cannibal Babe might be rendered impotent through the application of a muzzle or similar device, though attempting to affix anything to the monster's lethal lips is a hazardous undertaking. The monster might also be distracted by toys, bubbles, television, music, a balloon, slapstick violence, purple dinosaurs, or any other object that naturally captivates children.

Those wishing to avoid the Cannibal Babe should never respond to the cries of a child while roaming the woods of central North America. In fact, all infants throughout this region should be avoided in order to prevent accidental exposure to this terrible tyke. As the Cannibal Babe's appetite and ability to appease its hunger so quickly make it excessively dangerous, only the most well-armed monsterologists should seek this creature.

Even when well-prepared for this truly horrific being, remember that of all the North American monsters the Cannibal Babe is one of the most disturbing. Few creatures so shamelessly prey upon the human heart. The Cannibal Babe operates by eliciting such human qualities as pity, compassion, and affection. Upon finding a wailing infant in the woods, any of us would wonder at the identity of the base individual capable of abandoning such a beautiful child to the elements. We might even curse such a person as a monster when the monster is, in fact, at our feet.

THE DOVER DEMON

VITAL STATISTICS

DISTINGUISHING FEATURES: Peach-colored skin, luminescent orange or green eyes, long fingers and toes, and huge head

HEIGHT: 4′

WEIGHT: Unknown

RANGE AND HABITAT: Dover, Massachusetts

POPULATION SIZE: Unknown

DIET: Unknown

BEHAVIOR: The Dover Demon wanders back roads late at night on unknown errands. It is easily startled and quickly darts away from approaching humans.

SOURCE: Ufology, cryptozoology, Fortean studies

ENCOUNTERING THE DOVER DEMON:

Few cases in the history of cryptozoology have received as much attention as the peculiar Dover Demon affair, which began on the night of April 21, 1977, when seventeen-year-old Bill Bartlett caught a bizarre-looking creature in his car's headlights while traveling a darkened road in Dover, Massachusetts.

Bartlett, and subsequent witnesses, described the monster as a lithe, tiny creature with a head that vaguely resembles a watermelon sitting atop a thin neck. It lacks ears, a mouth, or a nose, and its enormous eyes alternately glow orange and green. Largely hairless, it is covered in rough, peach-colored skin. Its toes and fingers are long and nimble, and it frequently travels on all fours, using its enormous hands and feet to help it navigate even the rockiest terrain.

During the initial sighting, the monster stood in Bartlett's headlights for a moment, then disappeared into the shadows at the side of the road. Bartlett immediately sped past the scene, and two friends in the car, neither of whom had seen the monster, noted that Bartlett was visibly shaken. After he confessed the sighting, they encouraged him to return to the scene, but they found no sign of the monster. In later interviews, Bartlett insisted that he and his friends had not been drinking that night, although they had smoked small amounts of marijuana prior to the encounter.

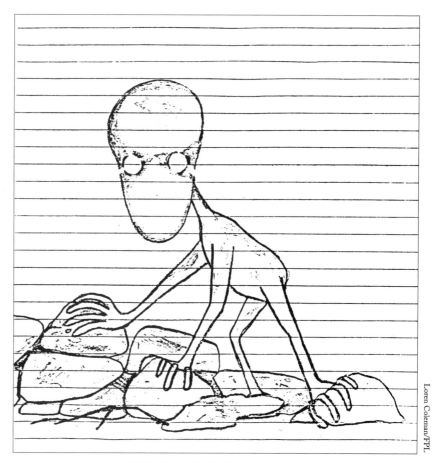

Bill Bartlett's sketch of the Dover Demon.

Loren Coleman/FPL

Just a few hours after the Bartlett sighting, fifteen-year-old John Baxter was walking home when he spotted a tiny figure in front of him. Mistaking the creature for a short friend, Baxter called out to it, then gave chase when the entity fled. After pursuing the mysterious being down a steep embankment, he realized he was chasing a monster and fearfully backed away.

Both Baxter and Bartlett, who had not conferred with each other, made sketches of the creature within hours of their respective sightings. The drawings were amazingly similar and consistent with later reports of the monster, which soon became known as the Dover Demon.

On the following evening, sometime after midnight, the Dover Demon appeared again. On this occasion, there were two witnesses: Will Taintor, eighteen, and his girlfriend, Abby Brabham, fifteen. Will, who had heard of Bartlett's encounter with the Demon earlier that day, was driving toward Abby's home when the pair noticed a small figure crouched on all fours near the road. Both witnesses were certain it was not a naturally occurring animal, such as a cat or raccoon. Terrified, the couple sped to Abby's home, where they told her parents and authorities about the encounter.

Soon after the teens came forward, investigators visited Dover in search of answers. Unfortunately, the Dover Demon failed to reappear for researchers scouring the area, and monsterologists have been left struggling with numerous questions about the beast. Most important, investigators have been unable to determine the Dover Demon's origins. Ufologists interested in the case still contend that the Dover Demon is an extraterrestrial, perhaps stranded on Earth or deposited on the planet to investigate human culture. Except for the monster's alien appearance, however, there is little evidence to support this theory.

More recently, the Dover Demon has been linked to creatures known to Native Americans as the Maymaygwayshi, a race of diminutive humanoids dwelling around the Great Lakes. But while the Maymaygwayshi do have large heads, they are generally described as hairy and foul-smelling, traits the Dover Demon does not share.

So what is this creature? While even the most experienced monsterologists are uncertain, it is most likely the Dover Demon is a member of an unidentified species that occurs naturally within the vast wilderness and enchanted backwoods of North America.

Sadly, future meetings with the Dover Demon may be impossible. The creature has not appeared since its short-lived initial visit to Dover in 1977. Still, the monster has become a very real part of monsterology, cryptozoology, and ufology, and should not be forgotten. Its sudden appearance, coupled with its equally mysterious disappearance, raises far too many questions.

In contrast to many other localized monsters, it may not be wise to begin a search for the Dover Demon in Dover, Massachusetts. If the monster was a visitor to the area, by accident or design, it has moved on, and a trip to Dover would be a waste of time and resources. Instead, scour the wilderness surrounding Massachusetts and range north into New Hampshire, Maine, and New Brunswick. As the monster has always been seen near bodies of water and amid trees, focus your quest on any forest punctuated by streams or lakes.

The Dover Demon has yet to prove dangerous, but it should be approached cautiously, if only to prevent frightening the creature. Though it usually darts away at the first sign of human life, the Dover Demon should not be cornered or captured. While it has not shown any "demonic" behavior thus far, the names we apply to monsters often prove prophetic. For all we know, the entity could have demonic powers of which we are unaware, including the ability to shoot flames from its mouth and roast humans in a blaze of fire and brimstone.

THE FLATWOODS MONSTER

VITAL STATISTICS

DISTINGUISHING FEATURES: Red face, green body, spade-shaped head, and foul odor

HEIGHT: Over 10′

WEIGHT: Unknown

RANGE AND HABITAT: Flatwoods, West Virginia, and other areas

POPULATION SIZE: One

DIET: Unknown

BEHAVIOR: The Flatwoods Monster only makes brief appearances, but in each case it is menacing toward humans and causes intense fear, although it has never actually attacked anyone.

SOURCE: Ufology, cryptozoology, Fortean studies

ENCOUNTERING THE FLATWOODS MONSTER:

The towering Flatwoods Monster first appeared on Earth on approximately the sixth of September 1952, when it frightened a pair of women traveling a road eleven miles outside the small Braxton County town of Flatwoods, West Virginia (pop. 300). The sudden shock sent one of the witnesses to the hospital, but the pair managed to describe their assailant as an extremely tall monster with a red face and glowing eyes.

September 12, 1952, marks the Flatwoods Monster's most dramatic performance. In Flatwoods that evening, a group of boys witnessed a flash of light in the sky, from which a red orb emerged. The sphere disappeared over a hill, but its glow was still visible and the curious boys decided to investigate.

After collecting a number of friends, including Kathleen May and her two sons, the boys arrived at the top of the hill. Immediately, the entire group, which consisted of seven teenagers, Mrs. May, and one dog, was affected by a horrible smell at the scene. Their eyes watered from the stench, and the dog turned and ran. Undaunted, Mrs. May suggested that one of the boys use his flashlight to scan the area.

The beam revealed the hideous giant that would become known as the Flatwoods Monster. Although they saw the creature for only seconds, the witnesses were consistent in several aspects of their reports. All agreed that the monster, which floated several inches above the ground, was at least ten feet tall. They also claimed that it had a dark red face, a spade-shaped head, and a bright green body, although some felt that it wore a bodysuit and helmet. Its eyes were luminous and projected greenish orange rays, but it did not seem to have a mouth or nose. As one witness stated, "It looked worse than Frankenstein."

After glimpsing the monster, the group scattered and ran. One boy fainted and had to be pulled away from the scene by his friends.

In her haste to escape, Mrs. May vaulted a six-foot gate in a single leap.

When the group returned to town, all witnesses were trembling and could barely speak. Several of the boys spent hours vomiting and sought medical attention. Armed adults and reporters soon rushed to the scene of the Flatwoods Monster's appearance, where they discovered flattened grass and detected a strange and irritating odor. They found no wreckage or other indication that a spacecraft had landed or crashed at the scene.

An hour after the initial encounter, the primary witnesses were interviewed by a reporter from the *Braxton Democrat,* and their story was quickly picked up by numerous wire services to appear in newspapers around the world. The resulting furor created unbridled excitement among ufologists. Noted saucer researcher Gray Barker interviewed the teens again for *Fate Magazine,* and at the behest of the North American Newspaper Alliance, famed cryptozoologist Ivan Sanderson also visited Flatwoods. These two men, and other investigators, discovered that even when isolated and questioned alone, the witnesses told nearly identical accounts of the encounter.

The sighting of the Flatwoods Monster quickly became a media sensation. Mrs. May and another witness even traveled to New York City to make television and radio appearances. Within a few years, however, all witnesses inexplicably became silent and refused to discuss the case any further. The Flatwoods Monster slowly faded from the public consciousness. However, the case of the Flatwoods Monster has become one of the most famous incidents in ufology and the subject of a country-and-western ballad titled "The Phantom of Flatwoods."

Although undeniably horrific to behold, the Flatwoods Monster has yet to actually attack humans, and monsterologists should feel relatively safe investigating this creature. Begin your search for the Flatwoods Monster in areas experiencing a high density of UFO sightings. While the entity may not be an extraterrestrial, it does have a tendency to appear only in areas with UFO activity.

While on the trail of the Flatwoods Monster, wear a protective face covering, goggles, and some sort of enclosed oxygen supply to prevent the effects of its stench. As in meetings with **Mothman,** if you do encounter the creature, attempt to establish communication. If it responds, ask where it has come from and what it wants.

FPL

THE GOUGOU MONSTER

VITAL STATISTICS

DISTINGUISHING FEATURES: Green hair, pointed ears, black scales, and wicked hiss

HEIGHT: Unknown

WEIGHT: Inestimable

RANGE AND HABITAT: Isle of Miscou in Chaleur Bay, Gulf of St. Lawrence

POPULATION SIZE: One

DIET: Carnivore/anthropophagus

BEHAVIOR: An aquatic giantess, the Gougou Monster delights in attacking ships and pulling sailors from their decks to consume.

SOURCE: Native American (Micmac) mythology, French-Canadian folklore

ENCOUNTERING THE GOUGOU MONSTER:

During his second voyage into the Gulf of St. Lawrence in the seventeenth century, the famed explorer Samuel de Champlain, who was the first European to observe **Champ,** had the opportunity to discuss the topic of monsters at great length with Native Americans. While conferring with the Micmac Indians, he heard of the terrible Gougou, a creature that filled the Native Americans with dread.

According to the Micmac and to Champlain's descriptions, the Gougou Monster is the most vile giant ever to roam the earth. She is incredibly large, towering over any ship that passes her hidden cave near the southern side of the Isle of Miscou in Chaleur Bay. The bay, which can be found in the Gulf of St. Lawrence between the northern coast of New Brunswick, Canada, and Quebec's Gaspé Peninsula, is an incredibly haunted stretch of water known for its fiery phantom ships, rough weather, and unpredictable winds. While these elements are cause for any sailor's concern, the Gougou Monster, often heard hissing loudly from within her cave, breeds absolute terror.

The Gougou's features are vaguely feminine. Much of her voluptuous body, including her face and hands, is covered in black scales. Her long hair is wispy and green, and when floating on the surface of the water, it appears to be seaweed. However, as the monster emerges from the depths, her pointed ears become visible, followed by her yellow eyes. When she opens her mouth to laugh at her victims, her dark, full lips part to reveal hideous fangs. Two huge fins extend from her shoulders, and her long fingers end in hooked claws.

In her distended belly, the Gougou Monster has a large pouch, where she stores victims. She will rise out of the water near a ship, grab handfuls of scurrying humans, and slip them into her fleshy pocket to free her hands so she may collect more victims. She then submerges and drowns her prey.

After discussing the monster with the

Micmac, Champlain found that many of his own men also knew of the beast. Captain Prevert, the commander of one of Champlain's ships, admitted that he heard the creature's hideous hissing whenever he sailed past her cave. Several other sailors also came forward with tales of hearing the beast or spying her kelplike hair.

Today, the Gougou and her terrible actions are rarely recognized. When sailors are snatched from the decks of their ships by this beast, they are assumed to have fallen overboard. When whole ships are lost to the monster's appetite, the vessels are declared lost, shipwrecked, or capsized. Until monsterologists come forward with concrete evidence proving the existence of this vile being, she will continue to take human life without reproach. However, she should only be sought by those with unfaltering courage, the ability to pilot a large ship, and a deep understanding of the ocean.

As only a handful of researchers actually possess the skills to seek out the Gougou Monster, monsterologists are much more likely to encounter the creature by accident while looking for other monsters in the same region. If this occurs, keep your wits about you and do not panic, despite the Gougou's astonishing size. Flight should be your first recourse, as battling the monster will do no good.

The Gougou's great size is also her sole weakness. She occasionally overlooks lone sailors swimming in the bay, just as a human might overlook a single ant crawling across a huge table. A quick escape into the water might allow you to elude the Gougou, although you will have to contend with the freezing temperatures of the Gulf of St. Lawrence. Unfortunately, if the Gougou does catch sight of your escape attempt, she may laugh and sweep the water with her arms, causing great tidal waves to pull you under. Since she can bear a lake in the palm of her hands, only the speediest swimmers will be able to avoid being scooped into her all-encompassing mouth.

GREMLINS

VITAL STATISTICS

DISTINGUISHING FEATURES: Oily skin, large ears, ducklike feet, and generally reptilian features

HEIGHT: Varies

WEIGHT: Varies

RANGE AND HABITAT: Most industrialized nations

POPULATION SIZE: Several million

DIET: Preference for gasoline

BEHAVIOR: Cruel and sadistic pranksters, Gremlins are a race of impish entities who delight in obstructing technology, especially planes and weapons of war.

SOURCE: Urban legend, and American, British, French, and Canadian folklore

ENCOUNTERING GREMLINS:

Gremlins were first recognized during World War I, when combat pilots in Britain's Royal Naval Air Service began documenting a host of malfunctions that could not be readily explained. Gradually, they realized that their planes were plagued by a race of malevolent entities capable of hiding in the machinery. In 1922, Gremlins finally received their moniker, which may derive from the Old English *gremian,* meaning "to vex," when an RAF pilot radioed the French airstrip Le Bourget for a weather report, but heard only an eerie voice repeating *"Gremlins sur la manche"* before his radio died.

After this report spread, the existence of Gremlins became common knowledge in many parts of the world, including North America. By World War II, it was discovered that they had completely infiltrated every military force around the globe: they now lurk in virtually every airplane produced, where they interfere with radars, radios, and onboard computers. They have also sneaked into tanks, battleships, submarines, radios, and even guns. As the decades rolled on, Gremlins branched out into nonmilitary machines as well, including televisions, satellites, and the space shuttle. Today, they are found in almost every piece of machinery in any household, from personal computers to washing machines to portable phones.

Gremlins are highly intelligent and possess an innate, almost supernatural understanding of the method and manner in which all machinery and technology works, and they use this ability to meddle with everything from transistor radios to nuclear bombs. The activity of Gremlins can be observed and measured as "Gremlin effect," a term abbreviated by mechanics, technicians, inventors, and others as GE.

Aside from their great knowledge of machinery, Gremlins possess a mild form of telekinesis (the ability to move objects with the mind). They employ this power to subtly shift steering wheels, move hammers slightly off course, unscrew screws, uncap bottles or fuel tanks, and generally create havoc from a distance.

As a whole, Gremlins seem to have some

common tricks, but rarely does a Gremlin repeat the same prank twice. Most household Gremlins enjoy stealing single socks from the dryer or disrupting a television's reception just as the final seconds tick away in an important sporting event. Automobile Gremlins leap about a car's trunk to create strange knocking noises, drink prodigious amounts of gasoline, and flatten the spare tire just before it is needed. Computer Gremlins crash hard drives and introduce viruses, while other workplace Gremlins steal pens, letter openers, and paychecks.

Without a doubt, Gremlins are most dangerous aboard airplanes. They ensure that baggage is mislabeled or lost, continually unbuckle seat belts or unlock lavatory doors, and shift luggage stored in overhead compartments to heighten risk of injury once these storage bins are opened. But these pranks pale in comparison to those Gremlins who delight in causing the airplane's radio, radar, landing gear, brakes, or engines to fail. Groups of evil Gremlins hiding in the belly of the plane also disrupt the plane's equilibrium by running, as a unit, from one wing to the other; such interference can cause pilots to lose control of the craft.

There are several different varieties of Gremlins, each with unique skills and physical adaptations. Aerial Gremlins, for example, possess membranes that enable them to glide safely to the earth, after abandoning a plane they have disabled. Spandules are a special variety of aerial Gremlin only found

> The Gremlins would go to any length to obstruct the navigator, even under extreme conditions shuffling all the stars in the heavens.
>
> —Richard Barber,
> *A Dictionary of Fabulous Beasts*

above ten thousand feet. They do not need to breathe oxygen and can survive in the cold darkness of space. Large numbers of these monsters currently occupy satellites, space stations, and the Mir space station. Marine Gremlins, who target submarines and boats, swim with the aid of webbed feet; they also have fins upon their heads, thick scales, and functional gills.

A few specific classes of Gremlins are known only in certain areas. Dingbelles are female Gremlins that only operate on the ground and usually target women. They were originally discovered by the Canadian Women's Division when they began interfering with typewriters and PA systems, and stealing personal effects such as photographs of boyfriends and lipstick tubes. Finfinellas are another female variety of Gremlins, but these tricksters prefer to hide near pilots and tickle them ruthlessly when they are about to land or perform other delicate maneuvers; on fighter planes; they molest bombardiers just before the young men drop their payloads.

Because gremlins are everywhere, the search for these creatures is quite rudimentary. Begin in your own home by looking within every appliance, machine, and piece of equipment. A radio incapable of achieving clear reception is a Gremlin habitat, as is the dishwasher that continually leaves spots on the glasses. When a drain clogs or a fuse box explodes, consider the possibility of Gremlin infestation before you contact a plumber or electrician.

HOPKINSVILLE GOBLINS

VITAL STATISTICS

DISTINGUISHING FEATURES: Glowing flesh and extremely large heads

HEIGHT: 3′6″

WEIGHT: Unknown

RANGE AND HABITAT: Area near Hopkinsville, Kentucky

POPULATION SIZE: Twelve to twenty

DIET: Unknown

BEHAVIOR: The Hopkinsville Goblins are a race of diminutive humanoids who possess numerous supernatural abilities and seem to enjoy harassing humans.

SOURCE: Cryptozoology, ufology

ENCOUNTERING THE HOPKINSVILLE GOBLINS:

During the middle of this century, a great many monsters were discovered in the heartlands of North America. At the time, the nation was gripped by a fascination with UFOs and aliens, and the majority of these strange entities were therefore identified as extraterrestrials despite a lack of data to support such claims. Such is the case with the Hopkinsville Goblins, tiny humanoids who first appeared in Kelly, Kentucky, just seven miles north of Hopkinsville, and now commonly believed to have heralded from outer space.

Also known as Kelly Creatures, the Goblins may have been misidentified as aliens because their appearance vaguely resembles the description of a traditional extraterrestrial: they are short, standing just three and a half feet tall, and have round, oversize heads, small mouths, and two thin nostrils in the center of their faces. Their rather large eyes are situated at the sides of their heads. The Goblins also have enormous, pointed ears, extremely elongated arms, and huge hands equipped with claws. Their skin has a silver cast capable of reflecting light, and indeed the Hopkinsville Goblins are surrounded by a dim glow. They are capable of floating several inches above the ground and have yet to be injured by any conventional means.

The Hopkinsville Goblins first appeared on August 21, 1955, sometime after 7:00 P.M. when they approached the farmhouse where Mrs. Lenny Langford, her son Cecil Sutton, and Cecil's family lived. The family was entertaining friends that particular night, and a total of eight adults and three children were in the house when someone noticed a bizarre light outside.

The men went out to investigate. They immediately encountered a group of horrifying Goblins and rushed back into the house to arm themselves. When one of the creatures peered into a window, Cecil Sutton fired at it. The gunfire caught the monster full in the chest, but after a few moments it stood up and ran away.

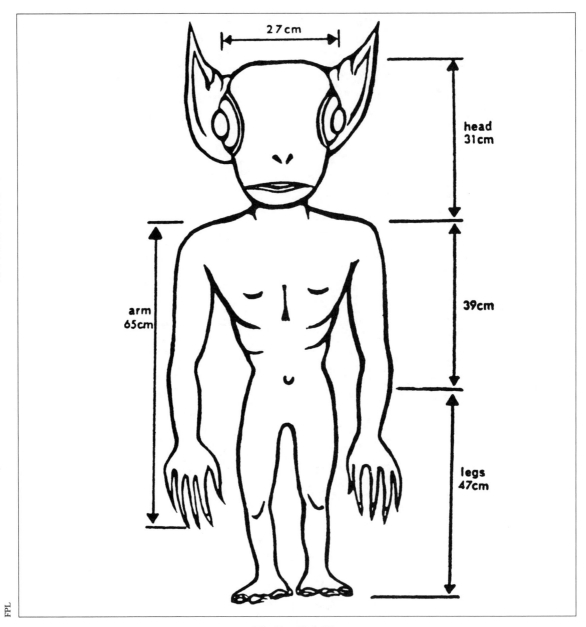

27cm

head
31cm

39cm

arm
65cm

legs
47cm

A Hopkinsville Goblin.

Moments after the appearance of the first Goblin, the farmhouse was under full assault. At least a dozen Goblins crawled around the house on all fours, investigating windows and doors in search of a way into the building. Sev-

eral imps climbed onto the roof, where they grabbed at one man's hair as he attempted to leave the farmhouse. A few also threw rocks at the building.

For over four hours, the humans battled

the Hopkinsville Goblins. The men fired upon the monsters, but the Goblins usually dodged the bullets, and when they were hit by a blast, they simply curled up and rolled with the force of the impact. Not a single Goblin was injured.

Eventually, the witnesses in the farmhouse made a mad dash for their vehicles. They drove directly to the police station and told authorities their incredible story. Police, private investigators, reporters, and even the military quickly arrived at the farmhouse to investigate. These individuals tramped around the site for several hours, but discovered nothing to indicate the existence of the Hopkinsville Goblins. It's entirely possible, however, that vital scraps of evidence were destroyed or stolen from the scene during this chaotic investigation.

By 3:30 A.M., the excitement had subsided and the Suttons had gone to sleep. Unfortunately, the Goblins decided to return to the farmhouse, and they were again caught spying into the windows. Cecil Sutton fired several rounds at the monsters, and the terrified family stayed awake until dawn, at which point the police were again called out to the farm. Several stray bullet holes were discovered, but no physical evidence that could be directly linked to the Goblins was recovered.

The U.S. Air Force's Project Blue Book, founded to examine possible UFO sightings, studied the case extensively but ultimately surmised that the event was unexplainable. Other Air Force investigators decried the affair as hysteria or a hoax. Yet the Suttons and their friends, upstanding citizens all, held staunchly to their story. Though neighbors and local authorities could not believe the entire incident had been a lie, the Suttons were eventually forced to relocate after their case

brought unwelcome notoriety and hordes of curiosity-seekers to the farm. Rumors persist that the family was kidnapped by the government, abducted by aliens, or spirited away by the Hopkinsville Goblins, who have themselves seemingly disappeared as well.

Today, few investigators can confidently identify the Hopkinsville Goblins, as the creatures have yet to reappear in North America. Ufologists claim that the monsters are aliens, largely because witnesses saw a glowing light in the sky shortly before the arrival of the Goblins. The family dog was visibly agitated by the glow, which is common in cases involving UFO landings. One man, Billy Ray Taylor, actually claimed to have seen a flying craft land in a gulch behind the Suttons' farm, but this sighting was never confirmed.

The Goblins may be extraterrestrials, but they are just as likely demons from another dimension, a naturally occurring terrestrial species, the product of a government experiment gone awry, or magical entities unleashed by a powerful witch.

The search for the Hopkinsville Goblins is probably in vain, but for those who do wish to pursue the creatures, begin by visiting rural Kentucky. The Goblins appear to be entirely nocturnal, always disappearing before sunrise, but they can be spotted at quite a distance by the bright glow of their bodies. Watch the night for signs of the Goblins' glow and stealthily follow the bobbing lights until an encounter occurs.

When the Goblins are spotted, all signs of hostility should be avoided. If met peacefully, they may not attack and could prove quite benign.

THE NAGUMWASUCK

VITAL STATISTICS

DISTINGUISHING FEATURES: Thin and ugly beyond belief

HEIGHT: 2″

WEIGHT: Less than two pounds

RANGE AND HABITAT: Coastal lands of Maine and Nova Scotia

POPULATION SIZE: Several thousand

DIET: Omnivore

BEHAVIOR: Although renowned for their incredible ugliness, the Nagumwasuck are actually kindly creatures who can be helpful and friendly when convinced to appear.

SOURCE: Native American (Penobscot, Passamaquoddy) folklore

ENCOUNTERING THE NAGUMWASUCK:

The Nagumwasuck, or Wanagemeswak, are a little people who live in a small tribal society along the coasts of Nova Scotia, Maine, and New Brunswick. Although rarely seen, they appear in numerous tales of the Penobscot and Passamaquoddy Indians, who uniformly describe the Nagumwasuck as extremely repulsive. Their bodies are emaciated, their skin is covered in warts and blemishes, and their heads are grossly misshapen. They are often described as "hatchet-faced," as they have sharp features, including long, pointed noses and thin lips. Their eyes are small, beady, and black.

Although horrible to behold, the Nagumwasuck are peaceful and have proven inordinately helpful in their rare interactions with humans. It was the Nagumwasuck, for example, who taught the Passamaquoddy and Penobscot Indians how to fish, trap, and raise crops. Unlike the Native Americans, who became closely allied with the Nagumwasuck, the first white settlers lacked the courage to face such hideous monsters and attempted to kill the ugly beings whenever encountered.

Quite understandably, Nagumwasuck now harbor a deep mistrust of all humans. They avoid mortals by hiding along the shores of secluded lakes, streams, and rivers, several of which have never been visited or discovered by modern man, where they subsist on a diet of acorns, fish, fruit, and small game, such as rabbits and squirrels.

The Nagumwasuck can also become invisible when surprised by humans. Because they are so thin, these beings only need turn sideways to "disappear." Unless a witness has extraordinary eyesight, a Nagumwasuck turned sideways is completely imperceptible.

Throughout the past several centuries, the Nagumwasuck have become increasingly distraught over the defilement of the forests, streams, and soil. A large faction of the Nagumwasuck even built a large stone canoe and set out into the Atlantic Ocean to escape humans. The fate of these emigrants remains unknown, but the rest of the Nagumwasuck remained in North America and continue to live hidden from humanity.

To find the Nagumwasuck, seek out a secluded body of water in Maine, preferably a lake with wide shores or a river sporting many fish. The signs of Nagumwasuck habitation are surprisingly obvious: these beings enjoy carving clay figurines, which they leave at the water's edge. Finding one of these figures not only proves that Nagumwasuck are indeed in the area, but it imparts good luck upon the finder.

When you do encounter the Nagumwasuck, be polite and respectful. Avoid showing signs of disgust at their appearance, and remember that they hold strongly to the belief that humans tend to violate and destroy all things of the natural world. You will need a strong show of good intentions to prevent the Nagumwasuck from disappearing immediately upon your arrival.

TWO FACES

VITAL STATISTICS

DISTINGUISHING FEATURES: Two faces (four eyes, two noses, two mouths), two enormous ears, and coarse hair

HEIGHT: 12′

WEIGHT: 1,800 lbs

RANGE AND HABITAT: Plains of central North America

POPULATION SIZE: One

DIET: Anthropophagus

BEHAVIOR: Two Faces is a grotesque giant who delights in capturing humans, whom he either eats or transforms into smaller versions of himself.

SOURCE: Native American (Sioux) mythology

ENCOUNTERING TWO FACES:

A frequent antagonist of the Sioux Indians, Two Faces is a hideous giant who stands well over twelve feet tall. He roams the plains of central North America and is especially active throughout Idaho and the Dakotas, hunting grounds where he allegedly stalked the Sioux ceaselessly in centuries past. As the monster's name suggests, the giant has two complete faces on its grossly distorted head. Each face has a twisted mouth, an enormous nose, and two shifty eyes. Thick, coarse hair covers the monster's entire body.

Although it does have two faces, the monster only possesses two ears, one on each side of its head. These bizarre ears are elephantine: each reaches ten feet in length when unfurled. Two Faces normally keeps these ears wrapped tightly against its skull, like two huge buns. However, whenever the monster finds a victim, it can extend its giant ears and use them as nets to capture humans. Each ear can efficiently contain three adult males. The monster's ears also act as its chief digestive organs. Instead of earwax, Two Faces' ears secrete digestive fluid that quickly reduces victims to a thick paste, which can then be absorbed through membranes in the ear.

Two Faces is entirely nocturnal and only hunts well after dark. When covering great distances, the giant travels on all fours, but he shifts to a bipedal stance when confronting humans. He can hunt with his sense of smell alone, but he also enjoys peering down chimneys or into windows in his search for victims. Like many other monsters, Two Faces is virtually indestructible. The creature can be stopped and vanquished for short periods, but it can never truly be destroyed.

As he travels across the plains, Two Faces delights in frightening animals. He will often kick up dust and screech or shout to drive owls from their nests and startle horses. Cows and other livestock are so terrified by Two Faces' nightly ramblings that many drop dead before morning. Although he is proficient at making noise and snorts and bellows like a buffalo when encountered, Two Faces cannot speak any known language.

Like **Vampires** and **Werewolves,** Two Faces is capable of producing offspring via infection. This infection is transmitted through the ear after a victim is captured. Transformed humans become miniature double-faced monsters within a few days. Although they do not possess Two Faces' considerable powers, they are physically strong and formidable beasts who unerringly follow their progenitor's orders.

Despite his fearsome abilities, the most widely retold Sioux encounter with Two Faces describes the monster's defeat at the hands of humans. The tale begins with one mother who watched in horror as her son was swallowed by the monster's huge ear. Determined to rescue her child, she hid near Two Faces' lair. When the giant returned home, she courageously leapt forward and grappled his thick legs. Her husband, upon hearing her cries, rushed to her aid, and the couple managed to topple the monster.

Once Two Faces hit the ground, the husband and wife stabbed the giant, bound him securely, and carved open the monster's ear to rescue their son. Unfortunately, upon freeing their child, the couple realized with horror that the monstrous transformation had already begun. The child was hairy, emaciated, and mute. His head was disfigured, and a second pair of eyes peered from the side of his face. The child quickly died, and the infuriated couple burned Two Faces' body.

After having his body reduced to ashes, Two Faces disappeared for several years. However, his corporeal body eventually reformed, and he returned to torment people living on the plains.

Two Faces is best studied by large groups of adequately armed monsterologists. If faced with a pack, it is likely that the giant will simply turn away, as he does not like to confront adversaries in large numbers. Still, his strength and savagery can overcome the most seasoned of warriors, and it's likely that even if the monster is slain, he will merely rise again in the near future.

Two Faces is prone to base emotions such as hatred, jealousy, and vengeance. Thus, if you encounter Two Faces in your prime and manage to defeat the creature, you must always be prepared to battle the monster once he has recovered from the battle. When you are elderly and incapable of standing up to the fury of this fiend, you may awake one night to find four hideous eyes staring through your bedroom window.

THE WATER BABIES

VITAL STATISTICS

DISTINGUISHING FEATURES: Pale skin and green hair

HEIGHT: 16–18′

WEIGHT: 20–50 lbs

RANGE AND HABITAT: Secluded lakes, streams, and creeks in the Great Basin of Nevada and surrounding states

POPULATION SIZE: Unknown

DIET: Omnivore

BEHAVIOR: Water Babies vary greatly in demeanor, but the most malicious enjoy drowning humans.

SOURCE: Native American mythology

ENCOUNTERING THE WATER BABIES:

In Native American folklore and mythology, Water Babies are a race of diminutive humanoids that occupy the Great Basin area, which includes most of Nevada and large portions of Utah, California, Oregon, and Idaho. The monsters are said to live in or near bodies of water, usually streams, rivers, creeks, springs, lakes, ponds, and serene pools.

Water Babies are similar to humans in many respects, but the tallest Water Babies stand only sixteen to eighteen inches tall. They cannot breathe water in the true sense, but they can remain submerged for hours at a time and are much stronger swimmers than humans. In addition, Water Babies are intelligent and are adept shamans, herbalists, animal handlers, hunters, and anglers.

Like humans, Water Babies are capable of good and evil. Benign Water Babies frequently spend their time tending to their own matters and only occasionally interact with humans. In rare instances, they will rescue a drowning child, but they intercede only infrequently on humanity's behalf. Some Water Babies are merely annoying, such as a Water Baby who spends his time tugging on fishermen's lines or stealing bait. These pranksters are essentially good-natured and rarely harm humans outright.

Evil Water Babies are cause for far more concern. Many spend their lives at least partially submerged in murky ponds, and their skin is pale, wrinkled, and coated in moss. Green algae clings to their teeth, and their hair is splotched with mud. The most unimaginative evil Water Babies lurk near shorelines and drown anyone who passes, but creative Water Babies might drill holes in canoes and boats, lure victims toward lakes inhabited by carnivorous monsters, or pretend to be a drowning child and murder any would-be rescuers.

A Water Baby's chosen habitat reflects its general demeanor. A boggy lake with frequent ground fog, ghost lights, and eerie noises will probably play host to a malevolent Water

Arkansas Department of Parks and Tourism

Scenic areas like this one in the Ozarks National Forest are prime spots for encounters with the Water Babies.

Baby; while a bright, bubbling spring visited by deer, rabbits, and squirrels is likely the home of a kindly Water Baby.

Searching for Water Babies requires knowledge of the particular individual's behavior, which can be gained through researching Native American folklore. For example, some Water Babies are said to remain in their marshy dens until dusk, but cavort freely all night long, while others only appear at midnight once a year.

However, folklore also reveals that Water Babies are most often encountered by accident, and few people seeking them meet with success. Begin your quest at a serene pond or gentle stream, a trip that will prove rewarding

regardless of whether or not a Water Baby appears. If such an entity does manifest, offer a gift of fresh fish, herbs, or flowers to establish trust and friendship.

Water Babies cannot perform certain physical tasks due to their size, and any donation of physical labor might be appreciated as well. You might offer to move a large rock to a more suitable location or help the entity lift a fallen tree. However, be warned that many evil Water Babies have been known to pose as their good-natured relations in order to dupe, kidnap, and murder humans. A malicious Water Baby can use its knowledge of black magic to imprison a human for life, dooming the victim to many years of hard labor.

Other Dwarves and Giants

Almost every region of North America has a long tradition of sightings of both towering and diminutive humanoids. Native Americans, in particular, have encountered a host of such beings, ranging from the benign to the truly bestial. Below is an overview of the diverse range of dwarves and giants known to inhabit the continent.

- **Amartoq:** A grotesque race of headless giants known to the Inuit of the far north. They have long arms and eat humans.

- **Apci'lnic:** Small skeletal humanoids living in the brushlands of Quebec and Labrador, where they are rumored to steal children.

- **Chenoo:** Mute giants made of stone who once battled the Iroquois. Generally described as clumsy and dim-witted, they frequently fight among themselves by throwing large boulders or tree limbs at one another. They can remain motionless indefinitely and are impossible to detect while sitting or standing among large rock formations.

- **Great Little People:** Helpful, fairylike beings allied with the Iroquois. They often impart wisdom and magical gifts, and it is said that one does not age while in the company of these entities.

- **Inland Elves:** A race of cannibalistic, one-eyed giants that hunt the Inuit Indians from Alaska to Labrador.

- **Leprechauns:** Dwarves who migrated to the New World with Irish settlers. Although they once appeared as dignified and well-dressed humanoids, in North America they have mutated into hairy, bestial creatures.

- **Maymaygwayshi:** Tiny humanoids living on the shores of lakes in central North America. They have long been known to the Ojibwa Indians, who describe the entities as hairy and rank, but generally harmless. In recent years, they have been associated with the **Dover Demon** as well.

- **Pixies:** Attractive dwarves who fled to the New World to escape a war with the Fairies of England. They live hidden in human homes, usually beneath beds and in closets, and enjoy playing pranks on their human neighbors.

- **Tommy Knockers:** A mine-dwelling tribe of dwarves who warn humans of impending cave-ins by rapping on the walls of mine shafts. Although notorious pranksters, they sometimes aid miners in the search for ore. Described as old men with huge heads, they first appeared in North America in the stories of Cornish miners, who as recently as the 1950s were known to place clay statuettes of the Tommy Knockers at mine entrances for good luck.

CRYPTID ANIMALS

CRYPTID ANIMALS, OR cryptids, are monsters that strongly resemble an animal already recognized by humans, but have one or more outstanding mutations that make them truly monstrous.

For example, the **Giant Gators** of the Everglades are similar in almost every way to normal alligators roaming those same swamps, except for their incredible size.

Cryptid animals usually possess the same natural abilities as their "normal" relations. The cryptid fish known as the **Fur-Bearing Trout** can breathe underwater, just like all other species of trout; while the **Jackalope**, a cryptid rabbit, has acute senses and can leap great distances. Cryptids typically share habitats with the normal animals they resemble and often have the same diets and behaviors.

As is the case with the Giant Gators, the most common mutation found among cryptids is immense size. In fact, almost every normal animal has its colossal equivalent. These giant animals can be relics from the past, scientific experiments gone awry, or the products of man-made mutagens such as pollution or radiation. Most are considered quite dangerous, usually because they possess voracious appetites.

The danger that cryptid animals pose toward humans varies tremendously. Some, such as the giant shark **Megalodon,** are inherently deadly, while others are only dangerous in extreme circumstances. Like any wild animal, most cryptids will lash out when cornered or in defense of their young.

This giant rabbit was killed by hunters in 1909.

Underwood Photo Archives, SF

THE CACTUS CAT

VITAL STATISTICS

DISTINGUISHING FEATURES: Feline body and face, thorny hide, and three-branched tail

HEIGHT: 2′ at shoulder

WEIGHT: 30 lbs

RANGE AND HABITAT: Cactus stands and chaparral in the Southwest

POPULATION SIZE: Less than fifty

DIET: Herbivore (primarily cactus sap)

BEHAVIOR: The Cactus Cat roams the desert, where it greedily feeds on cactus sap. Unfortunately, it becomes inebriated after gorging and can often be found wailing horribly as it drunkenly streaks across the sands.

SOURCE: American (cowboy) folklore

ENCOUNTERING THE CACTUS CAT:

In the Southwest of the 1800s, cowboys and their peers began telling tales of their terrifying encounters with the rare and reclusive Cactus Cat, one of the most unique felines on the face of the planet. From a distance, the Cactus Cat resembles a normal housecat, although it may be slightly taller at the shoulder than most domestic felines. Upon closer inspection, other differences between the two become obvious. First, the Cactus Cat's "fur" is actually composed entirely of thin, hairlike thorns. Large clumps of especially rigid and vicious barbs rest just above each ear. The animal's three-branched tail is also coated with these unique quills, and its forearms are covered in sharp, hooked spurs.

Unlike other cats, the Cactus Cat is not a carnivore. Its diet is limited to the sap running through common desert cacti. The Cactus Cat slashes open these plants with the knifelike adaptations on its forearms, then laps up the oozing sap with its thick, muscular tongue.

The Cactus Cat is oddly systematic in its approach to feeding, often attacking cacti in large circular patterns and eventually returning to the same cactus for a second feeding. Unfortunately, by the time the cat returns to the first few cacti, the sap has fermented. When the Cactus Cat drinks this fermented sap, it becomes thoroughly intoxicated.

In general, the Cactus Cat is only dangerous when it is drunk. While under the influence, it streaks across the sands, attacking anything in its path with its terrible tail and razor-sharp forearms. These vicious weapons leave red welts all over a victim's body, physical evidence that has often been wrongly attributed to sunstroke or heat exhaustion. Casualties of such lashings include roadrunners, coyotes, and humans.

While sober, the cat is merely obnoxious, often straying close to campfires and keeping cowboys and other travelers awake all night by wailing and rubbing its bony forearms together to produce an irritating rasp.

The Cactus Cat is native to Arizona, New Mexico, southern California, and other desert areas in which cacti of all varieties flourish. The animal is especially abundant between the Arizona towns of Prescott and Tucson, but even in this area a Cactus Cat is only seen about once every one hundred years.

Despite its limited range, the Cactus Cat is difficult to study because it is extremely quick, completely nocturnal, and survives in only small numbers. The entire population probably consists of less than fifty animals, most of which live in solitary dens that are well-concealed amid foothills, cactus stands, or dunes. The cats only venture out at night about once every fifteen days or so to feed.

Despite the monster's elusiveness, around the turn of the century, intrepid hunters set out to bag Cactus Cats and discovered that they could track the beast by following the trails of slashed cacti that the cat leaves behind. These hunters would hide near a wounded plant and wait, sometimes for several nights, until the cat returned. The hope was that the cat would be thoroughly sauced by the time it appeared and thus an easier quarry to capture. Yet the incensed feline always proved more than a match for even the most well-armed hunting parties.

Today, as in days past, you can attempt to track the Cactus Cat by observing its handiwork, but note if it walks with a stagger or slurs its yowls. Sober Cactus Cats may be glimpsed briefly before they disappear into their dens, but drunk Cactus Cats will charge without hesitation.

THE CANTEEN FISH

VITAL STATISTICS

DISTINGUISHING FEATURES: Water-filled hump on back

LENGTH: 6"

WEIGHT: 1 oz (when empty), 12 oz (when full)

RANGE AND HABITAT: Underground pools in the Mojave

POPULATION SIZE: Several thousand

DIET: Herbivore

BEHAVIOR: Canteen Fish spend most of their lives in shallow underground pools, only emerging to migrate to a new home.

SOURCE: American (cowboy) folklore

ENCOUNTERING THE CANTEEN FISH:

Since cowboys began roaming the 13,500 square miles of southern California's Mojave Desert roughly a century ago, they have reported sightings of the Canteen Fish, a curious animal living in pools of water hidden beneath the sands. According to such reports, Canteen Fish differ from other fish in that they are not proficient swimmers. Their pools are therefore extremely shallow. Canteen Fish are further differentiated from other species of desert fish by a prominent hump located just below the animal's short, spiny dorsal fin. Like a camel, the Canteen Fish stores a reserve supply of water within this small hump to protect it from dehydration during even the most difficult droughts.

Canteen Fish are adept at sensing any change or shift in their environment and will often migrate when their water holes begin to disappear completely. Fortunately, a Canteen Fish can detect water within a twenty-mile radius. With its hump brimming, a Canteen Fish can survive the desert heat for several weeks, which usually provides it with enough time to seek out a new habitat. Canteen Fish migrate across the desert in thin columns numbering anywhere between five and five hundred individuals, using their strong tails to cover several miles in a single day.

Because of their humps, Canteen Fish would seem to be the perfect source of water for thirsting humans lost in the desert, and they have indeed been used as such on occasion. However, many people report that the eyes of a Canteen Fish evoke strong sympathy, especially when the fish are caught helplessly adrift on a rain-swept desert after heavy rains flood their hidden ponds. This empathy prevents many people from killing the little animals and prompts many people to come to the Canteen Fish's aid. Those who have assisted struggling Canteen Fish have found that the monster harbors a degree of intelligence and a fierce sense of loyalty. Many of the fish's rescuers have gained pets far more dependable and faithful than any dog and blessed with the ability to lead their masters to water whenever thirst sets in.

Although it is impossible to discover a Canteen Fish's water hole during most seasons, these tiny dens often collapse after a heavy rain, forcing the six-inch fish to the surface. After a rainstorm, monsterologists can observe small groups of flapping and flipping fish struggling to find their way back underground.

However, Canteen Fish have remained a closely guarded secret for centuries because those who know of the animals are determined to protect them. If the secret of the Canteen Fish were to be discovered by the general public, the animals could become the water fountains of the desert and would likely die out within months. Monsterologists are encouraged to conduct their research carefully and surreptitiously to protect the species.

THE EARWIG

VITAL STATISTICS

DISTINGUISHING FEATURES: Tiny pincers and huge appetite

LENGTH: 1"

WEIGHT: Almost weightless

RANGE AND HABITAT: Central North America

POPULATION SIZE: One thousand

DIET: Carnivore (especially brain matter)

BEHAVIOR: Although a largely subterranean centipede, the Earwig feeds by slipping into human ears and burrowing its way steadily toward the brain, where it gorges on gray matter.

SOURCE: Urban legend

ENCOUNTERING THE EARWIG:

One of the most fearsome traits of monsters is their invasiveness. Their teeth and claws violate our flesh, their stealth allows them to sneak into our homes and hide beneath our beds, and they frequently pervade our dreams. Sometimes, they even manage to crawl beneath our skin and find homes within our very bodies. This theme is taken to incredible extremes by the tiny centipede known as the Earwig, a monster that crawls into human ears in search of food.

Earwigs usually gain entrance to the ear

when their prey is asleep, and many victims may not know for days that they have been infested. The Earwig makes slow but steady progress through the ear canal and ultimately pierces the eardrum, at which point victims begin suffering incredible pain. Unfortunately, the monster is seldom detected by even the most skilled physicians, and the creature is left to continue its bloody trek.

Eventually, the persistent Earwig burrows through the inner ear and makes its way to the brain. During its journey, it completely destroys the victim's hearing and sense of equilibrium by collapsing the eardrum and the ear's semicircular canals. Finally, it begins gorging on the outer layers of the cerebrum, devouring gray matter until it kills its host.

When not inhabiting ears, Earwigs live in small colonies found in soft, loose dirt. Like many bugs, Earwigs begin life in a larval stage, deposited by a queen Earwig. Queens are particularly dangerous because they can fly, thus allowing them to enter the human ear even when the victim is conscious. Once in the ear canal, the queen produces offspring, which digest earwax until they are large enough to begin consuming more solid tissue. Anyone infected by a queen is in grave peril, for it is nearly impossible to remove all the offspring, and the queen herself moves through the ear and the brain at an alarming rate. Fortunately, queens are rare.

As recently as fifty years ago, it was thought that the only cure for an Earwig infestation was to allow the centipede to work its way completely through the brain, while hoping it

destroyed only unnecessary cells. Most recipients of this "treatment" died, since the Earwig's progress cripples the central nervous system beyond repair. The few survivors were left with debilitating conditions such as severe memory or hearing loss, paralysis, speech disorders, and blindness.

Recently disseminated reports reveal a much more helpful method for dealing with the devastating Earwig. Victims are urged to lie against the ground, with the infected ear pressed against a patch of newly turned soil, preferably at the site of a fresh grave. Attracted by the smell of turned soil, the Earwig may give up its journey toward the brain and exit the victim. This process can take days, depending on how long the Earwig has been inhabiting the ear, but it is by far the most effective technique for dealing with the creature.

Outside the ear, the Earwig is completely harmless. Although it has small pincers, these cannot be used to any real effect until the creature can apply them to the soft tissue within an ear. The monster is not to be dismissed, however, for its invasion of the ear and brain causes tremendous, almost unbearable pain, and often death.

While studying Earwigs, eliminate the risk of infestation by wearing ear coverings at all times. This may make hearing difficult, but it will protect against an Earwig assault. If you do begin to feel discomfort within your ear, visit a plot of freshly turned soil and spend several hours with your ear pressed against the cool dirt.

THE FUR-BEARING TROUT

VITAL STATISTICS

DISTINGUISHING FEATURES: Thick white pelt

LENGTH: 2–4′

WEIGHT: 5–20 lbs

RANGE AND HABITAT: Cold rivers in the Midwest and upper Canada

POPULATION SIZE: Several hundred

DIET: Omnivore

BEHAVIOR: The elusive Fur-Bearing Trout lives in only the coldest lakes and streams, where it is protected from the chill by a woolly coat of white fur.

SOURCE: American folklore, creative taxidermy

ENCOUNTERING THE FUR-BEARING TROUT:

The Fur-Bearing Trout is a wonderful example of nature's adaptability and ingeniousness. Also known as the Beazel, the fish inhabits rivers and lakes of the Midwest and upper Canada, bodies of water notorious for their extremely low temperatures. To survive comfortably in these frigid waters, the Fur-Bearing Trout has developed a thick coat similar to the hide of the common rabbit.

Fur-Bearing Trout are highly prized by anglers, for they not only provide a hearty meal but their pelt can be fashioned into mittens or a warm hat, too. It's hardly surprising that many of the Fur-Bearing Trout populations have been fished to extinction, including those of Lake Superior, the Arkansas River near Salida, Colorado, and Iceberg Lake, Colorado. Legends also hold that the trout was common in various trout streams of Colorado, Michigan, Pennsylvania, and Maine, but it has since disappeared from these runs as well.

Today, the Fur-Bearing Trout exists only in the most far removed lakes and rivers, and only in the coldest and most desolate of climes. Large populations still thrive in the far north of central Canada and in a fair share of lakes scattered throughout the midwestern United States.

The most efficient method of studying the Fur-Bearing Trout is not in the field, as they are difficult to find and the environment in which they thrive is particularly harsh. Rather, mounted Fur-Bearing Trout are quite useful for research purposes and may be found in a variety of taverns, saloons, and bars in the trout's range. They can usually be purchased, although savvy barkeeps may charge a king's ransom for the fish.

Be wary of fraudulent Fur-Bearing Trout. Occasionally, an immoral taxidermist will wrap a large trout in the skin of a beaver, fox, or squirrel and try to sell this garish fake as a legitimate find. To avoid purchasing an imitation monster, remember that Fur-Bearing Trout have snow-white pelts.

Cold rivers like Wyoming's Gardiner River are the perfect habitat for the Fur-Bearing Trout.

THE GIANT GATOR

VITAL STATISTICS

DISTINGUISHING FEATURES: Mind-numbing size

LENGTH: At least 100′

WEIGHT: 60 tons

RANGE AND HABITAT: Swamps of the South, particularly the Everglades

POPULATION SIZE: Unknown

DIET: Carnivore

BEHAVIOR: The Giant Gators spend most of their time waiting patiently for prey, which they devour in a single bite.

SOURCE: Cryptozoology, urban legend, American folklore

ENCOUNTERING THE GIANT GATOR:

Like the **Megalodon** and the **Woolly Mammoth,** the Giant Gator is a relic of a primordial world that has long since vanished. Some 65 million years ago, just as the dinosaurs were fading from the earth, the swamps gave rise to the immense reptile known as *Phobosuchus,* whose scientific name means "horror crocodile." The horror crocodile may have contributed to the extinction of the dinosaurs, as it was the ultimate predator. It possessed the size and strength to kill anything it encountered: *Phobosuchus*'s skull was six feet long, considerably larger than the *Tyrannosaurus rex*'s head, and its body reached lengths of forty-five to fifty feet.

Scientists believe that *Phobosuchus* and all other large crocodilians are now long extinct. However, monsterologists recognize a similar monster known as the Giant Gator, which today thrives in the most removed reaches of the Everglades and other swamps.

One of the most dangerous predators ever known to the earth, the Giant Gator is twice the size of the ancient *Phobosuchus* and almost seven times the size of the modern alligator. Its head is over twelve feet in length, and its jaws, which can easily accommodate a tall human, contain dozens of teeth ranging in length from eight to twelve inches. The Giant Gator can easily kill and consume virtually anything.

The Giant Gator, like normal alligators, is a patient hunter. Because it has a slow metabolism, the monster can wait for years in the same spot until prey passes by. When it spies a victim, it moves like a tidal wave through the water, its black maw opened wide. Giant Gators feed on everything they encounter, including large bull alligators, deer, humans, and schools of fish.

Because Giant Gators spend such long stretches without moving, moss, plants, and even trees have been known to sprout on their backs. This foliage camouflages the leviathans and transforms the monsters into floating islands. Birds, rodents, turtles, and amphibians even make homes in the small jungles that grow atop the Giant Gators.

Giant Gators pose grave danger to anyone

A *Phobosuchus* skull.

or anything that comes near their mouths. No one who has run afoul of a Giant Gator has survived intact. The animal is exceptionally dangerous because it possesses an intelligence not common among its smaller relatives. It is far more cunning than most other animals and capable of outwitting humans. Furthermore, the monster's thick scales can deflect heavy artillery and fire.

Monsterologists must seriously evaluate the wisdom of pursuing the Giant Gator, given that an encounter means almost certain death. The truly suicidal researcher can seek the Giant Gator in the deepest, wildest portions of the Florida Everglades. Travel in a high-powered speedboat and search any muck-encrusted mass you may come upon for the Giant Gator's yellow eyes. The monster can also be located by listening for its thunderous bellow, which reverberates throughout the swamp whenever the animal is enraged or seeking a mate.

THE HODAG

VITAL STATISTICS

DISTINGUISHING FEATURES: Huge claws, bulging eyes, horns, and spiked back

HEIGHT/LENGTH: 5'/11'

WEIGHT: 2 tons

RANGE AND HABITAT: Swamps and marshlands from Wisconsin to Minnesota

POPULATION SIZE: Unknown

DIET: Carnivore (prefers porcupines)

BEHAVIOR: Although it primarily hunts porcupines, the Hodag is a truculent and easily incited monster known for attacking lumberjacks and other woodsmen without remorse.

SOURCE: American (lumberjack) folklore, creative taxidermy

ENCOUNTERING THE HODAG:

One of the most well-known and widely reported monsters from lumberjack folklore is the Hodag, an extremely ugly herd animal native to the swamps and marshes of the Great Lakes states. It was first reported in Maine in the early 1800s, but stories of the monster soon migrated westward until it had been encountered in virtually every state with dense woodlands. Today, the creatures are most often sighted in the forests of Wisconsin, Minnesota, and Michigan.

Similar in size and shape to a rhinoceros, the Hodag is exceedingly dangerous because of its powerful claws, large horns, and jagged dorsal spikes, which protrude from its spine and continue the length of its hooked, draconic tail. Although hairless, its thick, well-armored hide is covered in bony growth, stripes, and spots. It has stocky rear legs, but its front legs are thin and dexterous. All of its limbs end in sharp hooves, but lack joints of any kind, making it impossible for the creature to lie down. In addition, while the monster's large, bulging eyes provide it with excellent peripheral vision, its forward line of sight is blocked by a huge bony growth protruding from its snout.

The Hodag is an vovacious carnivore that will eat virtually any living creature. Its favorite quarry, however, is the porcupine. The Hodag hunts by slowly stalking the wilderness, scanning the treetops with its keen eyesight. Once it sights its prey in the limbs of a tree, it will use the spade-shaped growth on its snout to uproot the tree. It will then charge the tree, colliding headlong into the trunk. This attack unseats the porcupine, sending the helpless animal to the ground. With its sharp hooves, the Hodag tramples and kills the porcupine, swallowing the animal headfirst to avoid choking on the quills.

The Hodag is notorious among woodsmen for its mean streak. Easily angered, it attacks any creature that enters its territory. It also appreciates the flavor of human flesh; while the

Hodag does not actively hunt humans, it will kill and devour them given the opportunity.

While all Hodags are terribly dangerous, Wisconsin's Black Hodag is the most lethal. The Black Hodag is found only near Rhinelander, Wisconsin, where it inhabits deep caves hidden within the dense swampland. The monster feeds on a wide variety of animals, including mud turtles, water snakes, and muskrats, but prefers human prey above all else.

Because the Hodag has no joints and cannot bend its legs, it must lean against a tree whenever it wishes to sleep. Such "sleeping trees" are easily recognizable because they become gouged and slashed by the monster's spikes over time. In the past, Hodag hunters would seek out one of these sleeping trees and hack at the trunk until the tree was on the verge of toppling. They then waited for the Hodag to return from its daily wanderings. When the tired monster leaned up against the tree, it collapsed, toppling the creature onto its side. Unable to return to its feet, the Hodag was easily slain. According to lumberjack reports, in this manner Hodags were nearly hunted to extinction in the late 1800s.

Curiously, the Hodag is prone to uncontrollable weeping. These tears instantly harden and crystallize, forming long jewels that resemble exquisite chunks of amber. Hodag tears were once used in rings, necklaces, and other pieces of jewelry.

The Hodag is an egg-laying mammal much like the platypus or the **Sand Squink**. Female Hodags build large nests in the bowels of old trees and deposit clutches of up to fifteen eggs. These eggs hatch within weeks. Newborn Hodags are fully formed and capable of surviving without the aid of their mothers.

Interestingly, young Hodags are friendly and bright and can be tamed and trained to perform tricks. Such creatures have often been displayed at sideshow attractions and traveling cavalcades throughout North America. Unfortunately, as Hodags mature, they become unruly and will eventually turn on their masters.

Today, Hodags are fairly elusive. On rare occasions, dishonest taxidermists have been known to sew spiked hides onto the stuffed corpses of dogs, wolves, and large pigs to create false Hodags; but a live Hodag has not been reliably reported since the turn of the century. Still, monsters such as the Hodag die hard, and the creature thrives in extremely remote wildernesses.

Hiding near heavily gouged and scratched trees is the most foolproof method for sighting one of these beasts. Hodags can also be easily trapped within caves or rendered impotent if knocked to the ground. Using the tactics of former Hodag hunters, such as weakening a Hodag's favorite sleeping tree, can also provide monsterologists with a relatively helpless Hodag for study.

When seeking a Hodag, always carry a supply of lemons, as hunters and lumberjacks discovered that lemon juice acts as a highly corrosive poison in contact with the creature's hide. A few drops from a lemon will ward away even the most determined Hodag.

THE JACKALOPE

VITAL STATISTICS

DISTINGUISHING FEATURES: Large antlers

LENGTH: 4′ (including antlers)

WEIGHT: 15 lbs

RANGE AND HABITAT: Wyoming and surrounding states

POPULATION SIZE: Unknown

DIET: Herbivore

BEHAVIOR: A timid, rabbitlike animal, the Jackalope lives in dense forests, where it peacefully forages for food. However, it may attack with its huge antlers if threatened.

SOURCE: American folklore, creative taxidermy

ENCOUNTERING THE JACKALOPE:

The mysterious Jackalope makes its home in the dense forests of Wyoming, Montana, Utah, Colorado, and Idaho. The largest populations are found just outside Jackson Hole, Wyoming. A Jackalope's head and body are almost identical to that of the North American whitetail jackrabbit.

However, the pair of antlers protruding from the creature's forehead make the Jackalope truly wondrous. Both male and female Jackalopes wear such horns, although an average male's antlers are usually slightly larger than a typical female's horns. A Jackalope commonly reaches lengths of two feet, and its antlers, which are similar to those of the North American mule deer, often exceed this length. Most accounts portray the Jackalope as a gentle herbivore, but the animal uses its horns to ward away predators.

Aside from its antlers, the Jackalope is also well-known for its inordinate intelligence. It can disarm traps and steal away baits without being captured; legion are the stories of trappers who have returned to their lines only to find that all the baits have been carefully removed by this animal.

Unlike other species of rabbit, Jackalopes are unable to live in holes or dens because of their large antlers. Instead, they make use of the thick North American forests for shelter from predators and the elements. On rare occasion, they may be spotted on the open plain; they have little fear of airborne attackers, as such enemies would be impaled as they dropped down upon their antlered prey. Despite this relative sense of security, Jackalopes choose to remain extremely well hidden, perhaps fearing encounters with larger predators, such as wolves, bears, or humans.

Fortunately, newly uncovered folklore has revealed methods by which the wise monsterologist might lure Jackalopes into the open for further study. Evidently, Jackalopes are attracted to the scent of alcohol, which they can sense from miles away. Although considered an herbivore, the Jackalope is also fond of a bizarre mixture of human foods, which monsterologists can combine to make compelling

John Bonar/FPL

lures. Successful lures include mixtures of bourbon, baloney, and beer; moonshine, maggots, and marmalade; and whiskey, winter melon, and wasps. Any of these concoctions will attract a Jackalope or two, who will patiently wait to be fed, providing a monsterologist with a perfect opportunity to snap photographs.

For those whose search proves fruitless, most trading posts and souvenir stores offer a wide variety of merchandise featuring the Jackalope's likeness, including T-shirts, statuettes, coffee mugs, and postcards. In many places throughout the monster's range, mounted and stuffed Jackalopes, which are usually fakes, can also be purchased.

THE MEGALODON

VITAL STATISTICS

DISTINGUISHING FEATURES: Immense size and appetite

LENGTH: 40–100′

WEIGHT: 100 tons or more

RANGE AND HABITAT: Pacific Ocean

POPULATION SIZE: Unknown

DIET: Complete carnivore

BEHAVIOR: A single-minded eating machine, the Megalodon is a giant shark found roaming the oceans in search of food, which can include everything from whales to small boats.

SOURCE: Cryptozoology

ENCOUNTERING THE MEGALODON:

Most marine biologists, and anyone who has ever entered the ocean, would like to believe that this behemoth passed into extinction long ago. However, today the Megalodon is a thriving relic and still rules the seas.

The ultimate predator, the Megalodon possesses the instincts and abilities of the great white shark, whose voraciousness and stealth were made famous by the movie *Jaws,* coupled with a much greater size and hunger. Far more lethal than any other animal known to humankind, the Megalodon spends the bulk of its life on the ocean's floor, feeding on giant squid, giant octopi, sperm whales, and schools of fish. But when it surfaces, it devours entire killer whale pods and sea lion colonies. The Megalodon also feeds on other sharks, including the great white, as well as large tuna and sailfish and water fowl.

Although primitive, the beast is not stupid and does not make a habit of attacking nonorganic objects, such as buoys or ships. Still, the Megalodon may mistake the movement of small craft for prey and attack. Groups of scuba divers, surfers, and water-skiers are also vulnerable.

The Megalodon feeds ravenously and leaves few witnesses, but in 1918 a group of men

Over fifty thousand years ago, the world's oceans were home to the most fearsome predator that has ever existed: *Carcharodon megalodon.* More commonly known as the Megalodon (or "Meg"), this huge shark was a gigantic variation of the modern great white (*Carcharodon carcharias*) and is believed to be *C. carcharias*'s primeval predecessor. According to marine biologists, the monster fish easily surpassed lengths of fifty feet, nearly twice the size of today's largest great whites, and its jaws were capable of opening to an incredible six feet in diameter. Arranged in several rows within this awesome maw were hundreds of serrated teeth, each averaging eight inches in length and weighing up to three-quarters of a pound. The Megalodon could swallow even the largest sea lion whole or tear it apart with just a single bite.

fishing for crayfish from Australia's Broughton Islands, near Port Stephens, managed to survive an encounter with one of these giant sharks, which measured over 115 feet in length. The monster swallowed numerous crayfish pots and tore loose all moorings. The fishermen who observed the shark were experienced seamen familiar with all types of sharks and other sea life, but none had ever seen an animal of such size or ferocity.

Because it is so completely terrifying in every respect, monsterologists are warned against any pursuit of the monster shark. Interested researchers should be content with the analysis of fossilized Megalodon teeth, which are often dredged from the ocean floor and which illustrate the animal's great size without threatening the researcher's life.

For the foolhardy, the quest for the Megalodon should begin within the notorious Red Triangle, a portion of the Pacific Ocean so named because of the high percentage of shark attacks that occur there. The Red Triangle encompasses much of the northern California coastline from Monterey to San Francisco, and out to the Farallon Islands, about thirty miles offshore. If you wish to glimpse the Megalodon, frequent the Golden Gate Bridge on overcast days and keep your eyes affixed on the churning ocean below. Once in a lifetime, the massive dorsal fin of the Megalodon can be seen slicing through the water as the shark enters San Francisco Bay in search of windsurfers, sailboats, and other delights.

Sea World, Inc.

Reconstructed Megalodon jaws, on display at Sea World, California.

RADIOACTIVE FROGS

VITAL STATISTICS

DISTINGUISHING FEATURES: Varying mutations from glowing skin to immense size

LENGTH: Varies

WEIGHT: Varies

RANGE AND HABITAT: Swamps and woods throughout Tennessee

POPULATION SIZE: One thousand or more

DIET: Omnivore

BEHAVIOR: Radioactive Frogs tend to go about their business, unless molested. A small percentage may be particularly nasty, but most are harmless unless eaten.

SOURCE: Urban legend

ENCOUNTERING RADIOACTIVE FROGS:

Radioactive Frogs, or Hot Frogs, first appeared in the late 1940s when the Oak Ridge National Laboratory in Tennessee began using a small pond as a holding reservoir for nuclear research wastewater. Frogs maturing in the mud of the half-acre pond were exposed to absurd amounts of radiation and began showing mild signs of mutation. One spring in the late 1980s, a particularly intelligent batch of Radioactive Frogs was born and escaped the irradiated pond through a hole in the fence surrounding the lab. For the most part, the escapees appeared to be normal leopard frogs, about two inches long and brownish green in color, but they emitted enough radiation to choke a Geiger counter. Scientists claimed that the Hot Frogs were dangerous only if eaten.

The fugitive frogs were never recaptured and soon spread out into the swamps of Tennessee, where they began mating with normal frogs. The offspring of these unions showed distinct signs of severe mutation, the most common being immense size. Radioactive Frogs can reach lengths of five feet or more and may weigh up to one hundred pounds. While such large frogs are rarely dangerous, they do wreak havoc on crops and local fish populations. Other Hot Frogs have multiple eyes or limbs, have purple or red skin, or are capable of walking upright. The most fearsome mutant frogs bear fangs, secrete poisonous substances, spit acid, or use batlike wings to travel through the night sky.

It should also be noted that a small number of Radioactive Frogs have acquired a carnivorous appetite, which extends to humans. It is

Loren Coleman

Radioactive Frogs love to lurk in thick foliage, like the plants surrounding Silver Lake, in Athol, Massachusetts, where a giant frog has been spotted numerous times.

likely that as the frogs continue to mutate, the monsters will manifest even more deadly and horrifying mutations.

A reliable Geiger counter is an invaluable tool for tracking Radioactive Frogs. Each frog exudes massive amounts of radiation, and a group of the amphibians will register on even the most rudimentary radiation-detection device.

Hot Frogs tend to congregate in small ponds or bayous. Observing this habitat is a wondrous spectacle for even the most jaded monsterologist. As the researcher stands on the shore, glowing frogs croak from the reeds.

A frog possessing a unicornlike horn emerges from the brush, while a mammoth frog the size of a cow returns from hunting. Above the water, a frog with wings courts its lover, a two-headed frog with eyes the color of gold.

While it may be awe-inspiring to observe Hot Frogs in their natural surroundings, never handle one as they may ooze poisons and emit low-frequency radiation. If attacked by Hot Frogs, you may be able to ward them off with fire. In rare instances, intelligent Radioactive Frogs may attempt communication; if this occurs, use every effort to understand and converse with these fantastic animals.

Frogs and the Supernatural

The frog is one of the most widely recognized supernatural animals. Witches, voodoo priestesses, and shamans commonly utilize frog legs, tongues, eyes, and innards in potions, spells, and potent brews. Many witches can also enslave their enemies by transforming them into frogs, and trained frogs are loyal familiars who assist their masters in casting spells or spying. In the South, a croaking frog portends rain, approaching illness, or imminent death. Eating frogs' legs bestows agility and speed, and applying frog's blood to a wart will remove the blemish. However, killing frogs generally brings bad luck. One can reach a plane of altered consciousness after licking a frog; and, of course, kissing a frog produces staggering results.

THE RAZORBACK HOG

VITAL STATISTICS

DISTINGUISHING FEATURES: Sharp, spiny dorsal ridge

HEIGHT: 4′ (at shoulder)

WEIGHT: 400 lbs

RANGE AND HABITAT: Ozarks, Arkansas

POPULATION SIZE: Unknown

DIET: Omnivore

BEHAVIOR: The bane of the Ozarks, the Razorback is a violent pig that devours any living creature it encounters.

SOURCE: American (Ozarks) folklore

ENCOUNTERING THE RAZORBACK HOG:

The temperamental Razorback Hog is considered the most dangerous of the monsters lurking in the mountains and foothills of the Ozarks. A completely nocturnal animal, the Razorback Hog is so named for the sharp ridge that runs the length of its spine. It is omnivorous and will feed on virtually anything organic, including rodents, goats, sheep and other livestock, wolves, foxes, a variety of fowl, fish, bears, and humans. Victims are charged and knocked to the ground, trampled by the monster's sharp hooves, and gored by its six-inch tusks. It lacks any sense of fear or caution and will tenaciously fight to the death.

Killing a Razorback is difficult, for the beast has an extremely tough hide capable of withstanding claws, fangs, knives, and even bullets. In addition, its tremendous speed and agility allow it to strike

The Ozarks National Forest, home to many monsters, including the Razorback Hog.

Arkansas Department of Parks and Tourism

quickly and with a minimum of exposure despite its size. Ignorant of the Razorback's formidable abilities, many hunters have sought the hog in vain.

The Razorback's natural inclinations and habitat make it difficult to track or study in the wild, and capturing one of the beasts alive is nearly impossible given the monster's brutish nature. Razorbacks can, however, be lured into the open with prodigious amounts of food, es-

pecially sweet apples and piles of raw meat. With such bait in place, Razorbacks will make an appearance, but they will attack any humans in the area before turning their attentions to the food pile. Observation of the Razorback is therefore best done from a safe perch atop a sturdy tree. Be warned, however, that the Razorback may smell your scent, even in a high perch, and collide with the tree you're sitting in until it topples.

THE SAND SQUINK

VITAL STATISTICS

DISTINGUISHING FEATURES: Bushy tail and tendency to emit bursts of light

HEIGHT: 3′

WEIGHT: 15–30 lbs

RANGE AND HABITAT: Shores of Columbia River, Washington State

POPULATION SIZE: Unknown

DIET: Omnivore

BEHAVIOR: A coyote-bobcat hybrid roaming the Columbia River, the Sand Squink frequently releases sparks from its bushy tail to mesmerize travelers.

SOURCE: Lumberjack folklore

ENCOUNTERING THE SAND SQUINK:

The physical makeup of the Columbia River Sand Squink is a strange mixture. The hybrid's front end is pure coyote, while its back end has the makeup of a bobcat. Its spotted rump is adorned with a squirrel's long, bushy tail. Atop its wolfish head are two immense rabbitlike ears, with a small, round nub at the peak of each ear. The creature can only be spotted near the shores of Washington's Columbia River, where it stalks the riverbanks at night in search of food. With its padded feet, incredible stealth, and patience, it is a successful hunter. Its diet consists of frogs, tadpoles, trout, salmon, clams, larvae, and fungi, but the Squink is particularly fond of electric eels.

The Sand Squink possesses an amazing ability to generate electric charges by touching the tip of its bushy tail to either of the nubs at the tips of its ears. These flashes appear as brilliant sparks in the distance and often cause humans to wander blindly into the woods seeking the source of these mesmerizing and ghostly lights. Such unfortunates fall victim to the elements or wildlife and are never seen again.

Although the Squink's brilliant emanations have been witnessed on numerous occasions, few researchers have been able to study the monster more closely. However, a few Squink nests have been discovered. A typical nest is located about three feet beneath the ground and is insulated by old inner tubes, tires, rubber boots, and other similar items gathered from riverbanks and streams. Like the platypus, the Squink is a fur-bearing mammal that lays eggs, but a Squink's eggs have shells composed of a substance similar to plastic and are therefore incapable of transmitting electrical charges. This coating protects a nesting Squink from the electrical discharges of her developing offspring.

The Sand Squink is fairly easy quarry for monsterologists as it is relatively harmless to those researchers who protect themselves from falling victim to the creature's hypnotic light show. Protective eyewear can reduce the effects of the Squink's electric emanations, and rubber boots and insulated clothing will prevent any possibility of being electrocuted by the little animal.

Electric eels, the Squink's favorite food.

Sea World, Inc.

SEWER GATORS

VITAL STATISTICS

DISTINGUISHING FEATURES: Enormous size and a host of mutations

LENGTH: 25'

WEIGHT: 800 lbs

RANGE AND HABITAT: Sewers of New York City

POPULATION SIZE: One hundred to one thousand

DIET: Carnivore

BEHAVIOR: Sewer Gators spend most of their lives drifting through sewage tunnels but will attack humans when they happen by.

SOURCE: Urban legend

ENCOUNTERING THE SEWER GATORS:

The New York City Sewer Gators are huge alligators found floating silently among the chattering rats and human refuse deep within the bowels of the Big Apple. They first arrived in New York in the late 1960s to support a growing fad for exotic pets, but the majority of these helpless alligators found themselves flushed into the sewer systems by disenchanted children or angry parents. The exotic-pet fad died and the influx of infant alligators stopped, but a large population of the scaled babes had already been deposited into a warm environment with a plentiful supply of food and few predators.

The young Sewer Gators spent their formative years bathing in the sewers' strange soup of discarded radioactive materials, human wastes, and thousands of chemicals. They fed on a steady diet of raw sewage and irradiated rats, as well as large amounts of New York White, a rare strain of potent marijuana that took root in the sewers after drug users flushed massive quantities of the herb down toilets during police raids of the 1960s.

The first generation of Sewer Gators developed mild mutations, namely immense size. While the alligator species common to Florida and Louisiana rarely reaches fifteen feet in length, a Sewer Gator is likely to surpass lengths of twenty-five feet. Its teeth, tail, and fearsome head are sized accordingly, resulting in creatures that resemble the massive crocodilians from the Jurassic era.

As the Sewer Gator population continued to grow throughout the years, they interbred and their mutations became even more pronounced. Modern Sewer Gators often have multiple eyes, strangely colored scales, long tongues, two heads, and a host of other weird traits. A vast majority are also albino.

Due to their long years in the darkness, most Sewer Gators are blind and can only distinguish bright light sources such as open manholes, beneath which they often lie in wait for prey. However, they have an acute sense of smell and keen hearing.

Adult Sewer Gators spend most of their time wandering the sewers in search of food. They will consume almost anything that comes their way, from rubber boots to stray cats to maintenance workers. A large supply of edible materials and a lack of competition allows these gators to eat excessively, thus contributing to their awesome girth. While these alligators usually remain in the deepest sewer tunnels, far from human activity, they have been known to visit maintenance shafts, storm drains, and other openings when hunting larger prey.

It is widely rumored that, once it became obvious that alligators were living in the sewers of New York, the city's sanitation department ordered workers to enter the tunnels and eliminate the threat. As reported by Thomas Pynchon in his novel *V* (1963), the Sewer Gator hunters traveled in pairs, with one member holding a powerful flashlight and the other wielding a twelve-gauge shotgun.

After a large number of the beasts had been killed, the Sanitation Department deemed the situation secure. A clandestine museum was created to house stuffed alligators and photographs, but only top-level sanitation workers have actually visited the hidden alligator archive. Today, New York officials deny the existence of the Sewer Gators, yet they have installed cameras throughout the 6,200 miles of sewage tunnels.

To date, Sewer Gators have not posed a great danger to New Yorkers. The most common human casualties have been children venturing into the sewers in search of lost baseballs or on dares, maintenance workers, or transients seeking some legendary utopia hidden beneath the city. The reptiles have yet to strike out into the streets, and they seem content to roam the dank tunnels where food is plentiful and threats are nonexistent.

However, as their numbers continue to grow, the gators' food supplies will begin to dwindle and they will likely begin seeking prey more aggressively. Those who believe that the Gators will be contained by storm drains and manhole covers are sadly mistaken. If motivated by hunger, a Sewer Gator could easily use its sheer size and strength to smash through metal grates, steel covers, and asphalt. It is not implausible to imagine an invasion of giant alligators erupting through the streets of

New York City, pulling New Yorkers screaming from the sidewalks and dragging them into the dismal sewer world below.

Confronting the Sewer Gators is not an endeavor to be undertaken lightly. These are deadly beasts that live in a toxic environment, and finding their lair deep in the bowels of the sewer system is problematic.

If you must visit the Sewer Gators, travel with at least one other monsterologist and carry a powerful gun. Enter the sewers during the winter, when the alligators are cold and somewhat sluggish. Wear a radiation suit, gas mask, and thick rubber boots. Carry a Geiger counter to monitor the radiation levels and leave the tunnels if the level of exposure becomes too great. Use a waterproof flashlight to light your way, but never light matches or flares while in this methane-filled environment.

When the Sewer Gators are discovered, they will undoubtedly attack. Be prepared to face upward of twenty immense brutes with monstrous jaws and lashing tails. Their attacks will come at you from several directions at once, but refrain from screaming, as your shrieks will only attract the monsters in greater numbers.

THE SLIVER CAT

VITAL STATISTICS

DISTINGUISHING FEATURES: Long tail covered in spikes, red eyes, and tasseled ears

HEIGHT: 4' at shoulder

WEIGHT: 300 lbs

RANGE AND HABITAT: Forests of the Great Lakes region and central Canada

POPULATION SIZE: Under twelve

DIET: Carnivore/anthropophagus

BEHAVIOR: The mean-spirited Sliver Cat waits in trees for passing humans, whom the cat impales on its spiked tail.

SOURCE: American (lumberjack) folklore

ENCOUNTERING THE SLIVER CAT:

One of the most repugnant monsters discovered by lumberjacks is the devious and brutal Sliver Cat, a devoted man-eater. The beast is somewhat similar to a mountain lion, or puma, with a powerful body about five feet in length, retractable claws, and razor-sharp senses, including highly developed night vision. The beast, which lives only in the branches of tall trees, can reach up to 300 pounds and can be recognized by its low, ominous call.

Without a doubt, the Sliver Cat's most unique feature is its incredible tail. Reaching lengths of eleven feet, the animal's tail is prehensile and extremely muscular. It ends in a thick, round knob roughly a foot in diameter. One side of the knob is smooth and reinforced by thick bone, while the other side is studded with long, vicious spikes.

The Sliver Cat hunts humans by first finding a suitable roost in the shadowy boughs of a tree, about five to eight feet from the ground. When prey passes beneath the tree, the Sliver Cat lashes out with the hard, smooth side of its tail, moving with such speed and force that victims are rendered senseless and often suffer concussions and cranial fractures. After the target has been stunned, the Sliver Cat reverses its tail and strikes out again, impaling the hapless victim with its tremendous spikes. Once its prey is thus snared, the monster uses its incredible tail to hoist the body into the tree to devour it at leisure.

Because Sliver Cats are so malignant, lumberjacks ceaselessly hunted these monsters at one time. They discovered that, while agile and efficient amid the branches, Sliver Cats are clumsy and slow on the ground. Hunters exploited this weakness by felling trees believed to hide the beasts, but this practice is rarely repeated today.

Obviously, the Sliver Cat is a monster who enjoys human suffering, and therefore any in-depth study of the beast is extremely hazardous. Anyone traveling through the Sliver Cat's known territories should wear a sturdy helmet at all times.

After a Sliver Cat is spotted, chop down the cat's tree, cover the animal with a steel-cable net, or spook the beast with torches. Once grounded, the Sliver Cat is slow and clumsy and can be beaten to death or shot. However, as these creatures may be on the verge of extinction and will likely die out on their own, hunting Sliver Cats is a highly discouraged act. Furthermore, a would-be Sliver Cat hunter is likely to become the hunted and find himself painfully impaled by the creature's cruel tail.

The Snipe, a small bird that has appeared in reports from across the continent for the past two centuries, is one of the most abundant monsters in North America. However, few monsterologists have seen or captured a Snipe because the creature can render itself completely invisible at will.

The only description of a Snipe comes from noted monsterologist Henry H. Tryon, who allegedly spotted one of the birds while Snipe hunting in an undisclosed location around 1925. According to Tryon's description, the Snipe stands erect on two legs, to a height of about seven inches. A third, smaller leg juts from the bird's backside, which Tryon speculated may stabilize the Snipe when it runs. Its body is covered with feathers, which are blue, pink, and green with hints of gold. The Snipe's eyes emit a red glow and shoot small sparks. It has one vertical pupil and one horizontal pupil, and it uses a broad hooked beak to catch insects. The birds are largely nocturnal.

Most Snipes live in thick bushes near marshes, lakes, and swamps. Although researchers are unsure how the creature becomes invisible, it is likely that the animal simply fades into the surrounding foliage whenever it feels threatened.

The best known method for spotting a Snipe is the famed Snipe hunt, which has been conducted since the Civil War. As adults usually discount the existence of Snipes, Snipe hunting (or sniping) has been organized and conducted largely by

THE SNIPE

VITAL STATISTICS

DISTINGUISHING FEATURES: Three legs, multicolored feathers, and glowing eyes

HEIGHT: 7"

WEIGHT: 3 lbs

RANGE AND HABITAT: Almost any marshland, lake, or swamp throughout North America

POPULATION SIZE: Several million

DIET: Insectivore

BEHAVIOR: The Snipe, like most skittish birds, tries to avoid humans. When frightened, it becomes invisible and runs away.

SOURCE: American folklore

ENCOUNTERING THE SNIPE:

children, who have for generations preserved the following method for catching the birds.

Begin by gathering a group of six to twelve monsterologists and arm each with a large gunnysack and a flashlight. Travel to a nearby river, swamp, or marsh just before sunset. Direct one person to place his or her sack on the ground and position a flashlight at the mouth of the bag. Next, order the rest of the group to spread out into a large circle and begin beating the bushes while walking toward one another, shouting "Here, Snipe!" as they progress.

As the circle tightens, any nearby Snipes will be frightened from hiding and will race toward the nearest light source. As they blunder ahead, the Snipes, blinded by the powerful flashlight, will stumble into the gunnysack, which should be promptly closed. Upon capturing a Snipe, you may study the creature momentarily, but be sure to release it into the wild before it becomes traumatized by the encounter.

Though few Snipes have ever been captured, the joy of watching your friends wandering the bushes yelling "Here, Snipe!" usually justifies the excursion, as the testimony of children, lumberjacks, and summer-camp counselors can attest.

THE SQUONK

VITAL STATISTICS

DISTINGUISHING FEATURES: Warty, overweight, and ugly

HEIGHT: 3′

WEIGHT: 200 lbs

RANGE AND HABITAT: Hemlock forests of Pennsylvania

POPULATION SIZE: Ten to thirty

DIET: Herbivore

BEHAVIOR: The fat, flightless bird known as the Squonk spends its time weeping over its ugliness and hiding its shame from humanity.

SOURCE: American folklore

ENCOUNTERING THE SQUONK:

The Squonk, a pudgy bird native to Pennsylvania, has long been encountered by farmers, lumberjacks, hunters, trappers, hikers, and explorers, who uniformly describe it as an incredibly ugly beast. Its body is wrapped in loose, flabby skin marked with moles, warts, pockmarks, and clumps of wiry black hair. From its ponderous head stare two bloodshot and bulbous eyes, and its immense ears constantly drip wax. The animal's veiny lips part to reveal teeth coated in yellow plaque. A tiny piglike tail caps an enormous rump. The Squonk's hind legs are long and become easily tangled, and its nonfunctioning wings are short and weak. Its feet are extremely large, and its fat toes are webbed.

The Squonk is equipped with enough intelligence to know how grotesque it appears. It therefore remains hidden deep within Pennsylvania's hemlock forests to avoid any contact with other living creatures. Lonely and embarrassed by its appearance, the Squonk spends most of its life weeping over its fate.

An herbivore, the Squonk is active only at night, when the darkness conceals its hideous appearance. It spends its days curled in its small den, crying in its sleep. The Squonk also refuses to leave its lair whenever the moon is out, for fear the moonlight will reveal its ugliness.

Squonks are so self-conscious that they become consumed by self-loathing if they are seen, causing them to dissolve completely into a puddle of tears if they are cornered, surprised, or captured. Historically, those hunters who went after live Squonk would trap the animal in a burlap sack, but would realize after traveling a few minutes that the monster's weeping had ceased and the sack had lightened considerably. Upon opening the sack, hunters would find that a slick puddle of salty tears and a few bubbles were all that remained of the Squonk.

The Squonk can only be studied in its natural habitat by cautious and quiet monsterologists. When you enter the hemlock forests, listen for the Squonk's weeping, which is a low, steady sound that reverberates throughout the forests. Winter is the most opportune time to track the beast, as the monster's warm tears leave an easily discernible path in the snow.

Many Squonk researchers prefer to hide near small ponds, as the Squonk needs to drink frequently to stave off the dehydration caused by its constant crying. Because the Squonk fears catching sight of its own reflection in the water, it closes its eyes while it drinks and is unable to see any monsterologists hiding nearby.

Under no circumstances should the Squonk be confronted. If you alert the Squonk to your presence, it will surely break down, weeping uncontrollably until its sobs fade away into the sad silence of death.

THE TERICHIK

VITAL STATISTICS

DISTINGUISHING FEATURES: Immense size

LENGTH: 100' or more

WEIGHT: 150 tons or more

RANGE AND HABITAT: Huge burrows beneath Alaska and the Arctic

POPULATION SIZE: One

DIET: Carnivore/anthropophagus

BEHAVIOR: The monstrous Terichik is a huge, voracious worm that burrows beneath the tundra of the far north, only erupting to the surface to snatch human prey.

SOURCE: Inuit mythology

ENCOUNTERING THE TERICHIK:

One of the chief antagonists of Inuit Indians is the Terichik, a massive and disgusting worm that lives in burrows beneath the ground. It has all the physical features of a common earthworm swollen to epic proportions. However, it is a mindless devourer of mortals and is feared for its sudden appearance and unquenchable appetite.

Unlike a great many monsters, the Terichik's origins are clear. The monster first entered the world as a helpless larva born to a pair of unidentified human lovers. The creature's parents were horrified by their mutant offspring and left the infant to die in a snowbank. Before the creature could perish, however, a young pregnant woman found the larva and rescued it from the cold. Feeling sympathy for the mewling beast, the young woman nursed it, but the Terichik began to grow at a rapid pace, doubling in size within minutes.

Possessed by hunger, the Terichik nursed until its savior fainted from pain and exhaustion. The beast then devoured its surrogate mother and her unborn child. This gruesome double murder taught the Terichik to enjoy the taste of human flesh and sent it in search of more victims. Today, the Terichik, like a snowstorm or a plague, suddenly decimates entire villages to appease its unearthly appetite.

The Terichik's deep burrows are extremely difficult to spot, but it can be lured into the open with offerings of raw meat and live animals. Even when it is hidden miles beneath the earth, its sense of smell can detect the scent of blood, and it will rise from its subterranean home whenever it senses warm prey. Unfortunately, once the beast does break through the earth to feed, there is little you can do to escape its terrible hunger. No known weapons, poisons, or spells have been used successfully against the supernatural predator, and its speed prevents most victims from escaping. Fleeing to high, rocky ground might stall the Terichik for a short time, but ultimately the Terichik cannot be eluded.

THE WI-LU-GHO-YUK

VITAL STATISTICS

DISTINGUISHING FEATURES: Large incisors

LENGTH: 2"

WEIGHT: Almost weightless

RANGE AND HABITAT: Alaska, British Columbia, and the far north

POPULATION SIZE: One hundred plus

DIET: Anthropophagus

BEHAVIOR: The Wi-lu-gho-yuk, a shrewlike creature wandering the wastes of the far north, stealthily sneaks into the clothing of human victims, whom the monster rapidly devours.

SOURCE: Inuit mythology

ENCOUNTERING THE WI-LU-GHO-YUK:

Possibly the most terrifying of all monsters are those whose true natures are concealed by their seemingly innocent forms. Such is the case with the Wi-lu-gho-yuk, a small rodent resembling a harmless mouse or shrew. This meek disguise conceals a cunning and voracious devourer whose only food is human flesh.

The Wi-lu-gho-yuk hunts by waiting near paths or roads frequented by humans. When a victim passes by, the Wi-lu-gho-yuk darts from the brush and slips into the human's clothing, usually through a hole in a boot. The creature is so fast and small that it usually cannot be detected until it is far too late.

Once close to human flesh, the Wi-lu-gho-yuk begins to feast immediately. As it dines, its mouth secretes an anesthetic that numbs the pain of the little beast's vicious bites. Thus, the victim rarely realizes that he is being consumed. Unless killed within seconds of its initial bite, the monster rapidly burrows into its quarry's body in search of delectable organs. With a hunger that belies its small size, the Wi-lu-gho-yuk continues to gorge until it devours its victim completely.

In some cases, a victim may discover the Wi-lu-gho-yuk's presence before it finishes its grisly feast; when this unfortunate person removes his clothing, he finds that he is bleeding from a thousand wounds and then suddenly feels the little creature moving about beneath his flesh. Death (a blessing at this point) follows moments later.

Monsterologists should not seek out the Wi-lu-gho-yuk, for it too easily gains access to human flesh. But while traveling through Alaska and the Arctic in search of the **Woolly Mammoth** or other monsters, frequently inspect your clothing and footwear for holes and promptly patch them to prevent the Wi-lu-gho-yuk's invasion. If the monster is spotted, it can be crushed easily by a large rock, but once it burrows into human flesh, it is virtually impossible to kill. Your only recourse is suicide, which prevents the Wi-lu-gho-yuk from receiving any satisfaction from gnawing its way through your beating heart.

THE WOOLLY MAMMOTH

VITAL STATISTICS

DISTINGUISHING FEATURES: Small ears, long hair, trunk, and tusks

HEIGHT/LENGTH: 14'/12'

WEIGHT: 7–10 tons

RANGE AND HABITAT: Taiga lands of Alaska, Canada, and Siberia

POPULATION SIZE: Less than five hundred

DIET: Herbivore

BEHAVIOR: A relic from the last Ice Age, the Woolly Mammoth is content to wander the cold taiga of the far north. It will generally only become aggressive when threatened or in defense of its young.

SOURCE: Inuit mythology, cryptozoology

ENCOUNTERING THE WOOLLY MAMMOTH:

The Pleistocene era, some one million years ago, marked the dawn of humankind and the onset of a chilling Ice Age. It was also the golden era of the Woolly Mammoth, a shaggy behemoth similar in form and shape to the elephants known today. For several centuries, the Woolly Mammoth thrived in the colder regions of the world, including the far northern reaches of North America.

As the last Ice Age came to a close, mass extinctions plagued the large mammals of the Pleistocene epoch, and the Woolly Mammoth is considered to have disappeared from the planet over twelve thousand years ago. However, as is the case with so many creatures believed to be extinct, cryptozoologists have uncovered evidence to support the Woolly Mammoths' continued survival.

A typical Woolly Mammoth stands over thirteen feet at the shoulder and can weigh up to ten tons. The creature has a thick, durable coat, usually chestnut in color, for protection from the elements. Beneath the animal's coat is an insulating layer of fat roughly three inches thick. Mammoths also store fat in visible humps on their heads and shoulders.

Like elephants, Woolly Mammoths have short goatlike tails and prehensile trunks. Male Mammoths possess radically curved tusks almost sixteen feet in length, which are primarily used as shovels to break the frost-covered earth and uncover buried vegetation. When enraged, a charging Mammoth will use its tusks as bone-crushing weapons.

Woolly Mammoths are largely solitary animals and usually live alone. On occasion, groups of no more than four of these animals may remain together as a small family unit, but this must be rare as such herds would be easily detectable by infrared devices, satellites, or even low-flying planes. Most Mammoths have taken up residence in the taiga lands, vast expanses of dense forest that provide cover, consumable vegetation, and protection from the elements. In Siberia alone, where many Mammoths have been sighted, the taiga covers almost three million square miles, most of which is rarely crossed by humans. The North American taiga lands are equally impressive and isolated.

Sightings of Woolly Mammoths, which were first reported by the Inuit centuries ago, have occurred well past the date of their alleged extinction. In the sixteenth century, Siberian hunters reported stalking these huge, hairy elephants, which they called "the mountain of meat." In North America, there were also Woolly Mammoth sightings in the sixteenth century: in 1580, an English seaman walked from the Gulf of Mexico to Nova Scotia and reported seeing herds of shaggy elephants during his travels in the northern reaches of the continent. Throughout Alaska and Canada, similar accounts from Inuit Indians, fur trappers, and traders have been common and continue into the present.

Reported sightings of the monsters have been bolstered by the discovery of over one hundred thousand well-preserved Mammoth corpses within the past several centuries. The lack of decay in most of these specimens suggests recent death, although the extreme cold can preserve these massive cadavers for decades. Mammoth footprints, fecal matter, and hair have also been discovered on rare occasion.

Sadly, the Woolly Mammoths may be on the verge of extinction. Due to their small numbers, the species as a whole is poorly equipped to deal with a changing environment that includes a constantly growing human population. While the destruction of the Mammoth's habitat is occurring at a relatively slow pace in comparison to the decimation of other ecologies throughout the world, even the smallest disturbance in the natural order of the Arctic can adversely affect the species.

Human hunters are also a threat, and in 1899 it actually appeared the Mammoths had been hunted to extinction. That year, *McClure's* magazine published an article by Henry Tukeman entitled "The Killing of the Mammoth." Tukeman graphically described how he had hunted and violently murdered a

The Field Museum, #77641, Chicago

Woolly Mammoth in Alaska, then sold the Mammoth's hide and tusks to the Smithsonian Institution. (The Smithsonian, however, has no record of this purchase.) For many years, it was feared that Tukeman had killed the last of Alaska's Woolly Mammoths, but a smattering of sightings since the early 1900s have shown otherwise. Yet each death impacts the entire Woolly Mammoth population, and Mammoth murders could prove the creature's undoing.

Ironically, there is the strong possibility that Woolly Mammoths will thrive once again through the efforts of science. Many believe that the Mammoths found frozen in ice are not truly dead, but merely in suspended animation, and these creatures could conceivably be revived through the proper procedures. For decades there have been rumors of Soviet scientists, American zoologists, and Nazi madmen attempting to bring frozen Woolly Mammoths back to life.

Other tales have involved the use of frozen Mammoth sperm to fertilize the egg of a normal elephant. Today, such rumors have been replaced by hard fact: as of this writing, Japanese scientists are attempting to fertilize the egg of an Indian elephant with recovered Mammoth sperm.

The Woolly Mammoth can be tracked by careful observance of the creature's footprints and droppings. The creature typically leaves ominous circular footprints two feet across and eighteen inches long. The monster's droppings are even more impressive, collecting in mounds over three feet tall. Composed entirely of vegetable matter, these dung heaps are only mildly odorous and rapidly freeze solid. Also watch for signs of the Mammoths' passage: as they move through the taiga, they splinter trees and break branches as high as ten feet on the trunk.

Woolly Mammoths are fairly slow moving, unless angered or frightened, and experienced trackers should have little trouble overtaking the animals. Once a Mammoth is spotted, monsterologists would be wise to avoid alarming the animal in any way. An enraged and charging Mammoth can be deadly. Above all, never approach a young Mammoth, as Woolly Mammoth mothers are notoriously overprotective and will smother any threat to their children.

Other Cryptid Animals

The list of bizarre animals is far too long to contain in any single work and covers a diverse range of creatures from a wide variety of sources. Below is a cross section of such monsters.

- **Agropelter:** A vicious simian that enjoys killing lumberjacks by hurling dead tree limbs onto their heads.

- **Amarok:** A gigantic, intelligent wolf (with an appetite that far exceeds its incredible size) who stalks the Inuit.

- **Axhandle Hound:** A dog with a broad head resembling a hatchet, a thin body similar to an ax handle, and stumpy legs. It eats only ax handles, a unique diet that makes the animal the bane of logging and lumber operations.

- **Flitterbick:** A flying squirrel whose flight is so fast the creature is virtually invisible. It is known for colliding with lumberjacks at high speeds, resulting in the death of both squirrel and man.

- **Gumberoo:** A voracious, bearlike creature

native to the forests of the Pacific North-west. According to lumberjacks, it has a rubber hide and a tendency to explode whenever close to fire.

- **Hidebehind:** A monster that is never seen because it is always lurking behind a tree, boulder, or bush. It is an insatiable carni-vore and has been held responsible for killing and devouring many lumberjacks.

- **Hoop Snake:** A venomous viper that can form its body into a perfect circle and roll after prey.

- **Rubberado:** A tiny mole with a rubbery hide that moves by bouncing its body along the ground; also known as the bouncing porcupine. When consumed, its flesh be-stows incredible resiliency. Thus, cowboys who ate the animal were blessed with the ability to deflect bullets.

- **Saw Hog:** A docile pig native to the Ozarks whose extremely sharp back can be used to cut wood.

- **Snow Snake:** Perhaps the most venomous of all monsters, an Arctic viper whose bite causes death within seconds. Many lum-berjacks have been attacked by this menace.

- **Splinter Cat:** A manic feline who hunts raccoons and bees by ramming into dead trees with its dense forehead. Hikers and woodsmen often report that the Splinter Cat's attacks on trees resemble the damage caused by lightning.

- **Tirisuk:** A reptilian creature with massive jaws capable of snapping through virtually anything. It has four legs and two long, leathery feelers that it uses to capture prey, typically Inuit braves.

BEASTMEN AND BEASTWOMEN

BEASTMEN AND -WOMEN are monsters who appear surprisingly human but who possess many animalistic traits, such as the tail of a serpent or the face of a goat.

Mermaids, for example, are well-known beastwomen. Most of these creatures can temporarily conceal their monstrous aspects in order to interact with humanity, and a small number of beastmen, including **Werewolves,** are capable of completely transforming between a human guise and an animal form. All of these monsters represent the perfect marriage between animal and human: they retain all the intelligence of a normal human, but also have the natural instincts and abilities of the animal they most resemble.

Beastmen come in a wide variety of animal shapes and types, but they commonly have the attributes of those animals most feared by humans, including wolves and serpents. They are almost all inordinately dangerous and revel in slaughtering, kidnapping, or torturing humans. Beastwomen, in particular, enjoy seducing males, whom they often murder shortly after sex.

Most beastmen can mentally communicate with and command the animals they resemble. A few have such awesome powers as control over the weather and the ability to become invisible. All beastmen appear to be extremely long-lived, if not immortal, and are difficult to injure or kill. However, many of these creatures can be wounded with silver weapons, including silver daggers and silver bullets, and a large number are frightened by fire.

The Adlet, tall humanoids with wolflike features and a craving for human blood, first appeared centuries ago when they began hunting the Inuit Indians. They are covered in red fur, possess terrible fangs and claws, and have many other lupine features, including pointed ears, pronounced snouts, long tails, and yellow eyes.

According to Inuit monsterologists, the Adlet were originally spawned when an Inuit woman living on the shores of Hudson Bay married a massive red dog with supernatural powers. Eventually, the woman became pregnant and gave birth to ten children. Five were small, beautiful dogs in the image of her beloved husband. But the other five children were the Adlet: disfigured hybrids combining the worst attributes of both parents.

The five Adlet grew to adulthood within a matter of hours and immediately tried to kill their mother. Their father attacked and routed the beasts, but he was mortally wounded. After the battle, the grieving widow fled to the shores of Hudson Bay, where she set her five pups adrift on a piece of wood. The young dogs sailed across the sea, eventually landing on the coasts of Europe, where they too married humans and begot a race of pale-skinned humans who

THE ADLET

VITAL STATISTICS

DISTINGUISHING FEATURES: Wolfish face, fangs, and fur

HEIGHT: 7'

WEIGHT: 200–300 lbs

RANGE AND HABITAT: Wild regions of Quebec, Labrador, Newfoundland, and all lands to the north

POPULATION SIZE: One hundred to one thousand

DIET: Carnivore/anthropophagus

BEHAVIOR: The Adlet are merciless stalkers who hunt and eat anyone found roaming the northernmost reaches of the continent.

SOURCE: Inuit mythology

ENCOUNTERING THE ADLET:

returned to Hudson Bay centuries later. The Adlet, meanwhile, hid in the wild, intrabred, and multiplied.

Today, the Adlet roam a vast area of cold wilderness, beginning in Quebec and New-foundland and extending well into the north-ernmost regions of Greenland. Their chief habitat lies on the shores of Hudson Bay, but there are also large numbers of the monsters in Labrador. The Adlet are known to the Inuit living in several regions west of Hudson Bay as well.

Although capable of surviving on almost any organic matter, including fungi and roots, the Adlet prefer to drink the warm blood of freshly slain humans. Adlet hunt in large packs and attempt to overwhelm their prey. The approach of an Adlet pack is marked by their piercing, mournful howls, which paralyze prey. The feast that follows is grisly and bloody, and the Adlet rarely leave identifiable remains. Even skeletons are carried back to the huge caves that serve as the pack's lair, where the bones are cracked open and drained of marrow.

The Adlet, though powerful, do possess several weaknesses. As with the **Wendigo** and **Werewolves,** the Adlet are vulnerable to silver weapons. They are also deathly afraid of fire and will only attack a torch-wielding human when on the verge of starvation.

While wandering the Adlet's known terri-tories, travel in small, well-armed groups. Carry multiple torches, and large amounts of flint, lighter fluid, and matches. Load rifles with silver bullets and carry at least one silver dagger close at hand.

If confronted by an Adlet pack, light torches and a large campfire immediately. Wave the torches at any approaching Adlet, striking the monsters if necessary. Other members of your party should simultaneously fire silver bullets into the breast of the pack leader, identifiable as the largest and most feral Adlet. After the leader of the pack falls, the rest of the Adlet usually flee. If they do not, however, expect a long and painful death within the bone-breaking jaws of these beasts.

THE DEER WOMAN

VITAL STATISTICS

DISTINGUISHING FEATURES: Incredible beauty, deerlike legs, and hooves

HEIGHT: 5'5"

WEIGHT: 120 lbs

RANGE AND HABITAT: Nebraskan plains and some urban areas across the continent

POPULATION SIZE: One

DIET: Anthropophagus

BEHAVIOR: A seductive killer, the Deer Woman roams festive gatherings, where she lures men away from the party and tramples them to death.

SOURCE: Native American (Poncan) mythology

ENCOUNTERING THE DEER WOMAN:

The Deer Woman appears as an unbelievably beautiful woman with long black hair. She wears a white buckskin dress, which offsets her dark, deep eyes. These eyes have a hypnotic quality that, when coupled with her alluring figure and angelic face, discourage men from looking at her abnormal feet. If men were able to tear their eyes from her upper body, they would realize that she walks upon the hooves of a deer, a mutation impossible to conceal.

In centuries past, the Deer Woman would often manifest in Nebraska, during a Poncan celebration marking a great victory. During the early hours of the party, she would slip into the camp and join the human women dancing near the fire. Throughout the night, she would survey the men to find the most handsome and athletic of the group. When she chose her victim, she would use her vast beauty and mesmerizing eyes to tempt him into the woods.

Once away from the light of the fires, the Deer Woman would force her chosen mate onto the ground and ravish his trembling body until dawn approached. Then, just before her victim was overcome by ecstasy, the Deer Woman would leap to her feet and trample the supine man beneath her sharp and deadly hooves. With her powerful legs, she would kick his skull until it caved, and her foot would come down on his neck, tearing open his throat and spilling his blood onto the earth.

Today, the Deer Woman's tactics are much the same, although she has expanded her territory in search of more fertile hunting grounds. She is likely to appear at nightclubs, parties, and bars in any large city, where the darkness and crowds conceal her true nature. She will mingle and dance until she finds a suitable victim, whom she will lure into an alley or bathroom, where he is murdered. The Deer Woman's victims often appear to have been beaten to death, but can be differentiated from casualties of more mundane murderers by the oddly satisfied expression on their otherwise lifeless faces.

Aside from her powers over men, the Deer Woman can run faster than any natural deer, and she can leap over fences and other obstacles with ease. Also, like so many monsters attuned to the wilderness, the Deer Woman can will other animals to do her bidding. She has a special affinity with deer and other herd animals and can command large bucks to attack anyone who would do her harm.

The Deer Woman is easily studied by female monsterologists, for she has no power over women. The monster's feet will reveal her true nature to anyone with the willpower or inclination to look away from her face.

Male monsterologists who hope to survive an encounter with the Deer Woman must adopt a difficult habit: whenever surrounded by a large number of women, males must keep their eyes cast toward the ground and stare only at the women's feet. As men for the most part are quite capable of focusing their vision on extremely restricted areas of the female anatomy, this skill seems easily attainable. Unfortunately, the allure of the Deer Woman often overwhelms even those male monsterologists prepared for her presence. Such researchers are likely to be dredged from darkened rivers or pulled from beneath bushes, their faces crushed beyond recognition and their throats slashed.

THE BEAVER WOMEN

VITAL STATISTICS

DISTINGUISHING FEATURES: Extreme beauty, fur-covered legs, and seductive eyes

HEIGHT: 5–6'

WEIGHT: 100–150 lbs

RANGE AND HABITAT: Secluded lakes in Montana and other regions of central North America

POPULATION SIZE: Unknown

DIET: Unknown

BEHAVIOR: The Beaver Women are a race of seductive beastwomen with the ability to entice men into lakes, where they are drowned.

SOURCE: Native American (Blackfoot) mythology

ENCOUNTERING THE BEAVER WOMEN:

The Beaver Women are gorgeous water nymphs who, like many other water nymphs, enjoy seducing and murdering men. They always live on the shores of a lake and usually inhabit secluded areas infrequently visited by humans. Although few lakes are known to conceal these monsters, the Blackfoot Indians once knew McDermott Lake, in Montana's Glacier National Park, as Beaver Woman Lake.

Beaver Women hunt by standing waist-deep in the water, only a few feet from the shore. Often naked, they use their long, luxuriant hair to seductively conceal their breasts and face. They may also cover their bodies in red paint. Beaver Women will never leave the water or turn away from victims because their lower extremities and backs are covered in a beaver's reddish fur.

To entice men into the cold water, Beaver Women will sing sweetly, sway seductively, or even pretend to drown. Like a Greek Siren, the Beaver Woman has an almost supernatural ability to strip men of their wits and draw them into her clutches.

The fate of any man lured into the arms of a Beaver Woman is still unknown, as no one has returned to tell the tale. Some female monsters have sex with their victims, an act that is extremely pleasurable but ultimately fatal to the monsters' victims. Beaver Women may also eat their captives.

Lonely lakes like this one are said to be the haunt of the Beaver Women.

Wyoming Division of Tourism

Although Beaver Women primarily hunt men, they are extremely jealous of women and will attack any female they encounter. The only humans who are safe from the Beaver Women are infants and young children, as Beaver Women will never harm a child. They will even rescue drowning children and protect the babes from wild animals.

Unfortunately, Beaver Women are sometimes overly fond of children and have been known to kidnap youngsters. Both boys and girls are taken by the Beaver Women, who raise the children as their own. Over time, girls in the care of these monsters are themselves transformed into Beaver Women. Sadly, boys do not make this transformation and are eventually murdered by their captors.

The power of the Beaver Women should never be underestimated by monsterologists studying these creatures. Male monsterologists, in particular, should carefully assess their ability to withstand supernatural seduction, as only those with a true heart and iron will can hope to face the powers of the Beaver Women and survive. Male monsterologists determined to seek out a Beaver Woman must remain alert and attuned to their state of mind. If you find yourself wandering helplessly toward the lake and the nude figure standing on its misty shores, use all your willpower to avert your eyes and call for help. Those without this strength are sure to find themselves in a cold and watery grave.

THE LOVELAND FROGMEN

VITAL STATISTICS

DISTINGUISHING FEATURES: Froglike faces, leathery skin, and huge, bulbous eyes

HEIGHT: 3'6"

WEIGHT: 60 lbs

RANGE AND HABITAT: Rivers and waterways in Ohio River Valley, especially near Loveland, Ohio

POPULATION SIZE: Several dozen

DIET: Omnivore/insectivore

BEHAVIOR: The Frogmen enjoy lurking along quiet waterways, where they live out their lives in relative seclusion. On rare occasion, they venture away from their chosen stream or river, but will flee toward the nearest body of water when spotted by humans.

SOURCE: Cryptozoology, ufology

ENCOUNTERING THE LOVELAND FROGMEN:

The Loveland Frogmen are squat half-human/half-frog hybrids found roaming the banks of the Ohio River and its tributaries. According to several well-documented sightings, they have the faces of frogs atop wiry bodies covered in leathery flesh. Like frogs, they have bulging eyes and wide mouths. They are proficient swimmers, but can also use their muscular legs to hop great distances on land. In addition, they are extremely agile and have been known to dodge incoming bullets, leap easily over fences, and descend steep inclines without stumbling.

The existence of the Loveland Frogmen was first brought to the attention of cryptozoologists in March 1955, when a local businessman reported seeing a group of strange creatures beneath a bridge near Loveland, Ohio. He was unclear about what he had seen, variously describing the monsters as "trolls," giant lizards, and giant frogs.

After this sighting, guards were ordered to patrol the bridge, and the FBI launched an investigation, but no further evidence was encountered for almost twenty years. However, in 1972, again in March, a Frogman appeared in the headlights of a police cruiser. The officer later testified that the frog-faced creature quickly ran down an embankment at the side of the road and entered the Little Miami River. Immediately after his sighting, the officer contacted a second police officer, and both scoured the area of the encounter. On the shores of the Little Miami, they found several large scrapes leading into the river.

Ironically, just two weeks after the initial 1972 sighting, the second officer called to the scene was driving on a road near Loveland when he spotted a prone figure in his headlights. When he stepped from the car to investigate, he realized that he too had found a Frogman. As he neared the creature, it stood up and vaulted the nearest guardrail. Determined to prove the existence of the Loveland

Frogman, the officer fired at the fleeing creature, but his bullets either went wild or passed through the monster, and it escaped into the darkness.

After the two police officers came forward, cryptozoologists began uncovering a wealth of evidence to support the existence of the Loveland Frogmen. Researchers contacted local residents and farmers who had also seen groups of small froglike humanoids but had failed to report such sightings for fear of ridicule. More important, the Frogmen continue to be spotted along the Ohio River and nearby waterways. As recently as 1985, for example, two Loveland boys spotted what they described as a frog the size of a dog on the shore of the Little Miami.

Because the Frogmen are amphibians, it is unlikely that they would attack humans for food. However, the Loveland Frogmen may not be completely harmless. On August 21, 1955, Mrs. Darwin Johnson was swimming in the Ohio River near Evansville, Indiana, when she was attacked from below. The creature that grabbed her was incredibly strong and pulled her beneath the water twice before she managed to wrestle free. The attack left Mrs. Johnson with large scratches and bruises, but the most bizarre aspect of the case was the appearance of a strange green handprint on her leg. The print, which could not be washed away, resembled an oddly shaped bruise and lingered for several days. While it is unknown if Mrs. Johnson's assailant was actually a Loveland Frogman, the attack took place only a few hundred miles from Loveland and within only a few months of the first reliably recorded sighting of these humanoid amphibians.

The Frogmen remain near the Ohio River and most often roam abroad on cold, clear nights. They are most active in Loveland during March, but they seem to migrate west in preparation for winter. When searching for the Frogmen, spend March scouring Loveland and the surrounding region. As the month comes to a close, begin a slow six-month trek along the Ohio River, toward Evansville, Indiana, which should be the center of any search during August.

Although an attack by the Frogmen on humans is unlikely, the mere possibility of such an assault should be kept in mind at all times. Always swim with a buddy when you go for a dip, and never enter the water if you suspect a Frogman to be nearby.

Ron Schaffner/FPL

THE GATORMEN

VITAL STATISTICS

DISTINGUISHING FEATURES: Alligatorlike body

HEIGHT/LENGTH: 4'3"/6'

WEIGHT: 200 lbs

RANGE AND HABITAT: Dense swamps throughout the South

POPULATION SIZE: Unknown

DIET: Omnivore

BEHAVIOR: The Gatormen are a race of human-alligator hybrids who live in a primitive tribal society deep in the swamps, where they attempt to avoid any interaction with humans. They will fight ferociously if threatened or cornered.

SOURCE: Cryptozoology, urban legend, creative taxidermy

ENCOUNTERING THE GATORMEN:

Of all the beastmen, the Gatormen may be the most disturbing to behold, for they possess the upper torso of a small, pygmylike human, and the lower body of an alligator. A Gatorman's upper body is covered in a thin layer of scales, its fingertips end in stubby claws, and its mouth is filled with sharp teeth.

The Gatormen enjoy an aboriginal, tribal society that is largely migratory. Each tribe is exceedingly small, with but five or six members, and they travel only under cover of darkness. Using swamps and connecting waterways, Gatormen roam from eastern Texas to the Florida Everglades.

Gatormen have human intellects and communicate through a rudimentary language consisting of grunts, howls, gibberish, and extensive body movements. Gatormen have opposable thumbs and make extensive use of tools, and they will wield spears, knives, and nets when hunting. Although they can digest almost anything, Gatormen prefer the raw meat of deer, fish, turtles, small alligators, birds, frogs, and various rodents. In the absence of adequate game, they can also subsist on fruits and foliage.

The history of the Gatormen is varied and confused, but according to many reports, the beasts first came to the attention of researchers and reporters in the early 1990s, when a pair of hunters stumbled across a young Gatorman in the Florida Everglades. The hunters wanted to kill the monster, but a paleontologist who happened upon the scene begged the two men to spare the strange being. A wealthy Florida bureaucrat also passed by and offered the hunters a substantial sum if they would capture, but not kill, the Gatorman. The hunters agreed.

This first Gatorman was tagged and shipped to a mysterious marine lab hidden in the Florida Keys. The paleontologist and the bureaucrat joined forces with a team of trackers and set off into the swamps in search of more of the creatures, but they found no signs of the race. And then, as is the case with so many monsters, the account mysteriously ends. The marine lab and the Gatorman vanished, as did everyone involved in the hunt for the beasts.

Fortunately, the capture and subsequent disappearance of the young Gatorman prompted a few monsterologists to research the creature more thoroughly. Reported encounters with the Gatormen, some dating back to the late 1700s, were eventually unearthed, as were modern sightings from the Carolinas and Louisiana. More surprising, it has been discovered that a live Gatorman was captured and put on display in a New Orleans brothel sometime around the turn of the century. The fate of this unfortunate monster has never been revealed, but today, at least one Gatorman carcass is on display to the public at Marsh's Free Museum, in Long Beach, Washington. The monster, who is known as Jake to the museum staff, is often photographed by reporters, and his likeness accompanies most stories about modern Gatorman sightings.

The swamps inhabited by the Gatormen are extremely treacherous, and travel within these environs requires experience and fortitude. The rough terrain is made particularly perilous by an abundance of poisonous snakes, toxic flora, and irritating and venomous insects. In the Everglades, monsterologists seeking the Gatormen also run the risk of stumbling across other terrifying monsters, such as the **Giant Gators** and the **Skunk Apes.**

Before striking out into the swamp, prepare yourself well for the dangers presented by this habitat. Waterproof boots and jackets, insect repellent, and alligator nets are all must-have items. Also familiarize yourself with the Gatorman's disturbing appearance. If an encounter does occur, any show of fear or disgust—a natural reaction given the monster's countenance—could drive the Gatorman to violence.

Marsh's Free Museum/PhotoNeil

"Jake," the Gatorman.

Alligators and the Supernatural

The common alligator is often revered for its connections to the paranormal world. For example, it is widely believed that the alligator's roar causes rainfall, and many parts of its body can be used in various spells and rituals. The most powerful aspect of the alligator, however, is its teeth, which have a wide variety of apothecary applications. Carrying an alligator's tooth, it is said, will prevent snakes from striking, and if you are bitten, a single alligator tooth placed against the wound can neutralize the venom. A necklace of alligator teeth placed around an infant's neck alleviates the pain of teething, and an alligator's tooth is also thought to provide protection against witchcraft, voodoo, grief, and bad luck.

GOATMAN

VITAL STATISTICS

DISTINGUISHING FEATURES: Goatlike legs, face, horns, and beard

HEIGHT: 5'10"

WEIGHT: 160 lbs

RANGE AND HABITAT: Remote areas of Maryland, specifically Prince Georges County

POPULATION SIZE: One

DIET: Virtually anything

BEHAVIOR: Goatman is a horrible mutation known for terrorizing and murdering couples parked along secluded roads.

SOURCE: Urban legend

ENCOUNTERING GOATMAN:

Goatman is one of the most infamous of all the monsters roaming North America's lovers' lanes. A horrifying hybrid, he primarily stalks the secluded roads of Maryland, menacing young couples innocently enjoying the silence of the night and the splendor of the stars.

Coarse black hair covers the lower half of Goatman's body and also appears in sporadic clumps on his chest, back, and arms. His face is twisted, and a long beard dangles from his pointed chin. Two white nubs erupt from the pale flesh of his forehead, breaking through his skin like boils. Goatman's eyes are narrow and mean, his brows thick and bushy, and his teeth broad and yellow. His feet are cloven hooves and his fingers end in sharp claws. Repugnant in every way, Goatman is often mistaken for Satan.

When Goatman appears, he silently approaches parked cars and suddenly presses his hideous face against the windshield to terrify the occupants. Using his huge fists and sharp hooves, he then shatters the windows, caves in the roof, and collapses the car doors so they are impossible to open. Some victims have time to start the vehicle and escape, but others are not so fortunate. Goatman carries a large ax, which he frequently uses to slash the car's tires or batter through the hood and destroy the engine. Victims thus stranded are ripped from the vehicle, carried into the woods, and slaughtered.

When he is not hunting humans, Goatman spends his days sleeping, traveling, or foraging for food. Like a normal goat, Goatman's diet consists of anything he can find, including grass, leaves, shrubs, flowers, fruits, rubber boots, paper products, rodents, birds, human flesh, and a host of other organic and inorganic materials. Goatman is routinely blamed for the disappearance of neighborhood pets and the mutilation of livestock.

Although Goatman's origins are open to dispute, the most common accounts claim that he was once a biologist working for the government in nearby Washington, D.C. This anonymous scientist was researching a means by which human physical capabilities could be augmented through the exploitation of animals. Unfortunately, something went terribly amiss during an experiment involving a goat. After the smoke cleared, the biologist found himself transformed into a half-human, half-goat monstrosity. Infuriated by his failure, ashamed of his appearance, and driven mad by his plight, Goatman began to loathe humanity, especially the young and the beautiful. Thus motivated, the outcast embarked on his career of tormenting teenagers.

Although Goatman's range includes all of Maryland, monsterologists should limit their search to Prince Georges County, where the creature is spotted most often. Unfortunately, he is nearly impossible to track, as Goatman can travel for hours without tiring, leaping great distances to avoid leaving a distinguishable trail.

While traces of Goatman are difficult to find in the field, teenagers throughout the monster's range often try to warn one another of the monster's presence by spray-painting "Goatman was here" on walls or signs near the

Goats and the Supernatural

The goat falls into a category of the supernatural associated with sexuality, hedonism, and fertility. Goats are used by witches in fertility rites, and the Greek Satyrs, human-goat hybrids, were long venerated for their sexual proclivity and prowess. Goat genitals, tongues, eyeballs, and udders are used in a wide variety of spells, including potions for love, lust, impotence, and sexual endurance. A healthy goat inhabiting a farm is believed to protect livestock from disease and illness, and keeping a goat aboard a ship is thought to ensure good weather and strong winds. Finally, while killing a goat is rarely deemed wise, doing so on Christmas morning is a ritual performed to bring good luck throughout the following year.

area of an attack. If you stumble across such graffiti, interview the local teenagers and obtain directions to the nearest lovers' lane. Park alongside the secluded road at night in the hope of luring Goatman into the open. It is advised that you travel with a companion during this excursion, preferably one you are not adverse to kissing, as Goatman will sense an ambush if you are not engaged in a romantic interlude when he peers into the car. Of course, be careful not to become too involved in your amorous activities, lest you fail to hear the monster's approach and fall victim to his gleaming ax.

Letiche's habitat.

LETICHE THE MONSTER

VITAL STATISTICS

DISTINGUISHING FEATURES: Pale skin and webbed hands and feet

HEIGHT: 5′

WEIGHT: 100 lbs

RANGE AND HABITAT: Louisiana bayous

POPULATION SIZE: One

DIET: Carnivore

BEHAVIOR: Letiche, a twisted and lonely monster, haunts swamps, where he frequently overturns boats in search of human prey.

SOURCE: Cajun folklore

ENCOUNTERING LETICHE THE MONSTER:

Numerous malignant monsters are known to roam the mysterious Louisiana swamps, where they have long tormented Acadians and Cajuns living in the area. One such creature is a vicious ghoul known as Letiche the Monster. Letiche has sickly pale skin that is constantly wrinkled and waterlogged, and his hair is snarled and olive in color. Moss and muck obscures most of the monster's face, save for its luminous green eyes. His gnarled fingers and toes are joined by thick, translucent webbing, allowing the beast to move through the water rapidly. He also possesses heightened senses, a layer of tough scales, rows of sharp fangs, and three-inch claws on his fingertips.

Letiche is commonly believed to be an illegitimate and unbaptized child who was abandoned in the swamp by his shamed mother. He was raised by alligators and over time developed webbed feet and hands (the ultimate fate of anyone who spends too much time in the swamp), along with a deep hatred for humanity.

Letiche the Monster spends most of his time drifting lazily through the bayous. His glowing eyes peer above the surface of the water, searching for any sign of prey. He will eat anything he can catch, but particularly enjoys human flesh. The monster takes pleasure in overturning canoes and small craft to devour those within. He frequently shares his kills with alligators, snapping turtles, and large snakes, but reserves hearts and brains for himself. Fishermen, tourists, hermits, and alligator hunters are the monster's favorite victims.

Because Letiche only attacks or appears before lone humans drifting along in small boats, monsterologists wishing to observe Letiche should attempt a solo expedition. Unfortunately, given the dangerous nature of Letiche and his habitat, traveling alone is ill-advised and exceedingly perilous. Letiche can easily overpower a single human, and anyone who seeks the monster alone will soon fall victim to this beast's dark appetite.

THE SERPENT WOMAN

VITAL STATISTICS

DISTINGUISHING FEATURES: Great size and snakelike body

LENGTH: 100′

WEIGHT: Unknown

RANGE AND HABITAT: Great Lakes

POPULATION SIZE: One

DIET: Omnivore

BEHAVIOR: The Serpent Woman lurks at the bottom of deep lakes but emerges to seduce mortal males into her coils and transform them into "snake men."

SOURCE: Native American (Iroquois) mythology

ENCOUNTERING THE SERPENT WOMAN:

Of all the monsters known to the Iroquois Indians living on the shores of the Great Lakes, the Serpent Woman is probably the most formidable and frightening. A paranormal female entity with the upper body of a giant woman and the lower body of an enormous constrictor snake, the Serpent Woman is over one hundred feet long and can lift her muscular body to heights of more than thirty feet. Because of her great size, she spends most of her time hidden at the bottom of Lake Huron or Lake Erie.

Although she has a haunting beauty, the Serpent Woman's face, arms, chest, and abdomen are covered by silver scales. Her finger-tips end in sharp claws, and two distinct fangs protrude from her full lips. Nevertheless, the Serpent Woman possesses the ability to mesmerize humans with her movements, voice, and gaze. She will often use this power to lure a man into her lake, where she embraces him in her coils and forces him to become her lover. After only a few days in the company of the Serpent Woman, the captured man begins to transform into a scaled humanoid monster.

Surprisingly, the Serpent Woman was not always an evil, vile creature. In fact, she did not come to loathe humanity until she lost her one true love, a brave who was murdered by tribal shamans after they discovered his affair with the monster. Forever after she has been spiteful and vicious toward humans. She will not fall in love, for fear of suffering heartbreak again. Yet she still steals humans from the banks of the Great Lakes, to transform them into monsters for her own amusement and pleasure.

The Serpent Woman may appear to forlorn male monsterologists wandering the shores of Lake Erie or Lake Huron alone at night, but such researchers should be extremely careful when approaching the entity unless they wish to be transformed. The appearance of the Serpent Woman can cause almost any male to rush headlong into the water. A nearby female companion might be able to restrain a victim of the Serpent Woman's alluring presence, but the desire to be loved by the creature often proves far too compelling to be thwarted. Fortunately, life as a snake man may not be entirely painful. Certainly, being transformed by the Serpent Woman does prevent one from returning to normal society, but it is likely that most of her "snake men" live out the rest of their lives comfortably nestled within the coils of their monstrous mistress. Snake men never want for food, companionship, or physical pleasure, for all these needs are met by the Serpent Woman.

THE THETIS LAKE MONSTER

VITAL STATISTICS

DISTINGUISHING FEATURES: Scales, gills, huge eyes, and fishlike face

HEIGHT: 5′

WEIGHT: 120 lbs

RANGE AND HABITAT: Lake Thetis, British Columbia

POPULATION SIZE: One

DIET: Unknown

BEHAVIOR: The Thetis Lake Monster periodically surfaces to frighten people visiting its serene habitat. In the past, the monster may have eaten humans as well.

SOURCE: Cryptozoology, Native American (Kwakiutl) mythology

ENCOUNTERING THE THETIS LAKE MONSTER:

For centuries, Native Americans have reported encounters with various races of cannibalistic humanoids inhabiting lakes, rivers, and oceans. The Kwakiutl Indians of the Puget Sound region called these monsters the Pugwis and described them as fish-faced horrors with huge mouths and terrible fangs. Such monsters have reappeared in modern times, usually to be found lurking along some desolate stretch of coastline or in an isolated lake. One such beast is the Thetis Lake Monster, who was first reported in the 1970s.

Like the Pugwis, the Thetis monster is similar in appearance to the South American gill-man, made famous by such films as *The Creature from the Black Lagoon*. Its entire body is protected by tough, silvery scales, and a razor-sharp fin projects from the crest of its skull. Large webbed ears protrude from its rounded head, and its clawed hands and feet are also equipped with translucent webbing, an adaptation enabling the creature to move through the water at amazing speeds. It eyes are dark, bulbous orbs capable of penetrating the depths of even the murkiest lakes.

The Thetis Lake Monster can extract oxygen from both air and water, allowing it to travel on land. Although seemingly mute, the monster does make harsh gurgling noises, presumably as a result of forcing air through its waterlogged lungs.

The first recorded Thetis Lake Monster sighting occurred on August 19, 1972, when two teenagers on the shores of the lake observed a scaly, humanoid form suddenly rise from the water. The terrified teens fled the lake, but the beast pursued the pair and lacerated one boy's hand with the vicious barbed fin that adorns its skull. The boys immediately took their harrowing tale to the Royal Canadian Mounted Police (RCMP), who were so impressed with the sincerity of the witnesses that they launched a complete investigation into the attack. They found little evidence to corroborate the boys' story, but just four days later, two more witnesses were also frightened by the monster, and the RCMP were forced to increase its efforts. But after weeks of vainly searching the lake and the surrounding environs, the RCMP quietly halted the investigation.

While the monster has not been seen in the area for some time, any research into this particular beast should begin at Thetis Lake. Evidence in the form of footprints or discarded scales might direct researchers toward the Thetis Lake Monster's current whereabouts.

If you encounter the Thetis Lake Monster, remember its possible connections to the Pugwis and other fish-men, all of which are considered cannibalistic and extremely dangerous. Approach the monster only with the greatest caution.

In the event the creature attacks, there may be at least one effective method for dissuading the Thetis Lake Monster. South American gill-men, such as the monster featured in *The*

Creature from the Black Lagoon, and many other aquatic humanoids are deathly afraid of fire. Therefore, a monsterologist with a torch might be able to ward off the Thetis Lake Monster.

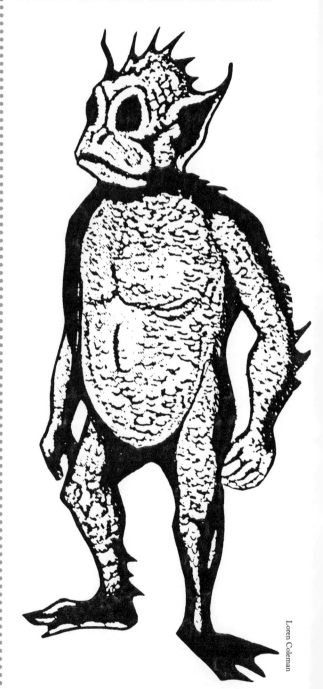

Loren Coleman

WEREWOLVES

VITAL STATISTICS

DISTINGUISHING FEATURES: Black fur, glowing red eyes, and huge teeth

HEIGHT: 5–7'

WEIGHT: 110–300 lbs

RANGE AND HABITAT: Any wilderness in North America, especially those on the edge of civilization

POPULATION SIZE: Less than five hundred

DIET: Carnivore

BEHAVIOR: Werewolves—men and women capable of assuming the form of a wolf—typically gorge on humans whenever they transform, although a small percentage only hunt woodland creatures.

SOURCE: Immigrant folklore, urban legend

ENCOUNTERING WEREWOLVES:

Like **Vampires**, Werewolves are known the world over and appear frequently in the folklore of North America. Immensely brutal monsters, Werewolves are normal humans who, through one of several methods, obtain the ability to assume the form of giant black wolves. In this state, they retain their human intellect but also gain the senses, strength, speed, and reflexes of a monstrous wolf. Such individuals usually revel in this power and spend the greater portions of their lives running through the wild, hunting deer, bears, and humans.

A variation of the common Werewolf is the Wolfman, a human who has the power to become half-man, half-wolf. These creatures stand upright, but have clawed hands and wolflike heads. They are frequently covered in hair and may possess tails. Wolfmen retain most of their intelligence and acquire great strength. A small percentage of Werewolves possess the ability to alternate between the normal wolf and Wolfman forms.

All Werewolves have incredible senses and can see clearly even in absolute darkness. Their sense of smell is unrivaled, as is their acute hearing. Most Werewolves regenerate rapidly from any wounds and can even regrow lost limbs.

In wolf form Werewolves are readily identifiable, but in human guise they are virtually indistinguishable from normal men and women. After a night hunting the forests, a Werewolf might have strange bruises and scratches and will be flushed and content, but many other nocturnal activities result in these same symptoms. Some believe that in human form Werewolves have excessively hairy hands, feet, palms, and eyebrows, but no conclusive proof supports this theory. While in human form, Werewolves can only be identified by their restlessness and violent tempers.

The transformation from human to wolf is a conscious decision and takes only a few minutes to complete. Contrary to popular belief, Werewolves are not forced to transform under the power of the full moon. This notion is especially popular in North America, but Werewolves are capable of becoming wolves at any time of the month and can even transform during the day. However, as the ability to shape-change requires a conscious effort, a North American who becomes a Werewolf but still clings to the belief that the change is caused by the rise of the full moon may subconsciously trigger the transformation but one night a month until he discovers the truth.

Although Werewolves as a species are almost as old as mankind, the origins of these monsters are uncertain. Roman mythology holds that Lycaon, king of Arcadia, was turned into the first Werewolf after he insulted the god Jupiter. In Lyceaon's honor, Werewolfism is today known as lycanthropy. An alternate theory from Icelandic lore suggests that several brave heroes became the first Werewolves after they donned enchanted wolf pelts.

In modern times, it is commonly believed that one can become a Werewolf simply by being bitten by one of these monsters. In actuality, few Werewolves are created through this method because so few victims survive a Werewolf attack. Rather, most Werewolves are people who have purposefully set out to become monsters and who devote themselves to the black arts and dark magics in this pursuit. In many arcane texts, there are rituals that enable one to gain the powers of lycanthropy. Common elements include drinking water or blood from a wolf's paw print and performing vile acts after eating roasted wolf's flesh or wearing a wolf's pelt. Most rituals also involve the herb wolfsbane and incorporate acts of cannibalism, such as drinking a lover's blood from a cup made from a wolf's skull. Native Americans have been known to repeat power-

ful chants while wearing a wolf's skin in order to effect the change as well.

Werewolves first came to public prominence in the Middle Ages when persecution of the beasts became extremely popular, especially in Europe. Although few actual Werewolves were captured and killed during this period, the furor that erupted over their discovery caused a mass exodus from Europe as Werewolves fled to Africa, South America, and North America to escape persecution.

In North America, immigrant Werewolves may have been surprised to discover the survival of a group of native New World Werewolves, commonly known as skin-walkers. Such beings were humans who became Werewolves by donning enchanted skins and who were often allied with Native American tribes, hunting alongside humans and protecting them from other monsters. Unfortunately, as American society grew larger, it created an atmosphere detrimental to monsters and forced all types of Werewolves to flee into the wilderness, where most remain to this day.

Although reluctant to emerge from the wild, a few Werewolves have been encountered in North America in recent times. One of the most exciting encounters took place in Greggton, Texas, and included sightings of the creature in both wolf and human forms. One night in July 1958, Mrs. Delburt Gregg of Greggton was horrified to spot a large, hulking wolf clawing at the screen of her bedroom window. The monster, which bared white fangs and had gleaming eyes, sprinted into the bushes when Mrs. Gregg retrieved a flashlight. However, in just a few moments, a large man emerged from the bushes at the exact spot where the beast had disappeared. The man calmly walked to the road and wandered away.

Other Lycanthropes

In modern times, monsterologists have expanded the term *lycanthrope* to include humans capable of shape-shifting into a variety of animals. While the most common lycanthropes are, of course, Werewolves, Werebears and Werepanthers are also frequently encountered. Other lycanthropic animal forms include rabbits, crocodiles and alligators, snakes, lizards, tigers, hyenas, bats, and foxes. Usually, the type of were-animal coincides with the known species of animals commonly found in the area. Thus, Werecrocodiles will be found in Africa, but are not likely to be present in Russia, where Werebears are plentiful. Most forms of lycanthropes will attack humans if hungry, enraged, or cornered.

In March 1967, a Werewolf was killed by Marvin Meade, who shot the large animal near Gorham, Illinois. Local authorities paid Meade a bounty of $15 and confiscated the corpse, which has since disappeared. Three years later, a similar monster was spotted alongside a road near Gallup, New Mexico. The Werewolf chased a car, exceeding speeds of forty-five miles per hour, whereupon one of the passengers pulled out a gun and blasted the monster. The Werewolf collapsed, but when the motorists returned to the scene of the monster's evident demise, not a trace of the creature nor any bloodstains were to be found.

Throughout February 1971, the small town of Lawton, Oklahoma, near Fort Sill, was plagued by a Werewolf. A startled housewife first spied the beast standing upright on her back porch, and another witness subsequently suffered a heart attack after spying the creature. The most prominent sighting occurred when two soldiers confronted the monster near a local cemetery. The Lawton Werewolf has never been caught, and authorities kept the case open well into the 1990s.

A female Werewolf who had the upper torso of a nude woman and the lower extremities of a wolf terrorized Mobile, Alabama, throughout the spring of 1971. More recent Werewolf sightings have been centered in Wisconsin, where one or more of these monsters has been stalking people since 1988. The Wisconsin Werewolf first emerged in Delavan on a dairy farm housing a large number of cows. Witnesses claimed that the monster had human hands but a wolf's head. It alternated between traveling on two legs and four. Since 1988, the creature has been investigated by numerous local authorities and featured on respectable tabloid news shows. It has also been spotted many times along Bray Road, where it lurks at night, and is implicated in the desecration of several graves in the local pet cemetery.

Because Werewolves are wild spirits moved by a desire to be free and unchained, monsterologists should search for Werewolves in the untamed wilderness. Any exceptionally large wolf, especially one with uncanny intelligence or glowing eyes, is likely to be a Werewolf.

Werewolves are not inherently evil or cannibalistic, and many researchers have spied Werewolves with no ill effect. However, if you are attacked, a silver bullet through the monster's heart can usually bring it down. After the beast has collapsed, the Werewolf's head must be removed and its body burned to prevent possible recovery. Upon being slain, the Werewolf will usually revert to its human form, and it is best to leave the scene before authorities arrive lest you be accused of murder.

If you manage to injure the Werewolf, but fail to kill the creature, the beast can easily be identified upon returning to human guise. If a Werewolf loses a paw, for example, he will be missing a hand when he next takes a human shape. Unless the paw was severed with a silver blade, the hand will eventually grow back, but for several days the wounded creature is clearly marked.

Other Beastmen and Beastwomen

In North America, there seems to be a beastman for every type of animal native to the continent, including those listed below.

- **Halfway People:** Creatures with human torsos atop the bodies of large, sleek fish living off the coast of eastern Canada. When storms are on the horizon, they sing loudly to warn their human neighbors, the Micmac Indians. However, when enraged, they can actually summon strong winds and rains.

- **Lizardman:** A tall bipedal humanoid covered in green scales. Its face is completely reptilian, with bulging eyes and an immense, lipless mouth. It enjoys frightening teenagers, as it did throughout South Carolina during the 1980s.

- **Lobo Girl:** A girl raised by wolves along the Devil's River in Texas in the mid-1800s. She mated with a wolf from her pack, spawning a race of intelligent lobo wolves with human eyes, which thrive in the Southwest today.

- **Loup Garou:** A French-Canadian Werewolf. Usually, a Loup Garou is someone who has turned his back on God and has been cursed with the compulsion to change into a wolf and hunt humans.

- **Mermaids (Mermen):** Monsters with the upper torsos of beautiful women (or handsome men) and the lower bodies of large fish. Although often associated with various European countries, a "Merman" was sighted in Lake Superior in 1812, and Mermaids have been observed in the Atlantic since the arrival of the first settlers.

- **Monkeyman:** A simian terror haunting playgrounds and schoolyards in Hoboken, New Jersey. He is blamed with kidnapping children and throwing teachers from third-story windows.

- **Rabbitman:** A half-rabbit, half-man monster who leaps onto unsuspecting travelers on lonely roads between Virginia and Maryland.

- **Sirens:** Female monsters that lurk on rocky shores and who have the upper torsos of a beautiful woman and the lower extremities of either a hideous bird or a giant serpent. Their singing lures sailors into the water, where they drown. Originally found in Greece, they have also been spotted by sailors in North America, especially on the Pacific Coast near Santa Barbara, California.

- **Worm Men:** Large, intelligent worms with the ability to take on the form of a man. Found throughout the far north, they use their vast supernatural powers to destroy Inuit villages by poisoning wells, murdering livestock, and killing crops.

SUPERNATURAL MONSTERS

SUPERNATURAL MONSTERS ARE those creatures generally considered to owe their existence to magical forces of some kind.

Some are created by spells or curses, while others are the product of mystical energies beyond human comprehension.

Although extremely diverse in form, supernatural entities nonetheless share a surprising number of traits. Most are cruel and vicious, and they often prey upon humans for joy or sustenance. The majority have a vast number of powers, including the ability to become intangible or vanish without a trace. They resist being caught on film, provoke great fear in animals, and rarely cast reflections or shadows.

Supernatural monsters also share a great many weaknesses. The larger number of these entities fear sunlight, which causes them intense physical pain and death. Almost all of these monsters are frightened by religious symbols, including crosses, and can be injured by holy water or similar ointments. Fire and silver are also effective weapons against these creatures. In addition, most are confined to relatively small habitats. For instance, a **Graveyard Dog** cannot stray outside the walls of its chosen cemetery, while the dancing ghoul **Ahkiyyinni** cannot wander far from bodies of water.

Most infamous among supernatural monsters are the undead, creatures such as **Vampires** and **Zombies,** who are little more than animated corpses maintaining a semblance of life. Undead typically show signs of being dead: they may have decayed or extremely pale skin, smell of the grave, and move about on stiff legs. Although they can often be injured through conventional methods, they can rarely be killed by any normal means and possess incredible regenerative properties that allow them to heal from any wound within minutes.

Other supernatural monsters include spectral animals. Generally taking the form of a normal and recognizable mammal (such as a dog or cat), spectral animals reveal their supernatural status by moving through walls, disappearing at will, and failing to leave footprints. They are often surrounded by powerful auras, which may cause fear or misfortune to afflict witnesses.

Finally, the collection of supernatural monsters also includes a few inordinately powerful entities who manipulate supernatural forces. The **Wendigo,** a monster created by dark, mystical forces and able to employ a host of incredible powers, falls into this category.

AHKIYYINNI

VITAL STATISTICS

DISTINGUISHING FEATURES: Glowing eyes, exposed bones, and deep voice

HEIGHT: About 5′5″

WEIGHT: 60–70 lbs

RANGE AND HABITAT: Shores of Arctic rivers

POPULATION SIZE: One

DIET: Unknown

BEHAVIOR: Ahkiyyinni is a vengeful corpse who controls the waters of Arctic rivers through his feverish dancing in order to drown any humans he encounters.

SOURCE: Inuit mythology

ENCOUNTERING AHKIYYINNI:

Ahkiyyinni is the animated corpse of a young Inuit man and was originally encountered only by these tribal peoples many centuries ago. He always manifests as a visibly decayed cadaver: rotting flesh dangles from his face, his eyes are shadowy pits, and his ribs protrude from his sunken chest.

More terrifying than Ahkiyyinni's appearance is his complete mastery over water, an ability that few other ghosts possess. Whenever this ghoul dances, his footfalls send supernatural energies racing through the earth, which cause rivers to rise and overflow. Anyone caught upon a river affected by Ahkiyyinni's dancing will be pulled under the water by the swift current, doomed to drown. Even those standing on the shores are likely to be swept into the rivers by massive waves.

Ahkiyyinni's origin is well documented by the Inuit. According to these early monsterologists, the terrible spirit was once an athletic and handsome Inuit hunter who, long ago, lived in a village on the shores of an Arctic river. His one true love was dancing, and his skill was legendary throughout what is now Alaska and northern Canada.

Ahkiyyinni died young and was interred atop a hill overlooking the nearby river, where he slept peacefully for many years. Yet, like many of the vengeful dead, Ahkiyyinni was reawakened by foolish mortals. In this case, a boatload of young men sailed past Ahkiyyinni's grave and made several jokes about the dead hunter's inability to dance within the tight confines of his burial mound.

After hearing these cruel cracks, Ahkiyyinni clawed his way from the grave and began to dance feverishly. He ripped off his own shoulder blade to beat it as a drum, and he cackled wildly as the young men on the river shrieked in horror. Magic coursed through the skeleton's limbs and brought chaos. Ahkiyyinni's footsteps caused the earth to shudder, and his drumbeats made the river rise. The young men pleaded for their lives, but Ahkiyyinni flashed a wicked smile, and the ghoul only danced more savagely. Responding to the relentless rhythm of Ahkiyyinni's footfalls, the thrashing river overturned the boat and the young men drowned.

Reveling in his newfound power, Ahkiyyinni was reluctant to return to his grave, and the dead Inuit thus set out to explore the world. To his dismay, he discovered that he could not travel far from the water's edge without feeling the pull of the netherworld again. Maddened by his plight, Ahkiyyinni vowed to murder anyone who crossed his path.

Ahkiyyinni still roams the shores of rivers and streams throughout Alaska and northern Canada, where he remains intent on mayhem. When encountered, the ghoul is incredibly dangerous. Because Ahkiyyinni enjoyed life so thoroughly, he has become enslaved by jealousy toward the living and now takes to murder in an attempt to appease this envy.

When Ahkiyyinni is spotted in the field, seek out solid ground as quickly as possible and passionately praise Ahkiyyinni's dancing abilities; when such compliments are made with the utmost respect and reverence, Ahkiyyinni may allow you to live. However, if Ahkiyyinni cannot be swayed or evaded, say a final prayer and prepare for a dreadful death within a frigid and watery grave.

BAYKOK

VITAL STATISTICS

DISTINGUISHING FEATURES: Exposed bones in face and body and audibly creaking joints

HEIGHT: 5'5"

WEIGHT: 90 lbs

RANGE AND HABITAT: Territory surrounding the Great Lakes, especially lands once inhabited by the Chippewa

POPULATION SIZE: One

DIET: Anthropophagus

BEHAVIOR: Baykok stalks the forests of the Great Lakes, armed with poisonous arrows that render victims helpless so that he may remove and consume their livers.

SOURCE: Native American (Chippewa) mythology

ENCOUNTERING BAYKOK:

Baykok appears as a skeleton wrapped tightly in transparent skin, complete with a skull-like face. His eyes usually glow an unholy red, although some accounts claim that Baykok's eyes are simply black pits, soulless and evil. The spirit preys exclusively on hunters and warriors, scouring the forests at night in search of lone victims.

Baykok's approach can only be noted by the sound of his bones popping and creaking as he moves through the darkness. Although there have been reports of Baykok striking down his victims with a powerful club, the ghoul most often hunts with a bow that fires invisible arrows. A poison coating these supernatural arrows sends Baykok's victim into a deep slumber, and once the warrior has been rendered unconscious, the monster begins a gruesome feast.

Among the numerous undead creatures found in North America, few elicit more fear than the ghoulish Baykok. A terrible harbinger of doom, Baykok has been encountered most often by the Chippewa, who spread out around the Great Lakes long before non-Native settlers arrived in the New World. The monster is also known to the Timiskaming Algonquin Indians and Timagami Ojibwa Indians, who refer to it as Paguk. Among all these peoples, Baykok is viewed as an unstoppable scourge who stalks and murders humans without compunction.

First, the spirit produces a small silver knife and makes an incision in the victim's abdominal region. The creature then removes the warrior's liver and eats it. After dining, Baykok shoves a stone into the victim's body, replacing the liver, and concludes the encounter by mending the wound with an invisible thread that magically heals all surface signs of the vivisection.

Most often, the victim wakes with no memory of the night with Baykok. More astonishing, Baykok's victims often survive for several days, sometimes even weeks, despite the loss of their livers. However, as would be expected, the warriors soon fall violently ill and, without exception, die.

Baykok's origins are not clearly understood, but some evidence suggests that the ghoul was once a hunter who starved to death in the wild. As he died, he vowed that his life force would never leave his corpse, and so it was that his remains rose again.

Baykok presents eager monsterologists with an interesting problem. To avoid falling prey to the monster, monsterologists must travel in groups. However, the ghoul never appears for more than one individual. Thus, the only monsterologists likely to spot Baykok are those intrepid enough to travel alone, and this is ill-advised.

If you do seek Baykok alone, be aware that there are no known methods for combating the creature once he is encountered. Holy water, religious symbols, and other devices usually potent against the undead have no effect on this monster. When facing the monster, flee toward the nearest human settlement, for Baykok never approaches civilization and is reluctant to leave the confines of the forest. Unfortunately, by running away from the ghoul, you expose yourself to a salvo of poison-tipped arrows.

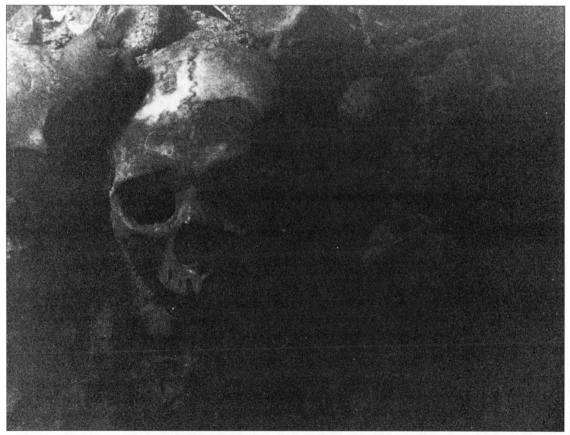

W. H. Blackman

Baykok's skull-like countenance strikes fear in all those who face the ghoul.

THE BLACK DOG OF WEST PEAK

VITAL STATISTICS

DISTINGUISHING FEATURES: Leaves no footprints and barks soundlessly

HEIGHT/LENGTH: 1'/2'

WEIGHT: Weightless

RANGE AND HABITAT: Hanging Hills, Connecticut

POPULATION SIZE: One

DIET: Unknown

BEHAVIOR: The Black Dog is extremely friendly and likes to approach humans. Unfortunately, it is surrounded by an aura of misfortune that brings death to those who encounter the beast.

SOURCE: American folklore

ENCOUNTERING THE BLACK DOG OF WEST PEAK:

The Black Dog of West Peak roams the spooky Hanging Hills of Connecticut, which rest behind the town of Meriden. The towering crags and peaks, which were formed by ancient lava flows, are positively primeval, and the region is littered with stories of mysterious disappearances. The summit of West Peak rises to one thousand feet above sea level, becomes slick with ice during the winter; dozens of hikers have slipped and plunged to their deaths while navigating the area. The eerie atmosphere of the mountains is further heightened by the names of various sites throughout the hills, including Black Pond, Lamentation Mountain, and Misery Brook.

Like its habitat, the Black Dog is a haunting creature. At first glance, it appears to be a normal and friendly terrier with soft eyes and a black coat. However, its spectral nature almost immediately becomes evident as the Black Dog leaves no footprints in mud or snow. In addition, while it opens its mouth and makes all the motions associated with barking, no sound emanates from its throat.

The Black Dog's most powerful aspect is its ability to bring disaster to those who encounter it more than once. According to author David Phillips, locals hold that "if a man shall meet the Black Dog once, it shall be for joy; and if twice, it shall be for sorrow; and the third time, he shall die." This third meeting with the Black Dog has reportedly caused almost a dozen deaths in the past one hundred years, often claiming the lives of experienced climbers and woodsmen.

The Black Dog's power is best illustrated through the most oft-told account of the beast. The prominent geologist W. H. C. Pynchon encountered the Black Dog on three separate occasions during the late 1800s. The first encounter took place in spring as Pynchon traveled past Lake Merimere on his way toward West Peak. At the lake, the dog appeared and instantly befriended Pynchon. The cheerful canine accompanied Pynchon throughout the day, following him deeper into the Hanging Hills, but vanished when the geologist returned to Lake Merimere near dusk.

Connecticut Department of Economic Development

A pond in Meriden, near the spot where Pynchon first encountered the Black Dog of West Peak.

In 1898, shortly after his friend's demise, Pynchon told his tragic story to the *Connecticut Quarterly*. He then inexplicably visited West Peak again, traversing the same route that he and his dead colleague had taken only weeks before. There, monsterologists believe, Pynchon encountered the dog a third and final time. On this climb, the geologist and experienced climber plummeted to his death, landing inches from the spot where his friend's broken body had been discovered.

The Black Dog continues to survive well into modern times, as evidenced by numerous accounts. On Thanksgiving Day, 1972, for example, the dog allegedly claimed the life of a successful and skilled alpine climber who was killed in a fall after spying the creature a third time.

For monsterologists, the first encounter with the Black Dog can be incredibly rewarding. Aside from the joy of meeting a spirited monster, you may receive some good fortune within a few weeks of the encounter. Possible outcomes of a single rendezvous with the Black Dog include sudden wealth, success, and love.

After an initial encounter with the Black Dog, however, avoid any subsequent meetings. Do not enter the Hanging Hills nor travel near the shores of Lake Merimere again. Wise monsterologists will avoid Connecticut altogether, for a second encounter is sure to bring deep sorrow. The risk of losing a companion, lover, or child is too great. And a third meeting, of course, will be fatal.

Several years later, in February, Pynchon visited the Hanging Hills with a colleague, who confessed that he had met a little black terrier during two previous trips to West Peak. Neither man knew of the Black Dog's curse, and when Pynchon told of his own encounter with the creature, they wondered aloud if they would find the animal again.

The following day, as they neared the summit of West Peak, the Black Dog poked its head from the rocks above them. Excitedly, the men continued toward the top of the mountain. Pynchon's friend misplaced a step on the ice, lost his footing, and fell several hundred feet to his death.

Soon after this tragedy, Pynchon was told of the Black Dog's powers, and indeed it did seem as if the canine's prophecies held true in his case: Pynchon's second sighting had brought him great misery in the loss of his friend, and of course his friend's third sighting of the beast had resulted in death.

THE BLACK FOX OF SALMON RIVER

VITAL STATISTICS

DISTINGUISHING FEATURES: Lustrous black pelt

HEIGHT/LENGTH: 2'4"/4'

WEIGHT: 40 lbs

RANGE AND HABITAT: Shores of Salmon River, Connecticut

POPULATION SIZE: One

DIET: Unknown

BEHAVIOR: The Black Fox uses its beautiful black pelt to hypnotize hunters and lead them into the forest, where they find they cannot kill the beast and soon become hopelessly lost.

SOURCE: Native American folklore, American folklore

ENCOUNTERING THE BLACK FOX OF SALMON RIVER:

The Black Fox of Salmon River is a ghostly animal that roams the banks of the Salmon and Connecticut Rivers in central Connecticut. It first manifested for Native Americans living on the shores of the Salmon River, but was quickly sighted by European settlers as well. By the 1700s, stories about encounters with the monster could be found throughout Connecticut; and in 1825, it was so well-known that the poet John G. C. Brainard devoted a work to the monster.

By all accounts the Black Fox is a beautiful animal, but its most striking feature is its gorgeous, soft pelt. The animal's fur is so alluring, in fact, that any who spy the creature are overcome with the desire to kill the animal and claim its hide.

Fortunately, the Black Fox possesses the ability to become intangible at will, thus evading arrows, knives, and bullets. Upon being stymied by this supernatural power, however, hunters take to pursuing the monster fox through the forest, illogically believing that they will be able to catch and kill the creature with their bare hands. The fox leads its victims on a merry chase over difficult terrain, sometimes ascending into high hills or crossing swift rivers.

Unfortunately, a small percentage of the Black Fox's pursuers do not survive their encounter with the creature. These individuals become lost in the wilderness, dying alone among the trees. Others are led over cliffs, where they fall to their deaths, or into strong rivers, where they are swept away and drowned.

The path of the Black Fox should not be crossed lightly. Although experienced hunters and hikers may not find the monster lethal, those who are less physically fit or who lack a knowledge of the wild may fare far worse when compelled to pursue the creature.

There is no known method for preventing

the effects of spying the Black Fox's luxurious coat. The urge to chase the creature is complete and overwhelming. If you succumb to this desire, which is likely, force yourself to remember that the animal cannot be killed or captured. *You will never acquire its beautiful black pelt.* This knowledge may be enough to break the creature's spell and avoid following it into oblivion.

> Covetousness warps—
> and sometimes even kills—
> the human animal.
>
> —David E. Phillips,
> *Legendary Connecticut*

The Salmon River.

Connecticut Department of Economic Development

GRAVEYARD DOGS

VITAL STATISTICS

DISTINGUISHING FEATURES: Varies, but usually includes fiery eyes, large size, and black coat

HEIGHT: Varies

WEIGHT: Weightless

RANGE AND HABITAT: Graveyards and cemeteries throughout North America; most often found in New England

POPULATION SIZE: One to four per burial site

DIET: Unknown

BEHAVIOR: Graveyard Dogs are spectral animals devoted to haunting and protecting graveyards, burial mounds, and cemeteries.

SOURCE: Immigrant (English) folklore, American folklore, urban legend, cryptozoology

ENCOUNTERING GRAVEYARD DOGS:

Graveyard Dogs are phantom canines charged with protecting graves from transgressions by grave robbers, disrespectful teenagers, members of dark cults, or others who would violate the dead. They also provide comfort for mourners visiting the graves of loved ones. Most encounters with Graveyard Dogs occur at night, when the eyes of these monsters glow fiercely through the darkness and their howls and moans drift through the ground fog.

Without exception, all Graveyard Dogs are localized ghosts, forced to haunt the same burial site for centuries without end. Their habitat is usually easily determined by man-made limitations, such as stone walls, iron gates, or roads. A large number of Graveyard Dogs also have strong ties to water and appear in cemeteries bordered by streams or creeks.

Graveyard Dogs appear in many varieties, largely dependent upon the type of burial site and the dog's specific duties. Graveyards frequented by the ill-intentioned are likely to be guarded by large, fierce dogs, while quiet and serene cemeteries will be inhabited by calm, friendly Graveyard Dogs.

Graveyard Dogs can be distinguished from real dogs by their behavior, size, and unusual physical traits. They are often large, sometimes the height and girth of a small cow. Almost all Graveyard Dogs have yellow, green, or (most often) red glowing eyes, a characteristic more pronounced in bellicose members of the species. Generally black in color, their fur is either extremely shaggy or inordinately smooth. A small percent of Graveyard Dogs are white, green, brown, or yellow. Graveyard Dogs are prone to prolonged periods of silence. When they do bark, it is far more terrifying and ferocious than the sound of a normal dog.

Graveyard Dogs move by teleportation, disappearing and reappearing at will. The effects of this vary: some Graveyard Dogs simply fade slowly into the darkness, and others sink quickly into the ground. Many disappear with a bright flash or a cloud of smoke.

Like ghosts, Graveyard Dogs can become intangible as well. Weapons, including bullets and fists, will merely pass through a Graveyard Dog without harming the creature. However, they are capable of initiating physical contact and can bite, scratch, and pin opponents to the ground, even though they are actually weightless. Because of their supernatural and ghostly nature, Graveyard Dogs do not produce the physical evidence associated with normal dogs, such as footprints, feces, or hair samples.

Almost all Graveyard Dogs exude a sulfur stench. Some have sulfurous bad breath, while others emit clouds of sulfur when they teleport, become invisible, or use any of their other powers. A graveyard haunted by a particularly nasty Graveyard Dog is likely to be inundated with this foul, rotting-egg smell.

Other animals are terrified of Graveyard Dogs and will attempt to flee any encounters with the ghosts. Horses have been known to throw their riders when confronted with a snarling Graveyard Dog, and large wolves have fled from these spectral canines. Any burial site inhabited by a Graveyard Dog will be devoid of birds and small woodland animals.

Along with their many other powers, Graveyard Dogs demonstrate uncanny and unsettling intelligence and can outsmart most humans. They almost always acknowledge the existence of a witness through a bark, smile, snarl, or stare.

Individual Graveyard Dogs exhibit unique, and often bizarre, inconsistencies that set them apart from the rest of the pack. Some Graveyard Dogs are headless or legless. Others possess inordinately large teeth, the ability to spit fire, or a bark that causes anyone who

hears it to drop dead instantly. A few Graveyard Dogs also travel with other ghosts, bear heavy chains, or only appear to those about to die.

The origins of Graveyard Dogs are as varied as the mutts themselves. Some are clearly the ghosts of dogs who have died, but have returned to protect their masters' graves. Others are said to be dog-shaped demons, the product of witchcraft, or a physical manifestation of a cemetery's supernatural energy. Many researchers also believe the dogs to be the loyal servants of Death.

Today, there are Graveyard Dogs in many cemeteries throughout North America, although the greatest concentration of these animals has always been in New England. The Graveyard Dogs of New England are fairly uniform: they are usually large mastiffs with black coats and blazing red eyes. Pugnacious and truculent, these monsters will attack anyone who enters their graveyards after the sun sets.

In Mississippi, there are numerous legends of a small white Graveyard Dog capable of growing to enormous proportions when enraged. Slave cemeteries were also home to numerous headless Graveyard Dogs.

When looking for Graveyard Dogs, research local legends to discover which nearby cemeteries are deemed to be haunted; such sites are almost always attended by a Graveyard Dog.

When encountered, most Graveyard Dogs will not attack or injure you unless you attempt to interfere with their intended duties. If, for example, a Graveyard Dog is meant to guard the cemetery gates at night to prevent any soul from crossing (in either direction), you may be attacked upon passing through these gates. In most cases, however, the Graveyard Dogs will simply ensure that you do not desecrate any graves.

If the Graveyard Dog does become violent or aggressive, be sure to note when, where, why, and how this anger manifests. If the dog reveals its fangs and utters a low growl whenever you approach a certain headstone, avoid that location for the duration of the encounter. In your follow-up research, be sure to investigate who is buried in that particular plot. You may find that the Graveyard Dog is guarding the body of a witch, the corpse of a murdered child, or a buried treasure chest.

Above all, throughout the encounter remain on guard. The behavior of these animals may shift radically without warning. Actions that we view as normal, such as taking a photograph or kneeling before a headstone, may be viewed as transgressions by the Graveyard Dog. If it does attack, run immediately from the burial site. Attempt to reach the outer edges of the Graveyard Dog's limited boundary as soon as possible.

Loren Coleman

This graveyard in Illinois, which houses the body of Mormon founder Joseph Smith, is a site of much Graveyard Dog activity.

JACK O'LANTERN

VITAL STATISTICS

DISTINGUISHING FEATURES: Huge eyes, hideous face, and brightly glowing lantern

HEIGHT: 5'10"

WEIGHT: 130 lbs

RANGE AND HABITAT: Swamps throughout Louisiana

POPULATION SIZE: One

DIET: Unknown

BEHAVIOR: Jack O'Lantern hates humans and enjoys luring them into dangerous swampland with his lantern.

SOURCE: African-American and Cajun folklore

ENCOUNTERING JACK O'LANTERN:

Jack O'Lantern, or simply Jack, is a malevolent spirit that haunts the swamps, bogs, and marshes of Louisiana. A humanoid, he has long hair, green skin, monstrous saucer eyes, and a wide, misshapen mouth. He also has the legs of a grasshopper, which allow him to quickly travel great distances. Jack always carries a lantern, which has a mesmerizing and hypnotic effect on anyone who spies its light. He uses the lantern to lure people into the swamps that pervade Louisiana, where he gleefully watches as they drown or are consumed by the swamp's voracious denizens.

Jack is a cursed soul who has been refused by both heaven and hell and is now trapped on earth. Long ago, Jack was a violent alcoholic who drank himself to death. Because of his evil ways, he was visited by the Devil, who wished to personally escort Jack to hell. When Satan entered Jack's shack, he was exhilarated to see that Jack suffered from delirium tremens, the uncontrollable fits and spasms that take hold of an alcoholic's worn-out body. The Devil knew that Jack's condition would make the long trip to hell arduous and painful.

After several hours of travel, Jack and the Devil reached an apple tree. Jack, who was hungry and tired from the trek, begged for an apple to eat before reaching hell. The Devil grudgingly agreed, as he too enjoyed apples. Because Jack's trembling condition prevented him from climbing the tree, the Devil hoisted himself into the limbs and plucked two bright apples from the bough. However, as the Devil started down, he watched in horror as Jack whipped a knife from his pocket and quickly carved a cross in the trunk of the tree. The Devil, who cannot pass any cross, was trapped in the branches. The desperate demon offered to leave Jack alone, forever, if Jack would cut away the offending symbol. Jack agreed, removed the cross, and wandered home.

For several years, Jack was the most wicked man on the planet. But after drinking and carousing his way through almost two lifetimes, his tired body could take no more and he resigned himself to death. He trudged to the gates of heaven, but was startled to learn that the angels would not let him enter because of his wicked ways.

The dejected Jack decided to seek out hell, where he hoped to find acceptance. When he reached the Lake of Fire and tried to cross over into the underworld, the Devil, who had sensed Jack's approach, was infuriated. The Devil told Jack that he could not enter hell and was doomed to roam the earth alone forever. But Jack thought that he could trick the Devil one last time. Pointing to the darkness behind him, Jack told the Devil that he had to be let into hell because the way back to the mortal world was far too dark for him to tread. The Devil smiled slyly, plucked a piece of coal from the ground, and tossed it to Jack. The flaming rock burned Jack's hands and transformed him into his monstrous form, but it also lit his way, and he was forced to return to earth. Later, Jack put the piece of coal into a silver lantern.

Now, Jack has become a forlorn night spirit, trapped between heaven and hell. Because of his loneliness, Jack O'Lantern has become incredibly spiteful toward humans and will hunt people, particularly the young or pure of heart, whenever they enter the swamps. He loathes those with a strong will, and he is also insanely jealous of drunks.

Although he is certainly strong enough to strangle his victims, and his awful appearance is enough to induce heart failure in many people, Jack relies largely on his enchanted lantern to torment humans. Those who come upon Jack first notice his blazing light bobbing in the distance. The lantern mesmerizes humans and compels them to follow Jack deeper into the swamps, where he leads them into alligator-infested waterways, sinkholes, and bear dens.

Although dangerous to those unprepared for the monster, Jack O'Lantern is generally a petty and stupid spirit who can easily be bested. He is dull and slow, driven only by hatred and self-pity. Such emotions can be manipulated by those well equipped, both physically and mentally, to confront the creature.

In addition, there are several methods for protecting oneself from Jack's influence. When seeking the monster, wear your coat inside out, as this tactic momentarily confuses Jack and can allow for a quick escape. A new knife, never before used to cut anything, should also be carried at all times. Although the knife may not actually injure Jack, the monster harbors a great fear of such weapons and will flee the moment he spies one.

Jack should only be sought at night, when his lantern can be seen shining through the trees, but avoid staring directly into his bobbing light. Calling out to the spirit with offerings of enchanted liquor, especially voodoo rum, will likely lure Jack into the open in the hope of finally being delivered into drunkenness again. Throughout any encounter, beware of Jack's sudden temper. If the monster becomes enraged, flee before he can engulf you within his monstrous mouth.

The Devil is said to be involved in the creation of numerous monsters and haunted sites throughout North America,
including the infamous Jack O'Lantern.

LA LLORONA, THE WEEPING WOMAN

VITAL STATISTICS

DISTINGUISHING FEATURES: Batlike face, long claws, sensuous black hair, and mournful wail

HEIGHT: 5'5"

WEIGHT: Weightless

RANGE AND HABITAT: Any body of water in the Southwest

POPULATION SIZE: One

DIET: Unknown

BEHAVIOR: La Llorona is an undead woman cursed to spend eternity weeping and wandering the shores of rivers looking for children to drown.

SOURCE: Mexican-American folklore, urban legend

ENCOUNTERING LA LLORONA:

Throughout the Southwest, the shores of lakes and rivers are haunted by the wailing spirit La Llorona, a horrific figure routinely blamed for the mysterious drowning deaths of children and young adults.

Known in some areas as the Weeping Woman, La Llorona can be found at night as she wanders near bodies of water, sobbing uncontrollably. From a distance, she appears to be an alluring woman dressed in white. Her lithe body and graceful movements are captivating, as is the long, beautiful black hair that seductively conceals her face.

La Llorona generally vanishes into a nearby body of water when approached. However, when she is encountered by a child, she grabs her victim with grotesquely distended fingers. She cradles the child to her breast and wades into the water, sinking below the surface to drown her quarry. Trapped underwater, the last vision the child sees is La Llorona's hideous, batlike face.

Unfortunately for many teenagers and young adults, La Llorona seems to loosely define the term "child." She has been known to capture and drown victims as old as twenty-five, although such unfortunates are usually described by their relatives and friends as "immature" or "childlike." Many of the older victims are taken while carousing along the shores of the Colorado River or while swimming at night.

According to most sources, La Llorona is the spirit of a mother who drowned herself and her children. The most widely re-told account relates the misfortune of a girl named Luisa, a sixteenth-century peasant who gave herself to the wealthy Don Muño Montes Claros. After bearing him three sons, Luisa found herself alone when Don Muño married a woman with a great deal of family money. Enraged, Luisa drowned the children to strike back at her fickle lover. She ran through the city wailing with grief, then returned to the river to join her sons beneath the cold water. Luisa's body was never recovered, but Don Muño found his three dead children on the shore the next day. He cursed Luisa and shot himself; as her name faded from Don Muño's dying lips, Luisa was brought back from the dead in the hideous form of La Llorona.

According to other sources, the ghost was once an irresponsible and negligent mother more attached to her carefree lifestyle than her children. The careless woman left her offspring unattended in order to meet her lover, but when she returned the next morning, she found that her children had drowned while playing on the riverbank. She was arrested for her crime and punished with death, but higher powers cursed the woman to life eternal as La Llorona. She now kidnaps and kills children to punish their inattentive parents.

In the most barbaric accounts, La Llorona was a woman who felt saddled by a horde of between eight and twenty children and opted to drown her brood to embark on a life of parties and levity. After murdering the majority of her children, she was furious to discover that a few had escaped. She searched the riverbank for them, but accidentally toppled into the water and sank to the bottom. La Llorona now returns from her watery grave in search of the children that escaped her grasp, but her memory has been corrupted and she claims any children whom she can find.

Although most dangerous to children left untended near bodies of water, La Llorona is also surrounded by an aura of misfortune that brings great tragedy or loss to anyone who encounters her. In a very few instances, however, an encounter with the Weeping Woman has actually benefited those present. Drunks are likely to reform their ways, especially if they run across La Llorona while under the influence; children who stray from their parents and almost fall prey to the ghost will be more wary in the future; and mothers and fathers who hear of the ghost become more responsible and protective of their young.

VAMPIRES

VITAL STATISTICS

DISTINGUISHING FEATURES: Pale skin, fangs, and red eyes

HEIGHT: 5–7′

WEIGHT: 110–300 lbs

RANGE AND HABITAT: Most large cities throughout North America

POPULATION SIZE: Less than one thousand

DIET: Anthropophagus

BEHAVIOR: Insatiable blood-drinking monsters, vampires are evil beings who stalk humans in every large city.

SOURCE: Immigrant folklore, urban legend

ENCOUNTERING VAMPIRES:

Vampires are humans who have technically died but still cling tenaciously to a semblance of life. This state of "undeath" is perpetuated only by drinking fresh blood, which Vampires obtain by using their sharp fangs to puncture victims' necks.

The most commonly recognized Vampires originated in Europe. These creatures are generally described as formidable entities who wield a wide range of powers. They can see clearly in complete darkness and possess acute hearing and olfactory powers. In addition, they are incredibly strong, heal rapidly from most conventional injuries, and are capable of flight. Vampires are known for their ability to hypnotize, seduce, and mentally control most humans. They also frequently befriend and command a wide variety of animals, most commonly dogs, wolves, cats, and large birds. On rare occasion, they have been known to transform into mist or a huge wolf, but the belief that they can assume the form of a bat is erroneous.

The Vampires currently found in North America are simply European Vampires who migrated to the New World with the early English settlers. Over time, the North American Vampires have adapted to North America, and while they still share all the powers associated with their European counterparts, they are much more resilient. For example, European Vampires need to sleep in coffins and must be in frequent contact with soil from their graves or native lands. This is not the case in North America, where Vampires can be found sleeping in caves, the trunks of cars, cellars, and attics. European Vampires are also unable to cross running water, such as a stream or river. But this rule does not apply to North American Vampires, who arrived in the New World by crossing the entire Atlantic Ocean. Garlic is believed by some to repel Vampires, but this is clearly not the case in North America. Finally, European Vampires need to be invited into a home before they can commit murder, but again this is not a common trait among North American Vampires.

Fortunately, North American Vampires still have numerous weaknesses. All Vampires, for example, are vulnerable to sunlight and can only move about during daylight hours under extreme duress. They can also be injured by fire and can be repelled by wolfsbane or wild roses. If religion played a significant part in the life of a human prior to his or her transformation into a Vampire, then that Vampire may fear holy objects, and holy water will burn its skin like acid. Furthermore, most Vampires will not cross consecrated ground.

It is commonly accepted that a stake through the heart will destroy a Vampire. However, this maneuver merely renders a Vampire indefinitely immobile, and other methods must be used to destroy the creature permanently. Silver bullets and silver-plated daggers can injure a Vampire and inhibit the creature's regenerative powers, but the only tried and true method of completely destroying a Vampire consists of beheading the creature, burning its body and head, and scattering the ashes over several different locations.

The method by which one becomes a Vampire is shrouded in mystery. In the Middle Ages, it was believed that only truly evil people rose again as Vampires. Today, it is assumed that Vampires can infect their victims with undeath through their bite alone.

Whatever the case, modern Vampires have learned to live among humans by hiding their true natures. Vampires will do their best to emulate normal humanity and remain inconspicuous. Therefore, contrary to popular belief, they do not wear capes, nor do they dress entirely in the color black. Instead, they wear the clothing of their peers and behave in a normal and socially acceptable manner. Vampires often have human friends and lovers, attend movies and the theater, visit amusement parks, and maintain steady jobs (of course, many of

these activities need to be scheduled at night).

Monsterologists can find Vampires living in any large city, but their activities are difficult to recognize. Begin your search for Vampires by wandering nightclubs, athletic clubs, movie theaters, and ritzy parties, all common hunting grounds for these fiends. Search police reports for recent murders that seem suspicious, but remember that, while a Vampire's victim will often have small puncture wounds on the neck, Vampires frequently try to conceal their attacks by mutilating the body after death. If possible, learn the preferences of any local Vampires: some prey exclusively on children, while others prefer criminals or the elderly.

As a monsterologist, never rely on the so-called confessions of Vampires, as a true Vampire would never willingly reveal its true nature. When faced with anyone who claims to be a Vampire, remember that a real Vampire does not cast a reflection or have a pulse.

If confronted by a true Vampire, do not fall prey to modern misconceptions, which tend to paint these monsters as tragic and sympathetic creatures. This is a complete distortion of the truth. These beings are incredibly powerful and corrupt. They will not hesitate to kill to sustain their own existence. Although many have relationships with humans, this is usually part of an intricate disguise, and most Vampires view themselves as being far superior to mere mortals. The harsh reality is that Vampires are ruthless killers who often receive a sexual thrill from butchering humans and devouring blood.

Finally, be aware that Vampires enjoy turning those who know of their existence into Vampires to ensure a witness's silence. Therefore, if you do seek out Vampires, it is highly likely that one day you will become a Vampire yourself.

THE WENDIGO

VITAL STATISTICS

DISTINGUISHING FEATURES: Generally horrific appearance, great size, and glowing eyes

HEIGHT: 7–10'

WEIGHT: 200–400 lbs

RANGE AND HABITAT: Forests of the Great Lakes region and central Canada

POPULATION SIZE: Unknown

DIET: Anthropophagus

BEHAVIOR: A being of vast supernatural power, the Wendigo enjoys tormenting humans lost in the woods, many of whom he eventually consumes.

SOURCE: Native American mythology

ENCOUNTERING THE WENDIGO:

The Wendigo, perhaps one of the most powerful entities native to North America, has long been documented by a wide range of indigenous peoples. Among the Native American and Inuit Indians, the beast was called by various names, including Windigo, Witigo, Witiko, Ithaqua, and Wee-Tee-Go, which can be roughly translated as "the evil spirit that devours mankind." In 1860, the German explorer Kohl translated *wendigo* as "cannibal" among the Great Lakes tribes.

According to the literally thousands of Native American encounters with this monster, the Wendigo is a human transformed by dark magics into an unspeakably evil spirit of the forests. Though each Wendigo's appearance varies somewhat, all Wendigoes have glowing eyes, but these can flare a wide array of colors from dark green to bright yellow. They have blood-flecked and twisted lips, long yellowed fangs, and dark blue tongues. Most have sallow skin, but a few have bodies covered in matted hair stained by gore. The vast majority of Wendigoes are tall, lanky, and extremely thin, perhaps as a reflection of an unholy hunger that drives them.

The hearts of Wendigoes are made of ice, and their claws are often described as icicles as well, reflecting their total dominion over desolate cold. Wendigoes can withstand debilitating temperatures and thrive in even the harshest climes. They frequently appear within the core of a snowstorm and prefer to steal their victims when the weather is at its most fearsome.

Wendigoes delight in eating human flesh, but many individual Wendigoes have a favorite type of prey. A Wendigo believed to inhabit Conqueror's Mountain, near Lake Chibougamou in Quebec, has a particular fondness for the sweet fat of children, while others of this monstrous group prefer the soft skin of women, the coarse muscles of brave warriors, or the brittle bones of the elderly.

Although the exact process is not clearly understood, a Wendigo is commonly created whenever a human resorts to cannibalism within the enchanted forests surrounding the Great Lakes. This vile act invites a malignant spirit of the wood to take control of the wayward human. The moment he is touched by such supernatural forces, the cannibal suffers from uncontrollable and continual retching and will eventually vomit vast quantities of blood. This blood loss results in death. However, the victim is soon reborn as a huge and monstrous beast overwhelmed by the desire to taste human flesh again, at which point conversion into a full-fledged Wendigo is complete.

The craving for human flesh does little to dull the Wendigo's intellect; it is not mindless, but it is an evil and cunning human blessed with the physical prowess and savagery of a monster. Wendigoes have been known to stash pots brimming with human remains high in the branches of trees in preparation for long winters, when few travelers are abroad. Wendigoes also invade cabins or tents in remote locales, killing the inhabitants and converting the dwellings into their own lairs.

Aside from its many other abilities, the Wendigo is incredibly attuned to its environment. It knows every tree, cave, hill, and bush in its territory and uses this knowledge to shadow its victims for hours without being spotted. It often makes itself known to potential victims by growling or shrieking. Wanderers spin toward the source of these sounds, only to see the dense forest closing in. This sense of being followed has driven the most stalwart adventurers insane, forcing them to fire rifles wildly into the bushes or to run haphazardly into the forest. Reduced to such a state, these victims are easy prey for the Wendigo.

The Wendigo excels at stealth, and it is often said that the creature moves upon the winds and breezes, because its approach is so silent and swift. A Wendigo can also fill the forest with an eerie siren by forcing air through its snarling lips, and when the wind rises, it might howl to terrify its victim before attacking. Usually such warnings occur far too late.

Although a bane to humanity, the Wendigo is closely allied with the animals of the forest. It often travels with other predators such as bears, wolves, and eagles, with whom the Wendigo seems to enjoy sharing its kills. Grizzly bears traveling with Wendigoes are treated to leftover bones, which they crack open to devour the marrow. Ravens likewise receive treats: a Wendigo might toss the bird a victim's head, so that the raven can pluck out the eyeballs.

As Wendigoes age, they become exponentially more powerful, and elder Wendigoes are skilled shamans with a vast array of abilities. Some can control the weather and create massive storms, while others call forth darkness hours before sundown. Animals can be summoned from the far reaches of the forest, wounds can be instantly healed, and huge distances can be traveled in a moment.

Another of the Wendigo's formidable powers is its ability to induce the dreaded Wendigo fever, a curse that overtakes a victim's body and mind. The first sign of infection is the sudden onset of a strange scent that only the victim can detect. After absorbing this disturbing odor, the afflicted will experience a terrible night of weeping and nightmares. Upon waking, a burning sensation in the legs and feet becomes so intense that the victim runs shrieking into the forest, throwing off clothes and tossing aside shoes. Most of those sickened by Wendigo fever never return to the human world, and it is speculated that most are consumed by the Wendigo.

Because they so feared the beast, a small number of Native Americans actively hunted the Wendigoes in the past. One of the most famous Wendigo hunters was Jack Fiddler, a Cree Indian who killed at least fourteen Wendigoes during his lifetime. The last murder, however, resulted in his imprisonment at the age of eighty-seven. On October 7, 1907, Jack and his son Joseph were tried for the murder of a woman who was a member of their own tribe. Both men pleaded guilty to the crime, but defended themselves by explaining that the woman had been possessed by the spirit of a Wendigo and was on the verge of a complete transformation. According to the Fiddlers, she had to be killed before she turned on the clan.

Despite the Fiddlers' successes, Wendigoes are notoriously difficult to destroy. They are immune to a wide range of weapons, including those made of iron or steel. Silver, however, has great power against a Wendigo, and a silver bullet or silver-plated blade can inflict terrible damage on the monster.

In general, a Wendigo can only be annihilated if its heart is shattered by a silver stake and its body is dismembered by a silver ax. The shards of the creature's heart should be locked in a silver box and buried in consecrated ground. Its decapitated head must be burned, and each piece of its body should be hidden in an inaccessible place, such as the bottom of a lake, chasm, or well.

Although surviving the experience may be difficult, Wendigoes are relatively easy to find. A small population of Wendigoes have lairs in the far north, somewhere near the northern lights. Caves, gullies, and canyons throughout central Canada can also provide suitable homes for a Wendigo. At least one Wendigo lives in the Cave of the Wendigo, near Mameigwess Lake in northern Ontario. Any other area named after the Wendigo, such as Windigo River and Windigo Lake in Ontario, is bound to be inhabited by this monster as well.

Kenora, Ontario, is viewed by many monsterologists as the "Wendigo Capital of the World." The monsters may have been attracted to this region originally because of the many Native American settlements scattered in the area. Throughout the past three centuries, Wendigoes have been spotted in and around Kenora by traders, missionaries, writers, journalists, explorers, trackers, and trappers. Sightings have occurred well into this decade.

Wendigoes should be sought with the greatest care. Properly prepared fetishes, amulets, enchantments, and protective spells must be employed to protect against Wendigo fever, and earplugs or headphones should be worn to block out the creature's maddening voice. A bright fire kept lit at all times might provide protection, but a rifle loaded with silver bullets is the most reliable means of self-defense from the monster's physical assault.

For truly brazen monsterologists who find the "average" Wendigo mundane, the quest for the "King of the Wendigoes" might prove more exhilarating. The oldest of all known Wendigoes, this fearsome beast roams Quebec's Windigo River. The King of the Wendigoes stands thirty feet tall and is a master of the elements and has full control over a wide range of magics. The beast has been known to assail hunters with raging fires and unrelenting storms, conceal itself in smoke or fog, and command the rivers to drown humans. Native Americans who once lived in the upper St. Maurice area would not fish on the Windigo River when they sensed that the monster was about, for fear of being overtaken by winds or rain summoned by the beast. Clearly, this is a monster that even the most fearless monsterologist would not want to encounter.

ZOMBIES

VITAL STATISTICS

DISTINGUISHING FEATURES: Stench of the dead, visibly decayed features, slack faces, and blank eyes

HEIGHT: Varies

WEIGHT: Varies

RANGE AND HABITAT: Conceivably anywhere, but most often New Orleans, Louisiana

POPULATION SIZE: Unknown

DIET: Varies

BEHAVIOR: Most zombies are mindless slaves to their creators, but a few are ravaging flesh eaters who blindly attack all humans.

SOURCE: Immigrant (Haitian) mythology, American folklore, urban legend

ENCOUNTERING ZOMBIES:

Also known as the living dead or the walking dead, Zombies are animated human corpses created through powerful magic or some other supernatural means. They are horrific to behold because they have been dead. Most Zombies are visibly rotting and may be worm-infested; they usually smell of decay; and they are frequently missing fingers, eyes, ears, or even entire limbs. Zombies are the least formidable of the undead because they can be wounded by most physical means, although they are immune to pain.

The great majority of these creatures are mute. They move with an awkward, halting gait, no doubt a product of their stiff limbs, and are usually seen shuffling or limping about. Despite their milky white eyes, Zombies have keen vision and can see perfectly in complete darkness. Most Zombies are considered mindless, and their slack faces never show a hint of feeling.

The most well-known of all Zombies are the Voodoo Zombies, corpses animated by the spells and rituals of evil voodoo priests or priestesses, also known as houngans. Voodoo priests animate corpses as Zombies for a variety of reasons, but most often the Zombie is to be used as a servant or slave. The creatures make ideal workers because they do not need to eat, drink, or sleep and they never tire. Once a Zombie has been directed to perform a task, it will do so without error until destroyed or ordered to stop by its master. A Zombie's duties usually include menial tasks and hard labor.

As Zombies are so obviously dead, Zombie masters must hide their slaves from the rest of the world. Zombies are usually put to work only at night, when darkness can conceal their decay. Factories that only operate after dusk may be driven by Zombie labor, and a field continually picked clean before sunrise is probably worked by Zombie slaves. For this reason, bakers, who work largely at night, were long thought to employ Zombies.

The exact means for creating a Zombie through voodoo has yet to be discovered, although there are a few detailed accounts of the process. Every Zombie recipe requires that the houngan have physical access to a corpse at some point during the ritual, and they all direct the houngan to instill the Zombie with fear by beating it harshly. If the spell has been cast correctly, the Zombie will be unable to harm its master and can easily be frightened into complete obedience.

In all cases, the experience of the priest and the type of spell will dictate the physical power of a new Zombie. Some Zombies are extremely fragile and continue to decay as they work, while the most formidable Zombies possess superhuman strength and do not rot away (although they cannot heal any decay that has already occurred). Some houngans know even more powerful versions of the spells needed to create a Zombie, enabling them to imbue their creations with dim intelligence. Although the creatures are still mute, these semi-intelligent Zombies can act as bookkeepers, chauffeurs, scribes, doormen, bodyguards, and gardeners. Zombies can even become assassins.

Most houngans only use fresh corpses to create Zombies, and it is rumored that some even resort to murder to procure healthy bodies. Despite the lack of decay, a Zombie constructed from a fresh corpse is still identifiable by its vacant stare and odd demeanor.

Oddly, the spell that holds Voodoo Zombies enthralled can be broken by ordinary salt. If the Zombie consumes food or drink containing even a dash of salt, it realizes its plight, becomes enraged, and kills its master before returning to the grave.

In general, Voodoo Zombies seldom pose a threat to most humans unless molested, prevented from performing their assigned tasks, or ordered to kill by their masters. In fact, most of these creatures hardly seem to notice the presence of living beings. But when they do become violent, they are virtually unstoppable and will continue to attack until destroyed. Complete and utter incineration is the only method of fully destroying a Zombie, although hacking off all of its limbs usually renders the creature ineffective.

In contrast to the relatively harmless Voodoo Zombies, the dreaded flesh-eating Zombies are thoroughly dangerous. Resurrected by some still unknown means, flesh-eating Zombies dig out from their graves in search of humans to consume. They almost always move in packs, and when they descend upon a victim, the feast becomes a grisly orgy of gore. The majority of these Zombies will eat an entire human, stripping it to the bone in minutes, but a specialized group known as the Brain Eaters only feed on brains.

Flesh Eaters are dirty and disheveled and surrounded by a rank cloud of putrefaction. Their skin is tinged a sickly green. Many continue to drop body parts and drip embalming fluid as they move about in search of food. Flesh Eaters are likely to have blood smeared on their faces and clothes, tattered strings of flesh hanging from their teeth, and skin trapped beneath their jagged, dirty nails.

Solitary Flesh Eaters are relatively impotent, for they are slow and clumsy creatures. But flesh-eating Zombies are never encountered alone, and in large numbers, these ghouls can easily overwhelm most victims. Moreover, Flesh Eaters will continue to move toward prey even after suffering massive physical damage. There are even reports of severed Zombie heads snapping at passing humans. When faced with fire, Flesh Eaters momentarily show caution, but this fades as their twisted hunger takes hold once again. The only way to completely destroy a Flesh Eater is to disrupt what remains of its central nervous system by piercing its brain with a bullet.

The manner in which Flesh Eaters become animated remains hotly debated. One theory argues that a passing meteor released undetectable radiation that periodically resurfaces and brings the dead to life. Some researchers suspect government experiments gone awry, and still others point to mutation-causing pollutants. It is also thought that a virus may be responsible for creating flesh-eating Zombies. This conjecture is supported by the fact that people who are bitten by Flesh Eaters but escape being consumed eventually become Flesh Eaters themselves.

Whatever force brings these gruesome automatons to life does so only infrequently. The few Zombie uprisings that occur are quickly and quietly put down by law enforcement authorities, usually through the deployment of crack sharpshooters, professional Zombie hunters, controlled fires, or small explosives.

Monsterologists researching Zombies should begin their search in New Orleans, Louisiana, where voodoo is most active. There, you are bound to find numerous Voodoo Zombies, which are active only at night. Flesh Eaters are more difficult to find as they seldom rise from the grave.

You may also look for Zombies on the back roads or in the bayous surrounding New Orleans, but be sure to carry a bag of salt and a high-powered rifle to defend yourself against whichever Zombie type you encounter. When you do spy a Zombie, watch for the telltale signs that reveal the Zombie's true nature. If the creature rushes forward, slavering and chomping its jaws, it is most likely a Flesh Eater, and you should shoot it through the brain or run with all possible haste. If the Zombie merely wanders past you, it is likely a Voodoo Zombie and should be fed salt or left alone.

Other Supernatural Monsters

Undead, ghostly animals and other supernatural monsters have been sighted across the continent for centuries. The sheer number and diversity of these monsters make them impossible to completely catalog, but below is a truncated list of such creatures.

- **The Bad One:** A demon who frequently appeared to Native Americans as a towering man with snakelike features, including scales and fangs.

- **Belarivo:** A Zombie who frequently appears at parties and weddings in New Orleans, looking for a chance to dance and revel, as he once did in life.

- **Black Hog:** A spectral shoat whose appearance presages death in the Ozarks.

- **Bone-Cleaner:** A haglike creature that lives in Washington's Lake Nuquispum and consumes anything that nears the water at night. It receives its name from its ability to completely strip a body clean.

- **Borego Phantom:** A towering skeleton with a lantern glowing in its chest who only appears at night to prospectors in the deserts near Borego, Arizona.

- **Cheeka:** A malevolent demon who once roamed Sproat Lake, British Columbia, where he consumed many Native Americans.

- **Demons of Newbury:** Invisible imps first reported in 1679 by English settlers and said to plague homes throughout New

England, particularly in Newbury, New Hampshire. They frequently slam doors, break windows, and throw rocks and dishes at humans. They also spoil milk, set barns on fire, and chase away livestock.

- **Gans:** Humanoid mountain spirits with huge heads, painted faces, and immense supernatural powers, including the ability to grant the wishes of Apache Indians.

- **Ghost Wrestler:** A burly phantom who appears to lone Native American braves or modern campers on the central plains at night. He is cordial, but insists on wrestling with anyone he encounters. If he wins, he slays his opponent; if he loses, he ensures that the victor's deepest desires come true.

- **Manitous:** A race of extremely powerful supernatural entities known to virtually every Native American tribe. Sometimes described as demons, they can be either harmful or helpful depending on their disposition and mood.

- **Plat-Eye:** A large spectral cat with flaming eyes and a terrible sulfur stench. It is typically found in the swamps and backwoods of Georgia, where it was originally encountered by African slaves before the Civil War.

- **Sea Weasel:** A small, ghostly mammal known to the Inuit Indians of the far north, who report that the creature's appearance causes misfortune and death.

- **Tree Husband:** A supernatural cottonwood with human intelligence and the ability to impregnate Cheyenne women with its quickly growing seed.

- **Vanishing Hitchhikers:** A collection of spectral men and women found wandering roadsides at night and believed to be the spirits of those slain in car accidents or while hitchhiking. When picked up by motorists, they seem normal, but they inexplicably vanish from the car before reaching their destinations.

- **White Fox of the Ozarks:** A supernatural canine appearing near Pevely, in Jefferson County, Missouri, where it has long been observed by farmers, motorists, and hikers along Highway 61. It can become intangible or change into a skunk or a short-haired black-and-white dog. Foxhounds can smell and see the White Fox, but will not pursue it.

- **White Horses:** Wild, untamed spectral horses that cannot be broken or ridden by mortal man. They are found throughout the United States and Canada and are generally regarded as the very embodiment of freedom.

ENIGMATIC ENTITIES

ENIGMATIC ENTITIES ARE those monsters who cannot be comfortably placed into any other monster category.

They are the completely inexplicable and often the most bizarre of all monsters because they rarely conform to rules and continually defy researchers.

As a group, enigmatic entities only share one commonality: they are shrouded in mystery. Their origins are largely unknown, and sightings reveal little new information about their motives, intelligence, or demeanor. Researchers are rarely certain how aggressive enigmatic entities may be, nor do we have concrete methods for combating these beasts.

For all these reasons, enigmatic entities may be the most dangerous—and unpredictable—of all monsters, and should only be pursued by experienced monsterologists.

THE BOGEYMEN

VITAL STATISTICS

DISTINGUISHING FEATURES: Varies, but almost all are male

HEIGHT: Varies

WEIGHT: Varies

RANGE AND HABITAT: Unlimited

POPULATION SIZE: Unknown

DIET: Varies (some anthropophagus)

BEHAVIOR: Although a diverse lot, all Bogeymen thrive on frightening, and often murdering, children.

SOURCE: Urban legend, American and Canadian folklore

ENCOUNTERING THE BOGEYMEN:

Children of North America share one common enemy. Whether in sleepy towns or sprawling cities, in backwoods or ghettos or suburbs, all children whisper tales of the dreaded Bogeyman (also known as the Bogieman, Boogieman, or Boogeyman). From California to Rhode Island, across plains and swamps and mountains, encounters with the nefarious Bogeymen are legion.

Bogeymen comprise a diverse group of maniacal entities. Almost every geographical area in the United States has its own individual Bogeyman, and the methods, appearance, and origins of each differs significantly. Some are extremely human, to the point of being indistinguishable in a crowd, while others are merely lithe shadows that slip under doors and into bedrooms. Some Bogeymen murder violently with hammers or knives; others use more subtle methods, such as drowning.

Bogeymen usually restrict their activities to a limited area, such as a small town, a section of a city, a portion of a woods, or a certain lonely stretch of highway. There are also instances of household Bogeymen who lurk in a home's closets, attic, and cellar. Overnight summer camps are frequently host to Bogeymen who stalk the staff and campers. Dilapidated houses and cemeteries are often home to Bogeymen, as are junkyards, parks, and schools.

In general, Bogeymen are immensely powerful. The most formidable can perform supernatural feats, such as entering dreams or moving through mirrors. Almost all Bogeymen are also immortal and invulnerable. It is possible to vanquish a Bogeyman temporarily, usually through highly specialized methods, but it will eventually reappear.

Many Bogeymen change shape and appear as the thing most feared by a victimized child. Because of this, Bogeymen are sometimes mistaken for ubiquitous monsters such as witches, **Werewolves, Vampires, Zombies,** and aliens. Bogeymen also use their shape-changing powers to imitate older siblings and trusted adults, such as teachers and parents, in order to lure victims closer.

Many notable Bogeymen are completely invisible until the moment they strike. Others use their horrific appearances to paralyze their prey. A haglike "Bogeywoman" reported in the Midwest scratches on the bedroom windows of her victims until the children die of fright. The most sadistic Bogeymen of all may be those who refrain from murder, but instead terrorize a few individual children for years at a time. A few Bogeymen seem to have some sense of morality and will only victimize bullies, liars, or cheats.

Most Bogeymen are brutal killers. In California beach towns, a Bogeyman is known to kidnap children from quiet sidewalks and stuff them into a white van, where he hacks their bodies into tiny pieces. The dismembered children are placed into burlap sacks and thrown into the ocean, to be discovered years later by other children building sand castles or digging for seashells.

Some Southern communities fear a Bogeyman with glowing green eyes and a proclivity for castrating young boys. He often makes eye contact with his victims weeks in advance so they realize he is pursuing them. The children of the region understand that, once this Bogeyman has chosen his next victim, there is no escape.

A Bogeyman's name is often indicative of its distinguishing qualities. The Shape, for instance, is a featureless humanoid, while the Shadow Men lurk solely in shadows. Dan the Chainsaw Man and **The Hook** are named for their choice of weapons, while Rawhead Rex and Bloody Bones are often associated with acts of cannibalism.

The Green Man of South Park, Pennsylvania, is named for the greenish glow that surrounds him. His face resembles melted wax, and he is frequently seen lurking along back roads, alleys, and side streets. The Green Man does not kill; rather, he uses his gruesome appearance to frighten children and teenagers.

Green and the Supernatural

A relationship to the color green is a trait shared by a large number of monsters around the world, including many Bogeymen. The color can be connected to a monster's eyes, skin, teeth, fingernails, clothes, or hair. Florida's **Skunk Ape** is described as having green eyes and a glowing green aura. New Jersey's disturbed **Grinning Man** wears a shimmering green costume. A great many monsters ooze green slime. The color also appears in the names of monsters, including Old Greenface, a Bogeyman who lurks beneath bridges in Washington; Old Green Eyes, a headless phantom roaming the Stones River Battlefield in Tennessee; Pennsylvania's Green Man; and the European hag Jenny Greenteeth. The color can be found in the names of evil places as well, such as Vermont's Green Mountain State Forest, a cursed area that boasts at least two mysterious ghost towns and several disappearances.

Loren Coleman

He is especially active on Halloween and prom night.

Although often relegated to the world of urban legends or childhood fantasy, Bogeymen have been encountered by reliable witnesses in recent years. The most terrifying of these cases involves the Killer Clowns of New England. In May 1981, several Bogeymen dressed as clowns descended upon Boston, Massachusetts, and attempted to lure children into black vans. The police were unable to capture these nefarious tricksters, and the sinister group expanded its activities to other cities throughout Massachusetts, including East Boston, Canton, and Cambridge. Within weeks, the Bogeymen had moved into Providence, Rhode Island, as well, where they continued to torment children and evade authorities.

By the end of May, at least one of the Bogeyclowns had migrated as far west as Kansas City, Missouri, and Kansas City, Kansas. The Killer Clown of Kansas City drives a yellow van, frequents elementary schools, and threatens victims with knives and swords. He also wears a black shirt with the Devil's face on the front. Similar phantom clowns have been encountered in Denver, Omaha, Pittsburgh, and elsewhere across the country.

Monsterologists seeking the Bogeymen are fortunate, for wherever you make your home, one of these monsters is sure to be on the loose. Begin the quest by interviewing children about the local Bogeyman. You will soon realize the community is overrun by these fiends. Urge the children to describe the living quarters, habits, behaviors, and general demeanor of the Bogeyman. However, be sensitive of the fact that children are easily frightened by any mention of the Bogeyman and may not willingly speak of the creature unless they are assured that he is not in the vicinity. The greater majority of children believe that the Bogeyman, like Santa Claus, knows what they are thinking at any time and will exact revenge against those who reveal the monster's existence.

When you do find children who will discuss the Bogeyman, they may be able to lead you into the monster's domain. If the children are not your own, be sure that you have their legal guardians sign appropriate waivers to release you from responsibility should the encounter result in injury or death.

Fortunately, children often know of the Bogeyman's weaknesses, which you may be able to exploit to destroy the creature. Perhaps the Bogeyman can be dissipated by a special chant or grievously wounded by holy water. Most of these monsters usually fear light, and some can be killed by sunlight alone. Other solutions are more unusual, as is the case with South Park's Green Man, who can be satiated for several weeks by gifts of alcohol.

When confronting a local Bogeyman, travel in numbers, as few Bogeymen attack groups or attempt to take more than one victim at a time. However, be warned: should you confront the Bogeyman but fail to destroy him, you are destined for terrible retribution. All the children who ever spoke the Bogeyman's name in your presence will be brutally murdered. If capable of traveling beyond local boundaries, the monster will haunt you until the end of your days.

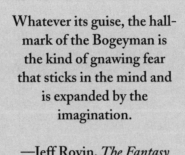

> Whatever its guise, the hallmark of the Bogeyman is the kind of gnawing fear that sticks in the mind and is expanded by the imagination.
>
> —Jeff Rovin, *The Fantasy Almanac*

CATTLE MUTILATORS

VITAL STATISTICS

DISTINGUISHING FEATURES: Unknown

HEIGHT/LENGTH: Unknown

WEIGHT: Unknown

RANGE AND HABITAT: Entire globe, but most active in the Southwest

POPULATION SIZE: Unknown

DIET: Unknown (presumably carnivore)

BEHAVIOR: Cattle Mutilators, monsters that have never been seen, viciously murder and disfigure livestock in the dead of night for reasons yet to be determined.

SOURCE: Urban legend, ufology, cryptozoology, Fortean studies

ENCOUNTERING THE CATTLE MUTILATORS:

The shadowy Cattle Mutilators, or "Mutes," are a group of unidentified entities who descend on farms and ranches to butcher cattle, horses, and other animals. They strike only after midnight but before dawn, and only in remote and isolated areas. How they arrive at a scene has yet to be discerned, for they do not leave footprints, tire tracks, or other evidence.

Mutes are silent in their attacks, and farmers and cowboys just a few hundred feet away from the victimized livestock are never awakened. But in the morning, the dawn reveals a bloodbath. Ranchers stride into their pastures to find anywhere from one to several dozen animals, usually cows or horses, butchered with surgical precision. The cause of death is often a proficient incision across the victim's throat.

Coroners and veterinarians who arrive at the scene can only retch or scratch their heads in awe as they study the mutilated cattle, which are usually bereft of brains, tongues, eyeballs, ears, udders, genitals, rectums, and other organs that common poachers or rustlers would not take the trouble to steal. Many victims are also completely skinned. In a small number of incidents, the cows are found alive, even after having had major organs removed. In almost all cases, the Mutes somehow manage to perform these complex violations without spilling a drop of blood onto the grass or the animal's hide.

While the methods described above are used most often, Mutes are also an inventive lot. For example, in Gallipolis, Ohio, in 1967, a cow was discovered neatly severed almost in two. In 1974, Sheriff George Yarnell of Elbert County, Colorado, found a mutilated cow whose udder had been drained of its natural contents and then filled with sand. Another brazen group of Mutes slipped into Colorado's Cheyenne Mountain Zoo, where they murdered and mutilated a 1,500-pound bison. They stole the animal's ear and udder, brutalized its genitals, and stripped away twenty-four square inches of hide.

While cattle are the most common victims of the Mutes, horses, cats, and dogs also frequently fall prey to these disturbed monsters. Snippy the Horse was discovered in Alamosa, Colorado, in September 1967 so badly mutilated that authorities speculated that the horse had either been struck by lighting or thrown into a vat of acid. It was later discovered that all of Snippy's brain fluid had also been removed, although the horse's skull had not been breached.

Throughout Ohio and West Virginia there remains an unusually high number of canine mutilations that bear a remarkable resemblance to the work of the Mutes. Dogs in this region are often found without any signs of physical injury, but have nevertheless been murdered and drained of blood. Completely dissected cats have also been found regularly throughout the continent, including a half dozen such felines discovered in Plano, Texas, in 1991.

Obviously, Mutes are amazingly efficient and frighteningly prolific. They murder animals across the continent with seeming impunity. Although a high number of incidents have come from Pennsylvania, Washington, California, Oregon, Ohio, West Virginia, and other states, the hotbed of mutilations seems to be the Southwest. Logan County, Colorado, suffers from an especially high number of annual mutilations, and Texas offers up many as well.

A 1978 Mute victim from New Hampshire, missing both eyes and rectum.

However, it is difficult to pinpoint the "center" of the Mutilators' territory because mutilations seem to occur in waves that afflict specific regions, sometimes for months at a time. In 1973, Mutes targeted the Midwest, murdering cows from Minnesota to Mississippi. In February of 1981, Decatur, Tennessee, was badly affected by Mutes with a fancy for the sex organs of the livestock they killed. Yet another band of Mutes obsessed with the genitalia of its victims has been plaguing the farms near Monterey, California, since early 1996; this group shows no signs of abating in its activities, despite a local effort to capture the fiends. Reports of mutilations are still being regularly received from Oklahoma, Alabama, British Columbia, and Alberta as well.

After spreading out across North America, Cattle Mutilators have also moved to other portions of world, including Africa, Sweden, South America, China, and Australia. Puerto Rico reports a high number of mutilations, as does the U.K., where the Mutes are particularly fond of slashing and crippling horses and have thus become known as the Horse Rippers.

Despite a wealth of documentation, the overall death toll attributed to Cattle Mutilators is almost impossible to calculate because a great many of these incidents go unreported or are concealed by local authorities. In North America, knowledgeable ranchers estimate about 10,000 animals are slaughtered *each year*

> It does seem as if many UFO and monster sightings are staged as distractions . . . while animal mutilations and disappearances are taking place almost unnoticed only a few miles away.
>
> —John Keel,
> *The Mothman Prophecies*

by unknown attackers, placing the total number of Mute victims at close to 450,000 since 1950. Dedicated researcher John Keel estimates more conservative numbers, with an annual total of 200 mutilations and the overall death toll at approximately 9,000 to date. In either case, it is obvious that literally thousands of animals have been killed by Mutes over the past few decades, numbers that constitute an epidemic.

In 1979 an ex–FBI employee, Kenneth Rommel, was granted $44,000 from the U.S. Law Enforcement Assistance Administration to solve the cattle mutilation mystery. After studying numerous bloodless and surgically mutilated corpses, Rommel concluded the murders were the work of predators. This highly unsatisfactory theory was embraced by the government, and research into the case was halted. More frightening, after four decades of horror and senseless slaughter, no arrests have been made in connection with cattle mutilations.

Among Mute researchers, there are many theories regarding the true identity of these murderers. The most widespread belief holds that cattle mutilations are conducted by extraterrestrials. Many ufologists support this theory because a large number of mutilations occur in areas recording a high density of UFO activity and mutilated cattle are frequently discovered soon after UFO sightings. However, many other monsters, including **Bigfoot,** the **Chupacabra,** the **Jersey Devil,** and **Mothman** are also sighted in areas famous for UFO activity. This coincidence is probably due to the fact that UFOs, Mutilators, and most other monsters prefer isolated habitats, and as these areas are continually shrinking in modern North America, the stomping grounds of such unexplained entities are bound to overlap.

Cattle Mutilators may, in fact, be much more human than we would dare suspect. While Blaine County, Idaho, was being rocked by cattle mutilations in 1975, several strangely garbed individuals were encountered near the sites of the killings. In September, a Forest Service employee spotted a group of humanoid figures in long, black robes near Cove Creek, and the following day mutilated cattle were discovered nearby. On October 9, a man had his car blocked on U.S. Highway 95 by a group of fifteen people in masks; he was forced to turn the vehicle around in order to escape. Again, cattle mutilations had occurred nearby during the night. In another case, a humanoid being wearing white coveralls was seen easily leaping a large fence near the site of a cattle mutilation.

Such sightings and other similar encounters from around the continent have given rise to the popular notion that cattle mutilations are the work of cultists. Authorities in several counties have blamed Satan worshipers and other dark cults for the deaths of livestock and family pets, the theft of animal organs, and other distasteful deeds. Yet, no known satanic cults have actually been uncovered in areas where mutilations frequently occur. In addition, as researcher John Keel points out,

most satanic cults and similar groups use the spreading of blood as components in their rituals, so it is unlikely that the rather tidy cattle mutilations are part of such ceremonies. The cultist theory cannot be discounted entirely, however. In New Jersey and a few other states, several instances of mysterious *human* mutilations have borne amazing similarities to cattle mutilations, and authorities eventually connected these murders to various cults.

Because the Mutes themselves are so reluctant to appear, monsterologists researching these monsters must devote much of their time to studying carcasses. This can be a daunting task, as Cattle Mutilators leave their victims horribly defiled. Hide and flesh is peeled away to expose muscle and bone; faces are stripped and pillaged. The stench of decay, dried blood, waste, and vomit hangs over the carcasses, and the drone of flies threatens the sanity of anyone who spends any amount of time near the rotting bodies. Studying the work of the Cattle Mutilators is one of the more disgusting aspects of monsterology and should not be undertaken by the faint of heart.

To actually spy the Cattle Mutilators as they go about their brutal business, it is best to hide in a large field or cow pasture at night, in an area known to have suffered recent cattle killings. Be warned, however: as no one has come forward to reveal the identity of the Cattle Mutilators, it is safe to assume that everyone who knows the truth behind this mystery is either involved in the practice or has been silenced.

THE ENFIELD HORROR

VITAL STATISTICS

DISTINGUISHING FEATURES: Three legs, pink eyes, and rough gray skin

HEIGHT: 4′6″

WEIGHT: 200 lbs

RANGE AND HABITAT: Enfield, Illinois

POPULATION SIZE: One

DIET: Unknown

BEHAVIOR: The Enfield Horror is often encountered scratching at doors or windows at night, trying to gain access to sleeping humans for unknown purposes.

SOURCE: Ufology, cryptozoology, urban legend

ENCOUNTERING THE ENFIELD HORROR:

The Enfield Horror is the name applied by monsterologists to a short, stocky being spotted romping through Enfield, Illinois, on rare occasion. The creature is known by a host of other names as well, including the Enfield Entity, the Enfield Imp, the Enfield Evil, and the Enfield Alien. Indeed, the Enfield Horror does seem exceedingly "alien" in appearance: it has three legs protruding from a squat body, two exceedingly short arms, and rough gray skin. Two pink eyes, each about the size of a flashlight, stare from its otherwise shadowy face.

The monster was first encountered in Enfield in April 1973, and soon after a panic erupted in the area, resulting in numerous false sightings of the creature and a massive influx of amateur monster hunters. The Enfield Horror failed to manifest for any of these armed yahoos, and the monster hunt was prematurely halted when local authorities jailed several of the weekend warriors in the interest of public safety. Since the 1970s, the creature has been spotted only sporadically.

The Enfield Horror is most feared for its tendency to approach isolated homes and spend hours scratching at doors and windows. Thankfully, its advances usually halt as soon as residents confront the creature. When spotted, the monster immediately leaps away: it has been known to traverse over fifty feet in two jumps.

As of yet, the Enfield Horror has not actually entered a home, but it is impossible to predict what the monster will do once it does invade a human dwelling. Its motives are completely unclear, and no one has been able to communicate with it. It always remains in the shadows and will never approach humans directly, but when cornered, it has been known to hiss like a wildcat or emit high-pitched and terrible shrieks. Although it has not exhibited any grasp of language, it does seem to have some intelligence and has eluded hunters throughout the past several decades. Several Enfield citizens have fired on the monster, but to no avail.

The exact origin of the Enfield Horror is

unknown. Many ufologists believe that the monster hails from outer space, but no evidence supports this theory. More likely, the Enfield Horror is a mutated human, forsaken by others because of its appearance.

Monsterologists investigating the Enfield Horror would do well to forget all preconceived notions about monsters and instead (cautiously) approach the creature with compassion. Tenderness might win the monster's heart, but hostility, disgust, or fear will engender its rage. Attempts at communication should include the presentation of food, shiny objects, and toys in order to establish trust.

Should the Enfield Horror live up to its sinister name, you must take any measure to ensure self-preservation. Sadly, the monster's speed may prevent even the most cautious researchers from defending themselves. Those who discover the Enfield Horror is indeed a terrible beast will probably never be able to share this secret with the rest of the world.

Loren Coleman

The Enfield Horror was spotted "hopping" along these train tracks in 1973.

THE GRINNING MAN

VITAL STATISTICS

DISTINGUISHING FEATURES: Perverse grin, green coveralls, and shiny bald head

HEIGHT: 7'

WEIGHT: 250 lbs

RANGE AND HABITAT: Roads and paths throughout New Jersey

POPULATION SIZE: One

DIET: Omnivore

BEHAVIOR: The Grinning Man is a disturbed individual who enjoys frightening children on lonely roads. He is also known to appear in the nightmares of those he torments.

SOURCE: Ufology, urban legend, Fortean studies

ENCOUNTERING THE GRINNING MAN:

During the 1960s, many ufologists became convinced that aliens walk among us. This belief was based largely on the fact that literally hundreds of people living in areas known for UFO activity were coming forward with reports of encountering weird strangers wearing futuristic clothing. One such case involved the bizarre Grinning Man, who appeared in suburban New Jersey in the late 1960s after a host of UFOs allegedly visited the area.

The Grinning Man is tall and extremely broad; many witnesses describe him as the largest man they have ever seen. His eyes are beady and widely spaced, and his nose and ears are exceedingly small. The Grinning Man usually shaves his head, but when he does allow his hair to grow, it is a shocking white. The monster wears a pair of shimmering green coveralls and a thick black belt.

The Grinning Man usually visits quiet towns known for their safety and tranquillity, and his arrival in the neighborhood is often followed by a marked increase in violence. Unexplained abductions and assaults are frequently attributed to this entity, and his presence seems to heighten tensions among a town's citizens, resulting in a dramatic increase in bar fights, murders, muggings, and general ill will.

Like many monsters, the Grinning Man particularly enjoys tormenting children. He often lurks near fences, behind walls, or in the shadows until a child unwittingly approaches him. As the carefree youngster nears, the Grinning Man suddenly steps from his hiding place and stands stock-still, grinning madly. His abrupt appearance, wicked facial expression, and intent stare frighten witnesses to near hysteria. The being has also been known to levitate and peer into second-story windows, or to manifest in the nightmares of a community's youngsters.

The Grinning Man was reported first in the suburbs of Elizabeth, New Jersey, in October 1966. For several weeks, unusual incidents of violence in and around the neighborhood sparked fear in the hearts of the community's children. Then, on the night of October 11, this palpable fear manifested when two boys spied a large man standing behind a fence near the turnpike. This attracted the children's attention because the man was standing in a largely inaccessible area wedged between the large fence and a steep embankment. The boys paused for a moment and took note of the figure's strange garb, but when the Grinning Man smiled wickedly, they wisely decided to flee. Later that night, the entity pursued a middle-aged man into a quiet street for no apparent reason. All three witnesses were impressed by the man's great size and disturbed by his continuous grin.

When these first encounters with the Grinning Man were reported, authorities speculated that the individual was a motorist whose car had broken down on the turnpike. However, ufologists investigating the case could find no reports of a disabled car along the turnpike that night, nor were footprints discovered on the embankment.

Late in 1966, the Grinning Man left New Jersey and was spotted numerous times in Provincetown, Massachusetts. He remained in New England until well into 1967, then moved south again. Throughout 1968, the Grinning Man visited Delaware County in New York, where he was seen running at amazing speeds and effortlessly vaulting wide ditches and tall fences.

Since 1968, the Grinning Man seems to have found a permanent home once again in New Jersey, where he is noted for terrorizing small children and teenagers with his wide, cracked grin before disappearing into the night. He has never been identified, but many ufologists still hold to the notion that he is a visiting alien, although there is little evidence to support this—or any other—theory about the monster's origins.

Like the **Flatwoods Monster** and **Mothman,** the Grinning Man seems to have an affinity for areas experiencing a number of UFO reports. Although probably not an extraterrestrial himself, the Grinning Man may be curious about alien life or enjoy the fear generated by UFO sightings. To spy the Grinning Man, plan to visit cities and towns inundated with recent UFO activity, especially those sections of New Jersey where such phenomena occur.

As is the case with **Bogeymen,** it is wise to interview children and teenagers while searching for the Grinning Man. Youths will often know a great deal about this monster, including details of recent sightings and encounters. Be gentle and persistent in your questioning, however, as children frequently avoid discussing the Grinning Man because they are so terrified of his powers. Many commonly believe that the Grinning Man will somehow realize he has been betrayed and will punish children who talk about him by giving them cruel and frightening nightmares. Adults are also subject to this torture. After sighting the Grinning Man, be prepared to experience weeks of restless sleep, your dreams punctuated by the Grinning Man's leering visage.

THE HOOK

VITAL STATISTICS

DISTINGUISHING FEATURES: Large, sharp hook replacing right hand

HEIGHT: 6'5"

WEIGHT: 200 lbs

RANGE AND HABITAT: Any lonely stretch of road

POPULATION SIZE: One

DIET: Omnivore

BEHAVIOR: The Hook has one goal: stalk, terrify, and brutally murder teens.

SOURCE: Urban legend

ENCOUNTERING THE HOOK:

The Hook is a maniacal sociopath who has been reported in virtually every portion of the United States and many parts of Canada. He is described as a large, overbearing fiend who delights in causing misery and death. In an accident long ago, he lost his right hand, but it has since been replaced by a large, vicious hook that he uses to gut his victims. Like many monsters, the Hook prefers to terrorize and murder children and teenagers, especially those parked along lovers' lanes on dark and stormy nights.

The Hook's origins are unknown, but reports about him follow one of several familiar patterns. The most famous encounter with the Hook occurred years ago, shortly after the maniac escaped from an insane asylum during a thunderstorm. A couple driving along a de-serted road at night heard a news report about the escape, and minutes later, their car ran out of gas. They came to a stop beneath a large tree, and the boyfriend offered to brave the storm to find help. Before slipping from the car, he urged his companion to lock the car's doors and forbade her to open them unless she heard three knocks on the roof, which would be the signal that he had returned.

Hours passed and the girl became more and more concerned. Finally, she was relieved to hear three knocks on the roof of the car, but her relief disappeared as the knocks continued steadily. Terrified, the girl crawled into the backseat and hid until morning, the rappings continuing until daybreak.

When authorities arrived at dawn, they helped the girl from the car and led her toward a waiting police cruiser. They urged her not to look back toward the stranded car, but these warnings only enticed the girl to turn her head. The sight that greeted her was gruesome indeed: her butchered boyfriend dangled from the branches of the large tree at the side of the road. He had been brutally ripped open from clavicle to groin. The knocks she had heard throughout the night were caused by her boyfriend's shoes as they lightly kicked the roof of the car when the wind pushed his lifeless form.

After a string of similar murders, the Hook began to attack couples in romantic trysts. Sometimes such assaults occurred in homes, but more often they took place along lovers' lanes. In at least one instance, a boyfriend and girlfriend parked at a local makeout point heard of the Hook's activities over the radio, became terrified at the prospect of an encounter with the killer, and promptly headed home. When the chivalrous boyfriend stepped from the car and rounded the vehicle to open his date's door, he was horrified to discover a bloody hook dangling from the handle of the passenger door.

The Hook has also been known to hide in the backseats of vehicles, especially those occupied by lone women. On occasion, he has raided summer camps and slashed through a collection of camp counselors, or murdered baby-sitters in full view of their terrified charges. He has also been reported on college campuses, at ski resorts, and on beaches. Clearly, wherever there are young people to slaughter, the Hook can be found.

Because of his relatively free access to all areas of North America, the Hook is difficult to track or corner. Except in legend, he rarely remains in an area after committing a murder, preferring to move on to communities that have not yet heard of his atrocious deeds. A man with a huge hook for a hand is fairly conspicuous, and yet there have been no reports of such a man being observed during daylight hours; therefore, it can be assumed that the Hook is completely nocturnal. His other habits remain undisclosed.

The most reliable method for spotting the Hook is to wait along secluded roads at night. Bring along teenagers to act as bait while you hide in the bushes and watch for the Hook's approach.

Although strong, bloodthirsty, and relentless, the Hook's most dangerous attribute is, of course, the curved hook projecting from the stump of his right arm. With this weapon, he can perform every mutilation imaginable.

THE MAD GASSER OF MATTOON

VITAL STATISTICS

DISTINGUISHING FEATURES: Gaunt face, black costume, and futuristic helmet

HEIGHT: About 6'

WEIGHT: Approximately 190 lbs

RANGE AND HABITAT: Mattoon, Illinois, and other areas across the continent

POPULATION SIZE: One

DIET: Unknown

BEHAVIOR: One of the most enigmatic of all monsters, the Mad Gasser enjoys exposing unwitting humans to a sickly sweet gas, which can cause extreme nausea and temporary paralysis.

SOURCE: Fortean studies, urban legend

ENCOUNTERING THE MAD GASSER OF MATTOON:

Few mysteries investigated by monsterologists are as puzzling as the case of the Mad Gasser of Mattoon. A mysterious figure that delights in sending toxic fumes into unsuspecting homes during the hours after midnight, the Gasser first achieved widespread recognition among monsterologists on August 31, 1944, when several residents of sleepy Mattoon, Illinois, awoke feeling violently ill. In the two weeks that followed, almost thirty people exhibited symptoms of exposure, including severe bouts of vomiting, extreme weakness, and partial paralysis. Fainting and respiratory difficulties were also commonly experienced.

Those exposed to concentrated amounts of the gas, which moves in blue fingers and has a sickening sweet odor, suffered the most severe symptoms. Eleven-year-old Glenda Hendershott was found unconscious in her bedroom after she was subjected to a toxic cloud on September 6, 1944. The day before, Beulah Cordes and her husband discovered a wet white cloth on their front porch, and when Beulah inhaled the fumes from the drenched rag, she was afflicted by instant paralysis below the knees, uncontrollable vomiting, and excessive swelling of the lips and face. Mrs. Cordes suffered from these symptoms for over two hours.

During the 1944 attacks, the most harmful effects of the gas were short-lived, lasting anywhere from thirty to ninety minutes. However, long-term effects, including a parched mouth and throat, burned lips, and a hacking cough, lasted for weeks in many instances.

After the first round of illnesses, local authorities made several attempts to discover the source of the toxic fumes. Homes were inspected for gas leaks, but none could be found. The investigators had few leads and even fewer theories regarding the sudden sickness sweeping Mattoon until several nights after the onset of the epidemic, when witnesses spotted a strangely garbed individual creeping near the windows of the afflicted.

FPL

was released. Detectives did manage to collect a few pieces of physical evidence from the crime scenes, including the gas-soaked rag found on the Cordes porch. At the Cordes residence, the police also stumbled across an empty lipstick tube and a skeleton key. Neither item, however, established the Gasser's identity.

Meanwhile, the Mad Gasser's attacks continued and public outrage mounted. Armed mobs tried in vain to hunt down the culprit. The FBI made quiet inquiries and conducted a short investigation, but the agents were also foiled by the Mad Gasser, and their top scientists could not identify the gas he used.

By mid-September, the Gasser was prying loose windows, cutting holes in screens, and pushing on doors in attempts to enter the homes of his victims. In every case, he was easily frightened away by screaming residents, but the escalating nature of his assaults drove the public to a heightened state of terror.

Exasperated and desperate, local authorities tried to mollify the public and the press by offering improbable theories. The first of these was that the gas was actually carbon tetrachloride, inadvertently released into the winds by the nearby Atlas Imperial Diesel Engine Company. This theory fell flat when it was discovered that tetrachloride was present at the Atlas plant only in the fire extinguishers.

The Gasser's attacks eventually ceased and the phantom left Mattoon as quietly as he had arrived. When it was clear the attacks had stopped and the panic subsided, frustrated

Based on information gathered from first-hand descriptions of the phantom, the Mad Gasser is a tall and haggard humanoid. He prefers to wear a skin-tight dark suit and a large gas mask, though he has also been known to sport a silver suit and a metallic helmet as well.

After the Mad Gasser was informally identified as an adult human male, Mattoon police searched the area for derelicts and escaped mental patients. Eventually, they happened upon a small shack that may have functioned as the Gasser's hideout. A single arrest was made, but the suspect passed a lie detector test and authorities attributed the rash of sicknesses to hoaxers and mass hysteria. The mainstream press accepted this theory, and the Mad Gasser almost became a footnote in the annals of monsterology.

Fortunately, ardent researchers managed to compile more evidence of the Mad Gasser's physical existence. It was discovered that the phantom had been active in other areas of the country before he arrived in Mattoon. Botetourt County, Virginia, was haunted by the Mad Gasser, or someone almost identical, from December 1933 to January 1934. And on February 1, 1944, just a few months before the Mattoon incidents, three people in Coatesville, Pennsylvania, were exposed to a sweet-smelling gas. All three died and the gas was never identified.

In addition, it seems that the Mad Gasser has remained active since leaving Mattoon as well. In 1961, during the Christmas service at a Baptist church in Houston, Texas, a sweet-smelling gas rapidly filled the building, forcing all the worshipers from the church. At least one hundred people suffered from severe headaches, profuse sweating, terrible nausea, and painful vomiting. Eight of the victims were hospitalized, but the gas remained unidentified. In 1997, an office building in Fort Worth, Texas, had to be evacuated on several occasions after workers were suddenly overcome by mysterious fumes. Again, dozens of those exposed were taken to hospitals for treatment of severe nausea, and the gas has never been identified. This pattern has been repeated on dozens of occasions in numerous office buildings throughout America.

Today, the Mad Gasser only makes rare appearances, and his activities are difficult to document as so many authorities readily accuse victims of suffering from hysteria. Monsterologists should watch local and national news for stories about mysterious deaths or sicknesses involving sweet-smelling gases.

Whenever investigating a bizarre death, regardless of whether you suspect the involvement of the Mad Gasser, always wear a gas mask to prevent possible exposure to toxic fumes. Similar precautions should be taken when interviewing witnesses involved in possible Mad Gasser sightings or encounters, as the gas may still cling to their clothing or skin.

In the unlikely event of a face-to-face encounter with the Mad Gasser, attempt to communicate with the figure. Ask questions about his identity, background, and motives. He will probably avoid answering, but observant researchers might glean information from the Gasser's mannerisms, tone of voice, and behavior when pressed with such inquiries.

Remain cautious, however, as the Mad Gasser has strived for many decades to keep his identity concealed and will be offended by anyone who seems to be nearing the truth. Be wary of any sudden movements, as the Gasser's slightest gesture could release a cloud of deadly gas.

PHANTOM FELINES

VITAL STATISTICS

DISTINGUISHING FEATURES: Abnormal size and intangibility

LENGTH: 4–9'

WEIGHT: 60–600 lbs

RANGE AND HABITAT: Various areas across the country, but most often centered around Illinois

POPULATION SIZE: Unknown

DIET: Carnivore

BEHAVIOR: Seemingly normal lions, pumas, and panthers, the Phantom Felines appear in urban areas before numerous witnesses and then vanish inexplicably. Many also attack humans and murder animals.

SOURCE: Urban legend, Fortean studies, cryptozoology

ENCOUNTERING THE PHANTOM FELINES: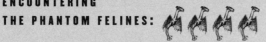

Cryptozoology is a confounding science, and dedicated cryptozoologists must contend with the bizarre, the inexplicable, and the unbelievable. Such is the case with the Phantom Felines, seemingly normal animals that have the ability to appear suddenly, become intangible, and vanish without a trace.

Phantom Felines are large cats that routinely manifest in rural and urban areas alike, most often in the Great Lakes states, where they appear before dozens of astonished witnesses before disappearing again. They come in many varieties, but the most common Phantom Felines resemble African lions, black panthers, or pumas. While such animals exist in the real world, Phantom Felines are differentiated from "normal" large cats because such cat species do not thrive on the continent. In fact, the only large cat native to North America is the puma (panther, cougar, catamount, or mountain lion), which is considered extinct throughout the regions where Phantom Felines commonly appear. In Illinois, where Phantom Felines are most abundant, the puma has been extinct for over one hundred years.

Phantom Felines leave behind few footprints, hair samples, or other physical evidence, and they seemingly cannot be captured, caught on film, or killed. In addition, they are often inordinately aggressive and will butcher livestock in great numbers.

The most famous Phantom Feline is arguably Nellie the Lion, a monster that appeared in central Illinois in July 1917. After an initial sighting in Camargo, Nellie soon moved to Decatur, where she attacked Thomas Gulliet, leaving him with minor injuries. Gulliet's terrifying encounter was followed by a month of consistent and reliable sightings, prompting roughly three hundred men to set out in search of the beast.

By late July, Nellie had become more

aggressive. On July 29, the lion charged a car and collided with the side of the vehicle before the frightened occupants could escape. Nellie continued to terrorize Decatur for several weeks, then the beast simply vanished. Investigators checked with local zoos and circuses, a common practice in all cases of Phantom Feline activity, but they found no indication that Nellie was merely an escaped lion.

While monstrous cats like Nellie have been spotted across the continent, Decatur, Illinois, is often identified as the nexus of Phantom Feline activity. Other areas experience short-lived Phantom Feline incursions, but mysterious cats manifest within Decatur and the surrounding communities more consistently and in larger numbers than anywhere else in the world.

In 1970, Phantom Felines virtually invaded Illinois, but the onslaught began in Decatur. Early in the year, a black cougar roamed near Decatur's Macon Seed Company, tearing through electric fences and leaving huge footprints. Shortly thereafter, Illinois became gripped in a Phantom Feline frenzy: by April, giant black cats were seen in Cairo and Olive Branch. In May, a maned lion turned up in and then vanished from Roscoe; and on September 19, a group of six people traveling in a car near Pana were astonished to find a large gray puma running alongside the vehicle.

Throughout December 1970, members of

> Now and then, rural communities in Illinois have a panther scare that reduces normal, thinking individuals into children that are afraid to step out into the dark.
>
> —Illinois Department of Conservation

the Clarence Runyon family reported seeing a large black panther and her cub in their fields, just outside Decatur. The Runyons had lost over forty chickens from their farm during the previous summer, thefts the phantom panther may have committed.

As evidenced by the attack on the Runyon farm, Phantom Felines frequently feed on livestock and farm animals, sometimes exacting a heavy toll. Champaign County, Illinois, was plagued by a brutal Phantom Feline in 1963, a creature that killed numerous farm animals, including dozens of chickens. A posse of three hundred men formed to capture the monstrous beast, but it eluded this group with ease. The cat's hunters did find large feline tracks, and sightings of the creature continued well into 1964 before dissipating. In June 1967, a mysterious mountain lion claimed the lives of over twenty sheep in Decatur.

One of the most bloodthirsty Phantom Felines appeared in Ohio's Richland Township in the spring of 1977, where it was credited with the deaths of over 140 sheep, dozens of fowl and other birds, and at least a few dogs and cats. Finally, a group composed of two local police officers and two county officials cornered the beast in a field just a few miles from Lafayette. The men, all armed with bright flashlights, surrounded the monster, but the beast remained calm until its hunters neared within twenty yards. As the men closed in, the phantom cat suddenly sprinted into the woods, where it disappeared forever.

The earliest recorded Phantom Feline attack on a human took place in December 1877 in Indiana. One evening, Mary Crane and a gentleman companion were walking a path near the village of Rising Sun. While passing through a heavily wooded area, they heard a frightening shriek emanating from the nearby trees. When Mary looked in the direction of the noise, she observed a huge lion with radiant eyes and a "tail as long as a door." The monster, described as the size of a large calf, promptly gave chase. Mary's companion bolted, leaving the poor woman behind.

The monster knocked Mary to the ground and tore into her dress, at which point Mary fainted. Fortunately, the sound of approaching rescuers caused the monster to dart into the forest before it could injure the woman. The area was thoroughly searched the following day, and a half-mile-long trail of six-inch footprints was discovered, but the monster was never seen again.

While Mary Crane's assailant was unsuccessful in its attack, other witnesses have not fared as well. When Ed Moorman was assaulted in June 1962 near Indiana's Monument City, his face was badly lacerated. Luckily, he managed to chase the beast away by firing his rifle into the air, but the cat returned to Moorman's farm later that month and killed ten of his pigs. When Moorman inspected his dead hogs, he found that the monster had punctured their necks and drained their blood before gorging on their hearts and livers.

Because of their aggressive nature, Phantom Felines are frequently hunted by humans.

Loren Coleman

Phantom Feline print collected from Durham, Maine, in 1973.

Loren Coleman

Head of the Meadow Beach, a well-known Phantom Feline haunt in Cape Cod, Massachusetts.

However, they have an uncanny ability to avoid capture and injury. In 1823, two marksmen in Russellville, Kentucky, cornered a large phantom tiger and fired at least twelve rounds into the creature from a distance of not less than fifty yards. The lion appeared unharmed by the attack and slowly wandered away before vanishing completely.

The 1950s provided a menagerie of Phantom Felines that could not be killed. Herman Belyea took an ax to a huge phantom cat in New Brunswick, Canada, on November 22, 1951, but the weapon seemed to pass through the monster. On October 25, 1955, game warden Paul G. Myers of Decatur shot a black panther on the run, but he could not lo-cate the body nor did he find blood smears or any other indication that the cat had been wounded. Two patrolmen in Atlanta, Georgia, met with similar failure when they encountered a black panther in April 1958. When the giant cat charged the two men, they completely emptied their revolvers into the animal. Silently, the phantom cat raced past the two astonished men and vanished around a corner.

While researchers have yet to procure a cadaver for study, monsterologists do have a small number of Phantom Feline footprints, which range from four to six inches in length. Unfortunately, such prints often baffle most investigators because they are vastly different from the footprints of normal large cats. The most common discrepancy is the appearance of distinct claw marks. Most cats walk with their claws retracted, and thus their prints do not exhibit such claw marks, but Phantom Felines seem to walk with their claws extended. Tracks found in Urbana, Ohio (1962) and Champaign County, Illinois (1963) followed this pattern, as have many other Phantom Feline footprints.

Phantom Feline trails are further confusing because, like the mystery cats themselves, they are likely to disappear and reappear without explanation. Sometimes a trail will stop at an obstacle but continue on the other side, making it seem as though the large cat simply passed through the fence, wall, or other obstacle without pause.

Phantom Felines continue to crop up across the continent today. Northern California; Decatur, Illinois; rural areas of Ohio and Indiana; and even the swamplands of the South have been invaded by Phantom Felines during the 1990s.

A Phantom Feline investigation can begin almost anywhere there has been a recent sighting, but Decatur, the heart of the Phantom Feline territory, is always a good place to start your search. Seek the Phantom Felines in August, as this is the time of year recording the highest number of sightings. Conversely, avoid

> We'll never catch them.
>
> —Cryptozoologist Ivan T. Sanderson

looking for the mystery cats during May, a month boasting few Phantom Feline reports. These monsters might be lured into the open with live bait, such as sheep, cows, or goats. Raw meat might also attract the beasts.

While finding the Phantom Felines may not prove inordinately difficult, be careful when actually encountering them. If you stumble upon a mystery cat, remain calm and avoid sudden movements. Cats enjoy attacking targets that are in motion, so do not turn and flee; instead, slowly back away from the creature. Once a considerable distance has been established, you may attempt photographs or video recordings.

During an encounter, always be observant of the Phantom Feline's behavior. A cat that growls, nervously twitches its tail, stares intently, or bares its fangs may be preparing to lunge. In a related vein, Phantom Felines have been known to hunt in packs, and you must therefore be wary of surprise attacks from behind.

After a Phantom Feline encounter, immediately contact all local zoos, circuses, and private collectors to ensure that a large cat has not recently escaped from captivity. Finally, never attempt to capture a Phantom Feline. Such endeavors are useless given the cat's amazing abilities and powers, but they can enrage the animal to the point of murder.

PHANTOM KANGAROOS

VITAL STATISTICS

DISTINGUISHING FEATURES: Abnormal size, odd behavior, glowing eyes, and intangibility

HEIGHT: 3'5"–5'5"

WEIGHT: 150 lbs

RANGE AND HABITAT: Various areas across the country

POPULATION SIZE: Unknown

DIET: Omnivore

BEHAVIOR: Phantom Kangaroos seemingly delight in appearing suddenly, astonishing witnesses, and then vanishing. They are often brutish and will not hesitate to attack humans and domestic animals.

SOURCE: Urban legend, Fortean studies, cryptozoology

ENCOUNTERING THE PHANTOM KANGAROOS: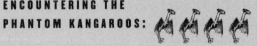

Like the **Phantom Felines,** Phantom Kangaroos are bizarre manifestations that cannot be completely explained and are thus pursued by cryptozoologists. Specifically, the Phantom Kangaroos, or mystery kangaroos, appear suddenly in areas that are clearly unnatural surroundings for the Australian marsupial. They have been spotted hopping through suburban backyards, rummaging through trashcans in urban alleyways, and wandering rural roads. While they have been encountered across the country, they are most active in Illinois and Wisconsin. They cannot be injured, can manifest suddenly, and often vanish without a trace.

At first glance, Phantom Kangaroos are almost identical to normal kangaroos. However, upon closer study, many physical and behavioral differences between the two become apparent. Phantom Kangaroos are exceptionally large and often act aggressively when confronted by humans. While it is true that all kangaroos can be dangerous if molested or annoyed, Phantom Kangaroos seem to *enjoy* attacking other creatures. Most distressing are reports of Phantom Kangaroos killing dogs, cats, rabbits, birds, and other small animals for no apparent reason.

Phantom Kangaroos are also much faster than normal kangaroos. In general, kangaroos can reach speeds of twenty-five miles per hour, but this pace can only be maintained for a short time. Phantom Kangaroos, in contrast, have been known to cover fifty miles in

> There is a strong possibility that the kangaroos are not real animals in the flesh-and-blood aspect of the word, but rather a transitional phenomenon —something only temporarily real.
>
> —Loren Coleman,
> *Mysterious America*

under a half hour and are capable of clearing huge fences and walls with little effort.

Since the late 1800s, Phantom Kangaroos have been hopping across the continent. The first reliably reported kangaroo sighting occurred on June 12, 1899, in Richmond, Wisconsin. The kangaroo dissipated before local authorities could corner the animal.

In January 1934, a particularly vicious Phantom Kangaroo appeared in South Pittsburg, Tennessee, where it was first spotted by the Reverend W. J. Hancock. That very day, a host of chickens and one large dog were killed and partially consumed, and another witness spied the kangaroo leaping away from a farm with a large sheep under each arm. Several other credible witnesses came forward before the mystery animal left Tennessee.

In 1957, the most famous Phantom Kangaroos leapt into Coon Rapids, Minnesota. The animal was first noticed by the children of Coon Rapids, who lovingly referred to the beast as the Big Bunny. The anomalous animal was encountered dozens of times throughout the following decade, and one woman even spotted a pair of kangas. Unfortunately, in 1967 the Big Bunny left Coon Rapids forever, leaving behind no evidence of its ten-year visit.

On October 18, 1974, hundreds of people on the northwest side of Chicago spotted an aggressive Phantom Kangaroo. Police officers eventually cornered the creature in an alley, but they backed away when it began kicking viciously. Before the officers could gather their

> People don't believe you when you see things like that. I definitely know it was a kangaroo.
>
> —Officer John Orr of Plano, Illinois, after seeing a mystery marsupial while off duty on November 1, 1974

courage to approach the animal again, it leapt over a fence and vanished. The puzzled authorities questioned local zoos, but no kangaroo escapes were reported.

In 1980, a Phantom Kangaroo took up residence in San Francisco's Golden Gate Park, and in 1981 the mysterious marsupials invaded the Appalachian, Ozark, and Rocky Mountain ranges. Phantom Kangaroos also appeared in Tulsa, Oklahoma, in 1981, where one of the monsters was reportedly killed on August 31. According to local authorities, a man was driving his truck down a darkened road in Tulsa when he suddenly spied a kangaroo in his headlights. He swerved to miss the animal, then collided with a second kangaroo standing on the side of the road. The anonymous motorist loaded the kanga carcass into his truck and proceeded to the nearest diner, where he showed the body to Tulsa police officers and a waitress. After finishing his meal, the man hopped into his truck and vanished forever into the darkness. This is the only known report of a Phantom Kangaroo actually being injured.

In the past two decades, kangas have continued to appear across the continent, popping up in Hollywood and other cities in California, as well as areas of Oklahoma, Ohio, and Indiana. They also make repeated and regular appearances in Chicago as well.

Monsterologists intrigued by the Phantom Kangaroos must watch a variety of media sources, especially small local papers and radio stations, for reports of kangaroo sightings.

A Phantom Kangaroo photographed at Waukesha, Wisconsin, on April 24, 1978.

Upon learning of a Phantom Kangaroo appearance, you should arrive at the scene quickly, as most of these animals disappear within days of their first appearance.

To actually spot a Phantom Kangaroo, the city must be scoured on foot. Researchers should ensure that all alleyways are thoroughly investigated as well, for Phantom Kangaroos often delve into trash cans and Dumpsters in search of food. Phantom Kangaroos might also be lured with such kangaroo-tempting treats as carrots or dry dog food.

If you actually spot a Phantom Kangaroo or interview others who have encountered these monsters, be certain to contact all neighboring zoos, circuses, and exotic-pet owners within several hundred miles in search of an escaped kangaroo. This is a standard procedure when dealing with any mystery animal. While there has never been a sighting of a Phantom Kangaroo that was later identified as an escaped kangaroo, monsterologists must still rule out this possibility before proceeding further.

Once encountered, Phantom Kangaroos should never be cornered. A hostile kangaroo can use its powerful legs to break your ribs, and its sharp claws can open extremely deep wounds. In addition, kangaroos are well-known for their ability to box, and Phantom Kangaroos often take swings at their pursuers. An angry kangaroo will often growl and occasionally emit a high-pitched shriek. Immediately flee from any Phantom Kangaroo exhibiting such behavior.

Other Enigmatic Entities

Although almost all monsters fit well into other categories in this book, a few creatures simply cannot be categorized because they seem so bizarre or out of place. Below is a partial list of such beings.

- **The Phantom:** A cryptic, darkly garbed man over eighteen feet tall originally encountered near Berwick, Nova Scotia, in April 1969. He can travel at speeds in excess of twenty miles per hour, and his sudden appearance has been known to cause traffic jams as curiosity-seekers rush to the area where he has most recently been sighted.

- **Phantom Crocodilians:** Alligators, crocodiles, and caimans appear in odd environments throughout North America. Like Phantom Felines and Phantom Kangaroos, these large reptiles are spotted numerous times and then vanish. Most recently, an alligator appeared in San Francisco's Mountain Lake in 1997.

- **Snallygaster:** A vicious and invisible Bogeyman in Maryland who steals and consumes children.

- **The St. Louis Thing:** A bizarre hybrid described as a "half-man, half-woman" entity with wild hair. It was first reported in St. Louis, Missouri, in 1963, where it was said to live in an abandoned building and haunt a seldom-used bus station.

Loren Coleman

Mysterious alligators seem to turn up everywhere: this one was pulled from a river in Stilwell, Kansas, in March 1979.

SO YOU WANT TO BE A MONSTEROLOGIST?

NOW THAT YOU have completed this book, you are ready to begin your career as a monsterologist.

However, there are still several skills you should develop before seeking out monsters of any kind.

Before Setting Out

You should be in fair physical condition and have a rudimentary knowledge of hiking and swimming. Tracking, horseback riding, wilderness survival, and crisis management are also valuable talents. You should learn to cast footprints using plaster and be able to identify different types of hair, feces, and tracks. An understanding of local customs and dialects is useful when visiting new regions of the continent.

You should also determine which creatures are most suitable to your current level of experience. Novice monsterologists should begin with beasts known to appear frequently and to lack aggressive tendencies. As you gain experience, you can begin questing after more dangerous and elusive monsters.

After you have selected your quarry, carefully choose the time of year to begin your search. The month of May should officially be recognized as the monsterologist's holiday from field study, as almost all of North America's monsters seem to disappear at this time of year. There is a marked decrease in sightings of sea serpents, lake monsters, **Phantom Felines,** and giant birds (such as the **Thunderbird** and the **Piasa Birds**). August, in contrast, is a particularly good month for monster sightings. Once you have arranged your travel schedule, plan to visit the areas where the monster has most often appeared. Any site of recent encounters is an especially auspicious place to start a search.

This site in the Hockomock (Devil) Swamp, Massachusetts, yields a high number of UFO and hairy humanoid reports, and is a good place for beginning monsterologists to start their search for monsters.

Interviewing Witnesses

At the scene of a monster sighting or known habitat, the first step in your field research is to interview witnesses and discuss the creature with knowledgeable locals. To conduct a thorough interview, contact witnesses within hours after a sighting. It is also wise to schedule at least one additional meeting a few weeks after your first interview, in the event that the witness recalls additional information. Also, in each interview, follow a detailed questionnaire, such as the sample list of questions provided in appendix A. Question a group of witnesses individually, but ensure that no one involved feels faced with unfair skepticism or interrogation.

It is also necessary to consider the type of witness to a monster sighting. An observer's educational background, composure, memory, reasoning capabilities, and physical and psychological condition should be determined before the accuracy of that individual's description can be gauged. Be sure to spend at least a portion of each interview discussing these topics.

Entering the Field

Once you have conducted any possible interviews and learned as much about the local monster as possible, you are ready to enter the field in search of the creature. While in the field, follow these important guidelines:

- **Be patient.** Documenting monsters requires long stints lying in wait for the creature to appear. Some cryptozoologists spend their whole lives staked out on the shores of Lake Champlain collecting a handful of sightings of **Champ.** Other explorers have traversed the Pacific Northwest for decades in their search for **Bigfoot.** Of course, knowing specific information about your quarry, such as the type of terrain the monster frequents, its favorite foods, and the time of day or year that it most often appears, can greatly increase your likelihood of an encounter. You can gather many of these facts through reading this book, but while the information supplied by this work is intended to be accurate, it would be impossible and foolish to *guarantee* that the information supplied will result in an encounter with a monster. Any crypto-zoologist will confess that, for the most part, spotting a monster is largely a matter of being in the right place at the right time.

- **Use caution.** Some monstrous environs, such as the vast Canadian wilderness and sections of New York City, can present threats to even the most seasoned explorer. Exposure to the elements, natural wildlife, and other "mundane" dangers should be a constant concern. Furthermore, the majority of creatures in this book are dangerous and often deadly. It is up to you to exercise caution and common sense: neither the author nor the publisher of this book may be held responsible for bodily injuries, deaths, or psychological trauma resulting from information provided within these pages.

- **Never travel alone.** Traveling in small groups provides more eyes and ears and affords some protection, as most monsters are reluctant to attack groups of people. Most important, if you do encounter your quarry, your recounting of the event will only be truly believable if bolstered by the testimony of at least one other person.

However, limit the size of your group to five individuals, as a larger pack can more easily alert a monster to your presence, and never travel with dogs or children.

- **Have fun.** Although often a serious endeavor, monsterology should also be enjoyable. Long stints of somber research can result in burnout and disillusionment. Savor the wonders of nature while in the field. When visiting new areas in search of monsters, take some time to visit local landmarks and attractions. Most important, thoroughly immerse yourself in any monster encounter you experience: the memories of this momentary glimpse into the unknown will remain with you forever.

Collecting Physical Evidence

Although you may not spot a monster while in the field, you will probably stumble across physical evidence, including hair samples, footprints, or photographs.

Hair samples and monster feces are best collected with tweezers or gloves and stored in airtight plastic containers, such as plastic Baggies. Blood, urine, tissue samples, and saliva should be sealed in airtight vials, frozen as soon as possible, and packed in dry ice. Avoid touching all physical evidence with your bare hands, as bacteria or flakes of skin can contaminate your finds, and always hand-deliver your discoveries to a notable laboratory for analysis. Do not trust such evidence to government institutions, and always demand a receipt.

When you stumble across footprints, first photograph them from a variety of angles. If you find a sety of tracks, photograph them in their order of appearance to show the move-

Loren Coleman

Something large and bipedal allegedly made these tracks in Wisconsin's Deltox Swamp.

ments of the monster. Whenever photographing any tracks, place a ruler next to the prints
to show their size accurately.

After photographing monster tracks, attempt to make plaster casts of the prints. A
casting plaster called Ultracal 30, which can be
found in most building-supply stores, is generally considered the best product for making
such casts. Allow Ultracal 30 to set for at least
thirty minutes before attempting to remove

the print. Footprints are most successfully pulled from dried mud.

If possible, carry two cameras into the field loaded with black-and-white and color film, respectively. While color photos are the most impressive, black-and-white photographs tend to capture many monsters with much greater definition. Routinely check your battery levels, light meter, and focus, and travel with the lens cap removed. When a monster first appears, snap several photographs quickly, then stop to focus before clicking another round of shots. Have the photographs developed by someone you trust, preferably a close relative who has a home darkroom. Always make multiple prints and keep negatives hidden.

Never send any physical evidence through the mail or entrust it to someone you do not know well. Physical evidence, like the monsters themselves, has a tendency to disappear inexplicably, so guard your finds well.

During the Encounter

When you actually come face-to-face with a monster, you may be overwhelmed by the sight and forget all you have learned in previous sections of this book. In general, the following advice should help you emerge from the encounter unscathed.

- **Keep your distance.** Unless the monster has exhibited extremely benign and friendly behavior, do not approach the creature. Almost all monsters tend to attack if they feel threatened or cornered.

- **Remain still and silent.** Most monsters react to loud noises and sudden movements by either vanishing or attacking.

- **Be observant.** Make mental notes of everything you see, hear, and smell during the encounter. Immediately after the sighting, write down as much as possible. Also, scour the area for physical evidence.

- **Be humane.** If you are interested in becoming a dedicated monsterologist, you must shun the methods of the monster hunter and embrace more benign means for spotting monsters. Specifically, devote yourself to protecting monsters rather than attempting to capture or kill them for personal gain. Remember that they have a right to live unhindered, and most are already endangered.

A Final Word

Even if you return from countless monster expeditions without physical evidence or the tale of an encounter, you can still consider yourself a monsterologist. True monsterologists, regardless of achievements in the field, are driven by awe, curiosity, and a fascination with the unknown. And, most important, they respect monsters for what they are: strange and wondrous aberrations that shatter our tidy conceptions of reality and force us to look at the world in a new way. As long as you recognize that monsters free us from stale routine and return to us a sense of wonder lost with the end of childhood, your search for monsters has been a success.

Loren Coleman

A resident of Decatur, Illinois, illustrates proper techniques for safely spotting a monster—in this case, phantom alligators.

APPENDIX A: SAMPLE QUESTIONNAIRE

It is important that you interview each monster witness with the aid of a detailed questionnaire to ensure consistency and receive the most thorough description possible. Following is a sample list of questions.

Sample Questionnaire

1. Witness data:
   Name, age, and sex:
   Occupation:

2. Describe the details of the sighting, including:
   Time, date, and location of sighting:
   Terrain:
   Weather conditions:
   Duration of sighting:
   Number of witnesses:
   Number of creatures sighted:
   The distance between witness(es) and
      creature(s):

3. Describe the creature's general appearance, including:
   The size and shape of the head:
   Color, size, and shape of the eyes:
   Mouth, gills, or other breathing holes:
   Fins, legs, or other appendages:
   Any ears, horns, or other facial features:
   Hair, mane, scales, fur, or skin color and
      texture:
   Tail, if any:
   Clothing, if any:
   Claws, spikes, fangs, and other natural
      weapons:

4. Was the monster in motion?
   If so, how did it move?
   How fast, and in which direction?

5. Did the monster make any noise? If so, describe:
   Did the monster speak? If so, what did it
      say?

6. How did the monster interact with humans or animals?
   Did it attack, flee, or remain indifferent?
   Were you frightened by the monster?

7. Did the monster exhibit any special abilities or powers?

8. Do you have any physical evidence (photographs, video footage, footprints, hair samples, etc.) from the encounter?

9. Did you ingest any form of alcohol, medication, or drug prior to the sighting?

10. Are you in good physical and mental health?

11. Is this your first monster sighting? If not, describe your previous encounter(s).

For Hairy Humanoids Only

12. Did the monster appear more human or more animal-like?

13. Did it appear to be male or female?

14. Did the monster have:
   Glowing eyes?
   A terrible stench?
   An eerie cry?

For Aquatic Monsters Only

15. How close to shore was the monster observed?

16. How many parts or sections appeared above water, and how high did these extend?

For Flying Monsters Only

17. How far above the ground was the monster observed?

18. Did it have wings or fly through other means?

19. Was it more humanoid or more birdlike?

For Dwarves and Giants Only

20. How tall was the monster?

21. Did it have:
Hair?
Glowing eyes?
An oversize head?

For Cryptid Animals Only

22. What other animal(s) did the monster most resemble?

23. Did the monster behave like the animal(s) it resembles?

For Beastmen and -women Only

24. Did the monster appear more human or more animal-like?

25. Did it appear to be male or female?

26. Did it talk or attempt any form of communication?

For Supernatural Entities Only

27. Did the monster's appearance cause intense fear?

28. Have you suffered from bad luck, nightmares, or other afflictions since sighting the monster?

29. Did it talk or attempt any form of communication?

For Enigmatic Entities Only

30. Did the monster appear suddenly and vanish inexplicably?

31. Did it leave behind any trace evidence (a stench, footprints, hair, etc.)?

32. Did it talk or attempt any form of communication?

APPENDIX B: STATE-PROVINCE LISTING

Below is a list of the monsters contained in *The Field Guide to North American Monsters* as they appear by U.S. state or Canadian province. Those few monsters with unlimited ranges, such as Vampires, are not included and should be considered cross-continental.

Alabama: Bigfoot, Cattle Mutilators, Gatormen, Giant Gators, Phantom Kangaroos, Zombies

Alaska: Ahkiyyinni, Bigfoot, Iliamna Lake Monsters, Terichik, Thunderbird, Wi-lu-gho-yuk, Woolly Mammoth

Alberta: Beaver Women, Bigfoot, Cannibal Babe, Cattle Mutilators, Fur-Bearing Trout, Thunderbird

The Arctic: Ahkiyyinni, Terichik, Wendigo, Wi-lu-gho-yuk, Woolly Mammoth

Arizona: Big Owl, Bigfoot, Cactus Cat, Canteen Fish, Cattle Mutilators, Chupacabra, Killer Bees, La Llorona, Thunderbird

Arkansas: Bigfoot, Fouke Monster, Phantom Felines, Razorback Hog, Whitey, Zombies

British Columbia: Bigfoot, Caddy, Cattle Mutilators, Columbia River Sand Squink, Ogopogo, Thetis Lake Monster, Thunderbird, Wi-lu-gho-yuk

California: Bigfoot, Cactus Cat, Canteen Fish, Cattle Mutilators, Chupacabra, Deer Woman, Killer Bees, La Llorona, Megalodon, Penelope, Phantom Felines, Phantom Kangaroos, Thunderbird, Water Babies, Zombies

Colorado: Bigfoot, Cattle Mutilators, Chupacabra, Fur-Bearing Trout, Jackalope, Killer Bees, La Llorona, Phantom Kangaroos, Thunderbird

Connecticut: Bigfoot, Black Dog of West Peak, Black Fox of Salmon River, Gloucester Sea Serpent, Graveyard Dogs, Phantom Felines, Winsted Wildman

Delaware: Graveyard Dogs, Jersey Devil, Phantom Kangaroos

Florida: Bigfoot, Cattle Mutilators, Chupacabra, Gatormen, Giant Gators, Skunk Ape

Georgia: Bigfoot, Gatormen, Giant Gators, Graveyard Dogs, Phantom Felines, Zombies

Idaho: Bear Lake Serpent, Beaver Women, Bigfoot, Cannibal Babe, Cattle Mutilators, Jackalope, Thunderbird, Two Faces, Water Babies

Illinois: Armouchiquois, Baykok, Bigfoot, Enfield Horror, Graveyard Dogs, Mad Gasser of Mattoon, Phantom Felines, Phantom Kangaroos, Piasa Birds, Sliver Cat

Indiana: Armouchiquois, Baykok, Beast of 'Busco, Bigfoot, Cattle Mutilators, Loveland Frogmen, Phantom Felines, Phantom Kangaroos, Thunderbird

Iowa: Baykok, Bigfoot, Earwig, Fur-Bearing Trout, Sliver Cat, Thunderbird, Two Faces, Wendigo

Kansas: Bigfoot, Earwig, Phantom Kangaroos, Thunderbird

Kentucky: Bigfoot, Cattle Mutilators, Hopkinsville Goblins, Phantom Felines, Piasa Birds, Thunderbird

Louisiana: Bigfoot, Gatormen, Giant Gators, Honey Island Swamp

Monster, Jack O'Lantern, Letiche the Monster, Phantom Felines, Zombies

Maine: Bigfoot, Gloucester Sea Serpent, Graveyard Dogs, Nagumwasuck

Manitoba: Bigfoot, Sliver Cat, Thunderbird, Wendigo

Maryland: Bigfoot, Goatman, Graveyard Dogs, Jersey Devil, Thunderbird

Massachusetts: Bigfoot, Dover Demon, Gloucester Sea Serpent, Graveyard Dogs, Grinning Man, Phantom Felines

Michigan: Armouchiquois, Baykok, Bigfoot, Cattle Mutilators, Phantom Felines, Phantom Kangaroos, Serpent Woman, Sliver Cat, Thunderbird, Wendigo

Minnesota: Armouchiquois, Baykok, Bigfoot, Fur-Bearing Trout, Hodag, Minnesota Iceman, Phantom Kangaroos, Sliver Cat, Wendigo

Mississippi: Bigfoot, Gatormen, Giant Gators, Graveyard Dogs, Honey Island Swamp Monster, Phantom Felines, Piasa Birds, Zombies

Missouri: Bigfoot, Graveyard Dogs, Momo, Piasa Birds, Razorback Hog, Zombies

Montana: Beaver Women, Bigfoot, Cannibal Babe, Flathead Lake Monster, Fur-Bearing Trout, Jackalope

Nebraska: Alkali Lake Monster, Bigfoot, Deer Woman, Earwig, Phantom Felines, Phantom Kangaroos, Thunderbird

Nevada: Cactus Cat, Canteen Fish, Cattle Mutilators, Chupacabra, Killer Bees, La Llorona, Penelope, Thunderbird, Water Babies

New Brunswick/Nova Scotia: Adlet, Gloucester Sea Serpent, Gougou Monster, Graveyard Dogs, Nagumwasuck, Phantom Felines, Phantom Kangaroos, Lake Utopia Monster, Wendigo

Newfoundland/Labrador: Adlet, Gougou Monster, Wendigo

New Hampshire: Bigfoot, Gloucester Sea Serpent, Graveyard Dogs

New Jersey: Bigfoot, Cattle Mutilators, Graveyard Dogs, Grinning Man, Jersey Devil

New Mexico: Big Owl, Cactus Cat, Cattle Mutilators, Chupacabra, Killer Bees, La Llorona, Thunderbird

New York: Bigfoot, Black River Monster, Champ, Deer Woman, Gloucester Sea Serpent, Graveyard Dogs, Grinning Man, Jersey Devil, Phantom Felines, Sewer Gators, Thunderbird, Zombies

North Carolina: Graveyard Dogs, Phantom Kangaroos

North Dakota: Bigfoot, Earwig, Fur-Bearing Trout, Thunderbird, Two Faces

Northwest Territories: Ahkiyyinni, Bigfoot, Terichik, Wendigo, Wi-lu-gho-yuk, Woolly Mammoth

Ohio: Armouchiquois, Bigfoot, Cattle Mutilators, Loveland Frogmen, Mothman, Orange Eyes, Phantom Felines, Phantom Kangaroos, Serpent Woman, Thunderbird

Oklahoma: Abominable Bigfoot, Cattle Mutilators, Chicken Man, Earwig, Phantom Kangaroos, Razorback Hog, Thunderbird

Ontario: Armouchiquois, Baykok, Bigfoot, Phantom Felines, Phantom Kangaroos, Serpent Woman, Sliver Cat, Wendigo

Oregon: Bigfoot, Caddy, Cattle Mutilators, Columbia River Sand Squink, Megalodon, Thunderbird, Water Babies

Pennsylvania: Bigfoot, Cattle Mutilators, Graveyard Dogs, Jersey Devil, Mad Gasser of Mattoon, Phantom Kangaroos, Squonk

Quebec: Adlet, Champ, Flatwoods Monster, Gougou Monster, Graveyard Dogs, Wendigo

Rhode Island: Bigfoot, Gloucester Sea Serpent, Graveyard Dogs

Saskatchewan: Beaver Women, Bigfoot, Cannibal Babe, Fur-Bearing Trout

South Carolina: Bigfoot, Gatormen, Giant Gators, Zombies

South Dakota: Earwig, Fur-Bearing Trout, Thunderbird, Two Faces

Tennessee: Bigfoot, Cattle Mutilators, Phantom Kangaroos, Radioactive Frogs, Zombies

Texas: Big Owl, Cattle Mutilators, Chupacabra, Killer Bees, Lake Worth Monster, La Llorona, Mad Gasser of Mattoon, Marfa Lights, Mothman, Thunderbird, Lake Zombies

Utah: Bear Lake Serpent, Cattle Mutilators, Jackalope, Killer Bees, La Llorona, Thunderbird, Water Babies

Vermont: Bigfoot, Champ, Graveyard Dogs

Virginia: Bigfoot, Graveyard Dogs, Jersey Devil, Mad Gasser of Mattoon

Washington: Bigfoot, Caddy, Cattle Mutilators, Columbia River Sand Squink, Gatormen, Megalodon, Phantom Kangaroos, Thetis Lake Monster

Washington, D.C.: Goatman, Graveyard Dogs, Phantom Felines, Zombies

West Virginia: Bigfoot, Cattle Mutilators, Flatwoods Monster, Graveyard Dogs, Mothman, Piasa Birds

Wisconsin: Armouchiquois, Baykok, Hodag, Phantom Kangaroos, Sliver Cat, Thunderbird, Wendigo

Wyoming: Beaver Women, Bigfoot, Cannibal Babe, Cattle Mutilators, Fur-Bearing Trout, Jackalope, Thunderbird

Yukon Territories: Ahkiyyinni, Bigfoot, Thunderbird, Wi-lu-gho-yuk, Woolly Mammoth

GLOSSARY OF IMPORTANT MONSTEROLOGY TERMS

Alien: An extraterrestrial.

Anthropophagus: Man-eater. (Plural: anthropophagi.)

Aura: The energy surrounding objects and individuals.

Beastmen: Humanoids with numerous animalistic features.

Carnivore: Meat-eater.

Creative taxidermy: The "art" of combining various animal parts to create monsters. For example, sailors have long concocted "mermaids" by sewing the upper torso of a small monkey to the body of a large fish.

Cryptid animal: An animal heretofore unknown to science. Also known as a cryptid, unknown animal, unexpected animal, or possible animal.

Cryptozoology: The study of cryptids. One who practices cryptozoology is a cryptozoologist.

Devil: An immensely powerful and incredibly evil being. The ruler of hell, he is also known as Lucifer or Satan.

Dwarf: A short humanoid monster, usually possessing supernatural powers.

Enigmatic entities: Monsters that do not fit easily into other monster categories.

Extraterrestrial: Commonly known as an alien, any creature not native to Earth. Although usually used in reference to entities from space and beyond, extraterrestrials can also be visitors from other dimensions or planes of existence.

Familiar: An intelligent animal that acts as a spy or assistant to an individual of great power, such as a witch or demon. Black cats are common familiars.

Flying monster: Any monster that can fly, often, though not always, through the use of large wings.

Fortean studies: A field of study that has greatly impacted monsterology. Named after Charles Hoy Fort (1874–1932), a researcher who cataloged thousands of bizarre manifestations, coincidences, apparitions, and manifestations.

Ghost: A spirit, usually of someone who has died, manifesting as a translucent apparition, specter, or phantom.

Ghost light: Any bobbing, elusive ball of light, usually found in packs of three or more, and often intangible and harmless. Most are capable of mesmerizing and misleading witnesses. Also known as will-o'-the-wisp or *ignis fatuus* (foolish fire).

Giant: A tall, humanoid monster, usually deadly and possessing mild supernatural powers.

Hairy humanoid: Any bipedal creature covered in hair or fur and usually, but not always, quite large. Also known as BHMs (big hairy monsters). **Bigfoot** is the most famous hairy humanoid.

Herbivore: Vegetarian.

Intangibile: Lacking a physical form. Intangible monsters cannot be injured by physical means. Many monsters can alternate between tangible and intangible forms.

Lake monster: A monster living in a lake.

Lovers' lane: Any secluded road frequented by amorous teenagers, and a common stomping ground for many monsters.

Lycanthrope: A shape-shifter, such as a werewolf. Many beastmen are also lycanthropes. A lycanthrope is said to be afflicted by "lycanthropy."

Magic: The art of tapping into supernatural forces to produce a host of effects. Those who use magic are known by a vast number of terms, including sorcerers, witches, magicians, and priests. The most vile form of magic, known as black magic, petitions dark and evil supernatural powers.

Monster: Any creature or entity (including humans) whose appearance or special abilities set it outside the commonly accepted laws of reality.

Monster frenzy: A common psychosis that grips communities after a monster sighting that can cause widespread panic resulting in traffic accidents, fires, riots, looting, and monster hunting. May be more dangerous than the monster that inspired the panic.

Monster hunter: Anyone who hunts monsters to kill or exploit them for personal gain.

Monster lake: A lake inhabited by a monster.

Monsterology: The study of monsters. One who practices monsterology is a monsterologist.

Night spirit: A specific type of ghost, often immensely evil, only found abroad at night.

Omnivore: A creature that eats both meat and vegetable matter.

Paranormal: Any event or object beyond current scientific understanding. Interchangeable with *supernatural,* although usually used to describe occurrences that are more firmly rooted in the physical world, such as telepathy.

Psychic power: Any talent or ability that originates in the mind. Well-known psychic powers include telepathy (the ability to send and read thoughts), pyrokinesis (the ability to control fire through thought alone), and telekinesis (the ability to move objects with the power of the mind).

Relic: An animal declared extinct by science but believed by monsterologists to still exist. **Woolly Mammoths** and the **Megalodon** are well-known relics.

Sea serpent: A monster (not necessarily serpentine) living in any of the world's oceans.

Supernatural: Anything beyond current scientific understanding. Interchangeable with *paranormal,* although usually used to describe events or entities that deal with the occult, magic, mysticism, and otherworldly powers.

Supernaturalism: The study of supernatural events, conducted by supernaturalists.

Teleportation: The instantaneous transportation of matter across any distance.

Ufologist: Anyone who studies UFOs.

Ufology: The study of unidentified flying objects (UFOs), usually believed to be alien spacecraft. By definition, winged humanoids, floating orbs of light, monstrous birds, and all other unidentified entities moving through the air can also be classified as UFOs.

Undead: Any creature that should be dead but still maintains a semblance of life. Includes **Vampires,** mummies, and **Zombies.**

Urban legends: Also known as friend-of-a-friend stories, tales that are a modern form of folklore. They often relate a horrible event, but are told as if the event actually occurred. Famous urban legends tell of encounters with the Hook and other **Bogeymen.**

Witch: A practitioner of any religion associated with magic and spells. Not necessarily evil, but capable of wielding devastating supernatural power. Male witches are known as warlocks.

SELECTED BIBLIOGRAPHY

The material in this book has been compiled over several years and from numerous sources, including newspaper and magazine articles, urban legends, the Internet, oral tradition, campfire tales, comic books, and stories told to me by my older brothers, barflies, friends, other researchers, and complete strangers. Below is a sampling of the wide array of recommended books that expand upon information contained herein. This list should not be regarded as a complete or comprehensive bibliography.

Barber, Richard, and Anne Riches. *A Dictionary of Fabulous Beasts.* New York: Walker and Company, 1971.

Baumann, Elwood D. *Monsters of North America.* New York: Franklin Watts, 1978.

Bord, Colin, and Janet Colin. *Alien Animals.* Harrisburg, Pa.: Stackpole Books, 1981.

———. *Unexplained Mysteries of the 20th Century.* Chicago: Contemporary Books, 1989.

Borges, Jorge Luis. *The Book of Imaginary Beings.* New York: E. P. Dutton & Co., 1969.

Botkin, B. A., ed. *The American People: In Their Stories, Legends, Tall Tales, Traditions, Ballads and Songs.* London: Pilot Press, 1946.

———. *A Treasury of American Folklore.* New York: Crown Publishers, 1944.

———. *A Treasury of Western Folklore.* New York: Crown Publishers, 1951.

Brunvand, Jan Harold. *The Vanishing Hitch-hiker: American Urban Legends & Their Meanings.* New York and London: W. W. Norton & Co., 1981.

Burland, Cottie, et al. *Mythology of the Americas.* London: Hamlyn Publishing Group, 1970.

Byrne, Peter. *The Search for Bigfoot.* Washington, D.C.: Acropolis Books Ltd., 1975.

Calkins, Carrol C., ed. *Mysteries of the Unexplained.* Pleasantville, N.Y.: The Reader's Digest Association, Inc., 1982.

Cavendish, Richard, ed. *Man, Myth & Magic: The Illustrated Encyclopedia of Mythology, Religion & the Unknown.* North Bellmore, N.Y.: Marshall Cavendish Corporation, 1995.

———. *The World of Ghosts and the Supernatural.* New York: Facts on File, 1994.

Clark, Jerome. *Encyclopedia of Strange and Unexplained Physical Phenomena.* Detroit: Gale Research, 1993.

Clark, Jerome, and Nancy Pear, eds. *Strange and Unexplained Happenings: When Nature Breaks the Rules of Science.* Detroit: UXL/Gale Research, 1995.

Cohen, Daniel. *The Encyclopedia of Monsters.* New York: Dodd, Mead & Co., 1982.

———. *Everything You Need to Know About Monsters and Still Be Able to Get to Sleep.* New York: Doubleday & Co., 1981.

———. *A Modern Look at Monsters.* New York: Dodd, Mead & Co., 1970.

———. *Supermonsters.* New York: Dodd, Mead & Co., 1970.

Coleman, Loren. *Curious Encounters.* London and Boston: Faber & Faber, 1985.

———. *Mysterious America.* London and Boston: Faber & Faber, 1983.

Colombo, John Robert. *Mysterious Canada: Strange Sights, Extraordinary Events, and Peculiar Places.* Toronto: Doubleday Canada, 1988.

Costello, Peter. *In Search of Lake Monsters.* New York: Coward, McCann & Geoghegan, 1974.

Cox, William T. *Fearsome Creatures of the Lumberwoods: With a Few Desert and Mountain Beasts.* Sacramento, Calif.: Bishop Publishing Co., 1984.

Dane, Christopher. *The American Indian and the Occult.* New York: Popular Library, 1973.

Drury, Nevill, and Gregory Tillett. *The Occult Sourcebook.* London: Routledge & Kegan Paul, 1978.

Eberhart, George M. *Monsters: A Guide to Information on Unaccounted-for Creatures, Including Bigfoot, Many Water Monsters, and Other Irregular Animals.* New York: Garland Publishing, Inc., 1983.

Ellis, Richard. *Monsters of the Sea: The History, Natural History, and Mythology of the Ocean's Most Fantastic Cratures.* New York: Doubleday, 1994.

Fitzhugh, William W., and Susan A. Kaplan. *Inua: Spirit World of the Bering Sea Eskimo.* Washington, D.C.: Smithsonian Institution Press, 1982.

Fleming, Robert Loren, and Robert F. Boyd. *The Big Book of Urban Legends.* New York: Paradox Press, 1994.

Giddings, J. Louis. *Ancient Men of the Arctic.* New York: Alfred A. Knopf, 1967.

Gordon, David George. *Field Guide to the Sasquatch.* Seattle, Wash.: Sasquatch Books, 1992.

Gray, Louis Herbert, ed., and Alexander Hartley Burr. *The Mythology of All Races, Volume X: North America.* New York: Cooper Square Publishers, 1964.

Guiley, Rosemary Ellen. *Atlas of the Mysterious in North America.* New York: Facts on File, 1995.

Hall, Angus. *Monsters and Mythic Beasts.* New York: Doubleday, 1976.

Hillerman, Tony. *Skinwalkers.* New York: Harper & Row, 1988.

Huevelmans, Bernard. *In the Wake of Sea Serpents.* New York: Hill and Wang, 1965.

———. *On the Track of Unknown Animals.* New York: Hill and Wang, 1965.

Keel, John A. *The Complete Guide to Mysterious Beings: A Revised Edition of Strange Creatures from Time and Space.* New York: Doubleday, 1994.

———. *The Mothman Prophecies.* New York: Dutton, 1975.

Kriss, Marika. *Werewolves, Shapeshifters and Skinwalkers.* Los Angeles: Sherbourn Press, 1972.

Lambert, R. S. *Exploring the Supernatural.* London: Arthur Barker, Ltd., 1955.

Leach, Maria, ed. *Funk & Wagnalls Standard Dictionary of Folklore, Mythology and Legend.* New York: Harper & Row, 1984.

Mascetti, Manuela Dunn. *Vampire: The Complete Guide to the World of the Undead.* New York: Penguin Books USA, Inc., 1992.

McCormick, Bob. *The Story of Tahoe Tessie: The Original Lake Tahoe Monster.* Kings Beach, Calif.: Tahoe Tourist Promotions, 1994.

McPhee, John. *The Pine Barrens.* New York: Farrar, Straus & Giroux, 1968.

Melton, J. Gordon. *The Vampire Book: The Encyclopedia of the Undead.* Detroit: Visible Ink Press, 1994.

Michelet, Jules. *Satanism and Witchcraft.* New York: Citadel Press, 1992.

Niven, Larry, and Steven Barnes. *The Barsoom Project.* New York: Ace, 1989.

Norman, Michael, and Beth Scott. *Haunted America.* New York: Tor, 1994.

Opie, Iona, and Moira Tatem, eds. *A Dictionary of Superstitions.* Oxford, England: Oxford University Press, 1992,

Page, Michael, and Robert Ingpen. *Encyclopedia of Things That Never Were.* New York: Penguin Books USA, Inc., 1987.

Phillips, David E. *Legendary Connecticut: Traditional Tales from the Nutmeg State.* Willimantic, Conn.: Curbstone Press, 1992.

Polley, Jane, ed. *American Folklore and Legend.* Pleasantville, N.Y.: The Reader's Digest Association, Inc., 1978.

Price, Vincent, and V. B. Price. *Monsters.* New York: Grosset & Dunlap, 1981.

Pyle, Robert Michael. *Where Bigfoot Walks: Crossing the Dark Divide.* Boston and New York: Houghton Mifflin Company, 1995.

Reinstedt, Randall A. *Mysterious Sea Monsters of California's Central Coast.* Carmel, Calif.: Ghost Town Publications, 1993.

Robinson, Herbert S., and Knox Wilson. *Myths and Legends of All Nations.* Garden City, N.Y.: Garden City Books, 1960.

Rovin, Jeff. *The Fantasy Almanac.* New York: Dutton, 1979.

Salmonson, Jessica Amanda. *Phantom Waters: Northwest Legends of Rivers, Lakes, and Shores.* Seattle: Sasquatch Books, 1995.

Summers, Montague. *The Werewolf.* New Hyde Park, N.Y.: University Books, 1966.

Sweeney, James B. *A Pictorial History of Sea Monsters and Other Dangerous Marine Life.* New York: Crown Publishers, 1972.

Todeschi, Kevin J. *The Encyclopedia of Symbolism.* New York: Berkley Publishing Group, 1995.

Tryon, Henry H. *Fearsome Critters.* Cornwall, N.Y.: Idlewild Press, 1939.

Underwood, Peter. *Dictionary of the Supernatural: An A to Z of Hauntings, Possession, Witchcraft, Demonology, and Other Occult Phenomena.* London: Harrap Ltd., 1978.

Wise, William. *Monsters of North America.* New York: G. P. Putnam's Sons, 1978.

Wolf, Leonard. *Monsters.* San Francisco: Straight Arrow Books, 1974.

Wylie, Kenneth. *Bigfoot: A Personal Inquiry into a Phenomenon.* New York: Viking Press, 1980.

NOTES

NOTES

NOTES

NOTES

NOTES

NOTES

ABOUT THE AUTHOR

W. Haden Blackman is a tall, omnivorous biped inhabiting San Francisco, California, where he forages for freelance writing assignments. He is largely nocturnal, has seldom been photographed, and cannot survive in captivity.